Praise for *The Inquisitors*

"[A] fierce and boldly imaginative artist. Arrogance, brutality, moral squalor—much here is reminiscent of another anatomist of tyranny's intimacies, William Faulkner."
—*The New York Times Book Review*

"Antunes's searing . . . novel about the 'Carnation Revolution,' in which young army rebels led Portugal from right-wing dictatorship to leftist social democracy. A great Portuguese novelist who uses the novel to illuminate individuals caught in the rip tide of history." —*The Plain Dealer* (Cleveland)

"A fiery and startling novel." —*The Seattle Times*

"Antunes . . . has created a character in Senhor Francisco . . . as complex in his cunning, blindness, selfishness and casual brutality as King Lear." —*Los Angeles Times*

"With this tapestry of harrowing testimonials, the supremely confident Antunes illuminates a dark corner of European history and produces a stunning piece of narrative art."
—*Publishers Weekly* (starred review)

"Remarkable for its descriptive exuberance . . . Antunes's razor-sharp eye dissects the outsized shadow cast by this fallen minister of state in all its paranoia-induced variations."
—*Library Journal*

the

inquisitors'

manual

the

inquisitors'

manual

by António Lobo Antunes

translated by Richard Zenith

grove press / new york

Originally published in Portuguese as *O Manual dos Inquisidores* by Publicações Don Quixote, Lisbon.

Published simultaneously in Canada
Printed in the United States

The publisher gratefully acknowledges the assistance of the Instituto Português do Livro e das Bibliotecas in funding the translation of this book

FIRST GROVE PRESS PAPERBACK EDITION

Library of Congress Cataloging-in-Publication Data

Antunes, António Lobo, 1942–
[Manual dos inquisidores. English]
The inquisitors' manual / by António Lobo Antunes ; translated by Richard Zenith.
p. cm.
ISBN 0-8021-4052-1 (pbk.)
I. Zenith, Richard. II. Title.
PQ9263.N77 M3613 2003
869.3'42—dc21   2002033858

Grove Press
841 Broadway
New York, NY 10003

04 05 06 07 08   10 9 8 7 6 5 4 3 2 1

I dedicate this novel to Ernesto Melo Antunes,

who for twenty-five years has been my captain,

an unfailing model of courage and honesty,

and to Marianne Eyre, who has put so much of her

remarkable talent and sensibility into

translating my books.

first report
(A clown who flies like some strange sort of bird)

REPORT

And as I walked into the courtroom in Lisbon I thought about the farm. Not the farm as it is today, with the garden statues all smashed, the swimming pool without water, the kennels and the flower beds overrun by couch grass, the old manor house full of leaks in the roof, the rain falling on the piano with the autographed picture of the queen, on the chess table missing half the chessmen, on the torn-up carpet and on the aluminum cot that I set up in the kitchen, next to the stove, where I toss and turn all night, afflicted by the cackling of the crows

   as I walked into the courtroom in Lisbon I didn't think about the farm as it is today but about the farm and the house in my father's day, when Setúbal

   (a city as insignificant as a provincial small town, a few lights dancing around the bandstand in the square, flickers in the dark night pierced by the dogs' anguished howls)

   hadn't yet reached the main gate and the willows along the wall but sloped straight down to the river in a jumble of trawlers and taverns, Setúbal where the housekeeper did the shopping on Sunday mornings, dragging me along by the elbow under the flurrying pigeons

3

the house and farm from my father's day with the staircase flanked by granite angels, with hyacinths growing all along the walls, and with a bustle of maids in the hallways like the people bustling in the lobby outside the courtroom

(it was July and the trees on the Rua Marquês da Fronteira twisted in the sun against the building façades)

in clusters that hurriedly formed and disbanded around the elevators, and amid all the witnesses and defendants and bailiffs, my lawyer, holding the sleeve of my sweater, pointed out the steps

"This way, Senhor João, divorces are this way"

and I, oblivious to him, oblivious to the courtroom, remembered that long-ago July in Palmela

(I must have been fifteen or sixteen years old because the new garage next to the beech trees was being built, the tractor rumbled beyond the vegetable garden, and the metal blades of the windmill creaked in the heat)

when I heard murmurs and whispers and steps in the chapel, not the sounds of chickens or turtledoves or magpies but of people, perhaps the gypsies from Azeitão making off with the Virgin Mary and the carved candlesticks

(women in black skirts, men blowing on flames under coffeepots, sad scrawny mules)

and I grabbed one of the canes from the stoneware umbrella stand in the foyer and trotted across the dining room

"This way, Senhor João, divorces are this way"

where the chandelier sprinkled glass shadows onto the tablecloth, I leapt over the flower bed with birds-of-paradise, I leapt over the petunias, the chapel door was open, the candles fluttered under the arches, but I didn't find the gypsies from Azeitão

(women in black skirts, men blowing on flames under coffeepots, sad scrawny mules)

I found the cook lying flat out on the altar, her clothes all tousled, with her apron around her neck, and my father beet red, cigarillo in his mouth and hat on his head, holding on to her hips and looking at me without anger or surprise, and on that same Sunday, after yelling his responses to the priest's Latin along with the steward, the housekeeper, and the maids, lighting up his cigarillos during communion, my father

(the wind shook the withered dahlias and the swamp's eucalyptus trees, which expanded and contracted to the rhythm of the algae's breathing)

called me into his office whose window faced the greenhouse of orchids and the murmur of the sea

"Let's hope your wife is on time, so the judge doesn't reschedule your divorce for the Greek calends"

(but there weren't any seagulls, you don't find seagulls on that side of the mountains)

and he stood up from his desk, walked around it toward me, pulled his Zippo lighter from his vest, and placed his hand around my neck as if he were inspecting a lamb or a calf from the stable

"I do everything a woman wants except take my hat off, so that she won't forget who's boss."

My father with his hand on the neck of the steward's teenage daughter, a dirty, barefoot redhead who squatted on a wooden stool while squeezing the cows' teats, my father grabbing her by the neck and forcing her to bend over the manger while still holding on to the pails of milk, my father once more beet red as he rammed his navel into her buttocks, the tip of his lit cigarillo pointing at the rafters without the steward's daughter ever once protesting, without the steward ever protesting, without anyone ever protesting or thinking of protesting, my father lifting his hand from my neck and disdainfully waving toward the kitchen, the maids' quarters, the orchard, the whole farm, the whole world

"I do everything a woman wants except take my hat off, so that she won't forget who's boss."

My father who on Saturdays, after lunch, would have the chauffeur buy half a pound of arrowroot cookies and drive him into Palmela, to the house of the pharmacist's widow up near the castle, a duplex with crocheted curtains and a plaster-of-Paris cat on the sideboard, and he'd return to the farm in the evening reeking of cheap perfume, within half an hour I'd hear him snoring in the living room, asleep in the easy chair with his hat covering his eyebrows and the last cigarillo hanging from his lips as the owls from the swamp *whooed* in the garden, and the lawyer, who dressed like an expensive lawyer, the color of his shirt matching that of his socks, tapped his fingernail against his watch

"If your wife is late for the divorce hearing, we're cooked"

the lawyer hired for me by my oldest daughter after she showed up at the farm and laid into me, shocked by the windows without windowpanes and the rotted floorboards, shocked to find a pot of cold soup next to the queen's picture on the piano, shocked to see fruit skins strewn on the rug

"How can you live all alone in a pigsty like this?"

the expensive lawyer whose hair was cut by an expensive barber and who received me in a fancy office with expensive pictures and expensive leather-bound books on expensive shelves, his expensive wife and expensive children smiling at me from out of a silver frame, and the furniture almost as expensive as my father's, the lawyer pretending not to notice the piece of rope I used for a belt, my unpolished shoes, my socks hanging limply at my ankles, my threadbare trousers, eyeing me with the same bored contempt my mother-in-law displayed when for the first time, knocking over bibelots and all embarrassed, I entered the mansion in Estoril, my mother-in-law who was playing bridge with her sisters-in-law, scooping up a trick in a blaze of flashing rings, and she raised her eyebrow as if at a gardener whose incompetence had ruined the shrubs on the terrace

"And do you have the means, young man, to maintain Sofia at the level she's accustomed to?"

the lawyer frowning at my sport coat that was too short, at the patch on my trouser seat, and at my joke of a mustache, playing with his silver mechanical pencil in a cloud of aftershave as he tried to pull out of my case without letting down my daughter

"We'll see what can be done, Senhor João, but I can't make any promises"

and when I left, the receptionist stared at me as if I were a Jehovah's Witness or sold encyclopedias, and my oldest daughter, poking through the kitchen drawers where my underwear was mixed in with the silverware

(the forks bent out of shape, the spoons turning green, the knives too dull to cut)

"Don't you at least have one decent suit?"

and Sofia brushing my shoulders with the back of her hand

"You could dress up just a little to meet my mother"

and my mother-in-law forgetting all about the cards when I knocked over a lamp

"Are you a moron, young man, or are you just pretending?"
I in the courtroom in Lisbon, escorted by the lawyer whose
fingernail tapped on his wristwatch and remembering the windmill's rust-darkened blades that no wind could turn anymore,
the vacant kennels, and the hungry German shepherds running
wild over the mountains or howling in the swamp as a court clerk
began to read out names, making an X with a pencil for each person who answered, remembering when I took my fiancée to the
farm in August and my father was in a rocking chair in the courtyard drinking lemonade with the sergeant's wife, a woman dressed
in baroque satins who caught the bus in Setúbal on the afternoons
when her husband was on duty at the barracks, and I said

"Dad, this is Sofia"

and from behind his drooping eyelids my father ogled her
as he ogled the cook, the steward's daughter, the gypsy women,
and the maids, pressing his hat down with a flick of his finger

"Do whatever she wants except take your hat off, so that
she won't forget who's boss"

and the nervous lawyer showing me his watch

"What do you suppose happened to your wife?"

Sofia shyly blushing and fiddling with her hair band, the
crows cackling in the beech trees, the house's reflection trembling in the swimming pool, the sergeant's wife offering us
godmotherly smiles, my father sizing up Sofia, speaking in the
same distracted voice he used when speaking about the animals
in the stable

"She's a skeleton, a coat hanger, you never understood squat
about heifers"

and the lawyer suddenly calm, suddenly serious, turning
toward the elevator while pulling on his shirt cuffs

"Here at last, Senhor João"

and there was Sofia not wearing a hair band not twenty years old not blushing shyly and not brushing my shoulders with the back of her hand, flanked by a lawyer who was the mirror image of mine, his replica, his twin, both with their hair cut by an expensive barber, both with custom-tailored Cheviot suits, both self-confident, authoritarian, severe, floating in the same aftershave with the majesty of conger eels, Sofia with my mother-in-law's ring on her wedding finger, Sofia with my mother-in-law's haughty effrontery

("Are you a moron, young man, or are you just pretending?")

not looking at me not smiling at me not telling me

"You could dress up just a little, João"

and I to my lawyer who looked just like her lawyer

"I should never have taken my hat off, so that no one would forget who was boss"

and the lawyer, bewildered, from the pinnacle of his Cheviot suit

"What?"

the lawyer who resembled the lawyers, bankers, finance managers, national assemblymen, and government ministers who came to the farm in my father's day, invisible in the opaque windows of their hearselike cars that proceeded up the cypress-lined drive leading from the main gate to the house, and they would distractedly stroke my chin and remark, without looking at me

"How you've grown"

before disappearing into the room with the piano for the rest of the day amid a whirl of trays carried by white-gloved maids, the housekeeper ordering me to play out back, the steward chasing away the crows and quieting down the dogs, the lawyers, bankers, finance managers, assemblymen, and government ministers who left in their huge cars when it was already night, vanishing from view on the road to Lisbon as my father, forgetting about them, turned back to the breathing of the swamp where the last turtledoves were already taking refuge, Sofia walking past me with her mother's haughty effrontery and my bewildered lawyer leaning closer to hear better

"Excuse me?"

I not in the courtroom but on the farm, talking to my father over the wailing of the frogs

"I should never have taken my hat off, so that no one would forget who was boss"

and the lawyer, whose startled eyebrows almost touched his hairline

"Excuse me?"

as if he weren't there in the courtroom but in Estoril, at the bridge game in Estoril where the window looked out onto the palm trees of the casino, and he had snapped at me in anger because of the lamp I'd just broken

"Are you a moron, young man, or are you just pretending?"

the mansion in Estoril where I took my father, who had dressed up like a hillbilly, with sheepskin boots, a copper chain on his vest, an old hat on his head, and a cigarillo between his teeth, who had left the Nash in the garage with the uniformed chauffeur buffing the chrome and had hired Palmela's only taxi, driven by a kind of clown who wore a peak cap with a shiny visor and who stopped at every tavern on the pretext of cooling off the motor while he spent hours among the vine bowers and flies, my father accompanied by the pharmacist's widow, who hid behind a pearl cameo, a Spanish fan with missing ribs, and a yelping, microscopic lapdog, the widow and I roasting inside the taxi that smelled like an old shoe box as my father and the clown with a shiny peak cap quaffed glasses of wine and cooled down the radiator with straw fans, their bodies covered with car grease, so that we didn't make it to Estoril until long after lunch, when they'd stopped waiting for us and were playing bridge on the terrace looking out onto the beach and the seagulls, and my mother-in-law didn't shudder at my father's bad manners as he pushed the widow and her microscopic dog into the house

"Are you a moron, young man, or are you just pretending?"

leaving the clown in the courtyard to reel among the hydrangeas and to screw and unscrew the engine of the taxi that shook in spasmodic fits of agony, my father with teacup in hand ogling Sofia's mother and her sisters-in-law from behind his drooping eyelids in the same way he ogled the cook, the steward's daughter, the gypsy women, and the maids, without taking his hat off or putting out his cigarillo, all set to push any one of them into the first vacant room, lift her skirt, and flatten her buttocks against a cabinet or a dresser whose drawers would creak, all set to tell whoever might walk in

"I do everything a woman wants except take my hat off, so that she won't forget who's boss"

my father with a teacup, the pharmacist's widow feeding cookie crumbs to her horrid little mutt, which was protected by a woolen sweater, and my mother-in-law not angered or outraged but indulgent

"What a pity your boy didn't inherit your sense of humor, Francisco" and past the palm trees lay the sea and the pontoon where white seagulls calmly perched, so different from the unruly crows on the farm

"What a pity your boy didn't inherit your sense of humor, Francisco"

my father quietly scrutinizing the sisters-in-law at the bridge table and looking as bored as when he inspected the cows in the stable, my father using his jackknife to scrape the mud from his boots, and yet I loved you, Dad, I really did, I was incapable of saying it but I loved you, Sofia's mother offering toast that my father, busy with his mud-caked soles, didn't even bother to refuse, Sofia's mother almost fawning

"My brother Pedro contacted you several times about problems with the bank when you were secretary of state, I'm sure you must remember Pedro"

and in the courtroom in Lisbon the lawyer to me

"The judge called your name"

the lawyer nervous and worried, imploring me, his suit suddenly cheap and drab, his haircut suddenly ordinary, as if he'd gone to a barber with a stairwell shop in Penha de França or Amadora

"Keep your mouth shut during the hearing, Senhor João, none of this crap about who the boss is"

a corridor full of clerks at typewriters, no-smoking signs and summonses on a bulletin board, people milling around, and at the end of the corridor a shelf with books, a calendar on the wall, stacks of files on the floor, a government desk covered with codes and proceedings, and the judge brandishing a pen and entrenched behind laws as if defending himself from us, just like a schoolteacher, the lower half of his face hidden by treatises with cardboard strips marking the pages, and he looked at me almost apologetically, the way I looked at my father when a week or two after the Revolution

(soldiers military parades guns prisons my mother-in-law and her sisters-in-law in third-rate hotels on the outskirts of Madrid without suitcases or passports, anxiously trying to call Lisbon and no answer, trying to call their country estates and the peasants screaming insults over the wire, my mother-in-law and her sisters-in-law in Spain wearing one fur coat on top of another and several gold watches on each wrist while my mother-in-law's brothers were being humiliated by armed civilians at the insurance company, humiliated by armed civilians at Guincho Beach, hauled off in meat trucks to the prisons of Caxias, Peniche, Vale de Judeus)

the way I looked at my father when a week or two after the Revolution he called me, Sofia, and our kids to the farm, where he'd barred shut all the windows, locked up the paintings and the silver, freed the German shepherds from their kennels, and dismissed the maids, and he waited for us at the top of the staircase, shotgun under his armpit and pockets bulging with cartridges, my father still wearing his hat and smoking cigarillos

"The first Communist who tries to enter gets his head blown off"

aiming his shotgun at the swamp, at the barn, at the orchard, and the cypress-lined drive while the German shepherds rolled in the flower beds, ravaging the daffodils

"The first Communist who tries to enter gets his head blown off"

and the lawyer in a low voice

"You can sit down"

the German shepherds galloping into the house and knocking over chairs, ripping up sofas and destroying drapes, returning to the garden in a tempest of pots and casseroles, shredded pillows, curtains, and towels, and my father firing at the frightened crows

"The first Communist who tries to enter gets his head blown off"

obliging me to help him patrol the barn, the vegetable garden, the garage, the eucalyptus trees in the swamp where the frogs wailed, handing me a pistol from his belt and snarling from under his hat

"Shoot if you see a Communist"

my father more alone than I'd ever seen him, with no wife, no friends, no subordinates, no associates, prodding the cows in the stables with the butt of his gun as he searched for revolutionaries in the mangers, in the milk cans, in the sacks of seed, in the straw, my father on his knees and then flat on his stomach in a pool of feces and urine, rummaging through garden tools

"Did you hear that? Did you hear that?"

and a German shepherd howled outside as my father tried to get up but slipped

("What a pity your boy didn't inherit your sense of humor, Francisco")

then tried to get up again

"It's them"

and the dogs increased their barking, the crows their cackling, the beech trees their soughing, my father bumping into a barrel, bumping into a rake, groping on all fours for the exit

"Shoot"

Sofia began to answer questions in her mother's tone of voice, in the bridge-game tone of voice, as if I didn't exist, as if I'd never existed, and the lawyer signaling to the judge

"Keep your mouth shut, Senhor João, let me do the talking"

but there was no one on the farm, no civilians with machine guns on the road to Lisbon, no Communists lurking by the gate, there was nothing but the stone angels and the crows perched on the eucalyptus trees, and the only one who lived on the farm after my separation was me, engaged in building a boat in the garage so that I could depart one day, Sofia had finished speaking, the schoolmaster judge nodded his chin behind the ramparts of proceedings as if to say, Don't worry, I won't flunk you on the exam, and my lawyer in his Cheviot suit that looked expensive again

"My client's only material asset is an almost worthless property"

and my mother-in-law in Estoril, forgetting about the cards and dubiously eyeing my clothes,

"And do you have the means, young man, to maintain Sofia at the level she's accustomed to?"

and so after the wedding they let me work in the bank provided that I sign my name on my monthly wage statement and have no dreams or ambitions, provided that I say nothing in meetings and not show up for work, provided, in other words, that I not exist there, even as I didn't exist for my mother-in-law, my wife, and my children

"How can you live in a pigsty like this?"

I building a boat in the remnants of the garage that was threatened by the remnants of an oak tree

(its branches pressing down on the roof and its roots lifting up the floor)

building a boat so that I could depart one day instead of ending up like my father in the stable, facedown in a pool of urine and feces and vainly groping on all fours for the exit

"Shoot"

and what I'll find when I get out are the fields gone to seed, the angels without arms or legs, the windows without windowpanes, the vegetable garden torn up by the dogs, the cot propped up by the wood-burning stove with no wood, and the echo of my cough in the empty rooms, the lawyer trying to reach the mountain range of legal codes where a fleeting glimmer of the judge's glasses occasionally jumped out

"My client, an engineer, gave up his private practice to manage a firm owned by his wife's family, being dismissed after years of service without the severance pay he was legally entitled to"

when in fact they didn't dismiss me, they simply told the clerk at the front desk not to let me in, I standing in the lobby and he waving his hands in the air

"I'm sorry, sir, but those are the orders I have, don't worry, your paycheck will be sent to your home address"

until they decided not to let me in my own home, informing me not through a company clerk but through two of my wife's cousins who blocked my way in the front yard in Estoril without violence or aggression or hostility, they were neutral

"Sofia wants a divorce, so we loaded all your stuff onto a van from the insurance company and sent it to Palmela"

a suitcase, a sack of clothes, a photo album, my mother's ivory crucifix, a crate with tools and drawings of ships, it was a rainy night in Estoril, the palm trees of the casino leaned toward the hotel, and I stood there with the key in my hand, unable to react, asking

"Why?"

exactly as I had asked the clerk in the bank lobby, while the receptionist and secretaries glanced with pity at the spots on my coat

(and my oldest daughter, poking through the kitchen drawers where my underwear was mixed in with the silverware

the forks bent out of shape, the spoons turning green, the knives too dull to cut

"Don't you have one decent suit?")

"Why?"

and before the judge's glasses reappeared between the plastic spiral rings of proceedings to glance at everyone sitting there, paralyzed like frightened animals, the other lawyer, the mirror image, replica, and twin of my own, presented auditors' depositions, photocopies, bills, numbers, drawings, and diagrams with colored arrows pointing up and sideways

"To manage a firm that went bankrupt?"

I who managed nothing, I just signed my name where they told me to and initialed the receipts and letters of credit presented to me by the personnel officer

"There on the dotted line, Senhor João, that's right"

I who understood nothing about loans or receipts or letters of credit, who never dreamed that the personnel officer would flee to Johannesburg with the bank's money, and my mother-in-law's brothers, released from the prison of Caxias or Peniche or Vale de Judeus, summoning me to a meeting and not asking me to sit down, shaking a handful of debts in my face

"What's this?"

debts, promissory notes, contracts, stock transfers, purchases, sales, fraudulent exchange operations, catastrophic transactions

"What's this?"

the judge's glasses surfaced from the legal codes, hovered for a moment, and resubmerged, Sofia now the same age and the same everything as her mother who forgot about the cards, forgot about the bridge game

"Are you a moron, young man, or are you just pretending?"

and the mirror image, the replica, the twin, expanding in his aquarium of hair lotion while pulling from his briefcase yet more certificates, more reports, more mortgages, more loans, more proof of embezzled dollars

"To manage a firm he forced or allowed to go bankrupt? That's water over the dam, we're willing to forget it, all my client asks is a mortgage on the farm in her favor"

the farm now gone to rack and ruin, with no cows, sheep, tractor or pigs, being slowly devoured by the swamp's monstrous eucalyptuses and the frogs' wailing, the trees in the orchard all gnarled and leafless, the irrigation channels swallowed up by couch grass, the beech and cypress trees stripped by the crows, the water in the swimming pool reflecting nothing, stagnating like a dead eye, not the farm and house of my father but the farm and house now, with the autographed picture of the queen on the piano without a single note in tune, the paintings on the floor, the rugs faded, the chapel overrun by creeping vines, with worms and lizards in the baptismal font, on the altar, and in the cabinet with tattered vestments, the lawyer and Sofia and Sofia's family getting revenge for what I didn't do, for what I couldn't have done even if I'd wanted to, and demanding a mortgage on nothing, since I have nothing but a sack of clothes, a photo album, an ivory crucifix, and this boat in the garage so that I can depart one day, a boat without motor or sails, as useless as the broken coal-burning boiler, as the bladeless threshing machine, as the mill with rust-soldered joints that no wind can move, and the judge, reduced to a faint myopic voice and an inkling of eyeglasses guarded by mountains of laws, granted them a mortgage on the farm, on shadows of destitution and the squawking of magpies, and when they come to foreclose, arriving with pomp and in the same hearselike cars that brought the lawyers, bankers, finance managers, assemblymen, and government ministers of yesteryear, they'll find me waiting for them on the front steps amid the shriveled hyacinth stalks and the German shepherds chasing the rabbits, digging into their burrows with their paws and snouts, and if they don't find me waiting on the front steps without even hearing or seeing them, aware only of Palmela's pigeons between the castle and the mountains, then they may find me groping on all fours, like my father, in the urine and feces of the stable

"What a pity your boy didn't inherit your sense of humor, Francisco"

bumping into milk pails, barrels, and rakes, brandishing a shotgun with no trigger or shot, drenched with urine, covered with manure, wiping the mud and straw from my face with a handkerchief, shouting at the revolutionaries from Setúbal and Azeitão armed with machine guns and besieging my house, flashing their court order, the order of justice

"Get out of here, don't touch me, go away, the first Communist who tries to enter gets his head blown off."

COMMENTARY

If you say it's true then okay, I believe you, but I don't see why Master João would say such terrible things about Senhor Francisco, who's got a mean temper, and he isn't dead yet, he could still recover from the stroke. It's none of my business, of course, and Master João has no doubt talked to the doctors to make sure his father has no chance of getting better and making his life hell, he'd be crazy to risk having the old man back on the loose, threatening everybody under the sun with his shotgun. That's how I see it but what do I know, I was just the steward's daughter, spending my life between the vegetable garden and the stable, milking the cows, cleaning the dovecote, changing the dogs' bowls and tending the hen coop, with no time left over for schools and books. When we arrived from Trás-os-Montes, Senhor Francisco made a place for us in the barn, with a partition that separated us from the corn, and we made a ceiling of sorts in order to keep out the swooping bats that talked like people, we put a stove in the corner, we used the sink in the wine cellar for our necessities, and I remember waking up in summer in the dark and hearing the frogs from the swamp, the sleepless dogs, the restless cattle, and my father's snoring, which made the same sound as the windmill, I remember seeing the light still on in Senhor Francisco's office, the oranges that glowed in the August calm, burning slow and steady like the oil lamps of saints, and I felt good, I felt eternal, I felt happy, because it seemed that time had stopped forever and no one would ever die. In the morning the oranges dimmed, the tractor began to drone, and with the return of death
(and, worse than death, time)

they yelled at me to get dressed, and with a milk pail in each hand, skinny as a twig and pushed along by the wind, I walked past the beehives and the pond with geese to the stable, where the animals turned their snouts away from the wall to look at me, and then a sound of boots crossing the wet cement floor, a cigarillo smell that made me sick, the hand of Senhor Francisco grabbing my neck

"Don't be afraid, little girl"

and I cringing in fear

(*he won't get better, will he? swear to me he won't get better, because if he gets better he'll beat my brains out*)

Senhor Francisco sprawled out on a sack of seeds, watching me without saying a word, or else watching the white foam seething in the buckets, and I without the courage to say

"Let me go"

without daring to say

"Get out of here"

since besides being my father's boss he was some kind of government minister, he was even visited once or twice a year by Professor Salazar

(*we knew when Professor Salazar was coming because the farm would fill up the day before with plainclothes policemen who shooed away the workers, snooped everywhere, even under our mattresses, and copied down the data from our ID cards, a National Guard jeep waited at the main gate, a second jeep by the swamp, and a third one on the other side of the wall, until finally a pair of motorcycles would climb the cypress-covered hill with sirens blaring, followed by an army truck, another pair of motorcycles, and at last the curtained car with Professor Salazar, dressed in an overcoat, even in summer, the plainclothesmen sprinkled among the rosebushes, a gentleman with glasses would get out of the limousine, open the door for Professor Salazar, and lead the way up the steps, prancing all around him as the crows in the distance mockingly cawed, and the next day the police returned to open fire on them)*

I without the courage to say

"Get out of here"

cringing in fear because he was the boss, because he was rich, because he was a government minister who had power over a lot of people in Lisbon, and I thought if I said

"Get out of here, let me go, get out of here"

(swear to me there's no danger or I won't say another word no matter how much you pay, because what good would the money do me?)

he'd order the National Guard to shoot me, just like when he heard about the Revolution on the radio and immediately seized his shotgun to kill us all, pulling back on the breech and aiming straight at us

"Scram, you commies, and I mean now"

as my mother and I scrambled toward the gate with a bundle of clothes and my father held out his pleading arms

"We're not Communists, Senhor Francisco, I swear to God we never tried to rob you"

Senhor Francisco all disheveled, his shirttail hanging out of his pants, his hat around his ears, threatening the tractor driver, the chauffeur, the housekeeper, the maids, even the cook who slept with him and hated me, Senhor Francisco hitting us with the barrel of his gun

"Scram"

as we all scrambled down the cypress-covered hillside to-ward Palmela, toward Setúbal, with the startled magpies flying

this way and that, the pigeons frozen with fear, and the German shepherds, let loose from their kennels, biting at our heels,
urged on by Senhor Francisco yelling

"Sic 'em"

(*before Professor Salazar's last visit a bunch of National Guard
jeeps commanded by a corporal spent a week gunning down the
crows, leaving dozens of them lying dead in the orchard, and the
corporal would kick them over with his boot*

"That'll teach you not to make fun of the Prime Minister")

one of the German shepherds knocked down the housekeeper, who was crying, her suitcase popped open on the gravel,
the dogs ran off with her skirts, her sweaters, and her shoes, my
father wanted to help her but Senhor Francisco wouldn't let him,
he pulled back on the breech

"I'll kill you, you swine, I'll kill you"

(*when Professor Salazar got out of his car the farm was a cemetery of birds and nobody made fun of him, not even the frogs from
the swamp with their algae-swollen throats*)

the German shepherds growling and snarling at each other
as they snapped at the suitcase and Senhor Francisco yelled

"Sic 'em"

my father shielding the housekeeper and vying with the
dogs for her sweaters and skirts, and from his face I could tell he
was almost weeping

"We're not Communists, Senhor Francisco, God strike me
down if we're Communists, we don't know anything about
politics"

the windmill searching for wind and Senhor Francisco
waving away my father with the butt of his gun

"Scram"

(Professor Salazar talking with his secretary, climbing the steps, shaking hands with Senhor Francisco, who didn't take off his hat or put out his cigarillo for anyone, not even the Prime Minister, Professor Salazar ignoring the National Guardsmen who stood at attention, stopping to admire the petunias, disappearing into the house)

and the German shepherds trampling the vegetables and the chickens, knocking over flowerpots, the tractor tearing up the rosebushes, the fleeing maids lugging their sacks on the road to Setúbal, stumbling forward as Senhor Francisco shouted

"Communists"

with a revolver tucked under his belt, pulling cartridges from his pocket, and when he noticed me he said

"You there"

separating me from my mother with his shotgun, grabbing my shoulder as my father, on his knees in the gravel and with the housekeeper's slipper pressed against his chest, whined

"You're not going to kill her, are you, sir?"

(and through the garden gate I caught a glimpse of Professor Salazar drinking tea in the parlor, and a plainclothesman motioned me away with his chin)

"Get lost"

the tractor going in circles inside the greenhouse and Senhor Francisco flashing his cartridges at my father

"Scram"

I heard the maids on the road, the bells of the sheep, the water overflowing the irrigation channels, the rose stems being ripped, and Senhor Francisco grabbed my neck and led me to the stable, prodding me with his shotgun against my bottom as the dogs jumped all around and my father, still clasping the housekeeper's slipper, watched from the gate, the wind shifted again, increasing the sound of the frogs' croaking, and I tried to plead but couldn't get out the words

"Don't kill me"

in the steamy stable with hills of dung on top of the straw and urine, Senhor Francisco bent me forward against a beam where turtledoves were sleeping, and the sheet metal in the roof rattled as he poked into my dress, found me lost me tried to find me again, and I forgot him, I thought of the oranges glowing in the August calm, burning slow and steady like the oil lamps of saints, and I wasn't afraid, I felt good, I felt eternal, I felt happy, because it seemed that time had stopped forever and no one would ever die, until the oranges dimmed, death

(and, worse than death, time)

returned, the tobacco smell faded, and Senhor Francisco stepped back

"That's so you'll never forget me, you rotten commie"

and outside there were no more German shepherds, no more pigeons, no more magpies, just the decapitated rose-bushes crackling in the silence and the tractor's final combustive sigh, I thought that the National Guard jeep would be waiting at the gate to take me away but there was no jeep, and the bus stop with its little roof against the rain was deserted as if it were Sunday, we went to my mother's cousin's apartment in Barreiro, which is where we always went on holidays, two cramped rooms behind the hospital, my father sitting on the enclosed balcony and refusing to eat, refusing to talk, still clasping the housekeeper's slipper against his chest, and my mother's cousin

"Heitor"

but my father just sitting among the shelves of Spanish dolls and miniature porcelain vases, my mother's cousin's husband offering him a shot of his favorite brandy but my father immovable, my mother taking away the slipper

"Heitor"

but my father just staring at the Tagus's rotting boats and little islands of grass without noticing the boats or islands, and soon there were fireworks, loud bangs and flashes and red streams of sparkles entered the window, the radio blared with songs of victory, cars honked their horns, the factories whistled nonstop, the café owner played his accordion on the sidewalk while dancing with his wife, my mother's cousin's husband guzzled the brandy but my father immovable, the whole neighborhood buzzing like during a Saturday fair or the Feast of Saint Peter's, the town hall deserted, the police station deserted, the ferryboats for Lisbon wagging their haunches against the pier, a hubbub of workers in nearby Lavradio, and my mother's cousin gave me a bowl of soup and an apple, through the skylight I could see the hospital and the patients in pajamas, just like the ones my mother's cousin's husband wore when instead of going to work he stayed at home drinking brandy and getting surly, and since I'd already forgotten about Senhor Francisco I ate the soup, I ate the apple, and after eating the apple I went over to my father, saying

"Dad"

and he lifted his eyes to me, leaned his head against my tummy, and began to cry, I'd forgotten Senhor Francisco but remembered the poor cows that hadn't been milked and had no feed in their mangers, the chickens and pigeons and peacocks without corn, and the earrings with the blue stones that I left at the farm, in the can with buttons, so that something grabbed me inside, I had to struggle not to cry, too, and my mother who'd removed her shoes and was sticking her nose into her ankles to dig a thorn out of her foot with a needle

"What happened to your earrings, Odete?"

and it wasn't just rockets, it was also cannons that shook the building's foundations and confounded the clock's cuckoo, which started announcing the hours without let-up, flinging open the tiny door, taking a bow, peeping, retreating, and shutting the door, flinging open the door, taking a bow, peeping, retreating, and shutting the door, my father crying with his head against my tummy and my mother's cousin's husband still chugging brandy, ticked off at the bird

"Any minute now I'm going to twist its neck off"

my mother showing the thorn to an old woman with a black scarf huddled in a shawl too big for her, ensconced in a corner of the enclosed balcony where the winter dampness had mildewed the walls with clusters of gray mushrooms

"Look at what was stuck in my heel, Dona Fraternidade"

and the old woman, paying no attention to her, alarmed by the cuckoo's frenzy

"Holy Jeezus"

the old woman, mother of my mother's cousin, grasping nothing, neither the rockets nor the cannons, neither the hubbub nor the music, grasping nothing and not caring to grasp, startled by the wooden bird's hysterical comings and goings

"Holy Jeezus"

there were band musicians in Lavradio, each playing his own tune, young men waving flags, a mulatto writing in blue paint on a wall, a man with a hard hat haranguing in the café from a stepladder, my mother, proud of the huge thorn and disappointed by the old woman's indifference, shaking the tweezers in front of my father's tears

"Look what I dug out of my heel, Heitor"

my mother's cousin's husband so incensed by the cheeping of hours that he swung his brandy bottle at the clock

"Motherfucking cuckoo"

the bird instantly stopped cheeping and dangled from a spring like a hung man, my mother's cousin took it down from the hook on the wall, pushed aside the dishes, gingerly laid it

(the cuckoo, the cuckoo's dwelling, and the weighted chains)

down on the plastic tablecloth like a patient recovering from back surgery, while her repentant husband, emerging from the mists of his brandy, made excuse

"I warned the bastard to shut up but he wouldn't listen"

the old woman with hands folded and fascinated by the spring

"Holy Jeezus"

my mother, hurt by the lack of interest in her thorn, angling for our sympathy by announcing forlornly to the Spanish dolls

"I'll bet I come down with a blood infection"

my father to my mother's cousin's husband as if he'd just woken up from an eight-month slumber or returned from far far away

"If there's any left, I'll have a tad of that brandy to calm my nerves"

and for a week my parents slept on the floor of the living room with my mother expecting to die from blood poisoning at any moment, continually asking for the thermometer to take her temperature, I slept on the enclosed balcony with the old woman who instead of sleeping spent all night staring wide-eyed at the cuckoo, marveling at the broken clockwork spread out on the plastic tablecloth, springs, chains, weights, chips of wood, wheels, and hands, the old woman who would furtively get up, shrouded in her widow's scarf, shrouded in her shawl, to touch the pieces with her finger

"Holy Jeezus"

until my father found a job as a custodian at a construction site where he kept track of the machines and tools, we moved to a third-floor apartment five buildings down, next to the hospital yard where patients strolled around on their crutches or with tubes in their noses or with IV bottles suspended from metal hooks, my mother, with a slipper on her left foot because of the thorn, suspiciously running her hand over my ears

"What happened to your earrings, Odete?"

I feeling sorry for the patients, watching the sparrows on the telephone wires and the seagulls on the river

"Quit worrying, I'll put them on tomorrow"

though from where we were living you couldn't see the river, just buildings as decrepit as our own, darkened by the years and the fumes of the United Factories industrial complex, a wasteland where men stacked bricks and raised scaffolds, you couldn't see the river, but you could hear the ferryboats for Lisbon and feel the cadaverous dankness of the ebb tide, my mother worked as a cleaning lady for an architect in between complaining about her poisoned blood and running her hand through my hair and over my ears

"What happened to your earrings, Odete?"

the fumes from the United Factories blackening the clothes we hung to dry, the sheets on our beds, and the casseroles in our kitchen, which was just a cubicle overlooking scrawny, leafless mulberry trees scorched by the ammonia from the smokestacks, my father fixed the cuckoo clock that my mother's cousin's husband had given us so as to be spared his mother-in-law's insomnias, when she would awaken the whole family with her astonished

"Holy Jeezus"

the bird, forever befuddled by the blow from the brandy bottle, cheeped imaginary hours and boreal middays, teasing us from the clock's door, until my father sealed it shut with a dozen nails

"Motherfucking cuckoo"

we could hear the animal peck in rage against us from inside the wood, and when it finally quite pecking, my father unnailed the door and we found the bird lying dead on a bed of screws and tiny wheels, we threw it in the trash, wrapping it in newspaper so it wouldn't smell, my mother, forgetting about the thorn, sniffled in grief before the empty box, and my father consoled her

"Don't be upset, Irene, at the end of the month I'll buy you another cuckoo"

and at the end of the month we had another cuckoo for the clock, painted red and yellow, only it didn't sing, it just opened its beak wide with a weary jerk, took a bow, looked at us with a kind of shrug, and disappeared without a sound, my father banged on the clock, took it off its hook, shook it hard

"The carpenter promised me it would sing"

the carpenter, summoned to explain, held the bird by its wings and examined its underside with a magnifying glass

"It looks like I made a female by mistake, my jackknife must have slipped, it happens with these tiny parakeets"

and my father, annoyed with the artist

"What do you mean a parakeet? I ordered a cuckoo bird"

and the artist, imperiously brushing aside all doubts with his chisel

"For me there's no difference between a parakeet and a cuckoo, they're equally lousy for eating with cornbread"

and without the squawking of hours and slamming of little doors at least we could sleep at night, at least there was no warbling to distract me from my dreams, the only sounds in the darkness, besides my father's coughing, were the kitchen faucet dripping water against the enamel sink, the stray dogs hunting for table scraps, the trains switching tracks in the station, and the speeches of factory workers on the street corners, and the workers called us comrades, promised us public housing, declared that we were free, and I thought

"Free from what?"

because the poverty remained, only now with more hullabaloo, more drunks, and more disorder, since there weren't any policemen, and the rockets and cannons gradually quieted, the workers got tired of smearing the walls with chalk, the café owner quit playing his accordion, the hospital patients continued their agonized procession along the fence, and my mother, returning from the architect's, running her hand through my hair and over my ears

"Don't tell me you sold your earrings, Odete"

I, pretending to be angry, curtsying in response to the cuckoo's speechless bow

"Yes, I sold them yesterday"

and so I finally returned to the farm to look for them in the can with buttons, catching a bus out of Barreiro that crucified my lower back every time we hit a bump, then another bus in Azeitão, with the radio at full blast and a stuffed bear dangling from the mirror, and when I got off at the town square in Palmela a poor people's funeral was leaving the church and proceeding up the hill amid chrysanthemums to the cemetery, with the family of the deceased pushing against the coffin to keep it from sliding off the wagon, life went on as before the rockets, cannons, the café owner's accordion, and speeches about freedom and public housing, the same retirees sat on the same benches, the same fish vendors tried in vain to sell fish, the same farmhands hoped for a farm manager who would hire them, there was the same deserted marketplace, the same chitchat among housewives, the funeral's chrysanthemums vanished around the bend, followed by a helmeted fireman with a hatchet, there was no Communism in Palmela, nor singing nor flags nor charcoal writing on the walls, there was just a hapless corpse that threatened to slip off the wagon on its sad climb up to the cemetery, the ruined castle on the summit, and row after forgotten row of olive trees, and past the aviary and the restaurant for truckers with an ice-cream chest at the entrance, the road curved left and came to the main gate of the farm, with its stone columns, its name inscribed on a tile, and the cypress-lined driveway that led to the house, but no dog barked, the windmill was still, the oranges in the orange grove rotted on the ground, and the tractor lay on its side amid the greenhouse debris, with one of its back wheels turning in silence, as it had turned for weeks and would turn forever

(the greenhouse windows shattered, the window frames crushed, the flowerpots smashed, the orchids' petals languidly hanging like huge purple lips)

and I saw a German shepherd trotting through the tomato patch and growling, the cows in the stable hopelessly licking their empty mangers, the garden statues missing arms and legs, the swimming pool without water, the charred remains of the burned-down barn, and not a sign of the earrings with the blue stones, not a sign of the can with buttons, I saw the pigeons' confusion and the magpies' anxiety, the chickens pecking at lettuce and hyacinths with the jerky motion of marionettes, the eucalyptus trees closing in on the garage amid a din of croaking frogs, the windows of the house wide open, the chapel with no Virgin Mary or carved candlesticks, and the canvas chairs of the terrace in tatters, I saw the memory of the plainclothesmen copying out our ID cards and thought

"The Communists carried off Senhor Francisco"

I thought

"The Communists came with rockets and cannons and accordions and speeches and carried off Senhor Francisco, putting an end to his shotgun, an end to his threats"

my mother in Barreiro, in an apartment even smaller than her cousin's, turning from the plastic tub with peas to run her hands over my ears

"Don't tell me you sold your earrings, Odete"

and as I passed the beech trees that talked to themselves just like the patients who walked in circles around the hospital yard I thought

"What happened to the crows?"

because I didn't hear their mocking, I didn't see their now small now large shadows flitting across the ground, I walked around the garage and saw the car's chrome all coated with dust, I reached the laundry tubs and the clothesline with its clothespins like so many plastic finches

(a peacock in a poplar shrieked as if it had just been stabbed)

the geese gabbled in the courtyard, wagging their tongues and stretching their dirty, irate necks in my direction, I thought

"What happened to the crows?"

my mother in Barreiro, plunging her hands back into the tub with peas as the red and yellow cuckoo gently shut its door after a soundless bow, my mother, loud enough for my father to hear

"Earrings worth at least three thousand escudos, it makes me sick just to think about it"

my father frantically rummaging in the bedroom

"Just my luck, I can't find my tie"

my mother violently shucking peas as a vein in her neck twitched

"You put on a tie and drench yourself in cologne to go see your whore and don't give a damn that your daughter has sold her earrings"

I imagining that the crows had migrated to Seixal or Amora but finding them at last in the walnut tree by the well, not a hundred, not fifty, not twenty, just ten or twelve, spying at me and flapping their wings like rags, while in the old water tank a pair of May storks nested, my father tying his tie in front of the tarnished piece of mirror

"What whore?"

I walked into the filthy clutter of the kitchen, the refrigerator bashed in, the stove covered with greasy pots and pans, the cupboards without screens and missing cups and glasses, the marble sink filled with rinds and bones, the pots of jam coated with mold and the pantry laced with spiderwebs, the red and yellow cuckoo opening its door to take a ceremonious butler's bow, and my mother, in a caustic voice, dumping pods into the garbage and running water over the peas

"The wench that sells tickets at the boat station and paints her nails gold, you were seen with her in the park on Saturday, don't deny it, you scoundrel"

the tables in the hallway with a thick layer of dust, the rug chewed to pieces by the dogs, the shelves without a single book, the lampshades in shreds, and the curtains and towels in tatters on the floor, my father whistling a tune, dressed in his Sunday suit, hair combed, clean-shaven, a Band-Aid on his chin, and with a paisley tie as big as a napkin, my father, in the clouds with joy, fishing for the shoe polish in the onion basket, dabbing the polish on his shoes

"I'm not going to see anyone, I'm going to work"

and in the parlor the chair where Professor Salazar sat as the housekeeper offered him plates of cookies or toast with the pomp of an altar boy extending cruets, the flower vases overturned, half the rug hanging off the verandah, a hole in the folding screen, the remains of a bedspread strewn across the floor, the radio without its cover, bristling with coils and lights and emitting a babble of voices, falling silent, more voices, then silent for good, inhabited by a multitude screaming for help and drowning, my mother drying the peas and lighting the stove, remembering the thorn and limping again

"One of these days I'm going to let her have it, one of these days I'll rip that braid right off her head"

the radio's voices dying and the cracked water tank dripping in the courtyard where the cook slit chickens' throats over a clay pot and I saw the blood and was afraid and started crying, afraid of their beady eyes staring at me, afraid of their claws, of their feathers, of the pink skin under their feathers, afraid the cook would grab me by the neck, seize the knife and slit my throat too, grab me by the neck like Senhor Francisco did in the stable, bending me forward into the cows' manger that reeked of oats and seeds, and I wanted to ask but couldn't get out the words

"You're not going to pour my blood into a clay pot, are you?"

Senhor Francisco with his belt unbuckled, his vest unbuttoned, clutching my waist with his thighs, laughing as he blew cigarillo smoke down the back of my neck

"Hold still, little girl"

I frightened by my blood dripping onto the grooves in the cement, by the cows' agitation, by the windmill's slow screeching on the south side of the farm, wanting to ask Senhor Francisco but unable to get out the words

"Don't cut my throat, please don't cut my throat, swear you won't cut my throat"

the papers from the office burnt to ashes on the terrace, magazines, newspapers, photo albums, the picture of Senhor Francisco with the Cardinal, of Senhor Francisco with the Admiral, of Senhor Francisco with Professor Salazar, of Senhor Francisco with the Pope, wearing a tailcoat with medals and kissing the Pope's ring, my father steeped in cologne, slamming the door and whistling on the stairs

"If I say I'm going to work, then I'm going to work"

the desk drawers overturned, the safe wide open and no money or jewels, a plaster bust lying on the carpet, the files ransacked in anxious haste, I thinking about the woman who sold tickets for the ferry, thinking about the bust and whom it might be

"He went away and won't ever come back to the farm, he went away"

and my mother tearing off her apron

"You'll be sorry, you liar, you'll be sorry"

a magpie calling me from the cypress trees, the daisies rattling their bony stems, the hangers swinging in the wardrobe without clothes, my mother to the woman with the braid

"You goddamn bitch"

Senhor Francisco letting me go and I shaking my dress, worried about the blood but relieved there was no clay pot or cook with a knife, I feeling happy

"I didn't die"

and then the piano started playing. It started playing not with the sound it used to have, back when little João would place a book with notes above the keyboard, then twirl the stool higher with his finger, then curve and stretch his fingers, curve and stretch his fingers, tilting his head back, and the music reached the barn, it reached the road to Palmela, if we were eating supper it changed the taste of the soup, and there was a sweet sadness in everything as when one has the flu or it rains on a September afternoon, it started playing not with the sound it used to have that unsettled the dogs and made the oranges glow brighter at night but with the sound of a wailing cascade, of a muddy outburst, of a stagnant rush, my father separating

37

the two women, careful not to mess up his tie or wrinkle his suit, my mother, barefoot and with her hair bun falling, entangled in the necklace of the ferryboat employee

"You goddamn bitch"

Senhor Francisco in the living room now without drapes, without sofas, without pictures, without the chess table, without the chandelier, without furniture, with the terrace leaning toward the neglected farm, the wilted flower beds, the heap of boards that once was a dovecote, the garage where a wheelless car sat rotting, my mother to my father, on the tips of her toes and slapping the other woman

"Let me go, you liar"

Senhor Francisco on the stool that went up and down, banging at random on the keys amid all the useless debris, swaying as if transported by the eighth notes, and my father, angry because his tie had got smudged, shoving my mother, who fell down on her rear end

"That's enough out of you"

Senhor Francisco insisting on the music, swaying faster and hitting the keys harder, dressed in faded trousers, a shirt, and socks, disheveled, emaciated, with white whiskers on his chin, much older than a month ago, incapable now of bending me forward against the manger

"Hold still, little girl"

of clutching me by the throat, of poking into my skirt, I didn't fear him or the clay pot or the knife or my blood on the cement, I felt no fear, no pity, no anger, nothing

"Hold still, little girl"

a crow passed by the window, a second crow, a third crow, their wings beating against the vines, against the columns, against the stone flowerpot with withered birds-of-paradise, a German shepherd howled in the orchard but no female answered, the night grayed the tops of the beech trees and soon there were bats, a blackness with no lights, the rattling of chairs

"Hold still, little girl"

I felt no fear, no pity, no anger, nothing, the piano was suddenly quiet, and my mother rubbing her back as she bawled at my father

"So you side with the bitch and attack me, you ingrate?"

the piano was suddenly quiet and Senhor Francisco speechlessly stared at me from behind the book of notes, and he kept staring at me for the longest time, until all I could see in the living room were the tip of his cigarillo, the piano's candlesticks, and the scarecrow of a silhouette wearing a hat and opening his arms in the form of a cross as he triumphantly sniveled:

"Tell your Communist friends they can come back, little girl, tell your scummy friends they can come back, because there's nothing left for them to take from me."

REPORT

One day a week I don't work on the boat. I lock the main gate to keep Sofia's cousins from entering the farm and evicting me the way they did from my house in Estoril, and I go to Lisbon to visit my father on the ground-floor clinic in Alvalade, where the farm plots of old have given way to houses, sidewalk cafés, and tree-shaded streets, and he speechlessly sits in a chair next to the window among the other old men who also can't speak, who also wear bathrobes, are immobile, rest their fingers on their knees, and silently stare at me with empty rage, my father who at night is dragged to bed by two female staff workers in an agony of shuffling slippers

"Who's the good little boy who goes to bed when it's time for beddy-bye?"

they undo the string on his pajamas, unbutton his fly, place a bedpan under his scrawny legs, all bones and hair

"Time to go wee-wee, Senhor Francisco, time for wee-wee, come on, come on, there you go, that's a good boy, tonight you're not going to be naughty and wet your nice clean sheets, are you?"

my father with his jaw hanging open, his buttocks flaccid, trying to wipe his nose with his trembling sleeve, and the staff workers, solicitous

"Isn't your hankie in your pocket, Senhor Francisco, yes here it is, look at your hankie, now tell me what your hankie is for"

my father quiet, submissive, useless, with no cigarillo, no denture, no lips, no hat, stretched out on the bed like a scarecrow, the staff workers tucking him in

"You rascal"

vanishing down the corridor, invisibly repeating everything in the next room, their voices muffled by the dividing wall, the rustling of clothes, the jangling of enamel

"Time to go wee-wee, Major, time for wee-wee, come on, come on, there you go, that's a good boy, tonight you're not going to be naughty and wet your nice clean sheets, are you?"

and another scarecrow stretched out on a bed, another quiet rascal, another submissive rascal, another useless rascal, the voices receding but with the same enthusiasm

"Time to go wee-wee"

my father's head propped on the pillow, the window behind him filled with the peace of the streetlamps on the square, building façades, a slide and a swing on a patch of grass that looks blue in the moonlight, I a little boy in the living room playing with building blocks and my father laying down the newspaper, pulling his watch from his vest, and pointing at the door

"Pack up your blocks, put the box in the closet, and off to bed, now"

the peace of the streetlamps on the square in Alvalade, the leaves of the trees against the lilac sky, the summer moths pressed flat against the windowpanes, the unaltered zeal of the staff workers' voices coming now from the opposite end of the clinic

"Time to go wee-wee"

I in the living room afraid of the dark, of kidnappers, of wolves

(*the housekeeper lying to me*

"There aren't any wolves, when did anyone see wolves on the farm?")

I holding back tears

"Let me finish what I'm building, Dad, just five more minutes, I promise"

my father with sunken cheeks, breathing like a sputtering teapot, his long fingernails resting on the fringe of the bedspread, my father with his legs crossed, engrossed in the paper, his hat gliding over the news in a cloud of tobacco smoke, sending me to my death

(*the cook thought I was crazy*

"Are you pulling my leg?")

my father

"Off to bed"

I terrified of the dark, of kidnappers, of wolves, trying to save my life by putting the blocks in the box as slowly as possible while the wall clock tolled my imminent doom, I walking to the closet with the box of blocks, gaining time with infinitely cautious steps, as if I were carrying a tray of glasses filled to the brim on a ship deck, and the hat lifting up from the newspaper, threatening

"I'm going to get up any second now, João"

the wolves perfectly still, waiting for me among the console tables with wide-open jaws, the masked kidnappers ready with their sacks to nab me and sell me at the fair to the gypsies from Azeitão

(stroking my ankles the way they stroked their mules)

I flicking on the light switches that separated me from my bedroom, because everyone knows that wolves and kidnappers don't like electricity, and I in the clinic, sitting on a stool and looking at him, his elbow propped on the nightstand full of pills and syrups, a storm door slamming, the staff workers' voices getting louder again, footsteps, a wisp of bangs peeking in, the corner of an apron, the lipstick of a smile

"Your father, poor thing, is a real saint"

the saint's chest rising and falling with a sound as of wet stones rubbing together, without him noticing me, without him worrying about me or the farm or the house or the Communists, without handing me the pistol tucked under his belt

"Shoot"

the saint transformed into a rattlebones, into a pair of dilated nostrils, into a worthless puppet, and yet I kept waiting for him to say I didn't know what, and he kept not saying it, nor would he ever, his case was hopeless according to the doctor who came to show me analyses and X rays, dark spots that he didactically circled with his pen

"We'll be lucky if your father doesn't get any worse, we'll try at least to prevent more attacks, the big worry is lesions, the big worry is he could catch pneumonia"

the doctor putting the analyses and X rays back into a brown envelope and I getting undressed as quickly as possible to try to fall asleep before my father came and turned off the light, since kidnappers and wolves lose interest in us when we sleep, they leave us alone and attack other children in other houses, but the sideboards and the dressers creaked in the silence, a murderer coughed somewhere in the darkness

(in the pantry? in the kitchen? in the office?)

my father in the doorway turning off the light switch

"Just what I needed, a son who's afraid of the dark"

I defending myself from the kidnappers by balling up under the covers, so tiny they wouldn't notice me if they lifted up the sheets, holding in my urine, holding my wildly beating heart, the woman who runs the clinic tapping me on the back, amused

"Wake up, Senhor João, it's one in the morning, are you planning to take up residence here?"

a woman who resembles the pharmacist's widow from Palmela, a woman who is likewise fat, likewise decked out in satins, likewise the owner of a microscopic lapdog, and she no doubt has a plaster-of-Paris cat in a house full of oriental bric-a-brac

(Chinese mandarins teacups platters)

on the outskirts of Lisbon, in Olivais or Prior Velho, Mem Martins or Cacém, the scarecrow who seemed to be powered by the barely turning motor of the broken lawn mower, my father who a year after the Revolution was still waiting for the Communists on the devastated farm, playing piano in the living room with the exultation of revenge, sucking on a spent cigarillo with his hat over his eyebrows, mocked by the magpies, by the crows, and by the seagulls that stray inland from the Arrábida coast

"There's nothing left for them to take from me"

the woman who runs the clinic, in her gauzy finery, helping me put on my raincoat in the lobby graced by a copper lantern and an elephant on a pedestal, handing me my scarf, worried about me getting cold

"Your sister came to see your dad yesterday"

my dad pounding the piano keys and shouting at me

"There's nothing left for them to take from me"

as the eucalyptus trees advanced toward him with a deafening din of frogs, the eucalyptuses with their croaking that will occupy the whole farm if Sofia's cousins and a court official don't show up one of these days with the police and a judicial order to evict me, that will occupy the whole farm with black leaves and the murmur of reeds, I sinking in the mud between crumbling walls, the sudden whining of door hinges, a ballet of footsteps, the sound of a shattered vase or plate, and the invisible staff worker with bangs

"Dona Cecilia, the Major just cashed in his chips"

the Major with a blanket on his knees whom they would sit up for his snack on the sofa in the sitting room among the other scarecrows, all with blankets, sitting in a semicircle to watch the soap on TV without enjoying the episodes, without making a sound, scarecrows with one or no teeth whom it's necessary to spoon-feed like decrepit babies, shouting in their ears

"Open up your mouth, sir, don't be a bad boy, it's time to eat"

until their teapot lungs stop whistling without warning, like the lawn mower that finally conked out, and the next week they're replaced by an identical scarecrow who also can't talk and has a blanket on his knees, who's also bald except for two or three strands of moldy hair like on an old doll in the attic, the woman who runs the clinic calling back to the staff worker with bangs

"Just a minute"

and while patting down my scarf and arching her eyelashes in resignation

"It's my destiny, Senhor João, if they last me a month, I'm lucky"

and although the scarecrows on the sofas constantly changed, for me they were the same, old age giving them all identical hands, noses, and foreheads, identical bodies and bristly hairs on their chests, dozens and dozens of scarecrows with bedpans pressing against their groins

("Some wee-wee, Professor, time to wee-wee, come on")

dozens and dozens of scarecrows drooling rice, pasta, and soup, washed with a sponge, dried with talcum powder, shaved on Saturdays, their ribs dancing in oversize suits and their neckties dancing in crooked collars

("All smart for your grandson, you vain son-of-a-gun")

on the day when their families visit, and one night like this one, when I was leaving the clinic, crossing the patch of bluish grass with the swing, the grass made bluer by the light of the streetlamps and the dew from the bushes, a car stopped smack in front of me and my sister leapt out onto the sidewalk, ready to strangle me

"You didn't tell me where Dad was, you didn't tell me he'd had a stroke"

my father on the devastated farm surrounded by ashes, surrounded by trash, mocked by the magpies, mocked by the crows, mocked by the seagulls that strayed inland from the Arrábida coast searching for fish in the empty pool, my father exulting

"There's nothing left for them to take from me"

ever more triumphant, ever more contented, his fingers stampeding over the keys, the ceiling lamp shaking, the autographed photo of the queen crashing to the floor, his hat flying off his head, the cigarillo falling on his shirt, the piano suddenly quiet, my father with drooping lapels, drooping arms, eyes bugging out at me, and I

"Dad"

a piano note playing on by itself, indefinitely, the magpies fallen silent, the crows silent, the eucalyptus trees silent, time congealed, the smoldering cigarillo tumbling in the ashes and trash, my father standing up from the stool, reaching for a portière without catching it, I rushing toward him

"Dad"

my sister on the blue patch of grass, pulling at my scarf

"You didn't tell me where Dad was, you didn't tell me he'd had a stroke"

(*"Time to go wee-wee, Senhor Francisco, time for wee-wee, come on, some wee-wee, there you go, that's a good boy, tonight you're not going to be naughty and wet your nice clean sheets, are you?"*)

my father hesitating, growing stiff, then flaccid, sticking out his stomach, shouting out the name he never pronounced

"Isabel"

slumping to the floor

"Isabel"

the magpies silent, the crows silent, the eucalyptus trees silent, the petals of the daffodils stricken with fear, my father on his stomach with his lips against the ground, with his denture coming loose, mumbling in secret, almost tenderly

"Isabel"

an albatross screeching next to the ceiling of the living room, my sister shaking with rage

"If you thought you'd end up with everything by not telling me, then guess again, you crook"

I running through the cypress trees to Palmela's first-aid station, with an examining table and an imposing dentist's chair that resembled a throne for shining shoes, for giving haircuts, for prince consorts or for capital punishments, next to it a dented bucket full of bandages, and on top of it a dead-drunk yokel wearing a smock, sprawled out with the dignity of an African chieftain, looking at me with impassive eyelids

"If he broke a shin, then apply hot compresses and forbear, because the doctor won't be back until next week"

an eye chart that looked like a message in code, a poster of the Palmela soccer team, a little stove for sterilizing needles that hissed like a goose, a peevish boy with a beret who appeared in the doorway with a message

"My godfather says you're holding up the quadrille game, Senhor Carlos, and he's tired of shuffling the cards"

I taking refuge from my sister on the slide and the swing that glowed in the grass of the tiny square in Alvalade while the staff workers in the clinic struggled with the unwilling corpse of the Major, wrapping it up in the suit reserved for family visits, and the smocked yokel slowly got down from the chair

"I can't wait on you now, as I've got an urgent call"

my sister retreating to her car, holding up her handbag like a shield, while a couple leaned over their balcony hoping for blood

(the blue grass, the blue slide, the blue swing moving back and forth on its own)

"Are you going to hit me, João, are you going to hit me?"

I returned to the farm accompanied by the smocked yokel, by the boy with a beret who stared at the irrigation channels in terror

"There're snakes in there, right?"

and by the quadrille players who strewed jacks in the couch grass, a heifer dazed by hunger whined outside the stable, the sparrows hopped around on the threshing floor, unnerved by the ever larger eucalyptus trees, the smocked yokel bumped into the piano

("Fuck")

and bent down over my father with a knowing air of seriousness

"It looks to me like he overdid it on the red wine"

and the godfather of the boy with a beret, his rings flashing

"The problem with this country is that there are people who can't even handle a four-ounce glass"

I as a little boy staring at the irrigation channels in terror

"There're snakes in there, right?"

striped snakes in the pond, spotted snakes in the well, water snakes in the swamp, rat snakes in the tractor shed, in the barn, in the stable, one Saturday when I came home on leave from the army, my father called me into his office, there was a girl with him, a girl with glasses and no makeup, no satins and no lapdog, a sad-looking typist or switchboard operator, and I thought

His latest lover, his latest conquest

(*the staff workers at the clinic covering him with the blanket "You rascal"*)

a girl sitting on the edge of the sofa as if she'd just arrived or were about to leave, the boy's godfather reeling as he categorically drawled

"If I were in charge of this country the first thing I'd do is outlaw alcohol, just look at that shameless sot sprawled out in your house with a hangover, if you want we can lug him out of here right now"

the girl with glasses who, intimidated, kept pushing them up her nose with her pinkie, I once saw a foot-long snake on the terrace, I went to get the housekeeper, who was giving orders in the sewing room, I forced her to come with me, but the snake had slithered off into the garage or the vegetable garden, the hyacinths didn't breathe a word, the turtledoves smoothed their feathers on their perches, the housekeeper poking through the geraniums with the tip of her shoe, chiding me

"Do you think I don't have enough to do without you playing tricks on me?"

the girl with glasses who was dressed like a sad typist or switchboard operator and didn't dare look at me, and all I wanted to do was leave the room, get out of my uniform and take a bath, my father as if informing me that it was going to rain or that he would be eating dinner in Lisbon

"Say hello to your sister, João"

one afternoon a snake slithered into the sewing room and curled up in the clothes basket, the gardener came and killed it with his hoe, the housekeeper almost fainted

"How disgusting"

and she didn't quit only because my father promised to recaulk the doors and windows and to cover the chimney with chicken wire, but she began to walk about with a broom in her fist and a rosary around her neck to ward off the vipers, I hot and itchy in the army jacket, wondering, Should I or shouldn't I give her a kiss, I with a smile that wasn't a smile but a frozen grimace

"Pleased to meet you"

I who instead of

"Pleased to meet you"

and instead of observing the crows through the office window should have grabbed the housekeeper's broom and driven out the switchboard operator with glasses who visited my father once or twice a year, full of ceremony and dressed as if she were older than she really was, holding on to her patent leather purse with both hands, sitting on the edge of the sofa as if she'd just arrived or were about to leave, a sister who was the daughter of I didn't know what mother, even as I didn't know who

(*"Isabel"*

my father on his stomach with his lips against the ground, mumbling in secret

"Isabel"

almost tenderly

"Isabel")

even as I didn't know who my mother was, I remember arguments, fighting, suitcases in the foyer, a car through the

cypresses turning onto the road to Lisbon, my father at the top
of the steps shouting

"Get out"

with nobody to hear him, with nobody interested in hearing him except for the pigeons and the frogs, the maids crying
in the kitchen, the housekeeper tucking me into bed and waiting with the light on until I'd fallen asleep

"Sleep tight, João, sleep tight"

my father yelling at the top of the steps to the car that had
left centuries ago

"Get out"

waving his arms in a cancerous rage

"Get out"

locked up in his office for days afterwards, without talking
on the phone, without giving orders, without inspecting the
vegetable garden or the stable, the maids leaving his lunch and
dinner on a tray outside the door and he not even touching the
soup, they leaving thermoses of tea he didn't drink, mail he
didn't open, and the godfather of the boy with a beret pulled a
deck of cards from his pocket, plopped down on the piano stool,
and invited one and all

"How about if we send the kid to Palmela for some beer
and play a round of quadrille while the old man decides whether
he wants to wake up?"

I didn't know who my mother was because I couldn't
remember her face, voice, or gestures, I remember a blue skirt
rushing down the steps, a raincoat, a closed umbrella, photographs that vanished from the furniture, Sofia asking me not
long after we met

"What was your mother like?"

and we went to dances, to dinners, to charity sales, and on boat rides, I went with her to Mass on Sundays and nodded off during the homilies, we played tennis in Estoril, we rode horses at the Marina Riding Club, my mother-in-law made me fill in at bridge when one of the players was missing, I didn't understand about discards and miscounted the trumps, my mother-in-law chewing on her cigarette holder

"You're a lousy player"

Sofia applying suntan lotion at Guincho Beach amid her cousins and sisters-in-law and their respective boyfriends, all taller than me, stronger than me, more handsome than me, richer than me

(*"And do you have the means, young man, to maintain Sofia at the level she's accustomed to?"*)

amid waffles, potato chips, giggles, and whispers that excluded me

"What was your mother like?"

amiably silent, showing polite interest, and in the wake of a steamer a crown of flamingos floating like a bridal veil, the smocked yokel opening up beers, shuffling cards on the piano lid, my father finally emerging from his office with his habitual stride, his habitual authority, I lying on the beach towel with my face turned away from them

"I never had a mother"

my father, with the weary disdain he exhibited when talking with the veterinarian, once more waving the maids off to the courtyard out back, summoning the cook with his finger, silently ordering her away from the stove, grabbing her neck, Sofia incredulous, her cheeks gleaming with suntan lotion, and in fact there were two steamers, not one, heading toward the harbor entrance, each with a crown of flamingos, the cousins and sisters-in-law blinking with surprise, and their boyfriends looking embarrassed

"You never had a mother?"

I with a vivid memory of arguments, fighting, suitcases in the foyer, a car on the road to Lisbon, a pastel skirt rushing down the steps, a raincoat, a closed umbrella, the housekeeper waiting with the light on until I'd fallen asleep

"Sleep tight, João, sleep tight"

but unable to remember her face, her voice

"I never had a mother"

the cook bent over the marble table, with a pastry board and a cake pan, my father raising her apron, madly groping with his fingers

(*snakes, snakes in the geraniums, snakes*)

the maids peeking from the courtyard, their noses pressed against the window, I searching for the cookie tin that said rice on the outside, as the tin with chick peas said sugar and the tin with beans said coffee, and suddenly I saw them, pressed against each other, pounding against the table, the kitchen full of wild shadows, I biting on a cookie when my father gave me a peda-gogical slap

"I do everything a woman wants except take my hat off, so that she won't forget who's boss"

I couldn't bring myself to kiss the sad switchboard opera-tor with a patent-leather purse who dressed like an ageless aunt

"Say hello to your sister, João"

and who visited Palmela twice a year, pushing up on her glasses with her pinkie, my sister who might have been the daughter of a hairdresser, manicurist, or dressmaker, or of a maid that my mother let go, and who might have been the cause of all the arguments, the fighting, the suitcases in the foyer, I in my army uniform, with the jacket that made me itch

(*snakes, snakes in the geraniums, in the geraniums, snakes*)

and all I wanted was to leave the room, get undressed, and take a bath, my belt made my waist itch

(*snakes*)

I just wanted to go to my room, read a magazine, a book, anything to forget about the car driving away through the cypress trees

"Pleased to meet you"

and I to Sofia as we came away from the beach, walking up the steps toward the hotel bar where our silhouettes waved in the aquarium with turbot

"I have no mother and no brothers, I'm an only son"

my father on his stomach with his lips against the ground, the smocked yokel studying the cards with cannibalistic fervor, the godfather of the boy with a beret offering me another beer

"When we finish this hand we'll pinch the beggar awake, and I promise that he won't bother you anymore"

the beggar whom we took to Palmela that night, tripping over each other as we sang raucous songs, I and the smocked yokel carrying him by the armpits, his head drooping and his heals dragging through the gorse, the beggar whom we sat on the dentist's or shoe shiner's or prince consort's throne, trying to revive him with sips of beer that ran out of his mouth gaping with shriveled aversion, the godfather of the boy with a beret trying to slap him awake

"If I were in charge of this country I'd outlaw alcohol and we'd be rid of idlers, I say we lean him up against the church wall and let the early morning cold wake him up while we get in a few more hands of quadrille"

on one of her visits my father left the office to watch a cow give birth, and so we were all alone, my sister and I, she pushing up on her glasses with her pinkie and clutching her purse like a handrail, and I scratching my navel, like two patients in a waiting room, two strangers in an elevator, the air got stuffy, the ceiling pressed down and the walls squeezed in on us, the clock on the bookshelf swelled into a gigantic globe, my sister opened her purse and started to fan herself with a piece of cardboard, I pulled my handkerchief from my pocket and blew my nose, she was sweating under her collar and I under my necktie, my back was all wet, my hair all wet, my stomach upset as if from fried food or octopus salad, I opened the window, the mocking of the crows hit us smack in the face, my father slid off the shoeshine chair as the ace of the trump suit overtook the king and the manille, and the smocked yokel tried to divert our attention to keep from losing the game

"How about if we take the beggar to the hospital?"

even with the window wide open to the papery rustle of the rosebushes, she kept fanning herself with the cardboard, my sister who wasn't after all a typist or switchboard operator but a legal assistant in Alcácer, without a husband or children or friends, cooped up in a dusky one-bedroom apartment crammed with dark furniture salvaged from a shipwreck, the godfather, who was on a winning streak, scooping up the cards to count points

"Hospital my ass, lean him against the church wall and let him sleep it off, that's all he needs"

a one-bedroom apartment by the river that she probably took over from her mother or from a relative who was a sailor and brought knickknacks back from Goa, an apartment that seemed to be underwater, with squid instead of birds outside, corals for trees, yellow refractions, a cat licking its vanity on the windowsill, embroidered cushions, my sister warming herself next to an electric heater, pushing up on her glasses with her pinkie, looking at me with widowish melancholy as I wondered

"By whom did my father have her?"

and I wondered if she was also the cause of arguments, fighting, suitcases in the foyer, my father shouting

"Get out"

my sister in her tiny apartment in Alcácer without a house-keeper to help her go to sleep, emerging from a pantry whose shelves were lined with paper towels, carrying a teapot covered by a woolen cozy and containing herbal tea, but she knew her mother, she didn't grow up amid moos, magpies, and frogs, the boy with the beret, bored of kibitzing the card game, feeling my father's cheeks with the back of his hand

"The geezer's as cold as a corpse, Godfather"

the godfather whose luck had changed, who was no longer winning any hands, and as his discouraged rings tossed the cards onto the examining table, he glanced over at my father with lethal intent

"Cold or not, the son-of-a-gun is jinxing my game"

the godfather pulling on my father to avenge his defeat, slipping on a beer bottle, both of them crashing to the floor of the first-aid station and knocking over syringes, the godfather banging his head into the bucket with bandages

"That swine shoved me, I swear he shoved me"

the doctor from the clinic in Alvalade laying down his little rubber hammer

"If the stroke happened yesterday, why did you only bring him here today?"

my sister offering me a cup of verbena tea in her tiny apartment in Alcácer, where the clothes drawers reeked of lavender, the cat jumping from the windowsill to the table like tumbling velvet, I drawn to the photograph of a woman framed by porcelain daisies

"Who could her mother be?"

I who had no mother and no brothers, I'm an only son, the photograph of a woman resembling the housekeeper who used to wait with the light on

"Sleep tight, João, sleep tight"

until I'd fallen asleep

"Could it be the housekeeper?"

a woman who also had the face of a seamstress or a sad switchboard operator, who also wore glasses, also dressed as if she were older than she really was, I pointing at the photograph as my sister pushed away the cat and the river of Alcácer swallowed up the square, freight trucks, outdoor cafés, stone steps, my father with his lips against the ground, almost tenderly

"Isabel"

I pointing at the photograph of the sad switchboard operator framed by porcelain daisies

"Is that your mother?"

I who have no mother, no brothers, no family

(*my oldest daughter, poking through the kitchen drawers where my suspenders were mixed in with the silverware*

the forks bent out of shape, the knives too dull to cut

"How can you live in a pigsty like this?")

I, tormented by the restless pigeons, building a boat so that I can depart one day, dozens of old men sputtering through their teapot lungs, dozens of scarecrows in bathrobes expiring in front of the soap on TV, the staff worker with bangs, undressing my father

"You smell like wee-wee and rancid beer, poor thing"

my father without his cigarillo, his denture, his hat, trying to wipe his nose with his trembling sleeve, and the woman who runs the clinic, solicitous

"Isn't your hankie in your pocket, Senhor Francisco, yes here it is, look at your hankie, now tell me what your hankie is for"

dozens of scarecrows with blankets on their knees, with strands of moldy hair on their bald skulls and white tufts on their scrawny legs, staring at me from their chairs with empty rage, scarecrows reminiscent of crows themselves, mocking me from their rooms with silent laughter, the doctor laying down his little rubber hammer

"If the stroke happened yesterday, why did you only bring him here today?"

old men mocking me from their rooms with silent laughter, hundreds of old men in the square of Alvalade perched on the buildings, perched on the streetlamps, skidding down the slide, dancing on the swing above the bluish grass, hundreds of elderly crows not on the farm, not in the vegetable garden, the orchard, or the tractor shed, not in the beech trees, but in that cellar of Alvalade, mocking me in that cellar of Alvalade, old men with fingers like claws, jaws like beaks, limbs like tattered wings, old men with bristling feathers who made fun of me, and the doctor, who also looked like a crow, writing a prescription, handing me the prescription

"If the stroke happened yesterday, why did you only bring him here today?"

and as I defended myself against the beaks, claws, and wings, as I covered my ears so as not to hear the cawing, the drunken godfather of the boy with the beret clasped me on the shoulder with his flashing rings, saying:

"We couldn't get here earlier, Doctor, because we had a little game of quadrille to finish."

COMMENTARY

I never went more than two or three times to the farm in Palmela. I don't like cows, I don't like pigs, I don't like the smell of manure everywhere you turn, and I didn't like my father-in-law eyeing me from head to toe as if he'd never seen me, as if I hadn't already been his daughter-in-law for ten years

"A skinny hothead without hips, you don't know how to pick out a heifer, João"

eyeing me without the slightest hesitation, shame, or scruple, indifferent to the housekeeper, to the maids, to our kids, and to the broad with a lapdog who sat next to him on the sofa, a sinister, incredibly tacky broad in her fifties, dressed up at five in the afternoon as if for a baptismal ceremony in Algés or some other nouveau-riche suburb, the widow of a small-town pharmacist or civil servant who liked to call me dear and touch my arm when she talked to me, I hate to be touched, and the old broad

presto

would grab my arm, which I jerked away, and she, taken aback, waving her fan with missing ribs to cool down her hot flashes

"Did I hurt you, dear?"

I making signs to João with my eyebrows that we should leave and João paying no attention, I fed up with the impertinent familiarity of the old broad, who insisted, God knows why, that I pet her little mutt

"Shake hands with this nice girl, Nero"

Nero with an imbecilic look, his paw in the air, licking my fingers with his disgusting tongue, and me feeling sick, on the verge of vomiting

"João"

my father-in-law with a cigarillo in his mouth, looking at me as if he'd never seen me

"What possessed you to take up with a broomstick, João?"

João keeping mum, João driving the car with the kids in the backseat fighting as usual over who would sit next to the window, João without the guts to do anything except swindle my family when they put him in charge of the bank after the Revolution, João defending his father instead of defending me

"That's how he is with everyone, don't take it personally"

and as we coasted down the drive to the main gate, dozens of birds kept crossing our path, cawing and hitting the windshield, swooping down on the tractor, swooping down on a half-naked girl coming out of the stable with a pail of milk in each hand, birds intent on breaking into the car to kill us, and I vowing to myself never to go back to Palmela, I forgetting all about the kids' bickering, I raising my elbows in self-defense, shouting

"Step on it"

and I had to stop in the town café to take a tranquilizer, a café with a slew of bicycles leaning against the wall on the outside and a slew of flies covering the pastries on the inside, where an employee in an undershirt wiped the dirty counter with a dirty cloth and shuffled under a row of soccer-team pennants

"Red or white, ma'am?"

while the kids demanded bubble gum, candies, and chocolates, enthralled by the sticky lollipops and addled cream puffs, the guy in the undershirt rummaging through filthy dishes, wiping a glass with his dirty cloth, filling it from a faucet elongated by a rubber tube, and sighing apologetically

"The source for the water is right behind the cemetery, so don't be surprised if it has a few particles of earth"

the kids

it was inevitable

filling their pockets with moldy caramels as the bicycle owners, likewise dressed in undershirts, played dominoes in a flurry of insults and I, spitting out the water, felt a tremendous urge to cry, I felt like being in Estoril with my mother and my brothers, in peace and quiet, without my father-in-law's vulgarity, without the widow and her fan missing half the ribs, without birds, without water containing dead people, without hassles, I felt like not being married or like being married to anyone but João, I who can't say I wasn't warned

"If you're stupid enough to waste your life on the first booby who comes along, that's your business"

the café proprietor probing his cavities with a splintered match and cleaning the match on the stains of his undershirt

"I warned you, ma'am, not to drink the tap water, which sometimes even has bits of bone in it"

so that I never went more than two or three times to the farm in Palmela. Years ago my mother took me to the Alentejo hinterland to attend the confirmation of the daughter of one of our seamstresses who got married, and what I saw was a multitude of bumpkins, men with mustaches and women with hair buns, all chewing with their mouths open and dumping platefuls of ham sandwiches into plastic bags, I clutched my mother's skirt in terror as she, frowning like a queen surrounded by unworthy vassals, shrugged in resignation

"However much we prod these people, this is how they'll always be"

in an abandoned roofless church or convent, with paintings of martyred saints above crumbling altars, stray dogs under the tables vying for a piece of chicken, a blind man playing accordion in the confessional, the godfather waving around a bottle of anisette and continually bumping into the sexton, and the seamstress with feathers dangling from her hat and carrying, like the other women, a plastic bag bursting with food, the seamstress leaning on my mother's fur coat and offering us a tray with toothpicks stuck into slices of blood sausage that an old woman, cheeping like a sparrow, stealthily slipped into her handbag

"Are you enjoying the lunch, ma'am?"

my mother furtively brushing her coat

(*"I'll bet I'm loaded with lice"*)

without smiling, expressionless, making a sign to the driver
who escorted us like a Swiss guard from the Vatican

"As much as I can, Aurora"

my mother already outside the ruined church, on a patio
where the guests' little boys ran around chucking stones at each
other and a group of confirmation girls, dressed like barrel-
organ monkeys, squealed with delight as they took snapshots of
each other under the leering glances of hooligans with sideburns
and sheepskin boots, my mother spraying herself with perfume
as if it were disinfectant

"My God, what a stench"

and no sooner did we arrive home at Estoril than she had
me take a bath and wash my hair on account of the bugs, diseases, and the smoke from the fried food, and each time I went
to Palmela it reminded me of that confirmation in the Alentejo,
the same people, the same hubbub, the same discomfort in spite
of the fairly decent furniture and paintings, the chinaware that
wouldn't be bad if it weren't all glued back together, and the
photographs of Salazar and the queen of England, in spite of
the shrubs and rosebushes, which needed pruning, in spite of
the tinny piano and the pretentious mirrors and the battalion
of badly dressed maids, one day I told my mother about the farm
and she, on her way to the massage parlor or the Catholic
Women's Association

"What did you expect from a bunch of provincials who
aren't even poor?"

whereas I had a poor person just for me on Wednesdays, a
poor person I was told not to give money to since he would go
right out and buy brandy, since that's what poor people do as
soon as they have a little change in their pockets, just second-

hand shoes and clothes, and food left over from last night's dinner that the veterinarian said was bad for our dogs because of
the spices, plus it would dull the sheen of their fur, and when
my poor person died of TB in the shack where he lived on top
of a windy hill that overlooked the sea and was covered by wild
grass, trash dumps, and white flowers, I noticed that there was
no light or electricity in his cabin but that there was a lamp with
glass pendants that swung from the ceiling, a canary in a bamboo cage nibbling at a lettuce leaf, and a pile of dirty rags on the
floor where the corpse lay, my brother Gonçalo's sweater serving as a blanket, and after my poor person died they offered me
a younger poor person who would live longer, who was healthy
and still had no cough, was baptized and duly vaccinated, and
who was recommended to me by the reverend prior because he
wasn't addicted to anything and wouldn't fail to respect me, but
by Christmastime I had to give him up and report his rude behavior to the Catholic Women's Association because I was dumb
enough to give him ten escudos, admonishing him

"Now don't go spend it all on liquor"

whereupon he, flipping the coin, rudely answered

"You can rest easy, miss, because I'm taking it straight to
the car dealer's to buy an Alfa Romeo"

which proved to me that the poor don't know their proper
place, they either run around with TB, coughing bacilli into our
faces, or else become absolutely unbearable, resentful because
they're poor and live in shacks made of boards and sheet metal
on the slopes facing the waves, with the sun shining down on
their poverty and reflecting off the empty cans and broken glass
strewn about the wild grass, so that I never cared to have another poor person, I have enough problems dealing with my own

life, with the idiot hairdresser who never does my hair right, and with the kids getting into drugs, the kids whom I raised single-handedly since João would spend weeks at a time at the farm in Palmela, which resembled a gypsy camp after the nightmare of the Revolution and my father-in-law's illness, João holed up in the garage building a boat for God knows what, as there's no water nearby, João who when we lived together virtually didn't exist, he didn't know how to play bridge, didn't know how to choose a tie that went with his shirt, and at one in the morning he'd fall asleep with his mouth open in the middle of conversations, right when someone had asked him a question, and my uncles, out of sheer ingenuousness or else good faith, relying on the fact that João's father had been a minister and received Salazar at the farm among the cows and birds, appointed him to the board of directors of the bank, where he went at the end of each month to sign his name and get his check, until one night one of my sisters-in-law woke me up screaming as if she were being strangled to death

"The Russians have overtaken Portugal, Sofia, turn on the radio if you don't believe me"

and then another sister-in-law, and a cousin, and my mother

"Don't ask questions, don't get hysterical, don't waste time, come here immediately with the children to Estoril, where the reverend prior is already hiding out"

and what we heard on the radio were military marches and songs about the people and freedom and the lack of bread, songs that couldn't possibly be more against God, according to the reverend prior who sat with his soutane unbuttoned and his head between his hands in my father's easy chair, the chair with the head rest next to the fireplace where my father read English golf magazines until he was hospitalized with cancer, my mother was in her bathrobe busily locking the silver in the safe before the poor people (who become more ungrateful the more you help them, warned the reverend bishop at the Easter mass) descended from the slope to rob us, to sleep in our beds, and to eat and belch in our dining room, despite the reverend prior's efforts to teach them good manners in his homilies at the 8 A.M. mass, which is the mass of the poor, who get up early since they don't have to go

lucky them

to the casino, to auctions, to the movies, or to deadly dull concerts on Saturday night, my mother rightly claimed that the poor are to be envied

(it might seem like a sin to say this, but it isn't)

since they don't have to go to Saint Vincent de Paula charity galas or to exorbitant Red Cross teas, they're to be envied for having no obligations except waiting for us to visit them and going to get their TB checked, so that they have entire days free to do precisely what they want, to beg, to cough, to have children, to rummage through garbage cans, to pick at their scabs, to let their teeth fall out, or whatever, and the reverend prior with his fork in the air, reprehending my mother as he took a second helping of soufflé

"It's wrong to be envious, Dona Filomena, and as penance you should say one Our Father and three Hail Marys immediately"

my mother ordered all the doors and windows to be locked so that the Communists wouldn't be able to just walk on in, she ordered the chauffeur to shut the cars in the garage, she had the maids say the rosary for the conversion of the Bolsheviks, a radio announcer interrupted some hymns against the Virgin Mary to report that revolutionary forces had arrested the president, whom the reverend bishop had compared to Saint Francis Xavier, and that they were going to let the murderers and rapists out of prison, the telephone rang nonstop with calls from my poor cousins at the insurance company, the real-estate agency, and the bank, where they had to defend themselves from clerks barging into their private offices as they desperately tried to transfer a few dollars to Zurich, clerks cursing and calling them crooks, vandals, fascists, addressing them not as sir but by their first names, as if they'd grown up in the same family, yanking the telephone from their hands and asking the revolutionary forces to take them away in handcuffs to be executed in Caxias, and João completely oblivious, without any consideration for my mother, without the slightest consideration for the reverend prior, he just kicked off his shoes and snored on the sofa as my mother, clutching a crucifix in the hope that Saint Expeditus would save us from the gallows, frantically shook him

"Are you a moron or are you just pretending?"

João in this respect was unfortunately not like my father-in-law, who stood his ground all alone at the farm in Palmela, ready to kill the muzhiks with his cocked shotgun, scanning the swamp, scanning the vegetable garden, scanning the dovecote, bravely defending Jesus under a swarm of nervous pigeons

"The first Communist who tries to enter will get it right in the guts"

the clerks from the insurance company, the real-estate agency, and the bank, joined by a pack of ghastly, unkempt soldiers with beards and long hair, insulted my uncles with every name in the book, confiscated their wallets and watches, tied their wrists together as if they were common criminals, and hauled them off to Caxias, to Peniche, to Monsanto, to prisons built for murderers who, along with the poor people, were now occupying buildings in Lisbon, and as the reverend prior says, why should a poor man want an apartment in Lapa, Príncipe Real, or some other fancy neighborhood, why should a poor man want air-conditioning, silverware, and elevators when he doesn't know what to do with these things, and we visited my uncles in jails next to the river, where my mother, searched by the guards, protested

"Are you young men morons, or are you just pretending?"

my uncles who never hurt a flea, on the contrary, they founded schools for teaching the blind to read holes, for people crippled in both legs, and for hunchbacked orphans, they did a lot for the blacks, who are equal to us, and for people who've had kidney transplants, my uncles without ties or belts or shoelaces, talking in English to my brothers and my cousins about problems in Miami, London, and Lyon, the river drowning out their voices as it crashed against the wall, my mother cupping her hand against her ear, unable to hear

"In Miami what?"

a bearded Communist who surreptitiously took notes rushing over from his corner with flashing eyes

"What the hell are you talking about?"

the Tagus River and the sewers that emptied into it, the green sand, fishermen on the pontoon, stones and sections of wall disclosed by the low tide, my uncle Pedro telling my mother to hush and addressing the Communist

"Family troubles, pal, I have a sick goddaughter who's going to be operated on in Geneva" the Communist desperately writing accusations in his notebook

"If you think you can stop the revolution, you're wrong, exploitation of the proletariat is over"

and that same night, in spite of it being May, in spite of the heat, we put one fur coat on top of another, put all the rings we could on our fingers, padded our bras with gold sovereigns and necklaces, went down the stairs with our bracelets jingling like loaded piggybanks, squeezed into two Mercedes-Benzes weighed down with trunks containing East India Company tureens and Italian candelabras, and didn't rest until we reached Madrid, hungry and scared, not knowing what to do next, and yet no one had stopped us during the trip, there were no Soviet tanks in the Alentejo, nor men with Astrakhan caps and Caucasus Mountain dancing shoes playing balalaika and patrolling the highways, we slept in a frightful hotel with a dance hall on the ground floor, a flamenco band and dozens of tragic-looking couples gleaming with brilliantine and shaking the floor with their heels, there were three of us to a bed and not so much as a lavatory, just an eternally occupied toilet at the end of the hallway which, when flushed, emitted the wail of a wounded animal followed by the clatter of a zarzuela, we ended up backtracking to the border town of Badajoz, which we were at least familiar with from going there to buy Spanish candies, and finally returned to Estoril, smothering in our coats and rings, to be greeted by the toothlessly cheerful gardener

"Good afternoon, ladies"

who was watering the plants as if nothing had changed, even though jeeps with young soldiers were parked under Estoril's arcades and poor people from the shacks on the hill were sun-ning themselves at Tamariz Beach, stretched out on canvas chaises longues with a lordly air, dribbling ice cream on themselves without any employee shooing them away, not to mention the dozens of houses that stood empty, most of our acquaintances having taken off for Brazil, meanwhile people from the bank brought papers for João to sign, and he didn't even lift his head from the couch where he snored twenty-four hours a day, he scrawled his name with his eyes closed, without reading anything, without waking up, João who swore that he never had a mother, but he had one, who convinced us all that he'd never seen her, but he'd seen her, and he continued to see her, and when the American ambassador met with the Bolsheviks, he gave them a good scolding and ordered them to stop harassing my uncles and the reverend prior, who went back to taking care of the poor and the Catholic Women's Association and discussion groups for married couples, who went back to the shacks on the hill overlooking the sea

(*it was July and the waves were so blue so blue so blue, you can't imagine how blue those waves were, bluer than this blouse, I swear I never, never saw a blue like that, not even in Sicily or Greece, I felt like being poor and living in a shack just for the sake of that ocean blue, what a waste it is on those people who lack the sensibility to appreciate nature and would prefer five escudos to a fabulous view, I don't know how God can stand to deal with uncouth people, what a chore*)

thanks to the reverend prior they had bingo, recreational activities, and free soup on Sundays at the Catholic social center, where we put on cute aprons to serve them, the poor people seated at table, we serving them even as Christ had washed the apostles' feet, they kissing our hands and asking for more soup, and if we'd let them they would have eaten a barrelful each, because what they want isn't the Bible or mass, it isn't for us to take them to the Hieronymite Monastery and the Coach Museum, it's to stuff their faces, they asking for more soup and kissing our hands

"Thank you, ma'am"

once more humble, respectful, domesticated, well-behaved, though when I mentioned this to the reverend prior he called me aside and cautioned

"Don't let their kindness fool you, Miss Sofia, they can't be trusted, they're as false as Judas, be on your guard and don't get too chummy, I'm only telling you this to keep you from getting disillusioned"

and it's absolutely true, so true that if we stop giving them food they immediately start to complain and snap at us, who are only there to make them happy, some of them even get obscene, I remember this one indigent, a huge troglodyte with a dog on a leash that was actually a piece of rope, trying to hug my cousin Filipa and muttering at her between bowls of cabbage soup

"You look really scrumptious, ma'am, you look really scrumptious"

the outraged reverend prior immediately phoned the police, my cousin's husband even considered divorce but finally just pulled some strings so that we never again saw the indigent, though his dog still showed up at the church once or twice, dragging the rope that served as a leash and raising its droopy snout to sniff our legs, until it too disappeared, they're probably both at a police station getting the punishment they deserve, the reverend prior did his best to console Filipa and her husband Nuno

"I promise you that he's going straight to hell, without so much as a whiff of purgatory, I've already arranged for an exposition of the Blessed Sacrament to make sure"

and as soon as my uncles were released from the prison fort of Caxias, next to the sewers of Lisbon and the fishermen's seaweed-covered pontoon that extended over the water toward the river's mouth, they summoned me to the office in Estrela, offered me a ginger ale, showed me file after file full of mortgages, letters of credit, receipts, and IOUs, all with João's signature at the bottom, and then waited with a serious look for me to say something, and since I said nothing my uncle Pedro grabbed my elbow and held it for a long time, as if I were about to faint or had just become a widow and he, full of compassion, felt it was his duty to take care of me

"Your husband robbed us"

the office heavy with silence, a muffled cough, worried faces, my cousins brushing invisible dust from their ties, examining the pleats in their trousers, staring at the ceiling, and suddenly a voice in the corridor

"Hey Zé Alfredo, hey Zé Alfredo"

I looking at the hieroglyphics of the file folders, at the unintelligible columns of numbers, at the photocopies, carbon copies, the variously colored sheets, at all that rigmarole

"What João did during these past months was snore and sign his name after the X while half asleep, like he was told"

a few hurried steps, the voice in the corridor getting louder

"Hey Zé Alfredo, hey Zé Alfredo"

my uncle Pedro releasing my elbow, his pity and compassion transformed into rage, rushing to the door and flinging it open

"What's all this ruckus, you animal?"

my uncle coming back all flushed, with the vein in his neck throbbing and his fingers still shaking, my uncle straightening his collar, straightening his shirt cuffs, once more taking hold of my elbow, once more caressing it slowly with his thumb, once more full of pity and compassion, determined to take care of me

"Asleep or awake, your husband robbed us, Sofia, it's all there"

more silence, more muffled coughs, more invisible dust, more pleats on trousers, more eyelashes raised toward the ceiling, where I found nothing of interest, just white paint, a thin jagged crack, and two halogen spotlights, each attached to a stem and pointing in a different direction, like the antennae of a cross-eyed lobster, I understanding nothing in the file folders, imploring once face after another

"He robbed us?"

when what I felt like doing was playing bridge in Estoril with my cousins and my mother, who acted as if needles were being poked into her rear end every time I played a card

"Hearts, Sofia, hearts, you're just like the maids: clever in certain things and plain stupid in others"

when what I felt like doing was being at the swimming pool with the kids, or at the hairdresser's, since my roots were already showing, or at the hair removal center, since I had a rallye the next day, or at the chinaware auction, where there were some teacups and vases I was interested in, and I thought that if I caught a cab right away and paid a high tip, I might still get those vases, I who was prevented from leaving by a stockade of uncles

"He robbed us?"

João who was after all a Communist, after all a Russian, after all a ruthless Bolshevik who wanted us to end up in Siberia, to shiver in the cold among the reindeer and be devoured by bears, João after all against us, hating us just like the poor, and in fact I remember João being dressed like a poor man at the farm that became as squalid and full of trash as the hill with shacks, his shoes were falling apart, he didn't have a belt, and he slept on a rickety cot next to the stove, João just like that troglodyte with the mangy dog, and my uncle Pedro caressing my elbow with the gentleness of a monk, my uncle Pedro calmly stating the obvious

"You can't stay married to a scoundrel like that"

and I glancing at my watch, afraid I'd miss out on those vases, agreeing with what I was told and accepting what I was asked to accept, including divorce, as long as I could make it to the auction for those teacups, I remembering the sea at Estoril, the snipes of Estoril, the palm trees of the casino, hastily making an appointment with my uncle's lawyer and asking them to lend me a car so that I could make it to the auction before the chinaware I wanted went on the block, my Uncle Pedro, full of understanding, turning to my cousin Rodrigo, who was in the back of the room smoothing down his lapels with the edge of his hand, fascinated by the stenographer's legs

"Have Augusto bring the Rover for Sofia, Rodrigo"

and luckily I now have those teacups on the sideboard and those vases in the living room, everyone thinks they're absolutely stunning, and they cost peanuts, people drop their mouths when I tell them what I paid

"You're kidding"

the vases that the reverend prior borrowed for the Easter celebration and that João never saw, because that same evening they took all his stuff to the farm, and my brothers forbade me from talking to him, and forbade him from entering our house in Estoril, João standing at the gate dumbfounded, jingling his keys on the other side of the shrubs, his arms open like the statue of Saint Rock at church

"What's going on?"

the maids all on the porch, stretching their necks to hear better, hidden by the stone table and the creeping vines, the gardener stationed behind the latticework of the arbor, and I'll bet that the seamstress, her thimble glittering, leaned out from the attic window, João knowing perfectly well that he robbed us but playing dumb

"What's going on?"

João who has never seen the teacups or vases, nor the remodeling I did to enlarge the back of the house, including a dressing room and a room with an insulated door so that the kids can have their friends over without disturbing me, I also enlarged the pool and covered the tennis court with a synthetic material, since the more they hit balls back and forth the less they'll do drugs, write bad checks, and make out with girlfriends in the halls at school, the less they'll be obsessed with buying little white packets from the gypsies, which the reverend prior blames on their not having had a real father, João never scolded them, never gave them any guidelines, never talked to them, he'd go to the farm to help my father-in-law with his cows and come home smelling like worms, and when he was staying in Estoril, he'd traipse off to Guincho Beach to fly kites, summer or win-

ter, in the cold and wind and rain, storms threatening, lightning everywhere, the albatrosses taking refuge in the fortress and
he skipping across the sand, drenched to the bone, with paper
stars at the end of a ball of string, my mother flabbergasted

"Is your husband a moron, or is he just pretending?"

João who never tried to get hugsy when we came home after
a birthday party, a cocktail at Turf Bar, or dinner at some fado
place, he would lie down without a word and turn out the light,
and if I tried to caress him he would sit up with a start and yell
as if there were a fire

"What was that? What was that?"

and I putting on my nightgown, sitting at the dressing table
to remove my makeup, and gazing at the peaceful trees in the
window

(the cotton balls black as soot, why does the cotton get so
black when I take off my makeup?)

blushing with embarrassment for having touched him

"It was nothing, go back to sleep, it was nothing"

João who never saw the teacups or vases

(*"What's going on?"*)

grasping the bars of the gate with his arms open like the
statue of Saint Rock at church, my brothers in the middle of
the begonias blocking his way, and the voices fell silent, I heard
footsteps heading toward the train station down by the water,
then an infinite calm, as if we'd all died without dying, as if we'd
stopped breathing but were still alive, the creeping vines motionless, the tea roses motionless, the flowering broom motionless, the house's shadow motionless, making the dark evening
yet darker, my uncle Pedro at his office, caressing my elbow with
his thumb

"You've made the right choice, don't worry"

and yet I'm not so sure, not because I love João, no, I stopped loving him a long time ago or perhaps, as my mother says, I never really loved him, it's not a question of love or of passion, it's something else, it's waking up suddenly, groping at the pillow and not finding him, it's this feeling of solitude like a deep well, it's the sound of his footsteps heading toward the train station in the depths of my fear, not the rustling of his clothes and not his breathing but his footsteps, the sound of his steps down the empty walkways, and when I tried to remember his face, his hands, his voice, what came to mind was a threatening sky, lightning and wind, the albatrosses taking refuge in the fortress and a silhouette skipping over the winter dunes with a paper star at the end of a ball of string, I don't feel any love, no, there's no more love, or perhaps, as my mother claims, there never was any love, since you can't love a clod who has nothing to do with us even if his father was an important assemblyman or minister and a friend of Salazar's, it was a whim, a caprice, a delusion, a delirium, it was pity, it was surely out of pity, and as my uncle Pedro pointed out, those who rob us don't deserve pity, they deserve to be punished for taking advantage of our kindness and ingenuousness, for it was ingenuousness, kindness, and concern for other people that caused my relatives to be locked up for a year at Caxias, next to the sewers and the pontoon, with the Tagus crashing against the prison wall, my uncles and cousins humiliated by the Communists, treated like animals, without shoelaces or neckties, my uncles and cousins without any insurance company, offices, real-estate agency, or bank, and the Bolsheviks and revolutionary troops insulting them

"Fascists"

so that as compensation for being robbed we kept the farm in Palmela, which amounts to a bunch of cows and crows and the foundations of a manor house sinking into the swamp, my cousin Martim says we're going to raze it all with bulldozers, level out the ground, and build a resort for spending weekends and holidays in the Arrábida Mountains, which are just a stone's throw away and fabulous, plus a sauna, a jockey club, and a golf course, none of which exists on the south side of the Tagus, just low-income housing, Indians and mulattos who come out after dinner wearing pajamas and slippers and reeking of onions to empty their trash into the Dumpsters, and since João has nowhere else to go, he'll end up moving to the slope with the poor people's shacks made of boards and sheet metal, with the sun shining down on their poverty and reflecting off the empty cans and broken glass strewn about the wild grass, he'll end up moving to the slope of shacks overlooking the sea, which my mother says is only right, and he won't even notice the blue of the waves even bluer than this blouse, a blue like you can't even find in Italy or Greece, an unreal blue, João coughing in a hovel without electricity or running water but with a canary, a lettuce leaf in a bamboo cage, and a useless ceiling lamp with dangling pendants, the north wind blowing through rags, scraps of newspaper, shredded blankets, tatters from umbrellas, a soleless boot, I standing at the door, nauseated by the stench of poverty

"João"

João refusing to answer, intently coughing over a pot of soup that I wouldn't eat for all the gold in the world, João wearing a worn-out coat, worn-out trousers, and a rope instead of a belt, looking as much like a beggar as he looked in the courtroom in Lisbon, João turning his head and standing up but too rheumy-eyed to recognize me, João hobbling toward me with outstretched hand, his wrist in a filthy cast, I not moving too close for fear of lice but opening up my purse and placing ten escudos in his palm

"Now don't go spend it all on liquor"

João staring at the coin, weighing it, wiping it on his knee, sticking it in his pocket among the ribbons, pieces of hardware, buckles, keys, and other useless items that poor people like to hoard for some mysterious reason, João to me, shaking his tatters in a joyous smile with missing teeth, João inexcusably rude, blowing his nose on his shirttail, João absolutely unbearable

"You can rest easy, miss, because I'm taking it straight to the car dealer's to buy an Alfa Romeo."

REPORT

I knew they would come to evict me, but I never thought it would happen like this. I imagined Sofia's family, policemen, uniformed guards, and her divorce lawyers bursting into the garage where I was finishing my boat or else rousing me at night from the cot I'd set up next to the kitchen stove, I imagined them pushing me out the main gate under the October rain, then watching me as I waited for the bus to Lisbon or Setúbal, since any bus would do, I imagined the eucalyptus leaves still calling me when I was already far from Palmela, the leaves of the climbing vines still calling me, two or three lonely notes from the piano, and then nothing. I knew that it was just a matter of time, that the court would sign the order, and that I would be evicted, but I never thought it would happen like this, by way of two unassuming men wearing civilian clothes and carrying leather briefcases, two mild-mannered men intimidated by the decrepit splendor of the sofas and the gilded picture frames lying in pieces on the floor, I pointing to a wicker chair full of holes

"Won't you sit down?"

it was January and the bougainvilleas blocked the sunlight, intensifying the silence, my father in the clinic of Alvalade unable to talk, with an enamel bedpan between his thighs

"Wee-wee, Senhor Francisco, it's time for wee-wee"

the empty swing swinging back and forth, the windmill by the well rusting away in the wind, the cows, pigs, and chickens all stolen or gone astray, leaving only the pigeons and magpies, the German shepherds on the crest of the slope, and I finishing my boat in the garage, expecting them to come and evict me but not like this, no sir, not like this, not two unassuming men opening up their briefcases, flipping through papers, showing me an eviction order I didn't bother to read, I showing them a wicker chair full of holes

"Won't you sit down?"

one of the men with a comedian's mustache groping in his pockets for a pen

"Please sign here"

and they didn't seem serious, they seemed like the clowns hired by Sofia for the kids' birthdays, the clowns who would come in through the kitchen door, shut themselves in the storage room to flour their faces, and then burst in after the cake and ice cream, greeting the kids with white gloves and playing two-steps on the saxophone, the clowns who looked like relatives of our maids, and Sofia would go to the kitchen to get them a slice of birthday cake and hand them an envelope, and then they'd leave, trailing their encased instruments along the garden wall, and before the court officials started telling jokes and speaking Spanish in jest, I felt like telling them

"You must have the wrong address, I don't have any cake, I don't have any money, today isn't my birthday"

the kids in a circle on the floor clapping hands, popping balloons, pulling on their enormous shoes, the clown with a mustache, whose pockets seemed to multiply like desk drawers, pulling out a pencil stub in the hope I'd think it was funny and laugh

"Please sign here"

I'd call to them from the fence, the buffoons would stop and turn around, the flour on their cheeks under the halo of a streetlamp once again highlighting their humility and submission, the waves gnawing the darkness beyond the trees from China, beyond all the yards, I handing them a hundred escudos each and they kneeling down on the sidewalk, opening their saxophone cases to show how grateful they were

"May we play you a two-step, sir?"

the same music that blind people play and that for some reason makes me cry, I running back to the house overwhelmed by a strange nostalgia and holding back tears, my mother-in-law putting on her silver fox in the foyer and frowning

"What a frightful racket"

the saxophones playing louder, the sound of fighting, arguments, suitcases, the engine of a car vanishing in the cypresses, my father shouting

"Get out"

the windmill searching for wind, the tractor straining in the cornfield with all its might, a row of turtledoves on the roof of the greenhouse, I wiping my eyelids

"It's a beautiful two-step, don't you think?"

my mother-in-law levitating in a cloud of perfume

"Are you a moron, or are you just pretending?"

the clown with a mustache placing the eviction order on the chess table instead of trying to move me with a two-step

"Please sign here"

a stone angel flitted over the rooftop without anyone seeing it but me, just as no one but me saw wolves and kidnappers in the dark nights of my childhood, the clown without a mustache offended because no one had offered them a slice of birthday cake

"We were instructed by the court to seal everything"

to seal the crows, the wind, the frogs, the eucalyptus trees, the whispers, and voices of the past, to seal the cook lying flat out on the altar and my father with his pants down

"I do everything a woman wants except take my hat off, so that she won't forget who's boss"

to seal my father in the clinic, too

"Wee-wee, Senhor Francisco, it's time for wee-wee"

the jester with the mustache tearing off a sheet from the eviction order

"This duplicate is for you"

I placing it like a piece of sheet music on the piano

"Duplicate of what?"

for there was nothing under the birds' sarcastic caws but brush and clay walls that would be washed away by next February's torrents, and they affixed their solemn seals on the doors, the windows, and the frames without windows, they taped shut one room after another instead of telling jokes and shaking my hand with white gloves and playing the two-step "Pisa Morena," and they managed to seal the crows, the magpies, and the frogs' wailing, they put a wax seal on the cows' mooing, and they sealed the cypresses one by one until we reached the main road, leaving the farm as still as a graveyard, and I to the clowns while pointing out the café frequented by Palmela's peasants, workmen, and traveling salesmen, who fell silent whenever I entered, as if I were my father and might have them arrested, I hearing a musical echo and feeling nostalgia for I didn't know what, as if my own birthday were being celebrated that very afternoon

"Sure you wouldn't like a slice of cake?"

a funeral proceeded up the hill to the cemetery in a bustle of chrysanthemums and widows pushing on the coffin to keep it from slipping off the wagon, the unemployed sat on the stone wall and smoked as usual, there were the usual fish vendors without customers, the usual poor people and mangy dogs, and the clown with the mustache retreated a step and pulled on the jacket of his partner while the funeral evaporated in a spiral of golden petals

"How do we know he isn't armed?"

and then I noticed a third clown at the wheel of a government car parked under the elm trees on the square, I saw what looked like Sofia's brothers in the backseat, and the two saxophonists got into the car without taking their eyes off me, as if they expected me to pull a pistol from my belt and start firing

(*my father trudging through the lettuce in the vegetable garden "Shoot at them, they're Communists, shoot"*)

but I have no aim, I'd be afraid to hurt someone, and I don't even know how a gun works

(*"Shoot, you dummy, shoot"*)

I who can't stand the sound of gunfire, the smell of gunpowder, the sight of blood, when I was little and my father hunted rabbits and partridges I couldn't bring myself to touch them or to look into their dead eyes, the car with Sofia's brothers sped away toward Lisbon and the petals of the funeral wafted around the square the way the feathers of the partridges used to waft around the shrubs, their hearts uselessly racing, slower and slower, and then a violent jerk, their bodies transformed into inanimate objects, and then nothing, my father folding his shotgun

"Go fetch it"

I walking toward it, touching it with the tip of my finger, and recoiling as if it had burnt my hand, frightened that it might start breathing again, that its blood would start flowing again, like a broken alarm clock that we shake and the mechanism revives, the second hand wakes up in a feverish start and hesitantly resumes its ticking, and to my father as I leaned over the confused mound of beaks and claws

"I can't"

perhaps if I were different and not so squeamish about death and blood then Sofia's brothers wouldn't have gotten the farm, they wouldn't have sent a couple of clowns to rob me, if I were like my father I would have planted myself with a shotgun at the top of the steps, and not a single machine gun or army jeep would have come through the gate, my father who if he weren't in the clinic would have stuck out his chest, aimed his shotgun, and not even raised his voice

"Scram"

and the soldiers, the Communists, Sofia's brothers, and the goofy saxophonists would have apologized and left with their tails between their legs, my father who would say to Salazar

"I think it's better this way"

and Salazar would nod his head, my father who would say to Salazar

"I think it's better that way"

and Salazar to his secretary, who would immediately set down his teacup and pick up his memo book

"Take note of Senhor Francisco's opinion"

Salazar next to the whistling roses, asking my father for advice about certain ministers, national assemblymen, the United States, the colonies in Africa, Salazar being introduced to the pharmacist's widow right after she'd removed her shoes to rub her aching corns and paying his due respects

"Pleased to meet you"

while the even more respectful secretary kissed her hand, ignoring the cracked nail polish

"My pleasure, madam"

and her lapdog in a fit of jealousy tried to bite the secretary, the pharmacist's widow strangling its neck until the animal changed color, then scolding the creature as it went away gasping through its wide-open jaws

"Nero"

and when the government car vanished from view on the road to Lisbon and the chrysanthemum petals subsided, I heard the church bells and remembered my father's cousin who lived with us on the farm and who brought me into town to attend funerals

"Just look, João"

fascinated by the pall over the casket and by the firemen's band that followed the wagon, the cousin who ate with us at table, on the side of the living room where the draft lifted up our napkins, and slept in a cubicle next to the chapel, the cousin who had no money, whose clothes were threadbare, who had a hat with a broken feather and a beadwork purse for when she went out, and whom the maids ruthlessly humiliated, refusing to make her bed or wash her clothes, turning up the radio if she tried to give orders, and sticking shriveled rats in her sheets, the cousin who knitted in a corner of the kitchen under the dish towels until the housekeeper, exasperated by that useless deadweight surrounded by balls of yarn on the floor, shouted at her to get lost

"Don't you see, ma'am, that you're in everybody's way?"

the cousin who would look for me at dinnertime when I was playing with the frogs

"Wash your hands, João"

I squatting in the mud with green slime on my shirt and breeches, poking at a frog's goiter with a twig and answering back

"You can't tell me what to do"

my cousin dragging me by the arm to the house, I trying to break away

"I want my mother"

the housekeeper's silhouette against the water tank

"Let the boy go, ma'am"

my cousin who one day asked me into her cubicle next to the chapel, locked the door with the secrecy of someone plotting a coup d'état, reached under the bed, pulled out her suitcase full of threadbare clothes, and rummaged through little boxes, veils for Mass, bundles of photographs and letters, a chinaware marchioness missing half her wig, and a tarnished silver ladle wrapped in newspaper, until she finally arrived at a velvet pouch containing a pearl cameo with a woman's profile in a nimbus of wrought silver, which she placed in my hand with trembling fingers

"It belonged to my grandmother and now it's yours, João"

and Sofia opening up the pouch, turning the cameo over in her fingers, then handing it back to me with a frown

"What am I supposed to do with a gewgaw like this?"

my cousin putting back her treasures into the suitcase, protecting the marchioness with a woolen cap, wrapping her silver ladle more snugly than before, my cousin in a choked voice

"It was my grandmother's finest piece of jewelry, she wore it in all the photographs I have of her"

her poor grandmother in a fifth-floor walk-up in Lisbon trying to stretch out her husband's pension till the end of the month and telling all the neighbors about her godfather the corporal, about the nag she once had and her vacation in Nazaré, where she walked down to the beach in the arm of her brother-in-law who was in charge of a deeds office, the grandmother who gave violin lessons and published sonnets in an almanac from Beja, and Sofia

"I'll bet she won this trinket in a box of cereal, give it to one of the maids, João"

my cousin pushing her treasures back under the bed, the hat with the broken feather balanced on the back of her head

"One day, when you get engaged, it will make a wonderful present for the lucky girl"

and for years she asked me almost every day about the cameo, calling me aside in the hallway in a conspiratorial whisper

"You didn't lose it, did you, João, swear you didn't lose it, don't lie to your old cousin"

and I to Sofia

"Gewgaw my eye, this is an antique piece of jewelry that's probably worth a fortune"

Sofia summoning one of her sisters-in-law as a witness and holding up the pearl cameo of a woman's profile

"Tell me what you think of this, Madalena"

the sister-in-law distractedly glancing over while shuffling cards and asking the score

"Since when did you start scavenging junk from the garbage like a beggar, Sofia?"

and when I caught the train at Tamariz Beach I threw the cameo into the river, and since it was night and the lights were on inside the train I couldn't see the embankment or the waves, I saw my own face in the window, and next to my face I saw a collar made of yellowed lace and a hat with a broken feather anxiously inquiring

"You didn't lose it, did you, João, swear you didn't lose it, don't lie to your old cousin"

and I to the lace collar and the ridiculous hat, my ire mounting as the stations fronting the sea sped by in a succession of platform lights and hexagonal clocks, I to the beadwork purse with missing beads while the conductor snapped his hole puncher in my face

"Your grandmother's precious piece of jewelry wasn't worth a counterfeit dime, you idiot"

more platform lights, more clocks, another stretch of sand that loomed and disappeared, me gesticulating before the startled conductor, who was about to raise his gold galloons to the emergency button

"Your precious cameo wasn't worth a counterfeit dime, did you hear, you idiot, it wasn't worth a counterfeit dime, did you hear, it wasn't worth a counterfeit dime, you idiot"

my cousin who lived with us until the housekeeper, exasperated by that deadweight surrounded by balls of yarn on the floor, shouted at her to get lost

"Don't you see, ma'am, that you're in everybody's way?"

my cousin who refused to obey, who said nothing, whose knitting needles stopped moving, and the housekeeper jingling the keys in front of her eyes

"Don't you see, ma'am, that you're in everybody's way?"

my cousin with her unmoving needles, not knitting and not getting up from the stool, refusing to obey the housekeeper, and the youngest of the maids, who sometimes spent a long time with my father in his office and wore a ruby ring given to her by I don't know whom

(*that's not true, I know exactly who gave it to her because I heard her say who, I saw her showing her bracelet and ring to the other maids*

"Just look"

and the other maids looking at her wrist, looking at her finger

"Play your cards right, for there's bound to be more where that came from")

the maid shaking my cousin's shoulder

"Are you deaf?"

the needles dropped first, then the beadwork purse, then the rest of my cousin, the housekeeper jumping back

"Oh my God"

and I accompanied the funeral up the hill to Palmela's cemetery where the deceased, on their tiptoes, can see the ocean, my father didn't yell or get mad at anyone, he chewed on a spent cigarillo during the whole ceremony, watching the prior say prayers, the grave-diggers shovel dirt, and the sack of quicklime being poured over the coffin, and when it was all over, the housekeeper blew her nose two or three times and we left the cemetery with the pall still draped over the empty wagon, my father spent the rest of the morning in the greenhouse with the orchids, arranging their leaves and petals like I'd never seen him do, as if styling their hair, and all for a cousin who made me shrivel with embarrassment in Estoril

"What am I supposed to do with a gimcrack like this?"

telling me tall tales that I was stupid enough to believe in

"It was my grandmother's finest piece of jewelry, she wore it in all the photographs I have of her"

about a junky cameo, making me look like a mental retard to Sofia's family, telling me that a piece of plastic trimmed with tin was mother-of-pearl and silver

"One day, when you get engaged, it will make a wonderful present for the lucky girl"

and as soon as I got home I went to the cubicle next to the chapel, pulled the suitcase from under her bed, carried it to the carport next to the garage, poured gasoline over it, lit a match, and in five minutes there was nothing left but ashes

"I'll bet this hideous gewgaw was the prize in a box of cereal, give it to one of the maids, João"

like my father did with the bracelet and ring

"Play your cards right, for there's bound to be more where that came from"

in five minutes there were just ashes, with the silver ladle being reduced to a smelly paste, and the chauffeur who shared the cook with my father appeared, worried about the flames and the smell of gasoline

"Did something happen, Master João?"

I wondering if my father knew about the cook and the chauffeur

"Don't worry, nothing happened, I was burning some manure, sweep this up for me"

and thinking that he probably did know, that he must have known, even as he knew about my mother and sent her away, and because he knew, he did whatever they wanted except take his hat off, so that they wouldn't forget who was boss, my father who as far as I can remember never talked to me, never gave me a kiss, never took me in his arms, suspecting that my mother had conceived me by another man, the chauffeur sweeping the ashes into a bucket

"With a fire like that and all this gasoline we're lucky, Master João, that the whole farm didn't go up in flames"

he lived in a room that looked out onto the courtyard where rabbits were flayed, and each morning he hung a little mirror on the latch to shave, bare-chested and whistling, winking at the cook and watching out for the maids through his open window, I never understood why my father, who sometimes fired employees for no reason at all, never fired him, a useless parasite, a philanderer whose job consisted of leisurely running a felt cloth over the car hood and a brush through his hair when he wasn't romping with all the women on the farm, I walking toward the dovecote

"You're the one who's lucky that the farm didn't go up in flames, since then you'd lose your monthly stipend"

imagining his resentment and the insults under his breath, he sweeping away the ashes and wishing he could sweep me away as well, I who made him deliver messages, run errands, mail letters in Palmela, get my signature notarized in Setúbal, pick up my coat at the dry cleaners, I who arrived home early one Sunday when my father was at a meeting in Lisbon and found him swimming with the cook in the pool, splashing about in a hoopla of slaps and giggles

"What the hell is going on?"

both of them stark naked, looking at me as if I'd just risen from the dead, the panic-stricken cook climbing the steps as plump, glistening drops streamed down her body

"I'm sorry, Master João, I'm sorry, Master João, I'm sorry, Master João"

I wondering why my father always called her into the chapel, grabbed her by the hips, lifted her apron, and laid her flat across the altar, when she spent all her wages on tie clips to appease the chauffeur, the cook taking cover in my brand-new towel

"I'm sorry, Master João, I'm sorry, Master João, I'm sorry, Master João"

the chauffeur on the air mattress stammering explanations, gathering up the pharmacist's widow's suntan lotion and my father's bottle of whiskey, marching like a penitent to his room with the little shaving mirror on the latch, I in my father's office, clutching the desktop so violently that my fingers turned white

"Fire them"

my father in silence behind the newspaper, his face swallowed by shadows in spite of the fluted lamp, my father suddenly vulnerable, fragile, passive, as I would know him years later in the clinic of Alvalade with a bedpan between his thighs

"Wee-wee, Senhor Francisco, it's time for wee-wee"

my father as if confiding a secret

"There are things you don't understand, João"

my father whom I preferred to see in his rubber boots in the stable, disagreeing with the veterinarian about the heifers being pregnant, ripping up the prescription, and tossing the bits of paper to the ground

"Nonsense, Doctor"

the doctor who taught classes in Lisbon, wrote books in French on foot-and-mouth disease, and terrorized assistants with his angry outbursts, the doctor as tall as my father, as corpulent and as explosive, slipping in the dung as he respectfully hopped to his feet

"You may be right, sir"

my father whom I preferred to see clasping the neck of the sergeant's wife, separating her knees with the tip of his shoe, bending her over the sideboard

"I do everything a woman wants except take my hat off, so that she won't forget who's boss"

my father as helpless as me when I was evicted, I who knew they would come to evict me, but I never thought it would happen like this. I imagined Sofia's family, uniformed guards, court officials, judges, and lawyers bursting into the garage where I was finishing my boat or else rousing me at night from the cot I'd set up next to the kitchen stove, but it was after all just a pair of unassuming men wearing civilian clothes and carrying leather briefcases, and I came away with them from the farm without putting up a fuss, without the slightest protest, as if I were accompanying the flour-faced clowns to the train station, stepping in time with a two-step played on the saxophone, I on Palmela's town square among the gypsies and the unemployed and the fish vendors without customers, here on a bench under the elm trees watching the funeral wagon go up the hill to the castle, I inside the coffin under a shower of petals, gazing at the evening turtledoves without really caring if they occupy my farm, if they occupy my house, if they sit in my chair at my table, if they sleep in my bed, not caring about all that, because there's always a place for an extra clown at the birthday parties of Estoril.

COMMENTARY

It was all very unpleasant for me and my family, which is why we hesitated, weighing the pros and cons and putting off the decision, thinking that we might simply forget what João had done to us, but when our analysts showed us a scale model and explained that the farm of Palmela could be made into a resort with an excellent return, we had to take action, not because of the potential profits

which in this case happened to be considerable

but because it would allow us to recover a little of what he stole from us

(and if we recover much more than what João stole from us, it will be due to hard work and careful management) as well as stimulate tourism, create jobs south of the Tagus, and improve the national economy, in spite of the unconscionable way the Portuguese government treated us after the Revolution, when we were crucified, insulted, condemned without trial or proof of guilt or the right to a decent lawyer, and locked up in a cell in Caxias with the worst riffraff imaginable, forever dreading the moment when the army or the Communists, who lost no opportunity to humiliate us, would rush in and kill us, dropping our bodies in the river to be devoured by cuttlefish, the army and the Communists sparing not even our wives, whom they tormented at 3 and 4 A.M. with cries of justice for the people, and taking from our homes whatever they felt like, furniture, paintings, silverware, saying they were proof of economic sabotage, as if an eighteenth-century oil painting or an Empire chest of drawers could have anything to do with Fascism, as for me

(worried about this nonsense called democracy and about the coloreds becoming independent, because the only thing those monkeys are good for is showing their teeth in big grins on missionary calendars, granting them independence is plain ludicrous)

as for me, I was in my office calmly speaking on the phone with our representative in Switzerland, trying to transfer a few measly dollars to Zurich so that we might make some sort of life for ourselves abroad, and suddenly my door sprang open without anyone knocking or even turning the knob, for a second I thought it might be my secretary, to whom I foolishly gave too many liberties and Italian dresses

(not to mention the two-bedroom apartment outside Lisbon, in Carnaxide) but it wasn't my secretary, because one hour before she entered the office I could smell the duty-free perfume that cost me twenty thousand escudos for one dinky bottle, it was a section chief from the bank who didn't bring his kids to receive their knickknacks at the annual Christmas party and who always pretended not to see me when I passed by so that he wouldn't have to stand up, an idiot whom with all the other problems I have to deal with every day I'd forgotten to fire, the idiot followed by a dozen screaming voices and frenzied pistols, I to the representative in Switzerland, cupping the receiver with my palm

"Just a minute"

astonished, dumbfounded, not understanding a thing, and least of all my secretary standing in their midst making hand signals of distress, not for my sake

(I never believed in the love she swore each time I left a check between the alarm clock and my picture)

but for the sake of her silver, two-seat convertible Honda on which I was making the payments, and the section chief, a pip-squeak from some godforsaken suburb who should have kissed my feet, yanking the telephone cord from the wall with no respect for my age, sixty-seven years if I'm a day, waving a typed sheet of paper and pointing me out to the pistols

"That's the head honcho"

I looking at them with the receiver in my hand and trying to understand my secretary's Morse code, she worrying that our trip to the Sierra Nevada was off, one of the pistols searching my pocket with such fury he ripped the alpaca

"Stand up"

just like that, without any "please" or "sir," I'm not exaggerating, a ruffian like I've never even seen on the streetcar

"Stand up"

I, with ripped pocket and still holding the phone against my ear, dragging the cut cord behind me as I simultaneously spoke to Zurich and the pistol

"Excuse me?"

and five minutes later I was walking down the stairs flanked by a bevy of unkempt soldiers who were applauded by the tellers, applauded by the Communists, applauded by the cleaning women, and even my slut of a secretary, after a moment's hesitation, started clapping louder than the rest, her fingers so loaded with gold that I still don't know how she was able to move them, on the street the applause changed to threats, a clerk kicked me in the rear end, an office boy spat on me, and I with the receiver against my ear, unable to distinguish if it was the personnel from the bank or the representative from Zurich who was insulting me, I talking to the mouthpiece while they pushed me into an army wagon

"Excuse me?"

and in the prison of Caxias I met up with my brothers, my nephews, my associates, each one clutching a telephone with a hanging piece of cord in the vain hope of transferring a few crummy bucks to Denver, Paris, Tokyo, Barcelona, all of them without shoelaces or neckties, speaking in unison to the dead receivers

"Excuse me?"

in the evening I was summoned to the second floor, where a cabin boy typed in a corner, his index finger like a beak pecking at the keys as at corn, and a weasel with glasses who could have passed for the husband of my wife's seamstress ordered me to confess my foreign bank account numbers, and I to Zurich, forgetting that the phone was definitively dead

"Be sure not to give away the account numbers, Carvalho"

the cabin boy, tired of pecking, made like he was screwing his finger into his temple to suggest to the weasel that I'd lost my mind, but the weasel, oblivious to the cabin boy's screwdriver, walked toward me with his arms angled like a grasshopper's, as if he were going to devour me

"Don't think for a minute that you're going to keep exploiting the working class"

I who never exploited the working class, on the contrary, I'm forever giving money to beggars at stoplights and donating sacks of beans to soup kitchens, and just look at the kinds of tips I leave in restaurants, and for weeks on end the illiterate cabin boy and the obstinate weasel haranguing about the exploitation of the working class, I eventually hearing reports that things were improving in our country in spite of the blacks who, masquerading as people, were jumping for joy in the African bush on the hope that they'd soon be ruling over their thatched huts, when the truth is that they continued to bow down and get pushed around, only it was no longer we who did the pushing but the Russians, I hearing reports that things were improving in our country, that the Church was finally acting to defend Christians and that the Americans were determined not to let us go down the tubes, I calmly answering with my legs crossed

"You'll have to call Zurich to find out the account numbers"

looking with pity at his cotton shirt, his serge trousers, his clearance-sale shoes, enduring his breath that smelled like meatballs and stale tobacco, exactly like the smell of a chauffeur's quarters, and it's not just the clothes and bad breath of subordinates that bother me, it's their having to pretend that they're different from what they are, it's their going into debt so that they can have furniture and Fiats just like other subordinates, it was September and the beach of Caxias was overrun by groups of kids in underwear wading in the sewer water and disturbing the mullet, and as I always say, what makes it hard for this country to become a civilized place is the Portuguese attraction to filth, proven by the fact that we tolerate the smell of niggers to the point of enlarging the world's population with mulattos, and the way things are going we'll reach a point when there's not a white person left in Lisbon, we'll all run around in corn-husk skirts, dance to tom-tom music, put rings in our noses, and eat boiled beetles, but to get back to subordinates, there are things the poor slobs never learn no matter how much we teach them, no matter how well trained they may seem to be, they still say belly instead of stomach, movie instead of film, slacks instead of trousers, supper instead of dinner, pass away instead of die, and to hear these words sends a paralyzing chill down our spines, so that when my secretary, for instance, would sit on my lap and call me sweetie pie, it made me lose my erection for a month, it's sad to say but there are three types of people, namely my type, the parvenus, and those whom the parvenus call the provincials, and so

I wonder

how it's possible for democracy to exist, for my vote to be worth no more than that of a joker whose bimbo wife gives two kisses instead of one and says

"What's new?"

when she runs into me and

"Toodle-oo"

before hanging up the phone, how it's possible for my vote to count the same as the vote of a clod whose idea of happiness is a yellow Mercedes-Benz and who refers to a pretty girl as a dish, in my own experience, after paying an interior decorator to make the apartment in Carnaxide acceptable, I discovered that the dish who was my secretary wouldn't rest content until she'd filled up the bookshelves with chinaware ducks and photographs of herself wearing a bathing suit and orthopedic sandals at Albufeira in the Algarve, where she spends her vacation among mosquitoes and Spaniards who clip their toenails in public, staying in one of those ghastly tourist complexes that cater to businessmen from Oporto, women who sell jewelry to their friends and coworkers on installment, and general practitioners with eight medical insignia on their windshields, and yet we're the ones, for some reason that's beyond me, who get thrown in jail when a revolution comes along, I myself realized the impossibility of democracy as a child, when I complained to my mother about a certain maid's stupidity, and my mother, engrossed in a *Paris-Match* article about the marriage of some princess or other

("Your petit-bourgeois side," lamented my father, "as if you'd been raised in Penha de França, Campo de Ourique, or some worse neighborhood")

"If she weren't stupid, she wouldn't be a maid"

in my opinion Salazar's greatest blunder was to ingenuously allow all these plebes to get rich, to let all these Fernandas, Fátimas, Victor Manuels, and Carlos Albertos buy condos in tasteless suburbs like Cacém, to enroll in the university, and to become officers in the army, and the inevitable result is calling cards with gilded letters, traffic jams, ugly high-rise developments and political parties, with the Communists practically gaining control, staging jamborees with speeches and guitar music on the dusty slopes of Ajuda and organizing excursions to northern Portugal to catechize the peasants, who, too attached to their cows to share them with their neighbors, quickly drove out the atheistic friars under a hail of stones, the Communists occupying buildings with the help of Lisbon's bums and outcasts, who are all too willing to abandon their park benches and loll on sofas that don't belong to them, provided they're not separated from their bottles of beer, I trying to look after the family's business concerns in prison, giving instructions on what to buy and sell during visiting hours, prompting calculated losses in the bank and the insurance company after they got nationalized, transferring our international operations to Brazil, persuading the French to stop aiding the Bolsheviks, propping up the real-estate agency with Australian capital, using my niece's half-baked husband, who never realized that we all made fun of him, to carry out some financial operations that enabled us to keep our heads above water, the half-baked husband of my niece Sofia, son of a churl who got rich as a government minister and administrator under Salazar and paid next to nothing, I kid you not, for a huge farm in Palmela where he raised pigs and orchids, a farm between Portinho and the mountains that will earn me a fortune if it's properly developed, a churl who, waist-deep in cow shit, fornicated with his maids without ever taking off his hat, as if it could hide the fact he was a cuckold, when everyone knew who the cuckolder was, I in Caxias fighting for my family so that my wife and the other women in the clan could keep spending a fortune on hairdressers and tureens and so that my imbecilic children and nephews could stuff enough cocaine up their noses to prevent them from coming to the office with business proposals and big ideas, to prevent them from tallying up their stock shares and trying to unseat me, the way I unseated my old man when I got tired of being a useless appendage who watched in agony as our stagnant assets slowly eroded, and so I made promises to various people, enticing them with a few seats on the board of directors, a few administrative positions, some discreet promotions and some vague guarantees until I'd secured 52 percent of the votes, whereupon I called a special shareholders' meeting

(and my dumbfounded father

"A special shareholders' meeting? What on earth for?")

and named him honorary president by unanimous acclamation, all of us clapping hands, my daughter Mafalda presenting him with a piece of expensive Venetian crystal, a few aunts who looked like bears in their fur coats feeling so touched underneath their facial creams that they had to dry their eyes with the tips of their handkerchiefs, my bewildered father, pulling on my sleeve without paying attention to the piece of crystal or to Mafalda, his favorite granddaughter

"Honorary president? Honorary president?"

I nodding to Mafalda not to worry, to go ahead and hand him the piece of crystal, Mafalda looking like she might hurl it to the floor and run away, a few managers showing signs of remorse, my brother Miguel shooting me a furious glance and walking out the door, I interrupting the clapping to hug my father, whispering into his ear with filial feeling, full of emotion

"I've got fifty-two percent of the votes and if you don't accept immediately I'll make your life hell"

Mafalda, without taking her eyes off me, walking forward with the piece of crystal that my father, who had taken his seat, refused to accept, and I with tender concern, putting my arm around his shoulders

"I'll make your life hell, Dad, I swear I'll make your life hell"

more clapping, more tears, more handkerchiefs, yet another infuriated brother storming out and slamming the door, my airhead wife looking puzzled, Mafalda once more hesitating, and I grabbing the bibelot from out of her hands and placing it like one of the three Magi

(the black one who, because he was black, must have been more subservient than the other two)

on my old man's lap, kissing him on the forehead before he could once more repeat, from out of his stupor

"Honorary president? Honorary president?"

I in an angry hiss between my smiling teeth

"Accept the gift, because I've got conversations on tape that will ruin your life if you don't"

my old man wanting to call me

"Scoundrel"

but not being able to, wanting to call me

"Traitor"

but not being able to, since he knew I'd cook his goose in a stew of scandals involving deception and embezzlement of the family's money over the course of thirty years, he knew I'd cook him like a quail in the casserole of his swindles without even bothering to pluck his feathers, he acknowledging the applause as if he were being shot, holding on to the crystal object with blind hands, walking out of the meeting room like a windup toy, my hands securing his sticky armpits with tender urgency, putting him in the car without accepting the driver's help, I with a final piece of advice to accompany my final kiss

"If you're stupid enough to breathe a word to anyone, then you can say good-bye to your pension as well as to your little hussy"

a typist forty years younger than my father and forty times more of a spendthrift than my mother, a blonde as crass as they come, a baker's stepdaughter who was crowned Miss Salvaterra de Magos in a beauty contest sponsored by the town's volunteer firemen and who was the joy of some junior economist at the bank when she wasn't escorting my old man to Rome or Bangkok, Mafalda in my private office, her lips trembling as they always did when she got mad, her upper teeth all showing, just like those of a growling puppy

"Aren't you ashamed, Dad, of what you did to Grandpa?"

and I as if I hadn't heard, taking all the time in the world to serve myself a whiskey and handing her a glass that she pushed away, her teeth growing yet larger under her upturned lip, she fuming as if on the verge of an epileptic fit

"You won't be satisfied until Grandpa's six feet under the ground, will you?"

I patiently explained to her that she was foolish and didn't understand, that it wasn't like she thought, that Grandpa was too old to be worrying about businesses, what with all the emotional stress, the physical strain, the conflicts that come up, his heart, his blood pressure, his diabetes, his last checkup at the Mayo Clinic, what he needed now was to rest, to take it easy, to have time to enjoy himself without problems or hassles, and besides, people's mental faculties diminish with age, they become narrow-minded and set in their ways, there were new methods and procedures that my father rejected, and the family's business enterprises can't be managed as if we were running a grocery shop, not that I'm comparing your grandfather to a grocer, heaven forbid, but you've always been a smart girl

(that's a lie, she's not at all smart, fortunately none of my children is smart, because if they were just a wee bit smart

not very smart, just a wee bit

then they would already have given me a piece of crystal, a pension handsome enough to tickle my fancy with the Miss Salvaterra de Magos of my choice, and the title of honorary president which, like all titles, is equal to no title)

but you've always been a smart girl and can see what I'm getting at, and Mafalda beginning to yield, her teeth growing smaller, her lips no longer trembling, I looking at her and thinking how easy it is to tame idiots by telling them that they're intelligent, and after I was done with Mafalda I went to the other private offices and did the same thing with my brother Miguel and my brother Gonçalo, swearing how much I admired them and how I thought they were geniuses, and I solemnly promised them a larger role in the insurance company and a larger role in running the bank, which is to say a larger car, an office as big as a recreation hall

(in which I'd gladly put a mambo band if they wanted it)

and a more pompous title for the two pieces of deadwood, I never again saw my father, because the ungrateful codger refused to see me, I was always told he had a headache, or was sleeping, or had gone out, I in the foyer hearing the squeals and giggles of the Miss upstairs, the Miss who came to see me at the real-estate agency decked out like a Christmas tree, with a bracelet around her ankle, rings on her thumbs, and an imitation-leopard dress made of Lycra, and if my memory serves me correctly I went with her once or twice to a quiet hotel to find out between the sheets, since that's where such things are discussed, if my father was plotting anything, and as soon as I started adding zeros to the check, the typist told me that my old man had made some phone calls and hung up in a rage, complaining between sips of gin about his nephews' disloyalty and cowardice, I signed the check

"If his nephews stop being disloyal and cowardly, it wouldn't hurt for me to know"

because it's important to monitor the vacillations in my cousins, a bunch of weaklings who do whatever their wives tell them, boobies who are too lightweight for their ambitions, if only I had a close friend in whom I could trust, the hotel wasn't bad, the mattress not bad, the service was acceptable, and the Miss, who had become more lovey-dovey since I'd signed the check, did coochie-coochie-coo on my chin and cooed

"Don't you trust me?"

while rolling around on the duvet and meditating on her future (because my father wasn't eternal), the Miss who wanted to be devoted to one man, "I swear I'm the kind of girl who wants to be devoted to one man, God strike me down if I don't want to be devoted to one man," the Miss who wanted to be a recording artist, to be a dancer in a theater, to have an acting career, just to keep her busy whenever the object of her devotion would, what a drag, have to work, because it's perfectly possible to be a performing artist and be serious, to be an artist and be faithful, to forgo the big dinners after performances, to refuse to hang out in bars and nightclubs, "you have no idea what a homebody I am, if I find a gentleman who treats me well I'll swear to him that no other man exists," and I tickling the nipple of her breast

"I'll have to talk to an impresario I know"

she running her fake fingernails through my hair, and I actually had to look twice before I could tell they were fake, while clarifying

"I'm more like a daughter to your father than a lover, I'm like his ward"

and so we occasionally returned to the hotel to discuss the duties of wards and my old man's phone calls, I reporting that the impresario was on a Brazilian tour, a week in Rio, a week in São Paulo, and a week in the Amazon jungle to offer Shakespeare to the Indians, but that we had exchanged telegrams, and as soon as he returned to Portugal he would start casting for a new play, a Broadway show in which the actors not only acted but sang and danced, and so he wanted to see some photographs and meet her as soon as possible, the Miss gave me an envelope with pictures of her making faces at the camera in her underwear, "pictures taken in front of my parents by a cousin of mine from Salvaterra de Magos who happens to be gay, if you don't believe me (but I'm sure you believe me, you have no reason not to, because you know what a serious girl I am) just ask them"

I stuffing the envelope into my trouser pocket, where it bothered my leg, to make sure I remembered to throw all that lingerie into the wastebasket, thinking about what Salvaterra de Magos must be like and how I didn't have the vaguest idea where it is, though we no doubt have a branch there with a dimwit teller behind the counter, I sweeping away Salvaterra de Magos with a magnanimous gesture

"Ask your parents? Don't be silly, of course I believe you"

I believed in her and she believed in the impresario in Brazil until I single-handedly controlled 70 percent of the family and no longer had to worry about the machinations of my old man, who gradually became resigned to his piece of crystal and stopped conspiring behind my back, and so one afternoon, while I was trimming my sideburns in the mirror of the hotel room and the typist got out of the shower with a towel tied in a turban on her head, I pointed to a check for double the usual amount and said

"This is the last time I'm coming here"

she hugging me from behind and brushing hairs from off my collar

"Did you get us a cute little apartment, sweetie?"

and I with my eyes fixed on the mirror to finish the knot, because I can't stand crooked knots on neckties

"I think you're better off with my father than with me, he has more time to take care of your acting career"

her hugs suddenly slack, her breathing against my neck suddenly faster, her turban coming undone, her voice like that of a baby consoling itself, talking to itself

"You're just joking, aren't you? You must be joking, sweetie pie, aren't you joking?"

when I left she was sitting on the bed, mouth agape and head between her hands, utterly incredulous

"What a fool I was"

and so I instructed my secretary not to transfer any calls and told security to put her on the street should she show up at the bank, she wrote me a threatening letter with more spelling mistakes than insults, and yet it must be said that she wasn't lying when she said she'd devote herself seriously to just one man, for she moved bag and baggage into my father's place in Estoril, to better love him with total loyalty and dedication, so that when my sisters and female cousins went to visit the old man, they were welcomed by an ankle bracelet and an imitation-leopard outfit that addressed them as "my little darlings," offered them chairs, and did coochie-coochie-coo on the chin of the honorary president with a conjugal familiarity that outraged my sisters and cousins, who promptly hired a lawyer to prevent the typist from entering the family and inheriting my father's 0.8 percent which they thought was 29 percent, and it was a good thing they thought so and didn't badger me with suspicions and innuendos when all I'd done was protect the family's interests, and given their stupid ingratitude, it's better that my relatives not know they're being protected, my sisters and cousins trembling with fear that they might become poor like the down-and-outers they gave sweaters to and served soup to on Sundays under the direction of the clever prior, a slyboots who wasn't even bad-looking, and every year he bought a new BMW at my expense, my sisters and cousins imploring me as they paced around my office in a whirlwind of face powder

"Now what do we do?"

and I, trying to do my work, weary of that cyclone of shantung dresses

"Isn't Dad, at the age of eighty, entitled to have a little fun?"

I told the lawyer to hold his horses and not make any waves, because waves make me seasick, to reassure the ladies and nod his head but do nothing, since I myself would resolve the matter in a discreet fashion that would make everyone happy, and so I had lunch with my father's doctor to find out how long the old man's diabetes, blood pressure, and heart would hold out and if it wouldn't be advisable to perform one of those complicated surgeries in which real arteries are replaced by rubber ones, with the convalescing patient being hooked up for months to three dozen machines with three dozen tubes going into his body while being spoon-fed cups of soup until a redemptory pneumonia liberates the poor slob from the machines, tubes, and soups, and the doctor, whom I had appointed director of the insurance company's hospital just a few days before, wavering between his salary and a few lingering ethical principles, remembering the mortgage payments on his house in Restelo, which made him lean toward his salary, but still with a smidgen of moral hesitation

"This type of operation tends to be more successful when done abroad, where they have more experience and better technology than we do, if you like I can contact a clinic in Los Angeles and your father will come back a new man"

I with determination, unwavering in my patriotism

"The example has to come from the top, if all our sick people are operated on in Los Angeles we'll never go forward, how can our surgeons progress if they're not given the chance?"

the doctor, who if he left the insurance company's hospital would have to return to the hubbub of Portela, next to the airport

"I have a colleague who studied in Scotland, but I doubt he'd operate on someone with your father's age and heart, he'd take one look at the test results and turn up his nose"

I persuasive, increasing the number of beds in the insurance company's clinic

"There are plenty of students fresh out of med school just waiting for an opportunity, we need to give young people a chance" and so an intrepid young man with a scrubby beard laid my father out on the table, and he didn't even make it to the machines and tubes, nor did he require the good graces of a pneumonia, he expired forthwith

(without suffering)

after the first whiff of anesthetic, would that I go so peacefully when my hour comes, falling asleep instead of weighing ninety pounds and moaning for weeks from the pain of lung cancer, and before he was under the ground, when his corpse was taken to the Basilica of Estrela in an endless procession of bootlickers and hypocrites, I sent a few expeditious types with experience handling ticklish situations on a diplomatic mission to my father's place in Estoril, where the typist, scantily dressed in ostrich feathers, fell on the sofa in distress as soon as they opened their mouths

"Don't hit me, take whatever you want but don't hit me"

and since she was what they wanted, they stuck her in a taxi, with her feathers but no luggage, headed for Salvaterra de Magos, where I'll bet that the Miss, who wanted to devote herself to one man, ended up marrying one of the firemen who elected her beauty queen or else the cousin who photographed her on all fours in bed wearing frilly panties as her parents looked on, for as I always say, life is sunny if we know how to take advantage of our setbacks, in my case, for instance, being in prison helped me arrive at 93 percent control, courtesy of some ingenious transfers that I laid to the charge of Sofia's husband, convincing my brothers and nephews that he'd converted to Bolshevism, convincing the judge of his Communist swindles, and as compensation for his thievery and illegal dealings, Sofia was awarded the farm, meaning that the family was awarded the farm, meaning that I was awarded the farm, I passed around some managerial posts to mollify the skeptics, for there are always those who, judging by their own lack of integrity, can't believe in anyone else's, and the development will get under way next month, with a golf course, tennis courts, and swimming pools just ten minutes from Arrábida, we've already leveled what was left of the house, we burned the couch grass, burned the geraniums, filled in the swamp, destroyed the eucalyptus trees, the vegetable garden, and the orchard, poisoned the crows and the magpies so that not one threatening bird will flutter about disturbing our guests, and we killed some scrawny, half-wild dogs that had trembling lips like my daughter Mafalda and that leaped every which way, barking at the cranes and biting the workers, last week I went to the requiem mass for my father, most of the family was there, along with a number of employees, a number of people who claim to have been his friends, and the opportunists who always show up in the hope of getting some leftover crumbs, the sly prior, whose ambition is to succeed the bishop, delivered a histrionic homily about camels and needles that filled the offering plate with ten-thousand-escudo notes, and my wife murmured to me from inside her Astrakhan grotto, my wife who goes to a shrink for her depression and whom I sometimes catch secretly observing me at breakfast with a look of resigned rancor

"I wish I were dead, I wish we were all dead"

and I swear there are times when, thinking about it, I wish so too.

second report
(The mischief of inanimate objects)

REPORT

I realized something was up when little João started crying. I was in the garden, fretting over the roses' fever, building a tent that would protect them from the wind, and at first I didn't think it was the boy who was calling me but a widowed pigeon in one of the cedars or a goose that had strayed into the boxwoods, and when I felt my skirt being tugged, I said

"Be still, Adamastor"

without turning around, and the wind suddenly died down, the blades of the windmill stopped creaking, the geraniums and the birds-of-paradise stopped whispering in the flower beds, I could hear the waterspout in the pool and the cackle of a crow in a beech tree, the German shepherd kept pulling at my skirt, whining all the while, I pushed the animal away with my foot

"Be still, Adamastor"

and was surprised by a soft, tear-choked voice that hung on to my clothes

"It's not Adamastor, Titina, it's me"

so I took him into my arms and looked for a scraped knee, since he was always running into a statue, or injuring himself on the stone borders of the flower beds, or tripping on the cement blocks that held up the umbrellas, and I nervously lifted his bangs, expecting to find blood

"Did you fall down?"

but there were no cuts, no scratches, no blood nor even a dirt stain, just his nose buried in my neck as he shook with tears and pointed his finger

"Mommy Daddy Mommy Daddy"

and so I realized something was up when little João started crying. Today I wonder if I shouldn't have done something when Senhor Francisco and Dona Isabel first started having problems, because they both listened to me, hardly a day went by that Dona Isabel didn't ask my opinion about one thing or another, the maids, the monthly expenditures, the house

"What do you think, Titina?"

and even Senhor Francisco, so different from the man he became later, would call me into his office and have me sit down like an equal to talk about the stable or the vegetable garden or certain changes in the orchard

"What do you suggest, Titina?"

little João with no cuts, no scratches, no blood nor even a dirt stain, just his nose buried in my neck as he shook with tears and pointed his finger

"Mommy Daddy Mommy Daddy"

and so I forgot about the roses' fever and walked to the house, my shadow and the boy's shadow mingling together as if he were mine, and even today, long after him growing up and having his own children, after Senhor Francisco sending me away from the farm, and after the people at court sending Master João away, so that I've lost touch with him, even today I feel that he was mine, that he is mine, for it was with me that he started to walk and talk, it was with me that he fell asleep, it was me he called for in the middle of the night, afraid of the dark

"The wolves are right outside, Titina"

I rocking him, fondling his hands, and stroking his cheeks until the wolves went away and the kidnappers vanished, until I thought he was asleep, I gently pulling away my fingers, standing up, walking toward the door, and little João's voice

"Titina"

the boy who belonged to me because he preferred being with me rather than with Senhor Francisco and Dona Isabel, the boy who went with me to the kitchen, the sewing room, the post office, the pastry shop, and the market in Palmela, who made drawings for me in the account book, who made paper boats for me from the bills, the boy whom I bathed and took to the doctor, for whom I peeled fruit, cutting it up in bite-size pieces, and for whom I crushed aspirins in a spoonful of sugar, the boy whom I washed and dressed, little João who didn't belong to his parents but to me, the son I didn't give birth to but who was mine, holding on to me with all his might

"What happened, João?"

Senhor Francisco and Dona Isabel arguing in the bedroom with the door open, she pulling clothes out of drawers and piling them on the bed, grabbing brushes from off the dresser, yanking dresses from their hangers, trampling blouses, trampling scarves, trampling those beautiful satin slacks that she wore when she had company and that now dragged behind her, caught on a heel, not one Dona Isabel but two or three Dona Isabels reflected in the mirrors from different angles, and Senhor Francisco was also two or three Senhor Franciscos, gesticulating at one another as if they were angry at themselves rather than at

Dona Isabel, whose way they blocked, and she, like I'd never seen her, threatening them with her hair dryer

"Let me go"

fighting with all those Senhor Franciscos

"Let me go"

Senhor Francisco grabbing the hair dryer and smashing it against the top of the dresser

"Tell me who the lover boy is, Isabel, I want to know who the lover boy is"

a shattered case of face powder, bottles of perfume on the floor, the lamp from the nightstand in pieces, and Dona Isabel looking for a sandal while taking slugs at Senhor Francisco

"Let me go"

the broken mirrors multiplying the two or three Senhor Franciscos into ten or twenty or thirty who repeated in unison

"Tell me who the lover boy is, Isabel, I want to know who the lover boy is"

Senhor Francisco shaking her until one of his reflections caught sight of me and little João, whom I held in my arms and who wasn't their son, he was mine, the only son I had, and the reflection looked straight at us

"Get lost, Titina"

Dona Isabel also looked at us as if her son weren't her son, and he wasn't her son, he was mine, holding me tight with his nose buried in my neck, Dona Isabel or a fraction of Dona Isabel in a fraction of mirror, just her hands, legs, forehead, and part of her chin, looking at us for a second as she pulled a trunk over to the bed to fill it with blouses, dresses, shoes, and shawls, her permanent all disheveled, with no lipstick or makeup or fingernail polish, not at all like when she would phone for a taxi and instruct me, while checking her stockings for runs

"If anyone asks for me, I went to do some shopping in Palmela"

while her husband was at the ministry in Lisbon, Dona Isabel walking down the drive through the cypress trees to a car that waited for her beyond the gate, under the elm trees by the square, and she'd come back humming without any shopping bags, I'd try to talk to her about dinner, and she, dancing about as she searched for the bath salts and turned on the faucet to fill the tub, unbuttoning her coat and twirling it over her head on the tip of her finger

"Fix whatever you like, Titina, it's all the same to me"

I'd try to tell her something about Senhor Francisco or the house or the maids, and she, pulling the plug with her toes and flicking a bit of foam at me

"Not now, Titina, hand me the towel and tell me about it later"

the bathroom tiles all steamed up, the shelves steamed up, the window so steamed up I couldn't make out the orchard or the magpies, just green patches beyond the glass, and a mark on her chest that she covered with some cream, tittering

"A puppy bit me, Titina, an adorable little puppy"

at first she shopped in Palmela once or twice a week, then three or four times, then five, the phone would ring on Saturday and Sunday, and if I answered they hung up, if Senhor Francisco answered they hung up, but if Dona Isabel answered she'd talk in whispers for the longest time, Senhor Francisco would ask who it was and Dona Isabel, cool as a cucumber, would say it was a girlfriend from high school whom she hadn't talked to in ten years, isn't it amazing how time flies, one of these days I'll have to go visit her in Coimbra, you could take some time off and we'll make a little holiday out of it, what do you say, Francisco, erasing his doubts, knowing full well that he wouldn't take time off from the ministry, and so on almost every weekend there was a girl from high school I haven't seen for centuries who would suddenly remember to call her friend in Palmela, and Dona Isabel giggling, wiggling, whispering into the receiver with her eyes closed

"Me too"

returning to the table as if she were floating, rolling a bit of bread into a ball instead of eating, the crows mocking in the vegetable garden, the geraniums mocking from the flower beds, Senhor Francisco suspecting nothing, glad that his wife's friends were so fond of her

"Your fish is getting cold, Isabel"

in August Dona Isabel, taking enough luggage for a hundred-year journey and beaming with so much excitement that she even kissed me, went on vacation for a month to Coimbra without leaving an address

"I've no idea where Luísa lives, I'll call you when I get there"

Dona Isabel patting little João on the head

"The only last name I remember is her maiden one, which won't do you any good, why the interrogation, Francisco?"

but Dona Isabel, who got the names of her girlfriends mixed up, what they did and their families mixed up, and the stories about her high school mixed up, never did call, she wrote a single letter from Spain explaining that she'd taken advantage of being in Coimbra to hop over to Madrid with her girlfriend,

I could tell Senhor Francisco missed her from the look on his face, all alone at the dinner table, alone in the living room with his books or leafing through the newspaper, smoking cigarillos while pacing up and down the hallway like a suffering soul, hands in his pockets, until Dona Isabel arrived home and in a foul mood, setting her luggage in the foyer and plopping down on the sofa without greeting anybody, frowning with disgust

"I'm exhausted"

the crows laughing their heads off, the frogs laughing their heads off, Senhor Francisco sitting down next to her and she moving away as if she'd been bitten

"Not now, Francisco, I'm exhausted"

looking at the paintings, the furniture, and the piano as if she hated them, as if they got on her nerves, picking up a fashion magazine and setting it back down, grabbing a cigarette and forgetting to light it, blowing out the lighter that Senhor Francisco held out to her

"Can't you leave me in peace for one minute, Francisco?"

slamming the door of the guest room, turning the key, and not coming out until the next morning, at eleven, when her husband was already at the ministry, she in her bathrobe, covered with cream for her wrinkles, cocking her head with disgust on the terrace where the gardener was pruning the creeping vines and the boxwoods

"My God, how ugly all this is"

I who could have helped her if I were smart, if I'd had some schooling, if I hadn't gone to Paços de Ferreira to be a servant when I was twelve, Dona Isabel ignoring João, not touching her tea, tapping her spoon against the jam jar, the butter dish, the teapot, taking a bite of toast and leaving the rest on her plate, muttering in French, the magpies pretending to pick lice from their feathers as they silently watched her from the railing, I with a mind to shoo them all away with the broom, and shooing them away with the broom is something I still have the strength to do, thank God, and the telephone started ringing, Dona Isabel dropped her spoon and jumped up, transfigured

"I'll get it, Titina"

the tractor now closer, the windmill turning so fast I couldn't make out the blades, just the glistening of metal enraged by the wind, and Dona Isabel, instead of whispering to her high-school classmates

"Me too"

knitted her eyebrows, puckering her lips so that I wouldn't hear

"I can't keep on like this, love, I swear I can't keep on like this, it has to be tomorrow"

and life was happy for her again, she drank the cold tea and ate the limp toast, got dressed, combed her hair, put on her makeup, spent hours polishing her nails, phoned for a taxi, and went shopping in Palmela, I at wit's end snapping at the maids, finding fault with everything, yelling at the cook, yelling at the dressmaker, chewing out the gardener over a wilted daffodil, the clock devouring the hours with an infinite hail of chimes, little João whimpering because he was sleepy or hungry

"Not now, child"

the beech trees turning dark, the driveway through the cypress trees turning dark, the crows retreating to the eucalyptus trees in the swamp, the lights of Setúbal, the lights in the mountains, a sort of halo over the ocean that couldn't be seen, a car in the courtyard, the sound of steps on the porch, Senhor

Francisco with a puzzled look, setting his briefcase on the table in the foyer, opening the door of the guest room, the door of the bedroom, the door of the living room, cuddling the boy who wasn't his boy, he was mine, because I was the one he called for when he fell down or was afraid of the dark, Senhor Francisco loosening the knot of his tie

"Where's my wife, Titina?"

Senhor Francisco in the chapel, in the greenhouse, in the roses, in the vegetable garden, circling around the house, and I hearing his soles on the cement, on the brick, on the gravel, on the soil, Senhor Francisco's eyes opened wider than I'd ever seen, and I couldn't help him because I'm not smart, I didn't have any schooling, I went to Paços de Ferreira to be a servant when I was twelve

"Where's my wife, Titina?"

picking up the phone, hesitating, pushing down on the hook with his finger, I feeling ashamed of I don't know what, all I know is that I didn't want to be there, and at that moment headlights coming up the drive, lighting up the cypress trees one by one, the sound of a motor getting louder, Dona Isabel's heels on the porch, Senhor Francisco with a face you had to pity

"What happened, Isabel?"

with a face you had to pity, I mean if I were Dona Isabel I would have stayed with him out of pity, Dona Isabel who didn't notice him, who didn't hear him

"Is dinner ready, Titina?"

who sat down at the table, took her napkin from its ring, and poured herself some water as if nothing were the matter, the dining room suddenly seeming terribly sad, a poor people's dining room in spite of the fancy furniture, Senhor Francisco lifting the pitcher that shook

"What happened, Isabel?"

she staring at him but not giving him the time of day

"The soup, Titina"

little João whimpering to be cuddled, to take a pee, for some candy, and no one paying him any heed, not even me

"Titina"

the maids hopping with curiosity in the kitchen, jostling each other in the excitement of an imminent tragedy

"He's going to hit her, isn't he, Dona Titina, he's going to hit her, how much do you want to bet he's going to hit her?"

the maids as happy as magpies, nudging each other in ecstasy

"He's going to hit her, isn't he, Dona Titina, he's going to hit her, how much do you want to bet he's going to hit her?"

and it began to rain, because I could hear the roof, the windows, the orange trees, and the stone angels calling me with a human voice

"Titina"

wings and branches tapping farewells on the windows, Dona Isabel locking herself in the guest room without a word as the first lightning struck, so close to us that it cut off all the lights in the house, transforming the rooms into a maze of dark shadows full of yet darker cabinets, empty mirrors, and blank spaces in the sculpted frames from where all the faces had vanished, lightning struck a second time, a third time, the dogs howling, the chestnut trees groaning in pain, and in the flash of a thundering discharge of still more shadows I saw Senhor Francisco at the door of the guest room like a crucified Jesus

"Isabel"

little João whimpering in the darkness to be cuddled, to take a pee, for some candy, and God forgive me but whom I wanted to cuddle at that moment wasn't the boy but his father, to cuddle him in my arms, to pull him away from the guest room holding him tightly against my chest, his nose buried in my neck, to undress him, to lay him down in bed, to tuck in the covers and hold his hand while rocking his body slowly, slowly, until Senhor Francisco was fast asleep.

COMMENTARY

Dona Titina can say what she wants, but it wasn't his wife that Senhor Francisco liked, it was me. He'd come into the kitchen wearing his hat, smoking his cigarillo, and pulling on his suspenders with his thumbs, his hand would wave the maids off to the courtyard where rabbits and chickens were killed, he'd stare at the seamstress with his drooping eyelids until she put down the iron and vanished down the hallway, and with his chin he'd point to the marble table where I was rolling out dough

"You there"

I'd make as if to escape too, heading to the pantry to hide among the pots of jam and sacks of rice, and Senhor Francisco would cross my path, with his cigarillo almost touching my nose

"Be still"

and it was me, not his wife, that he bent over the sink, me whom he grabbed by the hair as I pleaded

"Don't hurt me, please don't hurt me"

Master João peeking at us from the garden until his father went away shaking like a wet chicken, I went back to my risen dough, and the seamstress went back to her ironing, the clock striking five o'clock at midday, and in the living room the voice of Professor Salazar talking to Senhor Francisco

"Don't apologize, for heaven's sake, I completely understand that you had to phone the ministry"

so that Dona Titina can say what she wants and I don't care, she can say that Senhor Francisco only started messing around with me after his wife went away, even though their sheets, long before that, didn't have any stains when I went to wash them in the laundry tub, and she can say he had another woman here, another one there, the pharmacist's widow, the steward's daughter, a dancer or fado singer whom he maintained in Lisbon, she can say whatever she likes because I know

(even if Senhor Francisco, being a man of few words, never said anything)

that it was me he liked, Professor Salazar with his secretary and all those plainclothes policemen would come especially to Palmela to discuss our country's government, jeeps patrolling the farm, the National Guardsmen asking the tractor driver for his ID card and keeping people away with red rackets, and in the midst of the decisions concerning the overseas colonies, Portugal one and indivisible from the Minho River to Timor, Christian civilization, Afonso de Albuquerque and the Portuguese presence in India, the miracle of Fátima, the last bulwark against atheistic Communism, but leaving aside all the blah-blah-blah and getting down to business, should we give Africa to the coloreds or shouldn't we give Africa to the coloreds, Professor Salazar's secretary

(who had to be a pansy, judging by his mannerisms and how he eyed the chauffeur)

shrugging his shoulders as he set down his toast

"The coloreds don't even know what they want"

the March breeze wafting through the couch grass, a first hint of dampness seizing our bones, Professor Salazar tapping his pen against a file folder

"Tell me what else is new, Rodrigues, if the coloreds knew what they wanted there'd be no problem, they'd be white people"

a first hint of dampness creeping toward us in huge black splotches that didn't fool the turtledoves perched on top of the greenhouse nor my ankles already flaking with rust, Professor Salazar putting sugar in his tea as he weighed the pros and cons of giving Africa to the coloreds, suddenly it was dusk, suddenly the first drops fell on the rosebushes, Dona Titina turning on lights in a tizzy, Senhor Francisco getting up from the sofa and excusing himself to Professor Salazar

"Excuse me"

the secretary chirping with wonderment as he picked his toast back up

"I happen to know a colored who wears glasses and teaches French, can you believe it, Prime Minister?"

but I, checking the oven to make sure the rice wasn't burning, didn't hear the answer, because at that moment the maids all scrambled out to the courtyard, the seamstress hid in the hallway, Dona Titina, who had been sticking a fork into the soufflé, ran off to little João's room announcing in two notes, one high and one low

"Bath time"

the flypaper curled and danced with the onset of rain, I shut the oven door and stirred the soup, and a whiff of cigarillo smoke, a clearing of the throat, a voice behind me

"You there"

a voice that lifted my skirt and grabbed my hair

"Be still"

the window blown open by a gust of wind, a sheaf of branches waving into the kitchen, the flypaper sticking to my hair bun, the policemen and National Guardsmen wading in the flower beds, and again the secretary to Professor Salazar in the living room

"I have a message I forgot to give the Minister"

another window blown open by the wind, the carport next to the garage sinking into the mud, a trickle of water falling onto the rug, Professor Salazar looking green in the light of the fluted lamp

Professor Salazar smiling between Senhor Francisco and Professor Caetano* in a photograph in the office

defending himself from a second trickle that fell smack on his head

"Do something, Rodrigues"

the birds flitting from beech tree to beech tree without finding shelter, a National Guard jeep smashing an angel and knocking over statues, the secretary shouting on the terrace at the army vehicles

"The Prime Minister doesn't want any rain here"

the soldiers and policemen on all fours in the mud, firing their rifles at the clouds, and Dona Titina can say what she wants but it wasn't his wife whom Senhor Francisco liked, it was me, she can say that Dona Isabel was prettier than me and had firmer breasts since she never had to sleep with goats, she didn't have to beg from town to town in the Beira district, always afraid of the dogs' fangs, and she didn't have two pairs of shoes without soles and just one dress purchased from the gypsies in Azeitão, and yet when Dona Isabel left him it wasn't a woman with rings and necklaces he chose, it was me, who gave birth to a child all by myself when I was just fifteen, it was me whom Senhor Francisco ordered

"You there"

a child I buried with my own hands down by the river, she and I sticky wet with each other, warm with each other, bleeding the same blood, it was me whose thighs Senhor Francisco wrenched open with his fingers, ordering

"Be still"

and me perfectly still, empty, as when I abandoned my daughter who didn't call after me, who never knew me, and whom no one else ever knew about, just as no one knows about my second daughter except Senhor Francisco and Dona Titina, not the maids, not the seamstress, not the tractor driver, and not the chauffeur, who gives me what Senhor Francisco no longer cares to give even though I'm the one he likes, Senhor Francisco who stopped coming into the kitchen with his thumbs in his suspenders and sending away Dona Titina, the maids, and the seamstress on the day he found me plucking a chicken with a pan between my knees, pretending not to notice him, and he pulled me up by the hair with one hand and touched me where I was already showing with the other, tossing his cigarillo into the pan with the chicken

"What's this"

I looking at him and seeing not him but the pig merchant who took me past the tin goods and the pottery stand to beyond the school playground where the wild fig trees started, poking me in the butt with the stick he used for his pigs, and even without any wind the fig trees spoke, or it was the pig merchant who spoke, or it was my voice that spoke without any sound leaving my throat

"Let me go"

and Senhor Francisco feeling my pregnant belly as if I were a mare or a ewe

"What's this?"

all night long a German shepherd that had cut its paw on barbed wire howled in the kennel, there was an early morning fog and then the first crows shivering from the cold, the steward's daughter walking past the well and down the slope with her pails of milk, the chauffeur dragging the hose across the courtyard to wash the car, I feeling faint, dizzy, nauseated, and Dona Titina standing outside the door

"Senhor Francisco wants to see you in his office"

Dona Titina who can say what she wants, I don't care if it's not true, and I getting dressed and feeling dizzy, I holding on to the dresser as I looked for my shoes and the saint on the wall began spinning like the bumper cars at Sunday fairs

(*what I wanted more than anything else in the world was to buy some earrings made of Minho gold from the jeweler, but I had no money, the pig merchant promised me money and didn't pay up, he promised*

"If you come with me I'll give you some money"

and I wiping the dirt off my skirt

"So where's the money, you creep?"

I all ashamed wiping the dirt off my skirt and he poking me with his stick

"What money?"

and that was the only time, I swear by the memory of my departed mother that it was the only time)

and when the saint finally stopped spinning I walked along the wall, thinking

"I'm going to fall"

the hallway lurching this way and that, a porcelain Moor with a turban now near, now far, voices repeating themselves in an avalanche of syllables, and even before I reached the office I heard him

"Come in"

Senhor Francisco at his desk, clean-shaven and with a tie, wearing his suit for ruling the Portuguese, the one he wore when he appeared in the newspaper greeting assemblymen or inaugurating a hospital, his desk with a stack of books, the photograph of Professor Salazar, the photo of what looked like an actress wearing a fur stole that revealed her collarbones, the president of the Republic, the Cardinal,* the Pope, Senhor Francisco

"So how many months is it?"

and just as I was going to answer that I didn't know, that I hadn't been counting the time because I worked too hard to think about it, the desk started to sway, the president of the Republic and the Pope spun around like the bumper cars at the fair, I felt like lying down on the rug and dying, I felt my body growing in size, becoming much longer, then shorter, then longer, I felt a queasiness in my stomach, a surging wave, I tried to steady myself on the telephone, but it crashed to the floor, and then on the desk lamp, but it slipped from my fingers, Senhor Francisco scooting backward in his chair

"Control yourself"

but I was one of the bumper cars at the fair, I turned one way and glanced off him, then the other way and glanced off him, I saw the tents with pork sandwiches, chitterlings, fritters, music, doughnuts, I saw my father, I saw the jeweler showing me some earrings made of Minho gold, I saw the pig merchant and wanted to ask him for the money, but the whirl that spun me this way and that prevented me from protesting

"So where's the money, you creep?"

I wiped the dirt off my skirt and couldn't find my skirt, I brushed the dirt from my hair and couldn't find my hair, I saw the Pope smiling at me and the Pope disappeared, I decided to tell Senhor Francisco, but Senhor Francisco, rising from his chair and holding up his briefcase

"Watch out for my suit, watch out for my suit"

and my belly heaved like a snapped spring, I hung on to the curtain like a bell-ringer on to his rope, Senhor Francisco came toward me waving his arms as if a boulder were falling from a cliff overhead

"Watch out for my suit for Christ's sake, watch out for my suit"

I wanted to warn him

"Excuse me"

to tell him

"Excuse me"

to beg him

"Excuse me"

and despite Senhor Francisco's efforts to defend himself, the first heave hit him in the face, on his collar, on his tie, I threw up on his fancy coat for inaugurating hospitals, on his files, on his books, on the photograph of Professor Salazar, and in a corner of the office he squealed for help

"Titina"

I begging pardon, assuring him

"I love you"

and Senhor Francisco wriggling on the floor, whining like a child

"Titina"

I who had never loved anyone before, not the pig merchant, not the sexton of Mortágua, not the cripple from the Spanish civil war in the convent for lepers who gave me coins from his alms box for letting him touch my privates

"Let's see what we have here"

and not the jeweler with the Minho earrings who never gave me so much as a crummy bracelet for my favors, a man older than my father who would suck on a vaporizer for his asthma while motioning with his hand

"Wait a second"

and he took me inside his van crammed with his jewelry cases, his tent, and his wicker lunch basket but couldn't do it, he sucked on the vaporizer with all his might while motioning

"Wait a second"

and I thought he'd finally do it, but he couldn't, the jeweler who feared that his colleagues would make fun of him

"It must be the potatoes I ate that sapped my strength, I'll bet it was those damned potatoes, don't breathe a word to anyone and the next time I come I'll bring you a little present" but I never again saw his bumperless van with peeling paint among the other bumperless vans with peeling paint whose tailpipes dragged on the gravel, Dona Titina stepping on the Pope, the Cardinal, and Professor Salazar, I straddling Senhor Francisco, who lay flat on the floor and looked at her, at his son, and at me without seeing anyone, like the blind man from Pinhel, Dona Titina holding little João by the hand

"Holy Mother Mary"

and the walls and ceiling stopped turning, the carpet was again solid, my head screwed back into my neck and I could think, could talk, could tell Senhor Francisco

"I love you"

but it's impossible to say

"I love you"

when you're sitting on top of the man you love, I no longer felt dizzy or dazed, I felt like helping him get up, like cleaning his face and hair with my handkerchief, but it's impossible to say

"I love you"

to a man who looks like a tallow candle dripping tallow tears down his cheeks, Dona Titina arriving with a bucket and mop, which she ran up and down his face as if whitewashing a wall

"Holy Mother Mary"

Dona Titina who broke into tears over anything, whereas I cry the way the pine trees cry into resin pots, without anyone ever noticing, it takes years to fill a pot, and the tears are never seen, when I was little I spent day after day among the pine needles in the forest watching the clouds, the kites, and the men who robbed wood with carts and axes, and the liquid didn't increase by a whit, there was the same bit of sticky goo at the bottom and that was it, if only you understood, Senhor Francisco, that I'm like the pine trees, that it's not for lack of love that I don't say anything, it's not for lack of love that the chauffeur and I, it's precisely because I love you that I accept that the chauffeur and I, but if you said

"Drop him"

I'd drop him the way I dropped the cripple from the Spanish civil war, the pig merchant, the jeweler, and the rest, you'd only have to say

"Drop him"

not ask me but tell me

"Drop him"

because if you wanted me to drop him I'd drop him, if I suspected that you wanted me to drop him I'd drop him, but why is it that you never said

"Drop him"

why is it that you want me to sleep with the chauffeur, why is it that you watch the light on in his room at the same time I watch the light on in your office, and you hear the bed squeak, you hear us talk, you hear me come down the stairs at 2 A.M., shuffling my shoes back and forth in the hallway, hoping that you'll call me but you don't call, hoping that

"You there"

hoping to feel your hand on my neck, your cigarillo almost touching my nose

"Be still"

and after months of no one asking me questions because no one dared to ask anything, or to whisper in front of me, or to remark how I had trouble cooking and took twice as long to fix a rabbit or pluck a chicken, Dona Titina, the maids, and the seamstress pretended not to notice, little João didn't understand, and on the morning that the pangs arrived I felt so heavy I could hardly walk, it was June, the garage was finished, now they were working on the greenhouse, and the water broke out of me onto the sheets, and it was water, not the goo of the pine trees but water, my hip bones separated like floorboards, and I realized how much houses must suffer, and more water, more pangs, my torso sliding out of the covers and onto the floor, my joints snapping one by one as I moved forward, Senhor Francisco noticing me waddle, noticing my stained apron, realizing that I was suffering what houses suffer, picking up the phone, while outside the gardener was watering the birds-of-paradise, the magpies and crows were perched on the new scarecrow that couldn't scare a sparrow, I felt something huge and powerful rip the curtains of my womb and try to get out, and I who in all my life had never asked for anything asked him not to let me be killed by that thing in me that kept swelling, I in between two pangs, I in the moment I was going to die

"Help me"

the workmen weaving among the miffed orchids in the greenhouse like caterpillars in a cocoon, the pigeons rounding the edges of the dovecote with their wings, the frogs causing the surface of the swamp to swell, and Senhor Francisco leading me to the stable through the petunias whose buds were ready to burst

"Take it easy, girl, the doctor's waiting for you"

rows of cows looking at us with their jelly eyes, bales of straw, sacks of seed, the milk pails, some glass roof tiles showing a patch of sky with storks, and higher than the storks a kite, and higher than the kite a cloud gliding eastward, the morning dance of dust particles flitting from window to window, the steward's daughter straddling a bench just inside the door, the cypress trees that stopped existing as soon as the blackbirds deserted them, and the veterinarian with rolled-up sleeves and his instrument case

"I don't understand all your hurry on the phone, Minister, there's no heifer that's going to calve"

the storks and the kite and the cloud had vanished but I could hear the workmen in the greenhouse, I could hear the eucalyptus trees and the creaking wood of my bones, and the veterinarian, bewildered

"I don't understand your hurry, Minister, there's no heifer that's going to calve"

the Minister's eyelids drooping as they drooped when he grabbed my neck and bent me over the sink or the table, the Minister cutting the wires of a bale with pliers, spreading the straw around with his foot and making me lie down, the kite reappeared in the sky, one of the German shepherds sniffed me, the pangs came back and went away and came back again, I stopped seeing the kite, I saw only the scarlet of my pangs and the tip of his shoe pushing my head into the middle of the straw

"You didn't pay close enough attention, my friend, you didn't notice this heifer right here, now please go to work."

REPORT

I didn't say anything, because I knew Senhor Francisco would have to talk to me sooner or later, it was a matter of time, I did my usual duties, overseeing the servants, managing the household expenses, keeping the house in order, and on Monday evenings when he would arrive home from Lisbon and call me into his office for us to go over the accounts together, for me to bring him up to date, for him to tell me what he wanted and what he didn't want, I could feel him looking at me stealthily from behind the crescent-shaped glasses he wore to examine the bills and decipher the numbers, and I could tell he felt like asking me

"So now what, Titina?"

racked by indecision and with no one else who could help him, since no one respected or even pitied him, he'd gotten old, his body sagged, his hair was thinning, night had fallen over the trees, and Senhor Francisco sat there totaling the expenditures for meat, fish, gas, and the work done on the roof without noticing what he was totaling, indifferent to money, anxious to grab me by the arm and ask

"So now what, Titina?"

night having fallen over the trees, and I, who heard him in his troubled silence

"What?"

unsure if I should ask or not, I who was also wearing glasses, peering over his shoulder at the bills, adding in the payroll, the geranium bulbs, the sales of milk and chickens and pigs, cupping a hand to my ear as if some defect had prevented me from hearing what hadn't been said

"What?"

Senhor Francisco's eyes no longer focusing, he shaking his head and refocusing, irritated, verifying amounts with the tip of his pencil but getting them wrong, cross-checking the totals on a notepad, Senhor Francisco, realizing that I realized, not removing the cigarillo that burned his lips, so that I wouldn't notice how they trembled, and pushing the bills toward me

"I didn't say anything, I don't have the concentration for bills tonight, I'll look at them tomorrow"

I leaving his office and aware of his fear that I was leaving, just like little João's fear of being left helplessly alone in the dark, and it was as if they both called me at the same time, each one sobbing in a different part of the house

"Titina"

each one wanting me to sit close by, with the light on, protecting them from the wolves until sleep quenched their fear, daylight returned, and they could live again, and to this day they probably still call for me at night, but I can't help them, for when I get up to go be with them, right as I'm about to grab the doorknob, I hear the occupational therapist in Alverca's charity home for women

"Where do you think you're going, Dona Albertina?"

and she walks me back to the room for needlework and paper flowers as the trucks heading north shake the walls the way they do all the livelong day, I and my companions embroidering tablecloths and bedsheet borders from nine to noon and from two to six, or else sticking daisies onto wires, the occupational therapist making me sit down on my stool, handing me the needle

"At eighty years of age and with your arteries shot to hell, do you think you can just gad about, Dona Albertina?"

and what I see from the window is the highway of Alverca, the pillars of an unfinished overpass that's crumbling among the weeds, a row of buildings where no one lives except some beggars from Africa with their pots and their thin mattresses, entering by way of a field covered with rubbish and olive trees, what I see from the window is the bus station down below, the shadow of a cloud moving over the ground, and I flubbing up on the embroidery because my mind isn't in Alverca, it's on the farm

"Senhor Francisco and the boy need me"

Senhor Francisco, who when I brought him his whiskey before dinner would scoot forward in the armchair while wiping his forehead, I putting ice in the glass and thinking he'd said something

"Excuse me?"

feeling sorry for him, you understand, thinking it would be good to get him to talk, as when you prick an abscess to relieve the pain, as when they opened up my molar at the polyclinic and it hurt but the pain soon vanished, Senhor Francisco, just like a child, hiding behind the newspaper as if covering his face with his hands

"Nothing"

the pillars of the overpass of Alverca, one here and one there, like you find in those ancient monuments that people from far away visit to take pictures of and professors give lectures on, talking about Romans and Greeks, marveling over a few boulders worn away by time and completely useless, as well as ugly, the pillars of the overpass reduced to an iron skeleton with a few hanging tatters of brick and cement, no bearded fool having yet thought to assert "It was obviously a Phoenician temple," even as by a similar oversight the row of illegally constructed buildings occupied by African beggars still hasn't been declared a national monument, and the therapist, taking a daisy from the hands of one of my companions who couldn't find the hole and deftly hooking it onto the wire stem

"If they needed you, Dona Albertina, they wouldn't have stuck you in this dump"

but neither Senhor Francisco nor Master João have any idea I'm in Alverca, since otherwise they surely would have come to get me, for they don't know how to manage without me around to keep the servants in line, the accounts straight, and the household in order, and especially Senhor Francisco, so fussy about his shirts, so fussy about dust, running his pinkie over the top of a dresser and showing me a speck of fuzz you couldn't even see with a magnifying glass

"Look at this dirt, Titina"

Senhor Francisco who would yell for me if he saw a thread on the runner in the hall, a rug that was an inch out of place, a fingerprint on a platter

"Do you like things untidy, Titina?"

the occupational therapist undoing my needlework because she said I'd made a parrot instead of a turtledove

"Be sensible, Albertina, why would this Senhor Francisco need an old woman like you?"

instead of a turtledove from the farm, the turtledoves for which we had to build a box on posts to keep out the German shepherds, and it kept out the German shepherds but not the magpies, and so there was a pandemonium of different eggs and birds of every sort pecking at each other for the corn, and I may have been old but it was me who kept their servants in line, it was me they came to when problems arose, not their friends or family but me, the old woman

("If my father finds out he'll kill me, Titina")

who paid Master João's parking tickets in Palmela, the old woman

("I spent all my allowance and am clean broke, Titina")

who cleaned out her purse to lend him money for his tuition that he never remembered to pay back, the old woman

("Confound it, the governor just called to say he's coming for dinner, Titina")

who at the last minute changed the tablecloth, changed the centerpiece, invented menus and made the food stretch further, the old woman

("I don't want Professor Salazar's cops ruining my birds-of-paradise, Titina")

going out with a broom to chase away the young men with pistols who searched for assassins among the statues and the beech trees, hitting them in the rump and shutting the gate behind them

"Have a nice, quiet orangeade in the café and don't try to get back in, I'll let you know when Professor Salazar is ready to leave"

and so I'm sure that Senhor Francisco and Master João won't sit still until they find me in Alverca, I'm sure they've already called the police, the hospitals, and the morgue and have put ads in the newspaper offering a reward of five hundred escudos, like widows do for their French poodles and Persian cats, sooner or later they're bound to show up at Alverca's charity home for women, and they'll bawl out the therapist for not having written to tell them that I was here, next to the Etruscan cement of the overpass, and they'll take me with them so that I can deal with their problems as I dealt with Senhor Francisco's on the Sunday afternoon when he was correcting the ministerial report, railing against the typist who had jumbled everything up, I was changing the flowers in the vases, and a baby started crying in the cook's room the way blackbirds cry if their young should die, I taking care not to break any stems, the baby crying, and the sky so clear you could see the high rocks in the mountains and above them the hawks, like dots, circling in search of snakes, and Senhor Francisco slumping in the armchair, dropping the report, dropping his pencil

"Get me out of this mess, Titina"

Senhor Francisco who ordered people around in Lisbon, who knew the Pope and had received a medal from the Vatican, whom Professor Salazar would visit to decide what should be done in Portugal, who with a telephone call could put whomever he pleased into jail

("Nab that jerk for me, Major*")

and take out whomever he pleased

("Let the fellow go, Major")

Senhor Francisco to me, who am poor and never received a medal from the Pope

"Get me out of this mess, Titina"

who had no contacts, acquaintances, influence, or importance whatsoever, all I knew how to do was change the flowers in vases and run a household, I in my apron loaded with hyacinths as the baby got quieter, the cook rocking its crib, a crib with a broken bell that she'd dug out of the junk in the attic, I saw her carrying it at night, trying not to make noise, and I, playing dumb

"What are you stealing, Idalete?"

and she carrying the crib to her room, all out of breath

"I'm not stealing anything, ma'am, I'm not a thief"

the baby that she'd brought from the stable three weeks earlier wrapped in burlap, shielding it from the dogs' curiosity with her slippers, and that she didn't show anyone, as if it were a sore or a skin disease she was hiding, but I peeked through the keyhole and saw it, I saw the black hair and puffy eyelids, I saw the cook lifting her blouse to feed it, using scissors to cut diapers out of a pillowcase, sticking her thumb in the little girl's mouth for her to suck, I saw the face of the veterinarian putting away his tools and taking leave of Senhor Francisco

"I did the best I could, Minister, I'm not a doctor"

the veterinarian tearing out so fast that he almost crashed into the gatepost, his headlights on in the broad daylight, driving as if he'd drunk three bottles of vodka, I saw the baby as I saw the bloody straw, the dirty rags, and some gelatin in a bucket, I saw the steward's daughter digging a hole to bury the wet mess as magpies flew all about

"Get me out of this mess, Titina"

when he could have phoned the Major in charge of prisons

"Take care of this problem for me, will you, Major?"

and presto, but instead of that Senhor Francisco called on me, who had no contacts or Pope or influences to go to, as if I were the only person in the world

"Get me out of this mess, Titina"

when he could have sent the cook and the baby to Cape Verde

"Is there a ship sailing for Cape Verde tomorrow?"

and in my opinion the blame for all this lies not with Senhor Francisco but with his wife, with the car parked under the elm trees of Palmela, and I always knew whom it belonged to, as did Senhor Francisco, because on the day after Dona Isabel left him he called up the Major in charge of prisons

"I've got a pretty pickle for you, Major"

the hours ticking by, Senhor Francisco planted next to the phone, waiting for the Major to call back with an answer, little João in a pinafore, filthy dirty as usual, to this day I don't know how in two minutes flat he could get so filthy dirty in a clean house

"I want a banana, Titina"

the beech trees murmuring my name without letup, and Senhor Francisco to the Major, banging his fist against the wall

"Is this your idea of a joke or what?"

and not only the beech trees but now also the cypresses, the poplars, the flower bed of gladiolas, and the eucalyptus trees that warned me with their rustling leaves

"You're going to die"

little João pulling on my apron because it was suppertime and I'd forgotten him

"A banana, Titina"

and not only the eucalyptus trees but the vegetables in the garden, the orange trees in the orchard that hated me, the loquat that never flowered

"You're going to die"

its branches standing out against the wall of the farm

"You're going to die"

and Senhor Francisco banging his fist against the wall, deaf to his son, deaf to the tree's threat

"Is this your idea of a joke or what?"

and when the night falls in Alverca I still hear the eucalyptus trees and the gladiolas, even though there aren't any eucalyptus trees or gladiolas around, just olive trees and the pillars of the overpass gouged by the beggars from Africa, I hear the trees of Palmela, I stop embroidering so as to listen and soon the therapist at the head of the table

"Tired of working, Dona Albertina?"

here in Alverca, when I'm in the sitting room or on the patio after supper, they still talk to me and threaten me

"You're going to die"

if I look out the window, I see the abandoned buildings encroaching on the fields, but I also see the farm and the old house where I can't remember, after all these years, if I was happy or unhappy, I remember the winter cold and a heater with a gray-white coil that turned red and scorched me without warming me up, I remember the rain in January, I remember Master João's wedding, where I and the maids threw rice at him in front of the church, I remember that my heart sometimes stopped and I would fall into a tunnel until it started beating again, and yet I don't remember if I was happy or unhappy, I remember Senhor Francisco banging his fist against the wall as he said to the Major

"Is this your idea of a joke or what?"

and a cigarillo burned a hole in the carpet, I remember my godfather, no, excuse me, not my godfather, my godfather owned a drugstore, lived in Lisbon, and used a cane, and I believe he died before I went to the farm or shortly thereafter, I remember the Major saying to Senhor Francisco

"And that's why it's not possible for me to help you, Minister, it's best to leave certain matters well enough alone"

and Senhor Francisco looking at the Major as a match burned in his fingers

"It's not possible to help me? It's not possible to help me? Have I stopped counting for anything in this country, Major?"

the clock struck three times, meaning that it was 10 P.M., the maids all in bed, I thinking that I'd better put the fish back in the oven, little João starving and dead tired, alarmed by the talk of Senhor Francisco and the Major, pulling all the while on my apron

"A banana, Titina"

ten o'clock at night and the owls hooting, but I could never discover where they hid during the day, I looked for them in the storeroom, in the barn, and in the laundry tubs shaded by wild fig trees, the lantern in the chauffeur's bedroom went out but its reflection lingered in the courtyard tiles, the fat from the fish sticking to the platter, and the Major, who had come all the way from Lisbon in a car with policemen in front and another car of policemen behind him, placing his hand on Senhor Francisco's lapel in an effort to calm his rage

"Instructions from the Prime Minister, unfortunately there are certain people we can't afford to antagonize, both for the sake of the national interest and the regime's stability"

and that's when I became certain that Senhor Francisco knew exactly who waited for his wife under the elm trees, for he lost himself in thought, then murmured in a kind of echo

"I'll fix that bastard"

the piano played a note that made the living room curtains tremble, and a single gust of wind shook the twigs and pine cones in the fireplace

"You're going to die"

I could see glimmers in the mud that must have been way-ward souls in torment, or perhaps they were reflections from the moon or the porch light, the Major with his hand on Senhor Francisco's lapel in an effort to calm his rage

"The Prime Minister says that he'll talk to you himself, the Prime Minister says he's very sorry and begs you not to do anything rash that might compromise the current situation"

the piano on which a music teacher from Setúbal taught little João to play songs that make you want to lie down and close your eyes and that are like having the flu without any flu, here in Alverca I hear songs like that on the radio, I stop embroidering, and the occupational therapist

"What's wrong, Dona Albertina?"

I stop embroidering, and it's as if my whole life were that tearless tenderness inside just one tear, Senhor Francisco opening the front door without taking his eyes off the Major

"Get out"

the cars with policemen in coats and ties who chatted with one other, the German shepherds suspiciously growling in the kennels, the streetlights of Palmela, the halo of the castle, and the outline of the mountains, I'm sure Senhor Francisco and Master João will come get me, they won't let me stay here, twenty years have gone by and I haven't changed all that much, I get tired more quickly, I walk more slowly, but I haven't lost my touch for running a household the way they like, for taking care of the laundry and the housecleaning, and the Major in a hurt tone of voice, offended at Senhor Francisco for showing him the door like that

"These aren't my instructions, Minister, they're instructions I received from the Prime Minister, who assured me that you're a patriot and would be the first one to understand that we mustn't alienate financial groups, we need them on our side right now" little João pulling at my dress and on the verge of tears, and the Major opening his arms with the regret of a failed mission

"You're being unfair to me, you're throwing our friendship to the dogs, you know very well how I respect families and how if it depended on me I'd teach that fellow a lesson he'd never forget"

the sky was wider in Palmela than in Alverca, and wider than in Lisbon, too, it had more stars, more heavenly paths, more glittering dust, Senhor Francisco

"Get out"

never again talked with the Major on the phone, and if he called to the farm, Senhor Francisco would shout at me next to the phone so that the Major would hear

"Tell the gentleman that I'm not at home"

and he ended up getting revenge on the wealthy businessman who used to wait under the elm trees of Palmela, getting revenge without arousing the least suspicion in Professor Salazar, or in the Major, or even in the businessman, because years later Master João, ignorant of the whole affair, happened to marry the businessman's niece, whom Senhor Francisco received at the farm with his arm around the sergeant's wife, as if she were his own wife, unnerving the niece by acting like a manual laborer or a returned emigrant

"Too skinny and no hips, you obviously understand nothing about heifers, João"

and he visited his son's mother-in-law in Estoril accompanied by the pharmacist's widow and wearing sheepskin boots, with a hat pulled down to his ears and a chain with good-luck charms on his vest, talking to those rich ladies the way bums talk and behaving the way bums behave, Master João thinking it was to humiliate him but it wasn't, it was a final act of revenge, a vestige of hatred, nostalgia for his wife, because take my word it was his wife whom Senhor Francisco loved, I noticing his fork freeze in the middle of dinner, his eyes darken, his mind trail off, and I worried that the food wasn't to his liking, I who don't know if I was happy or unhappy, but I do know how to run a household

"Is something wrong with the stew, Senhor Francisco?"

I'm not great at embroidery, and I don't know how to stick plastic flowers on wires, but I know what a house needs, here in Alverca, for instance, there aren't enough forks on the table, there are yogurt and jelly jars instead of proper glasses, dish towels instead of napkins, and a spiderweb in my room that stretches from the lamp to the ceiling and from the ceiling back to the lamp, but I know I'm not going to stay here much longer, I can't believe Senhor Francisco and Master João would abandon me among olive trees and highway pillars, when I pointed out the spiderweb to the therapist she laughed so hard she turned lavender

"Would you prefer a luxury hotel, Dona Albertina?"

I just don't want them to come in May when they load us all on a bus to go to Fátima, and the road is lined with stands selling ham sandwiches and pilgrims crawling on their knees, last year I saw a man dragging himself to the sanctuary on his stomach like a lizard as his wife shielded him from the rain with an umbrella, and when the man, tired of being a snake, would sit down to rest, then she, exasperated, would poke him in the butt with the umbrella

"With the damn-fool vow you made, it'll take us at least a month to get there"

stands with ham sandwiches, wine by the cup, and priests who for twenty escudos will bless figurines of saints that turn the color of lettuce in the dark, I watched sick people in wheelchairs returning home as gaunt-looking as when they arrived but coughing a bit more and with back pains on account of the rain, the occupational therapist rejuvenated by the ceremonies, all faith and cheer, passing out tambourines and plastic flutes as we bussed back to Alverca and the Carthaginian cement ruins, snapping her fingers like a singer in a folk group before forty sleepy pensioners who were ready to collapse

"All together now, girls, all together now"

the bus passing by the priests who sold lettuce-colored Virgin Marys, startling them with the tambourines and flutes, and then it was towns in the middle of nowhere, the carcass of a mule on the side of the road, and I trying to stay awake in case Senhor Francisco and Master João were waiting for me at the charity home to take me back to Palmela, I missed the old house, the farm, Master João when he was a teenager calling me to his room but too embarrassed to look at me, spinning the globe on the bookshelf with his finger

"I spent all my allowance and am clean broke, Titina"

and I cleaning out my purse and lending him his tuition money that he never remembered to pay back, and I thought of how everything must have changed in the last twenty years, the pool now larger, more statues in the garden, the two men a tad older, with a few more wrinkles, one or another white hair, and I suddenly remembered the crying of the baby in the cook's room, like the crying of blackbirds when someone steals their young, Senhor Francisco slumping in his armchair, dropping the report, dropping his pencil, Senhor Francisco who ordered people around in Lisbon, who knew the Pope, and whom Professor Salazar would visit to decide what should be done in Portugal, Senhor Francisco trembling in desperation

"Get me out of this mess, Titina"

and so I went to Azeitão, to Setúbal, to Seixal, to Amora, to Montijo, to Sesimbra, knocking on the doors of houses, businesses, and out-of-the-way shops, I talked to people, explained, insisted, and I finally met the unmarried, childless dressmaker of Alcácer, I spoke with Senhor Francisco, Senhor Francisco called the cook to his office, and the cook, locking the door to her room and putting the key in her apron

"No"

refusing to let Senhor Francisco enter her room

"No"

the cook, without changing her expression one bit, like the figures in paintings that have been smiling for centuries

"No"

the cook who was capable of killing him, of killing me

"No"

Senhor Francisco pushing her aside, forcing the lock with his knee, breaking into the narrow compartment furnished with a bed, a saint on the wall, an empty wardrobe

(three hangers hanging from the rod but no clothes)

and the old, rusty, and rickety crib from the attic, lined with a bath towel, everything in bad repair, everything rotting, and when I bent over the crib and picked up the child she stopped saying

"No"

standing frozen, lifeless, as if she'd given everything up, looking on indifferently from between the wardrobe and the bed, walking slowly behind us, watching us go down the steps under the flutter of pigeons, the chauffeur bringing around the car from the carport, waiting for us next to the angel whose blind eyes read a book without letters, the tree whose branches stood out against the wall of the farm warning me

"You're going to die"

we in the car, on the driveway through the cypresses heading toward the gate, past the orchard, past the vegetable garden, past the steward's daughter who watched us from the stable, I in the backseat with the baby thinking how I really don't understand human feelings, because when I looked back, beyond the tailpipe and beyond the heat that paralyzed the roses, I saw the cook on the front steps getting smaller as we drove on and vaguely waving her arm in the air, bidding us farewell without horror or astonishment.

COMMENTARY

When the Minister called me at seven in the morning because of a heifer at the farm that was going to give birth, my wife, awakened by the phone that tumbled to the floor when I reached for the receiver, turned on the lamp by her side of the bed and made signs for me to cover the mouthpiece

"Who is it, Luís?"

and I suddenly realized that I'd been living for thirty-five years with a monster. I usually get up at nine o'clock, the venetian blinds already raised and the room lit by sunshine, my clothes half on the chair, half on the floor, since I get undressed in the dark, and the person who shakes my sleeping elbow awake is a woman in a dressing gown with hair more or less combed and face more or less presentable, a woman more or less bearable, and not the creature whose nightgown was sliding off her shoulder and who made signs for me to cover the mouthpiece, afraid her idiotic mother had suffered a heart attack

"Who is it, Luís?"

I incredulous, looking around and seeing that it was indeed my bedroom, my furniture, my jacket balled up on the rug, my empty shoe waiting to be filled with presents, but it wasn't Christmas, and if it were, the best present I could have had was to be a widower, I quelling the anxiety emanating from the pillow next to me

"It's the Minister calling about a cow, your mother's still alive, relax"

the morning light of Setúbal in the blinds was the amber color of a morgue where Christ, with the sunken cheeks of a pusher dead from an overdose, waited on the wall for his autopsy, the curtains resembled mortuary linens, and the brushes and cases were lined up on the marble-topped dresser like bones for the coroner's inquest, my wife slumping back down like an octopus going to sleep, plunging her arms into the sheets like tentacles into sand

"What a relief"

I, afraid she might devour me, getting quickly dressed before she could ask from out of her slumber

"Don't I get a kiss, Luís?"

obliging me to roll over into that squooshy body in a frilly gown and to rub my chin against a forehead smeared with moisturizing cream while a wet hand pinched my ear

"Bye-bye, Luís"

reminding me of the young chubby brunette placing the wedding band on my finger in the photo album, I heating up coffee in the kitchen and praying that she not shuffle in with her slippers to help me with the gas, to hand me the sugar, to open the cupboard above the microwave

"You'll never learn where the teacups are, Luís"

and to wave at me from the porch, ruining my morning by chirping bye-bye sweetie like a decrepit teenager, I hobbling across the lawn with my tie hanging from my neck, stooping to tie my shoelaces, backing the car out of the garage and banging the tailpipe into the wall as usual, and at that moment the living-room curtain moved slowly, theatrically, to one side

"Bye-bye sweetie"

as I imagined myself arriving home in the evening, ex-hausted after a long day of dogs barking by the dozen in the waiting room, and finding her in the foyer, shaking with en-thusiasm, her front paws on my chest while she licked my chin with slobbering joy, I pushing her away with my hands

"Be still"

and then, after our dessert of rice pudding, walking her around the block and stopping before every clothing boutique as if at a tree trunk, pulling her by my arm as by a leash, and then the soap opera, then the news, then bed, hearing her coo sweet nothings from her pillow

"Luís"

the effluvia of her desire mercifully subsiding thanks to the anesthetizing effect of the tripe we'd had for dinner, and as I got farther away from my house in Setúbal, I perked up, the streets took on color, I could smell the river and the netted fish beyond the smell of the factories, the world was once more pleasant and carefree, I passed by the statue of the poet, by the park, and by the high school to watch the young girls arrive, for with age I've become deeply moved by the sight of their legs, but at 7 A.M. the gate was still locked, the shutters of the pastry shop opposite were still shut, and all I could do was guess, from the stickers on the windows, which apartments they lived in and imagine their nakedness under the Mickey Mouse and Charlie Brown T-shirts they wore, the schoolgirls who, on my lucky days, show up at the animal hospital with their mothers and their mutts, and they don't sit still, they fiddle with the syringes, the stethoscope, and the bandages, prancing around the examining table without even noticing me, the mothers petting their dogs and cats the way I'd like to pet their daughters

"Does it have roundworms?"

I, oblivious to the dogs and cats, tripping over the anticavity, vitamin-enriched biscuits, the cans of food, and the rubber bones, with a mind to grab the schoolgirls by their gouache-stained sleeves, place a collar around my neck, and beg them

"Take me for a walk"

anxious to discover their secret universe of albums with stickers, comic books, and the names of boys who ride motor-bikes written on breath-fogged windows, forgetting my fifty-six years, ready to wear ragged jeans, grow a ponytail, and put a ring in my ear, like so many passports to a forbidden country of rap music and bubble gum, I

"Does it have roundworms?"

brutally reawakened to my daily reality of swine pox in which life's heaviness makes me sink into the sofa in front of the evening soap opera like one of the cats my cousin used to sink underwater with her bare hands, prescribing medicines even as my soul invisibly drips in stalactites, like the caverns of the Minho region

"Does it have roundworms?"

until the mothers go away, the mutts go away, and the schoolgirls, alas, also go away

"What are you waiting for, Cristina?"

my assistant cleaning the examining table with a rag

"Just ten more to go"

and in comes a woman my age, flushed from exertion, pushing a Saint Bernard the size of an ox. If the Minister hadn't called for me to help a heifer give birth, I would have parked the car opposite the high school and waited until the bell rang, gawking at the arriving schoolgirls while pretending to read a book on foot-and-mouth disease, or with my hood raised because of a supposed problem with the distributor, rejoicing in so many anklets, so much hair without hair spray, and so many chewed fingernails, trying to remember how my wife looked when I first met her, I'd sold some land in Barcelos to open up the animal hospital, and in the stationer's next door there was that chubby salesgirl who was so attentive when I ordered letterhead paper and receipts, stealing glances at me, ignoring the other customers, tripping over the stepladder when reaching for erasers on the highest shelf, and I examining her hips, I who in the empty, brand-new animal hospital was cursing my luck when the doorbell suddenly rang, I donned my smock, straightened my hair, and made ready to clip the fur of my first client, with a frown of veterinarian expertise joining my two eyebrows, and I opened the door to the salesgirl from the stationer's, who smelled of perfume and wore a slightly low-cut dress, she handed me the receipts I'd ordered with my name printed in fancy letters

"You look great in a smock, no kidding"

and so I got married because someone thought I looked great in a smock and because I was fed up with the boardinghouse where they scorched my shirt collars with the iron and ruined the elastic in my socks, her mother shaking her head with joy and my mother shaking her head with disgust before a throng of famished locals from Setúbal who devoured the codfish croquettes at the reception before you could say boo, my mother galled by such avid appetites, by so many garish vests and so many feathers, confiding to me in an outraged whisper

"Never in all my life"

my mother refusing to take part in the wedding pictures for fear she'd end up in the photographer's shop window between the army sergeant from the rations warehouse who addressed her as "dearie" and a woman capable of bending iron bars at the circus whose neck was choked by a mange-infected fox, my mother who returned to Barcelos on the train swearing

"Never in all my life"

who whenever we happened to talk would mumble

"Never in all my life"

like a stubborn refrain of disappointment, who died whispering

"Never in all my life"

to the astonishment of the priest, and my wife left the stationer's without any nostalgia for the stepladder, I left the boardinghouse with my clothes half-ruined, and since by then I had a steady flow of tapeworms and furred tongues, I bought the house near the stadium, without imagining that the chubby salesgirl would devote herself full-time to getting old as quickly as possible and to surprising me in the animal hospital so that she could see me in a smock

"You look great in a smock, Luís, no kidding"

as my assistant decorated Pekingeses with red ribbons for the community band dog show, and in the years following our marriage we spent several Augusts in Marbella, Spain, where we ran into Portuguese from Setúbal on every street corner, we slept for several winters next to an electric imitation fireplace with red plastic logs purchased at a fair along with the porcelain pauper who counts his change on top of the console table at the animal hospital, and when I finally stopped to think, I realized that I'd married a monster. It's easy to remember the date of this tragic discovery, for it happened on the morning that the Minister called for me to go to Palmela to help a heifer give birth, and although I hadn't seen any pregnant animals when I was at the farm three weeks earlier, I'd learned that whatever one of Salazar's protégés might say, no matter how strange, was either true or would be declared true in tomorrow's newspaper, which amounted to the same thing, and if we tried to contradict them, we'd end up at the police station with a flashlight shining in our eyes as the police chief used catechetical slaps to teach us on whose side the national interest, virtue, and truth lay. And so to top off all my troubles, I wasn't even able to see the schoolgirls arrive for their classes, which would have given me the strength to withstand the day's sadness, I cut across Setúbal and headed straight toward the square in Palmela where funerals go up and down the hill to the cemetery in a flurry of relatives and chrysanthemums

(the relatives taking consolation in the tavern as the parched chrysanthemums dangle from the palmettos)

·

with only me not having the pleasure of climbing the hill with my disconsolate wife and my mother-in-law's corpse in the wagon, and from the square I saw the town, the castle, and the mountains, the same dull panorama as ever, I wish someone could explain to me why nothing in this country ever changes, and after passing through Setúbal and Palmela and the elm trees that prompted a huge scandal a while back with some bigwig I'd better not mention to avoid problems, of which I've already got plenty, the principal of the high school having just filed charges that accuse me of harassing the schoolgirls, imagine how absurd, and after Setúbal, Palmela, and the elm trees by the square, I took a back road that was quickly paved after the Prime Minister started coming out here, and at the end of the road stood the stone columns of the main gate, with the driveway flanked by cypress trees leading up to the house I was never once invited to enter, apparently because the Minister saw me as just another employee, even though I'm a professor in Lisbon, a house where the Prime Minister went for tea and decided the fate of the Portuguese, under the protection of a dozen security cops who would lean me against my car

"Put your hands on the hood right now"

and check my pockets for regicidal grenades if they found me in the chicken coop taking the hens' temperature, the Minister who never invited me to take an afternoon stroll with him under the orange trees in the orchard, treating me as a subordinate not allowed to go beyond the rabbit hutch, the pigsty, and the stable, I who have opinions, who read, who could give some sound advice on the best way to run this country, I mean, what I think people need, especially the jackass high-school principal who calls me a lecher and has gotten me embroiled with the courts, is a tighter rein and a quicker whip, if Professor Caetano hadn't been such a wimp, if he had applied the brake and a few good slaps instead of going wild with liberalizing measures, then the tragedy of the Revolution would never have happened, and so I parked the car in the shade of the barn, grabbed my bag, found myself sniffed by German shepherds that jumped like grease in a frying pan

snouts eyes ears barks paws tails

and in the stable the steward's daughter who went barefoot in the manure, milking the cows' unwashed teats with her unwashed hands over pails containing bits of straw and dead flies, and the Minister pointing to her with his proud chin

"I do everything she wants except take my hat off, so that she won't forget who's boss"

a young thing with disheveled hair who might not have looked bad if we'd scrubbed her for a few hours with number three sandpaper and then left her for a week in a tub of bleach, above her some twenty turtledoves perching on the ridgepole, rats squealing in the lining of the roof, blowflies that stubbornly stuck to our faces, I to the Minister as I examined a calf with an ear infection

"Cute girl"

the eleven o'clock sun filtering through the boards, rakes, and shovels lying around to make us trip, a rusty fire extinguisher hanging from a nail, I thinking that they should wash the floor with creosote to decrease the stench of urine and dung, unless, as might well be the case, the stench comes directly from the cute girl, who lived with her parents in a part of the barn where they shared the night and the corn with spiders, snakes, and a poster of Saint Rock taped onto the wall and presiding over the mosquitoes, the crates that served as furniture, and the rusty pitchers, the Minister puffing his cigarillo under the din of the crows while considering his nymph

"She's not bad, she's not bad"

he who could have had elegant ladies in Lisbon but felt attracted to women without any class because of what happened with his wife, contenting himself with ruins like the sergeant's wife and the pharmacist's widow, whose clothes looked like colorful and frilly candy wrappers, receiving them in the living room where he never received me, and spending entire afternoons with them and a tray of spirits, contemplating the pink and blue glow of the orange trees, and I on all fours in the dovecote treating the baby pigeons' chicken pox, dying of thirst and coughing my head off because I'm allergic to feathers, I in the pigsty applying ointments to the piglets' sore throats, and yet if the Minister called me at seven in the morning to come and help a heifer give birth, I would get out of bed and go, even though he ignored and disdained me, even though he never shook my hand any more than he did the chauffeur's or the tractor driver's, I would get up and go even when my shoulder was stiff with arthritis, and in the stable, where the night lingered on in the bats flitting about the rafters, there was no heifer on its knees, no pregnant animal, no creature in pain, I to the steward's daughter while feeling the cows' bellies in bewilderment

"Which one is it?"

thinking that if there weren't many wagons with gypsies or trucks on the highway, I might make it back to Setúbal in time to rejoice in anklets, pigtails, and scraped knees, thinking that if I were the Minister I'd get off my duff and inaugurate a girls' school every other day, but since life is unfair, there I was in the stable asking the steward's daughter, who passed by with a hose that was ruining my shoes

"Which one is it?"

while thinking about Setúbal, thinking about the high school, and seeing by my watch that the bell had already rung, so that my only hope left was that the schoolgirls would come with their mothers and their mutts to the animal hospital in the afternoon, I checking the heifers one by one while swatting at blowflies, debating whether I should go up to the house, afraid the Minister might be annoyed to find me on the front steps without his permission, and then I saw a hat at the corner of the greenhouse helping a woman I thought might be the house-keeper but then realized wasn't, a woman who walked as if car-rying something heavy and fragile in her apron, something that risked breaking and excited the dogs, and by the time they'd reached the shed with flower bulbs I realized it was the cook, who helped me during the annual pig slaughter and whom I sometimes saw picking out a rabbit or a chicken for Professor Salazar's soup, when the farm crawled with troops and National Guardsmen, and the secret police traipsed through the flower beds, suspicious of the statues, the cook who always gazed at me in silence like the girl in the stable, neither of them answering me because they feared the Minister might get mad at them or because the crows

(or magpies or peacocks or geese)

could answer for them, I saying

"Hi there"

and not a peep out of them, I moving closer and they moving away, I who didn't have the slightest desire to touch them, I who couldn't imagine touching them any more than I could imagine touching the monster I live with, for they're equally, God forgive me, equally revolting, as if my mother were inside me fuming

"Never in all my life"

I who for all the world wouldn't touch the sergeant's wife or the widow dressed like candy who'd inherited her husband's pharmacy, their lapdog, and a plaster-of-Paris cat on the dining table, cheering up her grief with a panoply of satins and laces, and if the Minister takes up with shrews like these, I suppose it's because he had a bad time of it with other kinds of shrews and doesn't care to repeat the experience of being the town laughingstock, they even drew horns and obscene phrases on his wall, which he himself erased with a sponge, a paintbrush, and a pan of whitewash, like putting a bandage over a wound that still oozes onto the gauze, and so even though the horns and phrases are now invisible, I'll bet he still sees them and suffers on their account, since they still exist, though nonexistent, and are perhaps even larger, the charcoal lines even darker, and with grammatical errors that only magnify the insult and disgrace, the Minister who must see the steward and think

"It was him"

who must see the tractor driver and think

"It was him"

who when he enters the tavern of Palmela and sees the dominoes and quadrille cards suddenly freeze, the customers with their noses in their glasses, the owner behind the bar listening to the radio, the jobless waiting in vain for a farmer who would hire them, must think

"It was these bastards who called me a cuckold"

and he must have felt like clobbering them all with a stick, like seeing their arms break and their heads crack open, their bodies strewn on the floor among the sawdust and peanut shells

"It was these bastards"

but even if he killed them all, the drawings and words would still shriek with laughter, cracking through the layer of whitewash

THE MINISTER IS A CUCKOLD

because humiliation and outrage can't ever really be erased, and so I suspect he forbade his mistresses from talking to me in order to avoid more writings on the wall, more drawings, and the town's ridicule, as I suspect he forbade them from talking to anybody except the housekeeper and the maids, including his own son and Professor Salazar, when the latter happened to be at the farm, and I suspect he asked Professor Salazar to have the secret police keep tabs on the pharmacist's widow, with one agent posted in the den and another at the main gate, so that they could keep tabs not only on her but on each other, submitting weekly reports about each other to the ministry in Lisbon, the Minister approaching the stable, leading along the cook, who walked slowly, as if carrying something heavy and fragile in her apron, something that risked breaking and excited the dogs, the Minister shooing away the German shepherds as they entered, then bolting the door shut, the steward's daughter milking a cow six feet away from us, the bats hanging from the rafters, the turtle-doves along the ridgepole, the sound of water in the irrigation channels, and Palmela's church bell knelling not in Palmela, not at the farm, and not at the stable but in the heart of my terror, I thinking

"I don't want to do this"

thinking

"I can't do this"

thinking

"I won't do this"

while rummaging in my bag for some forceps, scissors, and thread, thinking

"I don't want to, I can't, I won't"

the Minister pushing me toward the cook's womb as white foam overflowed from the milk pail

"If there's a problem with the litter, I'll break your neck, now please go to work."

That afternoon, at twenty past three, I parked the car opposite the high school to watch the students come out, having forgotten the animal hospital, the bonemeal biscuits, the coats of fur in need of clipping, the waiting room full of scabies and tapeworms, my assistant baffled by my delay, inventing an emergency in Azeitão, I having forgotten about the farm, Senhor Francisco, the cook crucified on the pile of straw, the blood, the screams, and the final grunt that emptied her belly, I opposite the high school not just at three-twenty, but at four o'clock, five o'clock, six o'clock, opposite the locked school gate and next to the pastry shop where at seven-thirty they took away the tables and chairs from the sidewalk, took down the yellow umbrellas, closed the shutters, and went away, I remaining there on the deserted street, the streetlights coming on, the windows lighting up for dinner, silhouettes moving behind the curtains like shadows from the early cinema, I sitting in my car and determined to stay there forever, determined, once the high school and the pastry shop were no longer visible, once the windows had gone dark and the schoolgirls had stopped existing, to stay forever in the night of Setúbal, in the night of Setúbal's night, in the dark heart of the night of Setúbal's night, until in the silence of the square and the buildings and the trees I heard the whining of a crow, the anguished whining of a baby.

REPORT

I don't remember what day of the week it was, but I remember it was a day I was going to clean the chapel, and when I passed by the office, the blinds were raised, for I could see light under the door, the radio was on, and Senhor Francisco was talking on the telephone

"What's going on, for Christ's sake, what the hell is going on?"

and the kitchen clock struck a bunch of times, which meant it was already day. I don't remember what day it was, but it had to have been in April, for there were baby magpies in the orchard and white buds on the orange trees, Senhor Francisco had quit the ministry all angry at Professor Caetano, who visited the farm once or twice to try to convince him to come back, and he was received not in the living room with the piano and the photograph of the queen watching over all that was said, but in the room next to it, smaller and with hardly any furniture, where Senhor Francisco gave orders to the steward, the tractor driver, and the priest after Mass

since he considered a man who said Mass equivalent to one who plowed fields or tended flower beds

Senhor Francisco in an armchair pointing at a chair without arms for Professor Caetano, and if I turned the doorknob and appeared with the teapot, teacups, and a plate of toasts, he would wave me and my tray away before Professor Caetano could open his mouth

"This prime minister doesn't drink tea, Titina"

still furious that the Admiral* hadn't chosen him to lead the country, and on the day Professor Caetano spoke on television to thank the cheering crowds, Senhor Francisco took down the picture of himself and the Admiral smiling and embracing each other

"Throw that puppet in the trash"

Professor Caetano, who after an hour of pretending not to understand the humiliations, took his leave on the front porch, insisting

"Let me know if you change your mind, I was thinking of you for Defense or Foreign Affairs"

but Senhor Francisco turned around and left before his visitor even had time to go down the steps

"The next time that jerk shows up, sic the German shepherds on him"

Senhor Francisco, who could have bitten off the whole world's head, slamming the door to his office so hard that the startled pigeons disappeared into the swamp and a torrent of chinaware cascaded off the sideboard, Senhor Francisco flinging the door back open and running outside in the hope of finding Professor Caetano still among the statues

"Scoundrel"

Senhor Francisco pacing back and forth on the terrace for days, repeating

"Foreign Affairs, Foreign Affairs"

as if it were an insult, and if the Admiral called him on the phone, he would announce into the receiver, while tearing off a piece of wallpaper with his fingernail

"If it's not to appoint me prime minister, I'm not here"

so that Professor Caetano stopped visiting him and the Admiral limited himself to sending, on his birthday, a colonel with a basket of gardenias that Senhor Francisco would immediately and unceremoniously dump into the swamp in front of the shocked officer

"Scoundrel"

the baskets of gardenias stopped arriving, and it was aged army officers and old colleagues who came on Sundays and talked in conspiratorial whispers, meeting and sweating together in the greenhouse, asking in hushed tones

"This place isn't bugged, is it? Are you sure there are no hidden microphones?"

and what I heard when I brought them something to drink were coughs and wheezes, and what I saw as I handed them their glasses were harmless, withered old men in shirtsleeves on the verge of cardiac arrest, wiping their foreheads with handkerchiefs, and searching for reels and tape recorders in the little bags of seeds and in the soil of the flowerpots, army officers who enthusiastically promised defiant regiments, and colleagues who confidently envisioned entire villages getting off the bus in front of the National Assembly, bushy-haired abbots shouting from their pulpits in the backwoods of Trás-os-Montes, you'll see how easy it is, believe me, the Assembly will vote unanimously

unanimously, mark my words,

to oust the usurper, while a one-hundred-year-old gentleman who was dozing on a canvas stool with his nose in the
orchids would occasionally yawn himself out of his coma to
demand in a croaking drawl

"I'm not leaving here without the Treasury, I'm not leaving here without the Treasury"

and late into the night, when they could no longer see each
other, they divvied up cabinet posts, administrative posts, bu-
reaus, boards, and embassies, carving Portugal into pieces like a
slaughtered lamb, with the centenarian adamantly insisting

"I'm not leaving here without the Treasury"

until they finally went away, whispering as they passed the
pond in case the police had placed bugs in the gills of the goldfish, bumping into the arbor and the chicken coop, which caused
a to-do among the hens, pricking themselves on the roses that
swayed in the darkness, Senhor Francisco in a desolate tone of
voice

"A pack of doddering geriatrics, Titina"

Senhor Francisco, who had hung a map of the country in
his office to count up the number of administrative districts,
military bases, and assembly seats, who had invented a code for
secret messages, had written speeches for when he came to power,
had sent his tailcoat to the cleaners, given me his white bow tie
to iron, and unearthed his medals from the drawer, full of energy, enthusiastic, confident, asking for my approval with a
gleam in his eye

"What do you think, Titina?"

all cheer and expectation, making mysterious declarations
to the sergeant's wife and the pharmacist's widow, whose fin-

gernails would fish for specks that made their eyes water, Senhor Francisco rejuvenated

"The country is going to see a big turnaround, girls"

so that when I passed by the office and could tell that the blinds were raised, since I could see light under the door, and the radio was on, and Senhor Francisco was talking on the telephone

"What's going on, for Christ's sake, what the hell is going on?"

I thought it was the big turnaround, girls, that he'd been planning for a few years, I thought that the National Assembly had been invaded by the provinces under the leadership of the bishops, who threatened the traitors with their golden staffs if they didn't put the aged gentleman of the canvas stool at the head of the Treasury, which I imagined to be like a gigantic wallet bursting with money and with a photo-booth picture of the treasurer's wife in the clear-plastic pocket for loved ones, and so I forgot about cleaning the chapel, whose stained glass windows were badly spotted by the sparrows' disrespect, and stopped to listen in the hallway, with the detergent for scouring the Virgin in my hand, and Senhor Francisco shouting above the music of the radio

"What do you mean they're not our troops, Ambassador Nogueira? Whose fucking troops are they?"

Senhor Francisco desperately moving the radio dial but finding the same news and then calling for me as if he were drowning

"Titina"

he in front of the map of Portugal, sticking blue and yellow tacks in Oporto, in Ribatejo, in the Algarve, with the street map of Lisbon spread out on his desk, full of pencil marks and crosses, he dialing numbers that didn't answer, then checking them in his address book and redialing, oblivious to me, not seeing me standing there with detergent for scouring the Virgin in my hand, his eyes passing through me and searching for me beyond the doorway as his cigarillo dropped ashes onto his vest

"Titina"

and I thought

"The son went away and the father took his place"

for Master João had married years ago, lived in Estoril, and never asked about us, never wrote, and never came to the farm, I don't know how he managed to cope with wolves, kidnappers, and the darkness without me, and now it was his father who begged me to save him from the early morning shadows, from their terror that grew in the crows' shiny blackness and the beech trees' shimmer, in the orchard still without sunlight, or with a sunlight that was still struggling to free itself and the turtledoves from the eucalyptus trees, Senhor Francisco gesticulating on the telephone

"Is there no one who can tell me what's going on, for Christ's sake?"

I with the chapel to clean and the maids goofing off in the kitchen, waiting for me to come in and say you do this, you do that, you change the linens, you go to the butcher's in Palmela and be quick, because there's lots to do upstairs, and not only the maids but the chickens and pigeons likewise waiting, the German shepherds inside their kennels pressing their muzzles against the wires until their bowls of food arrived, the tractor driver in the courtyard because of a part that needed fixing, the gardener pruning the boxwoods the wrong way, the whole house depending on me, and Senhor Francisco now turning down the radio and looking straight through me as he called

"Titina"

now turning up the radio, sticking tacks into Penafiel, twirling around, grabbing the receiver, and crumpling the tailcoat that I'd left on the chair, turning milk-white with astonishment

"What?"

the tailcoat I'd just brought back from the cleaner's in a plastic wrapper for the glorious moment when he came to power, his medals lined up in order of importance, all ready to be pinned on his chest like in the photo of him with the Pope, his speech on a scroll tied by a ribbon with the colors of the flag, the gardener whistling as his shears hacked at the creeping vines without mercy, and his whistling floating into the office with implacable cheer as the branches fell one by one on the other side of the window, Senhor Francisco sprawled out on the chair, massacring the tailcoat

"Bring my pills from the bedroom, Titina"

his dancing fingers unable to hold the bottle steady or to take off the cap, the water spilling on his knees, the gardener's whistling drowning out the radio, drowning out the telephone, deafening me so much I felt like placing my hands over my ears, and Senhor Francisco suddenly purple, motioning me to hit him on the back, and in a voiceless moo

"It got caught in my throat, Titina"

and I hitting him on the back, softly at first, afraid I might hurt him, but then more willingly as I thought of the cook, of the sergeant's wife, of the pharmacist's widow, of the things he did in front of anyone and everyone, without worrying about

little João, without worrying about me, who would debone his
fish with my hair almost in his face, and he impassive, talking
with the sergeant's wife and the pharmacist's widow, I hitting
him for not thinking of me as a woman, hitting his shoulder
blades, his spinal column, his lower back, he with his hands up

"That's enough, Titina, I already spit out the pill"

I who sometimes used perfume and wore high heels and
had almost no wrinkles until I was fifty, but it was to the cook
that he said, right under my nose

"You there"

it was to her, the maid who'd just arrived the week before
on the train from the Beira district, still smelling of hunger and
goat turd, that he said

"Be still"

while knitting his eyebrows in a weary frown, and I pretending to be busy with the laundry basket, the canned raspberries, and the account book, when what I felt like doing was
vanishing under the floor, I who could have made all of them
into mincemeat but was submissive, obedient, trotting into the
living room or out to the pool whenever Senhor Francisco called

"Titina"

bringing juice for his mistresses, setting up chairs on the
terrace, ordering them ice cream, chocolates, and arrowroot
cookies, walking the hideous little dog of the pharmacist's
widow, who would hand it to me as if I were her slave, until it
peed three measly drops on the roots of a beech tree, I who
was already working for him when he got married to Dona
Isabel, with whom I preferred to share him rather than not have
him at all, not take care of him, not replace his soap when it got
used up, not keep him from spending money foolishly, not be

close by if he needed me, and Master João likewise didn't understand and went away without giving me a kiss

"Good-bye, Titina"

and never wrote, never called, never showed me his children, my grandchildren, not Dona Isabel's but my grandchildren, and never came to see me in Palmela, so that Senhor Francisco and I formed a couple without relatives or friends, growing old all alone in a huge house, he unmindful of me, but I attentive to the slightest twitch in his liver, his heart, or his lungs, worried about his uric acid, his cholesterol, his emphysema, whispering to the doctor while he got dressed behind the folding screen

"It's nothing serious, is it?"

I who hated to see him in bed with his mouth all twisted, able to eat only soup, and I know that one of these days he'll come to Alverca to get me, he'll march into the charity home with all the confidence, majesty, and authority I remember, whisking aside the occupational therapist as if she were a bothersome fly

"Where's your luggage, Titina?"

without even noticing the embroideries, or the cloth daisies, or my companions looking at him in awe

"Where's your luggage, Titina?"

a man whom everybody in Lisbon obeyed, who was consulted by Professor Salazar on how to run Portugal, who could have whomever he wanted arrested or released right from his own office, just by making a phone call

"Nab so-and-so for me, Major, and let such-and-such go"

and the Major kneeling, bowing down, kissing his feet

"Whatever you say, Minister, I'll have Barbieri* take care of it"

Senhor Francisco's car parked between the scrawny cement and brick pillars of the overpass, with the remnant of a poster committing suicide in the wind, the employees of the charity home flabbergasted to see the engagement ring he placed on my finger, with a pearl the size of an olive from Elvas, Senhor Francisco walking around the car to open the door for me, holding it open with his hat in his hand, waiting like a gallant prince as I pull in my dress and get comfortable, Senhor Francisco walking back around the car to get in the driver's seat and take me away with him to Palmela, Senhor Francisco in the office, taking his pill again without choking on it this time, helping it go down by shaking his head like a goose just as the last cluster of creeping vines fell and the gardener's whistling that decapitated my plants subsided, Senhor Francisco oblivious to the map of Portugal, to the map of Lisbon, getting up from the chair where his tailcoat had become a rag in order to answer the phone, talking with the dazed voice of an invalid

"A Communist coup and our troops aren't reacting, General Pina? A Communist coup and our troops are in the barracks?"

the voice on the other end said something about gunshots, about people staying off the streets and avoiding skirmishes, I imagined bombs, cannons, mass slaughters, corpses piled up on Commerce Square, the gardener's whistling, now farther away, was destroying gillyflowers and tulips with the ruthless calm of an executioner, I worried sick that the garden would be reduced to a common grave of deceased flowers, because the garden wasn't Dona Isabel's and it wasn't Senhor Francisco's, it was mine, I prepared the soil, I had it fertilized, I bought the shoots, I protected them from the sun, I yanked the weeds, I watered the flowers every morning and every evening in the summer, I kept the maids and German shepherds from trampling on them, I kept little João from plucking them by the armful, the garden belonged to me just as the house and its management belonged to me, just as every object in it belonged to me, just as Senhor Francisco belonged to me without knowing it, and on the porch by the pool the idiotic sergeant's wife, insolently ordering me around as she waved the sequins of her fan

"Go get me another lemonade, I'm burning up"

the sergeant's wife who crossed her legs like a slut, combed her hair like a slut, wore rings and earrings like a slut's

"Go get me another lemonade, I'm burning up"

and as I broke the ice against the edge of the marble counter, I decided to put cockroach poison in the pitcher, I imagined them kicking their legs and then dropping, and I even shook the skull-imprinted box to hear the grains inside, but I changed my mind, because these things get discovered, though I did put in too much sugar, since if she had a sugar problem like my roommate here in Alverca, who's forever dipping paper strips into her bedpan, she'd keel over a few hours later, with her husband at her side

"Gracinda, Gracinda"

and the police supposing that she'd carelessly eaten too many duchesses at the pastry shop, I placing her glass on the wicker table

"Would you like some more, ma'am?"

when the only madam around was me, who preserved myself for one man and didn't dress to attract dogs in rut, I was the only real lady, and the sergeant's wife didn't utter so much as a

"Thank you"

nor did Senhor Francisco bother to say

"Thank you"

as if I were there to satisfy their every whim, I who had tons of work to do in the kitchen and the sewing room, the crystal that needed dusting, the repairman who'd come to fix the roof of the garage, and the sergeant's wife, blowing kisses to Senhor Francisco like a commonplace slut

"Are you going to stand there all day, Titina?"

not Dona Titina but Titina, just like that, Titina

"Are you going to stand there all day, Titina?"

when everybody calls me Dona, it's a matter of respect, a matter of correctness, but the sergeant's wife, who didn't know me from anywhere because I'm not of her ilk, I work, I don't waste my time at sidewalk cafés chatting with girlfriends, flirting with the waiters, smoking cigarettes, and bad-mouthing honest people

"Are you going to stand there all day, Titina?"

and I regretting that I hadn't put poison in the pitcher

"If you ask me for more lemonade, you'll be sorry"

cockroach poison not only for the sergeant's wife but also for Senhor Francisco, who should have called her down and didn't, and who, if she paid no heed to principles, should have paid heed for her, I returning to the house in a cloud of desolation, accompanied by the German shepherds, whose heads drooped with pity, because animals at least can understand us, and Senhor Francisco on the phone, motioning for me to drag over the chair with his tailcoat so wrinkled it looked like an accordion, and the person who was there to drag it over wasn't the sergeant's wife but me, Senhor Francisco taking a second pill from the bottle and chewing it without water, he who wasn't able to chew pills

"Our troops went over to the Communists? Are you serious, am I hearing you right, what the hell sort of troops did you round up for me, General?"

Senhor Francisco calling the Ministry of the Armed Forces and no answer, calling the Ministry of Defense and no answer, swallowing his pride and calling the Major but no answer, the ministries all deserted, the secret police deserted, the phones of the army posts at Ajuda and Carmo disconnected, immoral songs on the radio, the announcer reporting that they had taken the airport and the TV station and had surrounded the national police, that Lisbon was now theirs, and as if that weren't enough to upset me, that blasted gardener was ruining the grass and butchering the gillyflowers while the maids, overjoyed to have a day off, were raiding the pantry, and Senhor Francisco on the phone, in a low, acid tone of voice

"Answer me with complete sincerity, Ambassador Nogueira, are the Communists in control or aren't they, because if the Communists are in control, we'd better move our asses on the double"

shrugging as he looked at his medals, smiling with scorn at his speech to the nation tied by a ribbon with the colors of the flag, gazing at the photos in the office as if taking leave of the Pope, the Cardinal, the nuncio, and Professor Salazar, who, poor soul, was already dead, as if taking leave of himself, Senhor Francisco picking up the tailcoat from the chair and hurling it to the floor with plastic wrapper and all, and only then did I realize how the time had passed and how he and I had changed during all those years at the farm, I realized that Master João didn't come to Palmela to visit us so as not to find ghosts in place of the people he had left, a second radio in the kitchen playing immoral songs, hundreds of radios all over town playing immoral songs, the steward's daughter abandoning the stable and her pails of milk, the windmill making a halting turn, two halting turns, then stopping, and yet

how strange

it seemed to me that the wind was blowing, that the hydrangeas were fluttering and the couch grass bending low, Senhor Francisco in a tone of voice I'd never heard, not even when he tried to convince his wife not to leave us

"Okay, Nogueira, I understand, the secret police has been neutralized, the government seized, and our joke of an army sold downriver to the Communists, meaning that tomorrow Lisbon is sure to be crawling with Russians who will either hang us from lampposts or pack us on trains for Siberia, don't worry about me, just vanish as fast as you can"

it must have already been late, because the turtledoves and the greenhouse roof now loomed large in the morning light, I could feel the sea in the glimmering clouds, and the house, gentlemen, patiently waited for me to get it going, because nothing worked without me, although only I was aware of this, even the occupational therapist, when I explain that over twenty people depended on my instructions, tells me to hush and just embroider, because I'm disturbing my companions, Senhor Francisco emptying the drawers of his desk into the safe, peeking out the window to see if the Soviet soldiers had come through the gate and were raising flags over the barn, turning off the radio, cutting the telephone wire, ordering me to bolt all the doors and free the dogs, tucking his pistol under his belt and taking his shotgun from the cabinet as he ordered

"I want everyone out of here, Titina"

banishing me along with the maids, the tractor driver, the steward, pulling the breech with a loud clack and firing at the cedars as the crows scattered

"Scram, you commies"

the greenhouse white, the turtledoves white, the sky white, and the eucalyptus trees pitch-black, Senhor Francisco pointing his cigarillo at me and shoving me with the butt of his gun

"Scram, you commie"

the dogs leaping in the garden, tearing through the rooms of the house and barking their heads off, the eucalyptus trees pitch-black and the breech clacking once more, the gun firing not at the cedars and not at the frightened magpies congregating in the treetops but in my direction

"Scram, commie"

and I realized that my suitcase weighed almost nothing, that I had almost nothing, as the occupational therapist noted on the day I arrived at Alverca's charity home for women

"Is that all you have, Dona Albertina?"

and I smiling to myself, because she wouldn't understand that that wasn't all I have, for I have a whole house and farm with trees and crows in Palmela, a stable of cows as well as pigs, turkeys, rabbits, chickens, turtledoves, and pigeons, I have a garden, a swimming pool, rosebushes, and a greenhouse full of orchids, twenty employees, including the maids, to direct and keep an eye on so that they don't rob me, because anyone with any brains knows how hired help is these days, and I don't expect to spend many months or even many weeks embroidering parrots next to the yards of the beggars from Africa and the pillars of the overpass, because one day soon, perhaps tomorrow, perhaps even tonight, Senhor Francisco will come get me in his car, he'll open the door for me, then walk around to his side, then get in the driver's seat, and then, as my companions peer through the curtains, he'll take me back to Palmela, he'll take me back to what's mine.

COMMENTARY

With unemployment on the rise, you take what you can find, and what I found was a position as an occupational therapist at the charity home for women in Alverca. After separating from Adérito I stayed on with our daughter in Odivelas, in a one-bedroom, ground-floor condo where she and I eat our meals in the kitchen, because I moved her bed into the living room, and with the sofa, chairs, bar, and stereo there's no room for the dining table. When Adérito still lived with us Tania was a baby and the three of us slept in the bedroom, but now she's eleven years old and I wouldn't feel comfortable, I need my privacy, so if I were still married

God help me

I'd have to get a larger place, but fortunately Adérito decided to leave, I got a bank loan to buy out his share, and off he went, not that we got on badly, we didn't, there were no scenes or fights, nor was he seeing other women, which I wouldn't have tolerated, the problem was that at a certain point I got tired of a person who could spend weeks in a corner just twiddling his thumbs and remembering the past, so one day I found myself wishing that he'd fall in love with someone else and clear out, I invited some of his female coworkers over to see if something might spark, but nothing did, I chatted with the girls while Adérito just sat there, without an opinion, a question, or a witty remark, but later that night his hand groped for my chest, I shoving it away

"Get your paws off"

Adérito insisting, as if he hadn't heard, I shoving some more

"I'm not in the mood, let me sleep"

and the next day I got up my courage and went to the travel agency, passed through a tunnel of desks and posters of Bermuda holidays and cruises to Tangier, and found Adérito with a client and the telephone pressed to his ear, searching for a flight to London on the computer, I pressing my fingers on the desktop with so much force that if I didn't use nail-hardening polish my pinkie nail would have cracked

"I want a divorce"

the client's charm bracelet jingling as she swiveled around, and Adérito, who knew how I was, imagining that I was imagining things

"There's nothing between me and this woman, Lina, I swear to God it's the first time I've ever seen her"

and the client, one of those bimbos who wear fishnet stockings and necklaces made of billiard-size balls, looking now at me now at him

"This is insane, I've walked into an insane asylum"

yelling for the manager, and the manager, who with his mustache and receding hairline happened not to be bad-looking, the manager, who didn't remember me although we'd stood next to each other at the end of the firm's annual party, where he showed me a picture of his kids and suggested we have lunch the following week at a nice little Italian place, the manager, who quickly took an interest in the bimbo's low-cut dress and held down her anger by the waist

"Is there a problem, Adérito?"

and before the manager and the bimbo left arm and arm to spend the rest of the afternoon in a seedy hotel on the Rua do Salitre, I, who have my own bag of tricks, batted my eyelashes and said

"No problem, Senhor Elias, I simply want a divorce from my husband"

and the bimbo, who was as artful as I was and no doubt liked to have her waist held, pretended to flee from me by throwing herself against the manager, in between a Russian doll and a framed Norwegian fjord, waving her charm bracelet's gold hearts, gold medallions, a horseshoe, and a huge sign of the fig

"This is insane, I've walked into an insane asylum"

Adérito pursuing me in the kitchen in Odivelas as I skipped from the refrigerator to the stove and lit matches to thaw the codfish casserole, Adérito switching from pleas to threats, from threats to apologies, from apologies to declarations of love, and from declarations of love to challenges

"Don't think I'm getting divorced and don't think I'm going anywhere, if you're not happy here, then you move out"

I had to endure a few uncomfortable nights on the couch, hearing him snore in the bedroom and waking up when he got out of bed coughing and turned the light on in the hall, and as if that weren't enough, from the unit above ours, since our building is like an echo chamber, I could hear the back of the divan banging against the wall as the gynecologist stimulated her husband with knife-stabbing screams

"Keep going, José, keep going"

a dozen frenzied humps, the springs squeaking, an exhausted pause, and then José, whom I sometimes saw carrying groceries up the stairs or else taking supermarket and we-deliver pizza ads out of their mailbox and surreptitiously stuffing them into ours, José pleading in a moribund voice

"I have to drink some water, Marina, my throat's all dried out"

and ten minutes later, with the whole building rooting for José's success, the divan started rocking again, the back part banging against the wall, the springs screeching this way and that, my sofa trembling from the shocks, the tireless doctor

"Keep going, José, keep going"

Adérito, startled and inspired by those marathons, trying to make up with me

"Move over, Lina, don't be mean"

I defending myself with a pottery plate from the Alentejo that served as an ashtray, promising to break his skull with a rustic scythe

"Get your paws off"

Adérito returning to the bedroom in defeat, pulling on his pajama string, I holding the scythe high in the air, in case he tried to come back, and from upstairs the tragic silence that follows catastrophes, the scattered sounds of survivors, the shuffling of slippers, a faucet, a trunk being moved, the whistling of the tea kettle, Adérito once more with his pleas, threats, apologies, declarations of love, and challenges, offering me bouquets of flowers, chocolates with hunting scenes on the box, a small blue case with a turquoise ring, and I insisting

"I want a divorce"

and Adérito slipping the blue case in his pocket with a pouty look of if you don't want it, then all the more for me

"I'm not leaving this condo, you have to leave"

Adérito whining to my parents that I was going to abandon him and ruin myself, that I didn't care about our daughter, and for two weeks it was you leave home because I'm not leaving, if you're not happy here, then you move out, I'm not the one who wanted to get divorced, mixed in with assorted jabber, jostling, and arguments over who would keep Tania, such as

"I insist on having custody"

or

"I won't allow my daughter to live with another man"

or

"Don't worry, Tania will grow up and I'll explain who you are"

and I worn ragged, because after these endless wars of words, pouts, slammed doors, and ominous prophecies, I couldn't get to sleep under the divan where the doctor kept spurring on her horse

"Keep going, José, keep going"

the doctor who last year finally got pregnant, quieted down, and brought peace to Odivelas, since the other neighbors are all normal, God bless them, just two or three hurried humps, which isn't bad, and I only went back to my bed when Adérito took up with a girl from the travel agency whose breasts pointed away from each other, in a kind of glandular sulkiness, and he moved with her to a development in Rinchoa, a cluster of crooked buildings in a pool of mud, miles from the train station and with boards over the holes for the sewer pipes, a place where I wouldn't have a condo if they gave it to me, and the two of them visiting me in Odivelas, in the hope they could walk away with half of the furniture and the wedding presents from his family, but I with my lawyer there and raising the scythe

"Get your paws off"

the lawyer who, instead of Adérito, ended up with the furniture and the wedding presents in payment for the bill he presented after the divorce, so if, when you finish reading this book, you feel like writing a novel about lawyers, just bring your tape recorder, we'll go to a quiet place, some little inn in the north, and I'll dictate it to you from the first to last chapter in a weekend, with plenty of time left over for us to visit Guimarães and play hide-and-seek in the castle, because you may not believe it, but at thirty-three years of age I'm still a girl, I still like

don't laugh

to play hopscotch and such, Tania always groans

"Come on, Mom"

when she sees me walking on the edge of the sidewalk, hopping like a maniac to keep from stepping on the cracks between the stones, and when I take her to the zoo it's not for her sake but for mine, I spend hours clapping in front of the cages and giving peanuts to the animals, Tania all embarrassed by my antics

"Come on, Mom"

and it's a shame I can't play at the charity home, but as the director says, and he's right, you can't trust the pensioners, forty-six women including thieves, whores, and drug addicts, ranging from thirteen-year-olds with more experience than me to eighty-year-old gagas, all of whom are trying to escape Alverca in spite of the free room and board, all of whom feel a vagabond impulse to return to a wretched existence in which they felt free, free to shoot up, catch diseases, wake up in alleys with their heads smashed in, and be unhappy, instead of the security of guaranteed soup, clean sheets, and professional training in embroidery and handicrafts, which they say is of no more use to them than the masses given in the dining room and the inspirational speeches of the director, who does everything he can to encourage them, don't tell me you're not happy with the installations and the cleanliness, the view may not be great but look how far it reaches, there's the new beltway, the overpass, fields, and even a bit of the Tagus in the distance, and what's better than a bit of the Tagus River to rest the eyes, in Odivelas all I see out the window are unemployed mulattos who scratch the paint off cars with nails, drunkards, and poverty, why do you think I keep the blinds lowered and the curtains drawn, drunkards, poverty, and ramshackle buses falling to pieces because of the potholes, I had to put bars over the windows, buy an expensive alarm that goes off with the slightest puff of wind, and install a lock with four bolts against burglars, and when I leave for work I sometimes find needles on the stairs, I don't dare go to the movies in Lisbon at night, to a bar with live music, to a discothèque or a show, I pick up my daughter from ballet at six o'clock, and we hole up in the kitchen like two castaways among thousands of other castaways with their own fears, their own barred windows, and their own locks, I helping Tania with geography and composition when a slight breeze suddenly makes the frigging alarm start howling, and the neighbors slugging away on my landing before realizing that they know each other, because around here even the lightbulbs on the stairs get stolen,

how am I supposed to feel like reading or like going out and
doing things, I lack the necessary peace of mind, I lack a partner, and at least at the charity home I don't have time to think
and don't have any hassles as long as I keep my distance from
the pensioners, who assemble flowers and embroider, my job is
to make sure they keep turning out daisies and needlework,
whether they be gagas or drug addicts, it's perfect socialism,
perfect equality, with all of them around a long table and me at
the head, keeping them from slacking off by tapping their arms
with a pointer like the ones from grade school

"What's wrong with you?"

forty-six pensioners, the young ones hate me and the gagas
don't even see me, their eyes staring blankly out of faces that
look even older if they smile, so gaga that when

"I have to pee"

I help one of them get up to go to the bathroom, I discover that her skirt is wet, her chair is wet, the floor is wet, I in
a reproachful tone

"Dona Fernanda"

or Dona Mécia or Dona Teresa or Dona Manuela, and all
completely alienated, with a Hindu impassiveness occasionally
broken by a toothless appeal

"Minervino"

and this gives you an idea of the torment I endure from
nine to one and from two to six to earn a third of what I deserve
to be paid, with the whores and drug addicts insulting me as
soon as I turn my back

"Bitch"

I unable to tell who it was among all the innocent little heads
bent over embroidery, the innocent little noses behind cloth pet-

als, and the innocent lips that dumbly sing along with the radio, the overpass of Alverca in the window, the unfinished buildings, the freight trucks on their way to Lisbon, a muddy smidgen of river, I pulling a handkerchief from my purse while thinking about my life because sadness, you know how it is, makes my sinuses act up, and a falsetto from the far end of the table

"Bitch"

me shaking the pointer at an angelic peace throughout the room, the peace of a nursery of newborns, I in the bathroom with my eyelids all puffy, because it's not easy, don't you see, it's not easy, it's not them calling me names that hurts, it's what I've turned into, it's the EKG two weeks from now, it's Tania who in no time will grow up and leave home

"Good-bye, Mom"

it's the condo in Odivelas, the alarm clock that yanks off bits of my skin at 7 A.M., and the endlessness of Saturday, that's the worst thing, Tania and I bored to death at the shopping mall, bored to death at a sidewalk café, bored to death watching *Cinderella,* let them call me bitch to their hearts' content but deliver me from Odivelas, the alarm clock, and Saturdays, with the evenings spent at my parents', where my mother complains about her varicose ulcer, you've no idea what Saturdays are like for a woman all alone, and as soon as I step off the bus and enter the charity home, as soon as I sit at the table for making cloth daisies and embroidering, as soon as I look over my left shoulder at a little boat on the Tagus River, at its smokestack leaving a trail that hovers over the mud, I hear a drug addict

"Bitch"

and one of the gagas, picking up the word the way seagulls pick up droppings in the air

"I need to pee, you bitch"

so that if I didn't have Tania to take care of I'd quit the charity home and split for Switzerland, where my sister-in-law, married to a rich man, is always inviting me to come live with them and take care of their boys, and she says I can take Tania along, but as silly as it may sound I wouldn't want to take Tania away from her grandparents, from her surroundings, her friends, her school, she's used to Odivelas, to its streets, its people, and to subject her to Geneva, to a strange language, strange food, all that snow, I don't know, if Tania were a different sort of girl, then okay, but as intelligent as she is, I'm honestly afraid, last year to ease my conscience I had her tested by a psychologist, who was astonished at the results

"Tania is a special child"

and I'm not telling you this because she's my daughter but because it's true, Tania really is a special child, with a maturity, a quickness, and powers of observation that frankly leave me breathless, and yet with all her sensibility she still watches the Disney Club at top volume on Sunday morning, the only day of the week when I can sleep late, she pestered me until I bought her eleven Barbie dolls plus Barbie dresses plus a pink, three-floor Barbie chalet with a plastic garden plus a heart-shaped Barbie swimming pool plus Barbie's square-jawed husband who looks so idiotic it hurts, she sticks bubble gum onto seats which hardens to the point that not even a knife will pry it off, she trails yards of toilet paper down the hall, ruins my lipstick, and uses up my perfumes, especially the French one that I spent ages saving up for, and she squeezes the toothpaste

I can't stand this, don't ask me why but I can't stand this

at the top rather than from the bottom, and I feel like tearing her to pieces, like sending her and her Barbies by parcel post to Rinchoa so that Adérito and his missus can put up with her until every one of their chairs has gum dangling from the seat bottom and I'll be free to invite João to Odivelas, to have dinner and listen to music with him in peace, to talk with him and feel less lonely, João who isn't young and isn't rich, he uses a rope instead of a belt and doesn't polish his shoes, but he's better than nothing, he worries about me, he talks to me, he tells me about his life on a farm in Palmela or Azeitão or Setúbal, wherever, because for me everything south of the Tagus is the same, it's all foul swamps, debris, and seagulls, João with a helpless air, as if he were afraid of the dark

(it's easy for a woman to tell which men are afraid of the dark)

João whom I met at the charity home for women, where on Tuesdays he would ring the doorbell to look in on his mother, who didn't seem to recognize him, even as he didn't seem to recognize her, at least not very well, João hesitating in the hall with the fruits or sweets he brought for his mother, looking at the cleaning women like a lost orphan, and finally asking me, the only person who didn't pass by him like a shadow or like someone who didn't even exist

"Dona Isabel?"

my mother who divorced my father when I was little and what I remember about her

Lina

are the sounds of fighting, shouts, insults, a trunk at the top of the steps, and a car on the road to Lisbon, what I remember about her are the flutter of pigeons, the tissue-paper crinkle of the rosebushes, the windmill searching for the wind in a daze, what I remember about her is the silence in the house, the maids whispering in the kitchen, my father locked in his room, Titina weeping in the shadows, the German shepherds barking all night, and the crows cackling in the orchard

Lina

and I bending over his mother

"Dona Isabel"

what I remember about her are the heifers in the dusky stable, the geese pursuing me in the couch grass with the whistling of their beaks, the kittens drowned by the cook without pity

Lina, Lina

in the washtub, with a few air bubbles rising from the water, what I remember is a headless chicken running around and around, just legs and wings, my father with his hat and a one-week-old beard

"Your son's here, Dona Isabel"

pulling on his suspenders and summoning the cook, what I remember about my mother is the rustling of the creeping vines, the hyacinths bowing down, the chatting of the dahlias, the plaster angels planted in the grass, the gypsies and kidnappers hiding in the courtyard

(dressed in black like smugglers, dressed in black like the dead)

armed with sacks to haul me away

Lina

and I

"Your son, Dona Isabel, your son's here to see you"

and the weird thing was how Dona Albertina, who's forever going on about a past filled with splendors, majors, and policemen, stopped moving her needle and glued her eyes on João, wanting to hug him, kiss him, call him young man, and go away with him

"Let's go, I've waited for you long enough"

and João, who of course didn't know her, who'd never seen her before, trying to break away

"Let go of me"

a creature

Lina

who's a complete stranger to me, and she hung on to me squealing, giggling, and sobbing until finally Lina and the maids dragged her to her room, tied her to the bed, and closed the door, I hearing her say

"little João"

without any idea of how she knew my name, fortunately it was time to leave, and I bought an orange drink for Lina in the café of Alverca, we talked a long while, she told me about Adérito, Tania, her condo in Odivelas and how Saturdays never end, and although I'm twenty years older, perhaps she doesn't dislike me, perhaps she can accept me, I made a date to have dinner with her and her daughter next week, we'll go to the amusement park, Lina pushed away the teacups, placed her hand in mine, asked me if I was afraid of the dark, and I felt something inside me, a solace, a rejoicing, a relief, the certainty of going home after an interminable journey, because when a woman asks a man if he's afraid of the dark, it's a sign that she wants to remain with him forever, it's a sign that she wants to remain with him for a long, long time.

third report
(on the existence of angels)

REPORT

One day, when I was nine or ten years old, my godmother
said

"Your father's coming to see you tomorrow"

and I didn't feel a thing because I didn't know what the
word father meant any more than I knew what the word mother
meant, I knew that other girls my age in the neighborhood and
at school lived with men they called father and with women they
called mother, but I had no idea what a father or a mother could
be, because if a father or a mother did what my godmother did

(feed me, send me to bed, take care of me, scold me)

then we wouldn't say father and mother on the one hand
and godmother on the other, we'd use the same word, so there
had to be something more or something less in a father and
mother that I didn't understand, even as I didn't understand why
I lived with an older woman in a home without a man and without the objects men place on the shelf in the shower, namely a
razor, a strop, a comb, brilliantine, and it wasn't only the objects of men that were missing but also the clothing of men, the
coughing of men, a newspaper on a chair, and above all the smell
of men in the places they inhabit, the smell of workshops, wine,

and the vomit wine causes, the smell of tobacco and sweat, the sour smell men bring home from the café on Sundays, men's smell, men's voices, their angry shouts in the kitchen, because men get angry to make their wives cry and get even angrier when they do cry, as I learned by listening to the fathers of the neighborhood girls shout at their mothers at night, and when the shouts and tears were over they would start grabbing their wives' dresses, and everything would hush except for the trees on the square, I'd feel a strange silence that made the darkness darker and the river larger and that I only understood much later, when César said to me

"Lie down here"

and my body transformed into a tunnel of silence that thumped with the echoes of my blood, whereas in our home there were no shouts or tears, the silences were all of the unstrange kind like when we go to sleep and can hear a bird in the treetops, water trickling, or a piece of furniture suddenly creaking, especially in summer, when the cabinets and wooden trunks would call me

"Paula, Paula"

so that when my godmother said

"Your father's coming to see you tomorrow"

I didn't feel anything because I didn't know what the word father meant, but since no man had ever entered our home with his cough, his anger, and his smell, it made me curious to imagine one in the living room, in the kitchen, in the backyard, I thought a man would be too big for where we lived, for at the age of nine or ten men seemed huge and awkward to me, a whirlwind of orders and body hair, it didn't make me happy to have a father, I was afraid to meet him, afraid of his newspapers and shouts, but it made me curious to imagine what my father would do in our home, what clothes he would wear, what chair he would sit in, whether he would pat my cheek with his hand and whether his hand on my cheek would hurt me, what he would talk about with my godmother, whether he would take me far away from Alcácer, and suddenly I was afraid he'd take me away and I began to cry and to see storks nesting on the notary's chimney, one of the them lying down on the nest and the other one perched perfectly still, without a flicker of movement, my godmother setting down the straw fan for the stove

"What's wrong, Paula?"

and assuring me that no one would take me away from Alcácer, I forgot about my father's visit, and soon it turned dark, the streetlights above us were round and still, those down below shimmered on the river, and soon I fell asleep, and soon, just a second later, it was daytime again, and again the window, again the square, again the bridge, because at that age my sleep lasted for one second if that much, and I marveled at how such long dreams could fit into such a short space of time, dreams in which I'd leap into the air and fly for centuries, dreams in which horned animals with an ox's body and a human face would gallop after me, and I unable to run, my feet so heavy they stuck to the ground, and right when the animal was going to hit me, bang, there was the sun shining in the window, my mother at my side, and my feet finally able to move

"What animal?"

the peace of the buildings, the peace of the trees, the cat looking at me from the windowsill, so pretty it didn't seem real, it seemed painted like the picture in my room and like the cookie tins that were prettier than life, my godmother's arms winding her braid on her neck like an amphora's handles searching for the head it doesn't have, my godmother, who had no time for horned animals, heating me up some milk, slicing me some bread, pouring food from a pan into the cat's bowl as the cat slid like silk from off the sill

"Hurry up"

my godmother who brought me a blouse, a skirt, and some brand-new socks from the drawer, combed my bangs, wiped a spot off my shoe with her finger, made me wear a sweater in spite of the heat, and set me on a stool like a piece of porcelain

"Don't get all rumpled, your father will be here soon"

my godmother ordering me to sit straight, tightening the bow on my waist, and snapping on my earrings like for Mass, I who hated earrings, once I lost a stone from an earring, a stone that was smaller than a grain of sand, since we didn't have money for boulders, and we hunted for it all weekend, praying to Saint Anthony and placing pairs of open scissors on the floor, because if you place open scissors on the floor you find what's missing, and in fact we found the microscopic coraline glittering in the threads of the rug, my godmother fiddling with the ribbon in my hair, brushing an eyelash from my face, noticing a hole in one of my socks, putting on her glasses and mending the hole, arranging my collar, turning round my skirt, bringing soap and a wet towel to wash my knees, tidying up the living room, changing the position of the table mats and the cat litter

"Don't get all rumpled, your father will be here soon"

buying a bottle of sparkling wine at the grocer's and placing it in the center of the table along with a wineglass she wiped on her apron, a dish of jam, and a pack of crackers, hiding the broom behind the laundry tub, hurriedly clipping my nails, hooking a tablet of lavender under the rim of the toilet bowl to make it smell better, pushing the chipped teacups to the back of the sideboard and covering them up with the plate that says Souvenir from Castelo de Vide at the bottom, replacing her slippers with sandals that pinched her, as I could tell by her sighs and by how she looked at them dreaming of the moment when she could take them off, dusting cat fur off the cushions, sitting down near the door, straight up like me, on the settee with a wooden seat that tortured her rear end, suddenly hopping up and anxiously running over to move a curtain but then putting it back like it was and rubbing her behind as she returned like a penitent to the rigors of the settee, my godmother and I, rigid like mummies so as not to ruin a single pleat, our eyes riveted to the door as we waited for a knock, heroically frozen until ten o'clock, eleven o'clock, twelve o'clock, and nothing, the cat nuzzling us because it was hungry, and my godmother, between her teeth, afraid she'd ruin her hairdo if she opened her mouth

"Be still, Benfica"

the cat, offended, vanishing down the hall, one o'clock, two o'clock, twenty minutes to three and me dying to get off the stool, my throat dry, my bladder bursting, and my godmother who watched from out of the corner of her eye

"Be still, Benfica"

dripping with sweat, the hot three–o'clock sun melting her fat and perfume and she without daring to move an inch, ten after three, quarter after three, three thirty-five, and the sound of a car engine increasing as we held our breath, then decreasing in the direction of Setúbal, Lisbon, or God knows where, I feeling my nose itch but not daring to blow it, feeling my back itch and enduring it, feeling the sun on my legs between my socks and my skirt, and my legs getting badly sunburned, I in a moribund voice as if I needed a hospital or the fire department, as if I needed oxygen, intravenous feeding, a machine to revive me

"Maybe my father forgot, Godmother"

and my godmother, who also needed oxygen

"Hush"

she saying

"Hush"

and someone knocking at the door as if

"Hush"

were a sign, a password, a cue, my godmother pulling me off the stool with infinite caution, smoothing my clothes, smoothing her clothes, walking to the door with a queenly stride, preparing a smile of cheerful deference, all set to laugh politely, to praise, to agree, turning the doorknob with the ceremony of someone unveiling a tabernacle

"Please step in, Minister"

and there was Alcácer, the river, the trees on the square, the truck drivers from the Algarve at the outdoor café, and the neighbor women stretching their necks toward us, itching with curiosity to see my father the Minister, but there was no Minister, it was the granddaughter of the priest's mistress in a pinafore with a cross-stitched Our Lady of Fátima on the pocket, an uppity nitwit who would hit me with a ruler during recess and who was forever threatening to poke me in the eye with the needle of her compass, who the year before had put a grasshopper in my lunch box for no reason at all, just because I'd said

"Your grandmother is the priest's girlfriend"

and my classmates began to thump their schoolbags and sing all around her

"Your grandma is the priest's girlfriend, your grandma is the priest's girlfriend"

my godmother and I on the threshold, sunburned and with our bladders bulging like blimps, our groins straining to hold back the urine, my dressed-up godmother and I all wilted, and it wasn't my father, it was the nitwit granddaughter of the priest's mistress, a girl who belonged to that class of people who have one long eyebrow running across their nose, and now both storks were lying down in the nest, their beaks tapping one against the other like castanets, the tide was going out, and as it went out a thin strip of beach without any footprints emerged and prolonged the embankment, the granddaughter of the priest's mistress to my godmother

"My grandmother wants to know if she can borrow two eggs, Dona Alice"

the priest's mistress who lived in an apartment just like ours with a backyard that amounted to a tiny vegetable patch and a withering walnut tree, the priest's mistress who was already old and never went out, who spent her days ironing soutanes and sashes and making chicken soup, rice casserole, sliced pork, and cod cakes for the priest, who at suppertime could be seen walking through Alcácer with a flask of strawberry liqueur under his arm, eyeing the waitress at the café, my disillusioned godmother looking at the mistress's granddaughter and unable to speak, breathing like a fish, and it occurred to me that, being protected, I could go get my ruler and hit her, go get my compass and poke her in the eye, and I went to my room and looked in my pencil case, I thought of using my penknife but the blade was dull and didn't cut, so I came back with my drawing pen, which had not just one big needle but two, I came back with the drawing pen in my hand and was oblivious to everything but the grand-daughter's death, although at the age of nine or ten I didn't really know what death meant, death for me was a rude person stretched out on a bed with his shoes on, whom no one got mad at for ruining the bedspread with his heels, death was a face covered by a handkerchief with lots of flies buzzing on top of it, and then everyone sighed, ate sandwiches, and took the naughty person to a boarding school where he wouldn't ruin bedspreads, or they handed him over to the gypsies, whose belongings are already all ruined, whose wives, mules, and lives are all ruined, and so I returned to the front door without paying attention to my embarrassed godmother, whose fingertips were straightening her bun as she idiotically, pathetically repeated

"Please step in, Minister, please step in, Minister, please step in, Minister"

I raised my arm, vaguely aware that the granddaughter had grown taller, wore a hat and suspenders, and smoked a cigarillo, that the neighbor women and truck drivers at the outdoor café looked at her in awe, and that the storks hovered over contrary winds, I vaguely noticed the cars of uniformed and plainclothes policemen sprinkled among the trees to keep watch over the square, I raised my arm feeling hungry, thirsty, impatient, and angry, I raised my arm

"Die die die"

imagining the blood, the handkerchief over her face, the flies, and with all my might I jabbed the needles of the drawing pen into my father's stomach, and he rubbed his stomach with-out complaining, he mauled his rear end on the wooden settee, accepted the glass of sparkling wine, crackers, and jam, grabbed me by the waist, and I, escaping to the window

"Don't touch me, I'm not going away with you"

and my godmother rolling herself up in apologies as if the whole world depended on him and moved or stood still according to his mood

"Paula didn't mean to hurt you with her drawing pen, Minister, I swear she didn't mean to hurt you with her drawing pen"

my father still wearing his hat and flicking cigarillo ashes into the Souvenir from Castelo Vide plate that my godmother brought over from the sideboard as if it were a priceless treasure, my father glancing with a sort of nostalgia at the ships through the window, motioning my godmother to be quiet so that he could hear the water lapping the hulls, the opposite of my classmates' fathers, for he had no newspaper, no sour smell, no wine on his breath, the policemen peering at us through the window as they circled the building to protect him, shooing the neighbor women away from their windowsills and the Communists from the outdoor café, throwing drowned bodies back into the water and preventing the trawlers from landing, climbing up the notary's chimney to handcuff the hidden Communists and send them off

way to go

to rot in the prison at Tarrafal,* and suddenly an authoritarian voice

"One, two, three"

the national anthem out on the street, and it was sung by my classmates, dressed up like me in their Sunday best, with new clothes like me, bows and ribbons like me, combed and brushed and stiff like me, waving paper Portuguese flags, lined up by height and with a teacher directing them, the granddaughter of the priest's mistress with a bouquet of flowers, and I thinking

"I'll kill her, I'll tell the police to shoot her dead"

the mayor unrolling his speech, the Brothers of the Holy Eucharist carrying lit candles, the volunteer firemen in their brand-new truck paying homage to my father with the siren, the whores with mermaid hair who worked the road to Setúbal shouting out in unison

"Long live the Minister, long live Salazar"

my father sighing on the settee of torments

"What a bore"

offering his thanks for the anthem, the flowers, the speech, the firemen's siren, and the long-live, my father

"What a bore"

embracing the mayor and promising a high school, a clinic, a beauty queen with a crown and scepter and blue eyes, a weather station, a Greek temple, a magazine of visual poetry, a housing development for workers, a Brazilian forward, and while the schoolteacher led the children in another round of the national anthem, my father drowned his weariness in the sparkling wine

"What a bore"

ordered the police to pick out a Setúbal road whore without lice or diseases to accompany him to Lisbon, and departed from Alcácer without remembering to take leave of me and my godmother, my father in the car waving without enthusiasm at my classmates

"What a bore"

protected by the policemen pointing their machine guns right at us, knocking down the crippled seller of lottery tickets for holding up the procession, shoving the schoolteacher to make her silence the anthem, clearing away the unemployed and the fishwives with the butts of their rifles and overturning their trays of whiting, and when the dust and fins had settled, the square was empty except for me and my godmother, she with her hands full of crackers and I with my drawing pen ready to murder the granddaughter, the storks in their nest on the chimney, and a drunk man happily staggering away, his patriotism ringing out amid the seagulls' outrage

"Long live Salazar"

my godmother and I had a sip of sparkling wine, which made my tongue tingle like a leg gone to sleep, the falling night swallowed up the river, and I looked at the cigarillo butts in the Souvenir from Castelo de Vide, thinking

"So that's what a father is, so that's all that a father is"

my father, who never came back to Alcácer lest he'd have to endure more speeches and anthems, who never built the clinic, the housing development for workers, the weather station or the Greek temple, and who never gave us a Brazilian forward or a beauty queen with latex eyelashes, my father whom I sometimes saw greeting archbishops or exhorting boy scouts on TV, and a few months later the cat puked up some strange things and we buried it next to the garden wall, and a few months after that the granddaughter stopped hitting me with a ruler, she became my friend, she taught me to pluck my eyebrows and remove the hair from my legs, she lent me some rings that weren't made of gold but looked like it, and they had diamonds bigger than the real kind, she took me to dances in Amora and Sines with a cousin who drove a car for hire, and as he drove he fondled my knees

"You're a pretty girl, Paula"

the cousin named César who said to me

"Lie down here"

and I put on the granddaughter's rings and necklaces and told my godmother that I was going to Grândola to look for work, to Vila Franca to apply for a job in the tax office, and César stopping his taxi in the quarry and pointing to the backseat

"Lie down here"

and what I felt must not have been pleasure, because if it were pleasure I'm sure I would have felt like crying and not have noticed the pine trees and our clothes and the marble dust that entered my ears, nor would it have mattered that César ripped off a button, and it did matter

"You ripped off a button"

I who never worry about buttons, and that button was as ordinary as can be, the kind I could get in any shop, and it was from a place on my blouse that my godmother wouldn't notice, I who couldn't care less about buttons, feeling confused by my anger, slipping out from under César like a lizard

"You ripped off a button"

and César touching me without seeing me, as if he'd been woken up at five in the morning

"What time is it, Adelaide?"

thinking he was at home, reaching for the alarm clock that wasn't there and for the window shade that didn't exist, recognizing me slowly, astonished to find himself with me in the midst of the pine trees, César combing his hair with his hand as if a visitor had surprised him in his bedroom

"Paula"

and the granddaughter in the pastry shop, enthusiastically whispering into my ear

"How did it go?"

César at another table with his wife, having a serious conversation with her and smiling on the sly at me, but he stopped
smiling when two policemen came from Lisbon, shut him up
with them in the station, took away his taxi license, and roughed
him up, so that his face was a mess and he limped for a week,
César stopped calling me, wouldn't answer my letters, and if I
phoned him he hung up, pleading in a terrified squeal
"Leave me alone"
the granddaughter likewise avoiding me after she was ques-
tioned by the police and laid off from her job, leaving the café
as soon as I entered, and crossing to the other side of the street
if she saw me coming, and when I tapped her on the shoulder
to ask why
"Please get out of my life before your father does me in"
so that I who had never again seen my father, who knew
nothing about him except that he inaugurated orphanages and
welcomed English princes, finally understood why people avoided
me or, if they couldn't avoid me, why they immediately agreed
with me, feared me, hated me with a hatred written all over their
faces, called me Miss Paula, made me pass in front of them at
the grocer's, the fish shop, the butcher's, and didn't accept my
money when I wanted to pay
"Out of the question, Miss Paula"
why the lawyer paid me twice as much as the other legal
assistants for doing a fifth of the work, gave me extra holidays
for no reason at all, placed a feather pillow on my chair, hung a
picture of Salazar in every office, changed my typewriter ribbon
every day, and said almost every ten minutes
"You needn't come in tomorrow if you're feeling tired,
Miss Paula"

why the mayor named the new fountain and the bandstand after my father, invited me to dinner whenever there were official visits, seated me at the head of the table as if I were rich and important, and praised the regime in my presence, since I represented the regime, I finally understood why our landlord never asked us for the rent, why presents of fresh fruit and meats always arrived, why I was asked to keep so-and-so from getting drafted, to get such-and-such admitted into a Lisbon clinic for a hernia operation, and to find an opening for somebody's aunt in a rest home because the March rains carried away her shack, I understood that no boy dared to date me since the police were apt to show up without warning, meet with the pretender, and leave him with a smashed-in face and a leg that hobbled for a week, I finally understood and I took the train to Lisbon, went straight to the ministry at Commerce Square, and there next to the Tagus River, under the stone arches full of beggars and accordion players with paper cups between their knees, I explained to the uniformed employee who blocked my way

"I'm here to speak with my father"

whom I remembered with a hat, cigarillo, and suspenders, giving thanks for the anthems, flowers, speeches, the firemen's siren, and the long-live, sighing

"What a bore"

and drowning his weariness in the sparkling wine, the first uniformed employee to a second uniformed employee with more silver stars on his collar, pointing a long, hesitating fingernail

"She says she's the Minister's daughter, she says she's here to speak with her father"

and behind me the city with slit veins bleeding bronze generals, pigeons, and dairy bars into the Tagus, ferryboats like diesel-powered houses plying between the two shores, the uniformed employee with more silver stars leaning toward a uniformed employee with a gold star, both of them looking at me sideways, then looking at each other, the one with the gold star addressing me reluctantly

"Your papers"

people entering and leaving with rectangular tags on their lapels, everything run-down and ugly, everything precarious like at the lawyer's office in Alcácer, the paint discolored, the plaster crumbling, an ancient desk falling apart in a corner, and I in the midst of the shabby walls, the shabby furniture, musing

"So this is what César's afraid of, so this is what the granddaughter's afraid of, so this is what the grocer, the fish merchant, and the butcher are afraid of"

musing on how a country could be ruled by officials steeped in trash, with beggars playing accordion under the arches of power, I to the uniformed employee, who was decrepit like the arches, which seemed not to be made of stone but of shredding cardboard

"Just tell my father to leave me in peace"

arches made of shredding cardboard, the statue of the king made of plywood, the castle with canvas battlements, and the castle garden with cheap wind-up peacocks, bought from a drugstore going out of business, and I thought

"If the granddaughter came here, if César came here, if the lawyer came here, if the mayor of Alcácer came here, what a disgrace for my father, what a disgrace for Salazar"

the drugstore peacocks whirling in a daze because their springs had snapped, to me the government resembled a drab and bankrupt traveling circus, a puppet theater operated by the miserable uniformed employees who slept in dilapidated buildings in between shows, and when I thought of the fountain and the bandstand they'd named after my father, what a joke, I felt like laughing at the Minister, at Salazar, at the boys who were afraid to date me

"Tell my father that I just want to be left in peace"

and that Sunday the police came to Alcácer to take me to a farm in Palmela with a cypress-lined driveway, an orange grove, a rose garden in which you could hear the petals jingle like tiny glass bells in the wind even when there was no wind, the house on the top of the hill, and at the top of the steps my father, who didn't kiss me or smile at me, who never showed any interest in me, a woman peeking at me through a chink in a window, the maids peeking at me through a chink in a window, the aproned cook holding a dead rabbit and a knife, the cook

you're going to think that what I'm about to tell you is strange, but coincidences like this happen every day

who had my exact same nose and chin, from my father's office I saw her cleaning the rabbit, I saw her apron covered with gray fur and my nose and my chin, I mean a nose and a chin identical to my nose and chin, bent over a clay pot with rabbit guts, my father who didn't notice anything, who didn't see the resemblance, my father who, if you'd pointed it out to him, would no doubt have dropped his jaw, my daughter with a cook's nose, don't be ridiculous, I'm sorry but that's impossible, who might well have had the police arrest you to teach you a lesson, and then a young man walked into the office, and my father

"Say hello to your sister, João"

a young man without a nose like mine or a chin like mine, with shoes that needed shining and a piece of rope for a belt, who stuck my father in a clinic so that he could keep my part of the house and farm, the young man disguised as a beggar from an operetta

(*"Say hello to your sister, João"*

and he rubbing one of his unpolished shoes against the other)

who hid my father in Alvalade on the hope that I wouldn't find out when he died, who ousted my father from Palmela so that he wouldn't have to give me half the estate, the chinaware, paintings, silver, furniture, money, I in Alcácer, alone in this minuscule apartment on the square since my godmother

I'd rather not talk about this now

alone in this minuscule apartment on the square exactly as my godmother left it, for I changed nothing, I still have her chipped teacups, the plate from Castelo de Vide, the settee, and the framed prints, my brother who sold the house and farm and kept my share of the money, because last week I took the bus to Palmela and saw that they had already torn down the barn and stable and were chopping down the orange trees, filling in the swamp, and cutting the eucalyptus trees at the root, I couldn't tell which way the wind blew because the windmill no longer existed, the emaciated German shepherds looked at us from out of the underbrush on the hill, and where there used to be flower beds they were already putting up houses and buildings, without the permission of my father, confined to the clinic of Alvalade and unable to speak, I furious at my brother as I gazed at the collapsed walls of the house, at what was left of the ceilings, at the courtyard that was now a pile of bricks and stone where no cook with my nose and my chin cleaned rabbits over a clay pot, and then

no, not then but later, when I left, when I walked out the gateway with no more gate and with the pillar that pointed to Setúbal, to Alcácer, now lying flat in the grass

I might be mistaken, which doesn't matter because it's not important, but I had the impression when I arrived at the bus stop that my father's cook, the one who resembled me, the one who had my nose and my chin, was waiting for me with a little package in her hand, as if she wanted to talk to me and give me the package, but I didn't have time to confirm that it was her and, if it was her, that she was indeed waiting for me, because the bus driver was closing the door and I had to jump on so as not to arrive at Alcácer at night, and when I tried to get a glimpse of her through the rear window, the bus stop had already been swallowed by a curve, so that I didn't see and would never again see whoever was standing there, for I had no intention of going back to Palmela.

COMMENTARY

The doctor in Luanda told me it was because of Africa that I couldn't have children, and Africa for me meant twenty-six years in the bushland of Angola, not in some city and not in a small town but in the middle of the bush, without electricity, creature comforts, or anything else, just the empty house where a Portuguese official had once lived, my husband's canteen, and a bunch of poor blacks who sat on their butts and scratched their bellies next to the river, and the doctor to me, shaking his head

"After twenty-six years in Africa, what do you expect?"

twenty-six years drinking filtered water, eating the dried fish we were unable to sell, languishing with malaria one week per month, and sleeping on a mat behind the counter until we moved into the empty house with a columned porch, engulfed by wild grass and without the least hint of a windowpane. My husband drove the truck to Malanje and returned a week later with a few pieces of junk and his mind pickled in alcohol, shouting like an excited newlywed that he'd bought me a complete set of furniture, but it was a complete set of useless debris that no mulatto with any sense would accept for free, a cushionless sofa, a rocking chair without the wicker, and a table made of wood from a discarded barrel, and my husband, aided by the Indian who was as broke as we were and as lazy as the blacks but who liked to call himself our employee, plopping the things down on what was left of the plank flooring

"You're going to have a first-class palace, Alice"

meaning a dilapidated building in which it rained as much as on the street, the floor with holes the size of lynx traps that continually caught our feet, a rusty telegraph that we used as a cabinet and that now and then, just like a retired person, remembered its old job and started feebly tapping out SOS's, my husband beaming in the rocking chair as his behind scraped the floor, with a beer breath so strong it could kill geckos on the ceiling

"So what do you think of our little palace, Alice?"

and the doctor prescribing vitamins and a cruise to Greece, the vitamins costing me almost as much as the cruise would have cost, if I'd had the money for historical heaps of stone

"After twenty-six years of crocodiles and mosquitoes, what do you expect?"

crocodiles and mosquitoes were the least of my troubles, one gets used to tertian fevers as one gets used to those giant lizards that appear as a single beady eye peeking out of the river and that would occasionally swallow a black man as if he were a throat lozenge, which was no great loss, since the blacks had babies by the broodful, I even wondered if the women, instead of getting pregnant, laid a dozen eggs in their huts and hatched them during the night, giving rise the next morning to a new band of black infants jumping through the grass, and so crocodiles and mosquitoes were the least of my troubles, worse was the fact that no one bought anything from the canteen except my husband, who became his one and only client, polishing off a crate of beer in a trice with the help of the Indian who, like his Hindu gods, seemed to have eight arms for holding eight bottles at once and arriving that much sooner at nirvana, which consisted of him ecstatically drooling in a monsoon of saliva with his eyelids turned inside out, crocodiles and mosquitoes were the least of my troubles, much worse was to find myself sailing on the raft boards that were our bed for eight days of moon cascading down my legs as the telegraph interrupted my agony with delirious messages and the mango trees broke down in tears because of the November rain, much worse was the wholesaler in Malanje, a cold little Chinaman whose ruthless eyes resembled crooked slots in alms boxes and who would eat his mother with chopsticks and a bowl of fried rice were she stupid enough to owe him a red cent, his Chinese partner having already done just that, to judge by his flab and his contented smile, the wholesaler cutting off all credit and merchandise, my husband almost on his knees

"Don't leave me without beer, my friend"

and the Chinaman, who if the bush were Lisbon would have worn canvas slip-ons and kowtowed to the whites without ever making waves, pointed at the crates while addressing the partner whose mother was already under his belt

"No beer either"

and with no more nirvanas in the canteen the Indian, reduced to the sad lot of having just two human arms, took off for Luanda to search for an oasis of draft beers and peanuts or else ended up as a cough drop in the throat of a crocodile, and my husband and I didn't know what to do among the blacks who did nothing but have children that scratched themselves next to their parents on the bank of the river, observed by the floating eyes eager for any food that might slip, I watching the weeping rain in the mango trees, and the doctor using a diagram from an encyclopedia with the organs all numbered to explain that my tubes had withered, his mechanical pencil tracing the path followed by cells and stopping at a flesh-colored diamond called thirty-seven

"After twenty-six years in Africa, the train ends here, your plumbing's stopped up"

my beer-deprived husband having lost, it seemed, his love of life, reduced to sighing and moaning among the lazy blacks, my husband frequenting the black settlement to brood, I thought, on his melancholy amidst the manioc, returning home and falling into the wickerless rocker, holding his forehead with his tortured hand

"Don't say anything, Alice"

because, I thought, he was silently suffering while planning suicides, which were the only thing he ever planned, due to the Chinaman who had pulled the plug on his dream of becoming a successful businessman at the very moment he was nearing the summit of financial ruin, my husband who didn't sleep with me and didn't touch me, he'd get up in his pajamas in the middle of the night and go out like a sleepwalker, seized, I thought, by a desperate impulse to offer himself as a vitamin to the crocodiles, until I began to notice some mulatto children I'd never seen before making believe they were canteen owners in the grass, until I began to notice some coffee-colored children discoursing next to the counter with a shopkeeper's eloquence, and my husband, ever more exhausted when at home, sprawled in the wickerless rocker, overwhelmed by his business troubles

"Don't say anything, Alice"

my husband seeing me approach with an elephant tusk the size of a shepherd's crook

"Take it easy with that tooth, Alice"

forgetting his depression, bursting with the will to live but unable to extricate himself from the chair, raising his knees to defend his incubator of mulattos and crossing his arms to shield the shamelessness written on his face

"Be careful, Alice, or you'll injure me"

and the doctor in Luanda, putting the encyclopedia back on the shelf among the other volumes with illustrations of tapeworms and other kinds of snakes that sleep in our bowels as peacefully as a priest after feasting on our dinner of cuttlefish with ink

"After twenty-six years in Africa and all that you've been through, what do you expect?"

and perhaps I did injure my husband with the crook-size tooth, for my anger was fierce and the elephant huge, and to be perfectly honest I can remember the scream he let out, the shattered chair, his final plea

"For the love of God, Alice"

to be perfectly honest I can remember my husband running through the grass and causing the blacks who distractedly
scratched their bellies to stare in shock at so much commotion,
and since from the porch I could see the river, where beady eyes
floated among the reeds, I can remember the crocodile next
to the shore whose jaws suddenly yawned, I remember with a
snicker my husband tripping on a root, my husband flipping
in the air and losing one of his sandals, I remember as if it were
today his final scream, a second before he vanished down the
animal's esophagus

"Alice"

and the doctor in Luanda, imagining the scene and how
much I suffered, clearly feeling moved and patting my hand with
understanding, since fortunately there are sensitive doctors

"You poor thing"

the crocodile locked its lips shut with my husband inside,
dove into the mud to digest its meal, and voilà, I was a widow,
abandoning five dozen mulattos to the horrors of orphanhood,
giving away our junky furniture to the blacks, who stared at it
while scratching their groins, apparently miffed because it wasn't
Empire, and retreating in mourning to the capital, where the
accumulation of garbage and coffee planters hindered circula-
tion on the streets, with the shore road lined by palms and
prostitutes, one per tree, leaning against the trunks and magnanimously prepared to help the planters launder their money
in the island's dirty sheets, a city where the blacks scratched
their bellies a little less and moved their butts a little more than
in the bush, thanks to the pedagogical arguments of a good swift
kick and an occasional slap, a city where they were crammed into

wretched neighborhoods along with dogs that they in turn thrashed, because the educational instinct is contagious, blacks, dogs, and dead donkeys amid zinc and cardboard shanties that shook like pudding with the slightest wind, blacks with perfect eyesight indulging in the luxury of wearing bifocals on Sundays, a refinement that afforded them the satisfaction of groping their way down the street and bumping into lampposts, I waiting at my cousin Alda's house in the neighborhood of Cuca until my ship left for Lisbon, I next to the laundry tub, looking at the baobab trees as my cousin Alda pined for the town of her birth in Portugal

"If only I could be in Cova da Piedade, Alice"

Cova da Piedade, which, take my word, is the same as Angola, the only difference being that the blacks are us, the same trash dumps, the same vacant lots, the same decrepit buildings, the same dead donkeys blocking our way to the door, and the same people without work scratching their bellies, inventing meals out of bones and rinds, my cousin Alda married to a barber who, for lack of Portuguese clients, tied his towel around the neck of whatever poor black happened to walk by

"Come over here"

and trimmed his hair with pruning shears like a gardener his shrubs, my cousin Alda whose tubes had also withered because of Africa but who didn't especially mind being childless, since all she wanted in the world was to die of hunger in Cova da Piedade instead of dying of hunger in Luanda, as if dying of hunger where the poor blacks are us were better than dying of hunger where the blacks are other people, as if she enjoyed being mistreated, humiliated, and beaten, as if Portugal were a country excuse me while I laugh

worth living in, with the sun lighting up the poverty and with the sea everywhere you turn, especially where you don't want it, if there were less sea at least we could plant a few turnips and cabbages, if there were less sea we could grow potatoes and eat dinner, if Portugal had a smart government, it would sell off the idiot sea and hot weather to the Swiss, who are rich, or to the gypsies, who are clever and would figure out how to sell the waves retail, a smart government would sell off the sea to the Swiss, who need iodine, and buy us a good thick piece of salt cod for dinner, my cousin Alda who preferred Cova da Piedade to paradise

"If only I could be in Almada, Alice, if only I could be in Feijó"

and she sent a letter to me in Alcácer one Christmas telling all about her husband's emphysema and how with his lungs swollen up he could no longer prune their black neighbors' hair like a gardener, and so he spends the afternoon lying under the baobab tree and breathing like a toad, you can't imagine how depressing it is to see him lumber around the house wheezing, Alice, lifting his nose to me but unable to talk, begging me to stick the bread knife into his guts to end it all, and one day I'll end it, but in the meantime tell me how everything is in Cova da Piedade, Alice, how's my sister, how's my mother, and I wrote back saying that her mother at least had no complaints, without adding that at the cemetery, particularly with a few shovelfuls of dirt in your mouth, it's difficult to complain, saying that her sister had a well-paying job in public relations, working the night shift, but without adding that her workplace was a bawdy discothèque in Lisbon and her uniform a pair of tight-fitting, imitation-panther slacks and that she received moral support from a young benefactor whom she in turn supported, since love is a system of exchanges, buying him some English suits and making the monthly payments on a yellow convertible, Alda in her next letter, deeply touched by the family's prosperity

"Give them my greetings"

and I squatting down to knock with my knuckles on her mother's tombstone

"Alda sends her greetings, Aunt"

I waving at the yellow convertible, the low-riding kind that resembles a cigarette case, with eyelids covering its headlights during the day, the kind with seats in which you almost lie down, and lying down happened to be the panther's usual position by trade, I waving at the yellow convertible that whizzed through Cova da Piedade like a comet

"Alda sends her greetings, Idalina"

Alda who presumably carried out her vow, sticking the bread knife into the barber's guts in a euthanasic fit and ending up in jail, because she stopped writing, sparing me from having to knock on the gravestone, which hurt my knuckles, and from waving at the convertible, which threatened to run me over, not to mention other family duties that obliged me to waste entire mornings going to Cova da Piedade from Alcácer, which is where, on the square with Algarve-bound truckers, stunted mulberry trees, and squawking seagulls, I found a one-bedroom apartment when I arrived from Luanda, volume thirty-seven of the doctor's encyclopedia having resigned me to being childless, and to keep myself company I bought some jingling bracelets and took in a white cat, as lean as a budget, which I won over with some eels strategically purchased from the fishermen down by the river, resigned to being childless until the day the Minister's housekeeper arrived in a chauffeured car with little Paula on her lap, to sound out all the widows in town, and since a child, despite the headache of diapers, baby teeth, and vaccines, provides more company than bracelets, with the added advantage of us being able to scold and spank it when something gets on our nerves, such as a broken faucet or a fruit vendor who overcharged us for some bananas, I went with the housekeeper to Palmela to talk with the Minister at a weird farm full of birds and cows, I who'd never known any official higher than the navy ensign who drew up on the larboard side of my youth, offering me aquarium mermaids and miniature ships in soda-pop bottles, which I still have in some drawer or other, along with a photo of the mariner taken at the fair in Castelo de Vide, his face framed in cardboard as Vasco da Gama hugging me, a nymph from the ninth canto of *The Lusiads,* though the flirting never made it to the book cover of Camões's epic, let alone the racy verses inside it, a weird farm that was partly kept up, partly neglected, with a deafening swarm of birds and a housekeeper who dressed the way nuns dress when not in their habits, looking even more nunnish than when wearing caps, hoods, crucifixes, and all those complicated skirts, the housekeeper leading me to the Minister's office through a kind of rich man's junkyard, a maze of rooms in which piles of crystal, statues, pictures, and furniture languished with the ruthless inertia of things, the housekeeper sticking her respectful neck through a plaster archway, where someone's bronchitis was hurling coughs like so many stones

"May I, Senhor Francisco?"

and the Minister, what a letdown, wasn't wearing a uniform with medals, a minister's crown, and a minister's ermine cape, but a corner druggist's suspenders and the hat of a retiree who plays quadrille on a public square, and instead of a minister's scepter he held a smelly cigarillo like you can buy at Alcácer's dingiest bar, the Minister to the housekeeper

"Is it this old dame, Titina?"

the Minister whom my husband, if he weren't in the stomach of a crocodile in Africa, would have hit over the head with a bottle of beer to teach him to respect me, the Minister hanging on the wall with Salazar, the Pope, the Admiral, and others, kissing children and ruling the people, for you can measure a man's authority by the number of kids he holds in his arms with a grandfatherly smile, the Minister opening a folder full of papers with the seal of the Republic

"Twenty-six years in Africa?"

the swarm of birds pecking at the curtains, I hoping to twist one of their necks so I could fry it for a sandwich, thinking how the thrushes would be great in a rice casserole, not to mention the turtledoves that in Angola were a dime a dozen, and besides the birds the creaking of a windmill that hadn't been oiled since the monarchy, the Minister holding my life written forward and backward in his hands, beginning with the mountains of Castelo de Vide, the icy winters, my deceased mother, who sometimes ate blackberries to stave off hunger, walking toward me among the cork trees, the period when I met my husband, the ill-fated Easter that I knew I'd come to regret, I having been duped

(eighteen years old, you understand)

by his song and dance, I stupidly going with him to the notary's winepress, I in tears signing my name before the justice of the peace, and my stepfather enraged because I no longer had what he thought I should have

"You slut"

and I spent three weeks vomiting among sacks of tomatoes in the hold of an Angola-bound freighter to learn to be virtuous and uninterested in winepresses, and on docking in Benguela there was a multitude of blacks so eager to help me with my suitcase that I never saw it again, which at least solved the problem of dealing with heavy luggage, the Minister underlining my existence with a red pencil while the birds for thrush and rice casserole kept pecking at the window

"You didn't bring back any contagious diseases, I hope"

the Minister whose folder contained not only my life but that of my parents, brothers and sisters, cousins, nieces and nephews, plus the two-month trek I made with my husband across savannas and shallow pools, past nightmarish gorillas, festering rhinoceroses, and hordes of leprous apes, in a truck that gradually lost wheels as we lost our nerve, stopping once we reached the ramshackle canteen, because the land was flat and undoubtedly close to the edge where, had we kept going, we would have careened down a precipice without any handrail and into the starry void, the unoiled mill creaked irregularly, spreading peace with each push of the wind, a shuddering owl kept the trees awake, there was a muttering sound as of jealous roses, the framed Pope with a stern look, the framed Cardinal with a stern look, and the Minister with his retiree's hat as if it were a crown, his corner druggist's suspenders an ermine cape, and his cheap cigarillo the scepter of his power, the Minister to the housekeeper, who stared at him with the kind of awe usually reserved for astronauts and tax auditors

"Have the cook bring in the baby, Titina"

a seagull glided like an airborne rat over the beech trees as a creature wearing an apron and slippers shuffled into the office, holding a bundle of sheets pressed to her bosom, and with the housekeeper right behind her

"Here it is"

I stooping under the weight of the eucalyptus and beech trees, wondering if the aproned creature whom the Minister called the cook might not be the baby's wet nurse, I marveling at the house's order and disorder, the angels of passage perching in the yard like ducks among reeds, the smell of orchids coming from I didn't know where and wrapping us like a corpse's shroud, I deciding that she must be the wet nurse, since the housekeeper had told me in Alcácer that the baby was an orphan, I, who had seen my withered tubes in the doctor's encyclopedia in Luanda, deciding that a child is better company than a pair of bracelets, and the Minister to me

"Go ahead and hold it"

I taking the baby in my hands as a girl outside walked with two milk cans toward the stable, and the housekeeper to the aproned creature, the wet nurse, the cook, who looked ready to kill me since handing over the baby

"Isn't it time you fixed the chicken for Senhor Francisco's dinner?"

and as I left I saw her slit a chicken's throat over a tin tub and stir the blood with her knife while struggling with the jerking animal, cleaning out its guts as if the animal were me, even though I had never seen her before and didn't have the time to do her any harm, I who'd come to free her from diapers, colic, crying, and ear infections, I whom she should have thanked for taking the child off her hands, but instead she seethed with

implacable rage, her knife dancing around until my bowels fell
into the tub, then my liver, then my two lungs, first one and
then the other, like shoes being kicked off the edge of a bed, I
doing her a favor and she plotting revenge as she cut me up over
a pot, so that I didn't rest easy until there were a few dozen cypress trees between me and her knife, and the next month the
housekeeper appeared in Alcácer with a bundle of sheets

"Here"

and since I had no one I could give my affection to except the bracelets, which could talk to me but not listen, I got
attached to the girl, we slept in the same bedroom, we shuddered at the same thunderbolts, we got mumps and measles at
the same time, and since we were both orphans we strolled
together along the river in the late afternoon, watching albatrosses eat grilled steaks in the wake of luxury liners, looking
at the drowned men who crashed against the wall to see if the
crocodile, sick of my husband, had decided to give him back
to me, one night there was someone at the door, a shadow
breathing in the needlework of the portière, and it wasn't the
neighbor, a gypsy, a beggar, or a burglar, nor was it the priest's
mistress asking for garlic or olive oil, it was the hat, cigarillo,
and suspenders on the threshold, then in the living room, then
on the settee that tortured people's buttocks, and I without
any sparkling wine to offer him, without crackers or a dish of
jam, wearing my house clothes and old shoes, my hair un-
combed, I who if I'd known the Minister was coming would
have pulled the tub out of the closet, heated up some water,
and taken a bath, I looking at my hands thinking

"I'll go to my jewel box for a second to put on my ring
and my necklace"

I getting up from the wicker chair and the Minister stopping me with his imperious lips

"Be still"

the Minister in a poor person's sitting room filled with a poor person's furniture and pictures of saints on the wall, I fretfully noticing the fraying rugs, the teacups without handles, the shepherdess who'd lost her lamb, the rusty pipes, the chipped ceiling light, the crooked burner on the stove, the Minister walking toward the bedroom where the cat was sleeping, where Paula was sleeping in the only bed we ever had, under the only bedspread, between the only sheets, I, ashamed of the enamel washbasin, the cardboard in place of a broken windowpane, the loose floorboard, and the missing roof tile, blocking the Minister's way to the bedroom, the sheets, the bedspread, the bed, and the Minister pushing me aside like an obstacle, a roadblock, an impediment, as if I'd robbed something that rightfully belonged to him

"I want to see my daughter"

he said.

REPORT

All I want is what's rightfully mine: a slightly better life than what my godmother was able to give me on the truck drivers' square in Alcácer between the river and the bridge, watching the cars heading to the Algarve and wishing I were going with them. All I want is an apartment in Lisbon, no matter if it's small, no matter in what neighborhood, and not to have to pinch pennies all month long, not to have to shop at the cheapest supermarket, to be able to go occasionally to a restaurant and eat a lunch I didn't have to cook myself, to go to the movies on Saturday and forget that when I turn the key in my door there's no one waiting for me on the other side, no one for me to take care of, to buy clothes for, to go on holiday with me in July to southern Spain, which isn't so expensive now, we'd ask a foreigner to take our picture in front of a statue, arm in arm and with straw hats on our heads, then paste the picture in the photo album with tissue paper to protect the snapshots, the two of us in a hotel with another couple we're friends with

(Fátima and Feliciano, Fernanda and Dimas, Elisete and Amadeu)

then place the album between the stereo and the three volumes of *The Family Encyclopedia,* all I want is a decent winter coat, because the one I have is out of fashion and doesn't keep me warm, to go to the hairdresser on my birthday, to be addressed as "Dona Paula" rather than as "you" or "Miss" or just plain "Paula," all I want is a slightly better life, and my attorney

"Your father didn't legitimate you, he left no document, no declaration, there's not much I can do"

my father didn't legitimate me but everyone knows I'm his daughter, the Fascist's daughter, so that the very next day after the Revolution, because democracy is urgent and won't wait, the lawyer I worked for who'd always licked my boots and fawned all over me, doing everything but kneel when I walked by, suddenly sported a hammer and sickle on his lapel and handed me an envelope with a month's salary

"And not a peep out of you, it's more than you deserve, now get out" the granddaughter of the priest's mistress who had become my friend and borrowed books from me spat in my face

"Traitor"

the neighbor women trampled my cabbages, killed my poultry, dumped pails of rubbish onto my yard, shattered my windows with stones, and although I managed to glue back together the plate from Castelo de Vide, it's not the same, the kids on the square tried to hit me and make me trip

"Exploiter"

I who never exploited anyone and never had any money, I lived in a tiny apartment without a tub or toilet, doing my business in a shed with a hole that was freezing in February, traipsing through the lettuces with an umbrella, and yet the neighbor women wrote

"Nazi"

on my wall, and when I entered Vergílio Ferreira's pastry shop everyone suddenly hushed to stare at the criminal, at the murderer, while Senhor Vergílio, who was calmness incarnate, served his customers as if he hadn't seen me, and César, drinking coffee at the counter with Adelaide, turned to Senhor Vergílio, whose face flushed so red it was pathetic

"Since when do you wait on Fascists, Ferreira?"

the granddaughter jumping up from her table, disgusted by my presence, hitting me in the back with all her might as she stormed past, indignantly shouting next to the shopwindow filled with bean pastries

"I didn't know Ferreira worked for the secret police"

and Senhor Vergílio, afraid they might destroy all his pastries and plastic napkin dispensers, Senhor Vergílio who in December had forced me to accept for free

"I wouldn't hear of you paying"

a Christmas basket wrapped in cellophane with a blue ribbon and a bottle of port that tasted corky, Senhor Vergílio growling at me with rage

"Get out"

a basket with a Christmas cake, little bags of walnuts and pine nuts, liqueur-filled chocolates, and a frozen turkey wing, Senhor Vergílio all smiles when he passed by me in the square

"How was the Christmas basket, Miss Paula?"

who praised my father in the local paper and always bowed, was always polite, treating me after the revolution the way he treated gypsies, the boy with the wasted leg, or the seller of lottery tickets, Senhor Vergílio showing me the door with his finger as if I'd entered his shop to beg or steal

"Get out"

and for two years I silently put up with my chickens being poisoned, my garden being used as a trash dump, and my furniture getting smashed to bits, until one month, when I was especially hard pressed, I finally went to Palmela to ask my father for help, and I found the farm in such a shambles that the greenhouse and rose garden were beyond recognition, it was only by the crows' squawking that I knew I was at the right gate, at the top of the drive stood the house, a shot whizzed through the trees, my father waved his shotgun on the steps

"Fucking Communists"

there was a second shot, then a howl, a leaping dog, the irrigation channel shattering at my feet, my father pulling cartridges from his pockets and loading them in his gun, I blinded by a cloud of pulverized cement from the irrigation channel, branches falling, the echo of lead hitting the dented bucket from the well, I who for two years had silently endured humiliations and insults, smeared windows, painted walls, the landlord who used to refuse my rent money

"For heaven's sake, Miss Paula"

lodging a complaint at court alleging damages I didn't cause, the mailman handing me the summons with triumphant glee, the courtroom full of truck drivers and neighbor women with raised fists who called me a Fascist, I without water or electricity, without any money, who ate God only knows what, thinking at least my godmother was spared all this shame, this scorn, the barrage of stones, the granddaughter talking about justice for the people, about surplus value, about dictatorship, calling everyone comrade, yelling threats at the judge, who didn't dare answer back or order her to be silent, the judge adjourning the trial on some pretext or other, starting up his car, fleeing amid snorts, spitting, and swiping canes, at the farm in shambles a third shot, a fourth shot, a fifth shot, I at the bottom of the steps next to a flower vase

"Dad"

and my father smiling at me from under his hat's brim

"Isabel"

my father likewise without water or electricity, likewise with his phone cut off, as hard-pressed for cash as I was, offering me the vestige of a chair in the living room

"Isabel"

while he sat down at the piano, on the verge of tears and in a whirl of notes

"Stay with me, Isabel"

and since I assumed that he didn't want me to see him cry, I crossed the room, walked down the steps, and was halfway down the cypress-lined drive when I heard the clack of a breech and a gunshot in the irrigation channel, my father waving his shotgun

"Fucking Communist"

I to my attorney

"All I want is what's rightfully mine"

and the attorney pushing on the bridge of his glasses

"I don't doubt that it's rightfully yours, but tell me how we can prove it"

I who don't have rich habits, who don't want to be rich, I just want a slightly better life than what my godmother was able to give me in Alcácer, all I ask is an apartment in Lisbon, no matter if it's small, no matter in what neighborhood, and not to have to pinch pennies all month long, not to have to shop at the cheapest supermarket, to be able to go occasionally to a restaurant and eat a lunch I didn't have to cook myself, to go to the movies on Saturday and forget that when I turn the key in my door there's no one waiting for me on the other side, no one to buy clothes for, no one to go on holiday with me in July to southern Spain, which isn't so expensive now, and my brother lying through his teeth, my brother, who always hated me, making up excuses

"Divide what down the middle, if my wife's family ended up with everything?"

giving me a song and dance about his ex-wife and how a clever uncle of hers cheated him out of the farm and the house, how the uncle pulled some strings and pocketed Palmela, and I, not buying a word of it

"Blah blah blah blah blah"

my brother acting the part of a bum so well that if someone saw him on the street they'd put a coin

"Here, buddy"

in his hand, my brother sticking our old man into a clinic in Alvalade so that he could screw me out of the inheritance without me even suspecting, or so he thought, my brother living in Odivelas, in a condo that, compared to my place, was a palace, with a breezy gal who could pass for his daughter and with the gal's obnoxious little girl who could pass for his great-granddaughter, the kind of little girl

(frequently found at the dentist's office or the line at the bank)

considered brilliant by her mother and impertinent by everyone else, inquisitive by her mother and meddlesome by everyone else, highly observant by her mother and downright rude by everyone else, the kind of girl whom, even before she opens her mouth, we feel like pinching on the cheek, a nice round cheek that's perfect for pinches, the kind of girl who's irksomely full of bright ideas, who sometimes wears glasses, sometimes braces, and nearly always a necklace, who sticks her nose into everything, steps on our toes without begging pardon, and not only doesn't she beg pardon, she looks at us as if we were to blame for being stepped on, the kind of little girl who when she grows up will dye her hair purple, use costume-jewelry earrings, work behind a counter or a service window, and tell us, as soon as it's our turn to be waited on after hours in line

"Just a moment"

while setting down her lipstick-stained cigarette and proceeding to tell her coworker all about the skirt she saw that morning at a shop downtown, then refuse our forms because we filled in one of the little boxes incorrectly, forcing us to start over again at the end of the line, my brother in a nifty condo in

Odivelas, with bamboo furniture and brick tile flooring which I'd be thankful to have just for a day, to throw a party, and which he bought outright with the sale of the farm, my brother taking me for an idiot and throwing dust in my eyes

"The condo isn't mine, it belongs to Lina, I swear my ex-wife's family got everything"

as if a woman my age or younger

"Blah blah blah blah blah"

and on top of that a good-looker, tall, and with a place of her own in Odivelas, which with the bus is as good as Lisbon, would marry a paunchy older man who dresses badly and is flat broke, as if a smart young woman who felt like hooking up with an indigent wouldn't find one her own age as easy as pie, a slim and muscular indigent with smooth skin and no wrinkles, I in the condo looking at a poster of a bear which I have to admit was cute, at a collection of terra-cotta windmills and a collection of miniature chrome scales on top of the video-cassettes, at the enclosed balcony with a basket of magazines, plants, straw blinds, and a false ceiling made of pinewood, at the smoked-glass table where they ate their meals, I looking at all that without

of course

believing a single word my brother said

"Blah blah blah blah blah"

the good-looker's daughter, sitting on one of those expensive rugs from Arraiolos, I mean give me a break, changing the TV channel every five seconds until I thought I'd go mad, cartoons, a handball match, a Mexican soap opera, a beauty contest, and then, as if I'd been waiting for nothing else

"I'm going to show you the play I was in at school"

a cavernous sound, lines floating up the screen, a smiling teacher badly out of focus, more lines, and then, camera jiggling, a panoramic shot of the captive audience, little girls dressed as bunnies with pom-poms for tails, long ears, and the rest, somersaulting at random across the stage, my brother so absorbed by the rodents that he forgot I was there, the good-looker enthralled by the rodents, the good-looker's daughter stopping the video and pressing her proud hand on the hopping varmints

"This one is me"

the bunnies lined up by height and singing some ditty or other in unison while gesticulating every which way, the good-looker's daughter stopping the video again and pointing out the eighth bunny from the right, a rodent that frenetically clapped and wiggled its haunches, with a gold bracelet on its paw and lavender sneakers

"This one is me"

the good-looker proudly straightening the ribbon in her daughter's hair

"Your teacher promised that next year, if you're a good girl, she'll put you on a throne and make you queen of the bunny rabbits"

my brother who with the money from the farm bought the mongoloid her bunny suit and squandered the rest on terra-cotta windmills, false ceilings, and chrome scales, plus the bamboos, smoked glass, and a bed all swirls and arabesques, with satin pillows like TV stars have, plus of course the condo itself, on a quiet, residential street in Odivelas with grass and trees and mulatto children

because contrary to what people think there are mulattos who aren't bad off skating and bicycling down the sidewalk, and my attorney looking mystified, my attorney who I'm convinced understood no more about prices than he did about the law and whom I, like a gullible voter, was stupid enough to count on, my attorney

"A one-bedroom condo in Odivelas isn't all that expensive"

the bunnies with zero coordination, led by their teacher who'd spent at least a month teaching them to prance around while clapping their hands and waving their arms, shaking pompoms among Styrofoam coconut trees and plastic sunflowers, the bunnies acknowledging the applause with confused curtsies, except for the second one from the left, who bawled for her grandmother, and the good-looker's daughter to me, while freezing the curtsies with the remote control and rewinding the cassette

"You don't understand a thing, you dummy"

I, the owner of a prehistoric, black-and-white TV without remote control whose image and sound are adjusted by whacking it until the faces and voices return, so that if I feel like watching an interview or a movie I spend the whole evening on my feet banging away at the TV, which spouts out foreign languages every time I turn it on, giving me the speech of Bolivia's president or the weather report for the Philippines, I slapping the contraption with my sore arm while my brother lolls in an armchair and enjoys having his bald crown fondled by the good-looker who's in love with his capital, my brother with a parabolic antenna, twelve channels, a thirteenth channel via cable, and stereophonic sound, it's not that I'm envious, I'm not, I don't want to be rich, the rich can drown in their bank notes, I just want what's mine, I don't think it's too much to ask for a slightly better life, a little apartment in Lisbon, not to have to pinch pennies all month long, not to have to shop at the cheapest supermarket, to be able to go occasionally to a restaurant and eat a lunch I didn't have to cook myself, to go to the movies on Saturday and forget that when I turn the key in my door there's no one waiting for me on the other side, no one for me to take care of, to buy clothes for, no one to go on holiday with me in July to southern Spain, which is gorgeous, we could take an excursion by bus with hotel and breakfast included, we'd make lots of friends with cheerful people who shake tambourines and jingle triangles the whole way, and we'd see a bunch of castles and Moorish churches for peanuts, I may not look it but I'm thirty-nine years old and entitled to enjoy life, there are always some single and divorced men on the excursions to Spain, insurance agents, pharmaceutical representatives, an occasional engineer and the like, if girls worse than me, and I may not be fantastic but I'm not crippled, can date army sergeants and get married, why do I have to live alone in Alcácer spending Sundays at the pastry shop with the granddaughter whose explanations and apologies I accepted when she showed up one afternoon at the lawyer's office and gave me a bouquet of birds-of-paradise

"I got sucked in by what other people said, I'm sorry"

and now we're friends again, we visit each other, talk, trade recipes for sauces, look at what César's up to, he has three children and ran in the last municipal elections as a Christian Democrat, but most of all we get bored together, what a drag, and get old together, what a bitch, the granddaughter has to get operated on for a myoma and I suffer from headaches every morning plus high blood pressure, while my brother is healthy as a horse in Odivelas, with a sky-blue cell phone and a rug from Arraiolos to knock your socks off, and my attorney with this tic of twisting his chin toward his shoulder

"The only solution I can see is you making a casual visit to the clinic and trying to bring your father around"

I told the granddaughter in the pastry shop about the condo in Odivelas, about the good-looker and the swank bamboos, I wanted to see what she thought, and she and Senhor Vergílio were outraged by my brother's selfishness

"A real swine"

the clinic of Alvalade, between Avenida do Brasil and Avenida de Roma, on a square surrounded by buildings full of architects and personnel managers, even nicer than in Odivelas, with slides and swings and a balance beam from which little brats can fall and break an arm and which, if I could, I'd wrap in some gold foil for the bunny rabbit's birthday, the clinic with its name on a plaque, THE REST AND REJUVENATION INSTITUTE, and occupied by a bunch of skeletal mummies, all rested up and rejuvenated, dripping soup from the corners of their mouths, wheezing gibberish, and urinating in their long johns, a dusky ground-floor clinic reeking of ammonia and rancid béchamel sauce, littered with beds and invalids in wheelchairs, all of them wearing diapers under their pajamas, regaining their strength as they wheel along, dentures in their pockets so as not to eat them by mistake during their rejuvenating lunches, I absolutely stunned by that cemetery of fanatics, crutches, slippers, and bedpans, the staff workers in ratty smocks and with nurse caps coming loose from their hairpins as they tried to stimulate the corpses' bladders yelling

"Time to go wee-wee, Major, let's have a nice little wee-wee"

while the corpses stared blankly at the ceiling, with two or three strands of hair on their white skulls, indifferent to the

beauty of emptying their bladders, to the aesthetics of the ure-
thra, to the charms of kidney filtering, the corpses stacked on
sofas like upside-down chairs on the tables of a bar and grill
after closing, a blaring radio drowning them in dance music and
airplane crashes with no survivors, my father rejuvenating in a
tiny room that in previous incarnations was probably a pantry
for storing beans and sausage, my father without any majesty,
whom no one consulted on how to run the country, whom no
one asked

"And what, Minister, should we do about Europe at this
time?"

or

"And what, Minister, should we do about Africa at this
time?"

who had power over no one, who wasn't a state minister,
an assemblyman, or a regional governor, who would get laughed
at if he instructed, as in the old days

"Nab that character and ship him to Cape Verde, to the
prison at Tarrafal"

people would think he was crazy, and if he said, as in the
old days

"Release this fellow and make him the ward chairman of
Calvário"

they'd slap him on the back and recommend that he quit
drinking, my father nourished on syrups and spoonfuls of stewed
fruit, with a strip of linen around his neck to catch his baby's
vomit, and me explaining to him that all I want is what's rightfully mine, a slightly better life than my life in Alcácer, not to
have to pinch pennies all month long, to be able to go occasionally to a restaurant and eat a lunch I didn't have to cook myself,

to forget at the movies on Saturday that when I turn the key in my door there's no one waiting for me on the other side, I showing him the papers that my attorney drew up, sticking a pen between his fingers

"All I need is for you to sign right here, a nice little signature on the dotted line"

and my father turning his head from the buildings and rooftops and trees, his lips pursed in a series of wrinkles with stubble here and there, my father suddenly sitting up, growing taller, getting heavier, my father almost on his feet and baring his gums

"Come with me to Palmela, Isabel"

the rumpled papers falling to the floor, the pen rolling underneath the bed and vanishing in a crack between the planks, a staff worker in a ratty smock and with her nurse cap coming loose from its hairpins suddenly appearing in the doorway

"Is there a problem?"

my father puking up a brownish liquid, which no doubt meant that he was rejuvenating in the Rest Institute, that he would soon return to Palmela, put the farm in order, fix the pool and the greenhouse, hire a chauffeur, a steward, a tractor driver, and maids, and sit down with me on the terrace overlooking the beech trees, and I would have the money for an excursion by bus to Spain with hotel and breakfast included, I'd make friends with cheerful people who would sing Alentejo folk songs the whole way, I'd ask the granddaughter to be my maid of honor when I got married to a fellow who was already set up, an insurance agent, a pharmaceutical representative, an engineer or the like, I'd paste a picture in my photo album of me with a straw hat hugging him in front of an Arab church, and I'd be happy happy happy like I've never been in all my life.

COMMENTARY

When I open the curtains in the morning, I sometimes see the caravels anchored in the sea right outside our apartment. It's not the red boat of the Life-Saving Patrol, nor trawlers, canoes, or pleasure boats that I see, but the caravels of Prince Henry the Navigator, with bearded men in doublets carrying sacks and barrels, it's the king with a huge ring on his finger sitting on a velvet chair, fanning himself with ostrich feathers amid page boys, ladies-in-waiting, astrologers, dwarfs, and dogs, it's a count on his knees unrolling a map and explaining India to the king

a map you can buy on the Rua de São Bento, and hang up in a frame in the living room, to reach Goa without ever departing from the sofa

the caravels decked with flags and banners and emblems in the sea right outside our apartment, and the captains of the caravels, with yellowed incisors loosened by fevers and scurvy, leaning against the gunwales, swords in their scabbards, and I to my mother

"Look at the caravels, Mom"

and my mother, who has to get up at the crack of dawn to tidy up the apartment before catching the bus to Sines for her job, she works like a slave since my father passed away, my mother wiping her hands on a cloth while walking into my room

"What caravels, Romeu?"

without believing me, putting on her glasses and looking through the curtains in the wrong direction, where there were just some fishermen's huts, a gallows, and barefoot people, I pointing at the beach on the right, where a canopy was being raised to protect the king from the sun and where three yoke of oxen, in the foam almost up to their horns, were pulling a cannon to go aboard

"There, in the sea"

my mother, who stubbornly insists that in Alcácer there is no sea, just the river, the bridge for the Algarve, a few buildings, and the crumbling castle, completely oblivious to the wind, the black waves, and the captain with graying oakum hair and a tricorn who was measuring the horizon with a shiny instrument, my mother saying

"We're going to the hospital, Romeu"

and she took me to the doctor's in Lisbon, where we waited in a room full of people sitting in pews

"He's dreaming of caravels again, Doctor"

because she didn't understand that it wasn't a dream, that the ships, as slow as nightmares, really were setting sail for Brazil and for India, she didn't notice the monks with their huge candles, the bishop's incense, and the Gregorian blessings, she made signs to the doctor, twirling her index finger around her ear, and the doctor to me while patting her with a reassuring palm

"I know of some great pills to take at night against caravels"

but the pills, besides taking away the caravels, took away all my energy, they made my legs wobble, they made me tongue-tied, and the lawyer got angry because I kept falling asleep on top of the legal cases

"Would you prefer a pillow to lay your head on, Romeu?"

and Miss Filomena and Miss Paula laughed, last year Miss Filomena got married to Senhor Vergílio's nephew and invited everyone she knows except me to the reception where there was dancing and all, but Miss Paula who wears glasses and isn't very pretty didn't get married to anyone, and the lawyer, encouraged by their laughing, said in the sing-song voice of a kindergarten teacher

"A pillow and a pacifier, Romeu?"

and since this time neither Miss Filomena nor Miss Paula laughed, the lawyer, whom my pills had turned into a trembling blob, stood firm, opened his legs, deepened his voice, and stuck out his chest like a toreador daring the bull

"You have half an hour to finish that petition, and if there are any mistakes you're not leaving until nine o'clock"

the lawyer who didn't fire me because he knew a cousin of my deceased father and felt sorry for me

"A hapless lummox who can't do anything right, what do you expect, I keep him on out of charity"

so that my work consisted of copying cases, going to the post office, sticking stamps on envelopes, and buying aspirins for Miss Filomena

"I've got an absolutely splitting headache, Romeu"

and I wished Miss Paula needed aspirins, I wished she would beckon me with a painful frown

"I've got an absolutely splitting headache, Romeu"

in which case I would have skipped right across the square to relieve her pains because I liked Miss Paula, she was quieter, more discreet, wore longer skirts and no makeup, she lived alone since her godmother had committed suicide by climbing on a stool, hanging a rope from the ceiling lamp, and adios, the lamp came a bit loose from the weight, but since it was made of plastic, not glass, it didn't break, and Senhor César, who had said he would go there to fix the kitchen faucet, found the door ajar, and on the other side of the door a pair of shoes swinging at eye level, and with screwdriver in hand he showed up at the lawyer's office to break the news to Miss Paula, who was so nearsighted she had to stick her eyeglasses into the pages to be able to read anything

"Your godmother's dangling from the ceiling lamp, Paula"

and everything became instantly and perfectly still, even the tides, the seagulls, and the trucks on the bridge, the lawyer walking in my direction to chew me out suddenly freezing with his foot in midair, everything so silent you could hear the knitting of the woodworms in the floorboards, so quiet you could hear the blinking eyelids

bleep bleep

of Miss Filomena, you could hear Miss Paula extracting her glasses from the pages she was reading, I noticed for the first time that there was dust in the office, whose furniture was so gloomy that even in August we turned the lights on soon after lunch, Miss Paula lived alone, spending her Sundays in the pastry shop with a sweet roll, a lemon tea, and no one to talk to since Miss Filomena got married, and on the weekends I, with caravels on the brain, would sometimes enter the shop with my mother to buy a half-pound of Christmas cake for our dessert, when we had the money, Miss Paula frowning like a Pekingese as she wiped her glasses with her hankie, looking at everyone with the proudly erect head of a blind person, I elbowing my mother, who stared at the scale to make sure we didn't get cheated and then painfully pulled coins from out of her purse, one by one, as if they were scabs, to pay Senhor Vergílio, I to my mother as if I were announcing Prince Henry's caravels anchored in the sea just outside our apartment

"There's Miss Paula, Mom"

and my mother distracted, jostled by other customers, hunched because of her bone disease, asking Senhor Vergílio to put twine around the package, because she liked to carry it by her pinkie

"What Miss Paula, Romeu?"

and if I turned to what she called the river and that was actually the sea, I saw bearded men in doublets carrying sacks and barrels, the king sitting on a velvet chair swatting the heat with an ostrich-feather fan amid page boys, ladies-in-waiting, astrologers, cockatoos, dwarfs, and dogs, I saw the count on his knees and three yoke of oxen in the foam almost up to their horns, pulling a cannon to go aboard, the fishermen's huts, the gallows and barefoot people, and my mother, who didn't want me to talk to girls or go out with them

"You're fine the way you are"

lest they use me and make fun of me, my mother greeting the priest's mistress and pulling me by the arm

"Let's go home, Romeu"

I saying good-bye to Miss Paula, who looked over her shoulder, thinking I'd said it to someone else, but since there was just the wall behind her, yet still afraid she might be mistaken, she hesitantly smiled back at me, and my mother, who may be distracted but who's no fool, noticing the smile and pulling me harder

"Let's go home, Romeu"

a decrepit ground-floor apartment on the courtyard with the tavern where they play foosball on the porch, an apartment leased by my parents a few months before I was born, twenty-five years ago, with the front door opening onto the kitchen where we eat and watch TV, then a room on the right and another on the left, and the toilet outside, a courtyard inhabited by widows like my mother who all feel they have to look after me and lecture me

"You be careful about that"

and who are periodically hospitalized with broken hips, returning home even thinner and older-looking, limping and complaining about the nurses, the shots, and the food, the courtyard where if I arrive just slightly later than usual I find the widows in an uproar and my mother tearing her hair out, with a glass of water and the bottle of anticaravel pills, a dozen of which she empties onto a saucer

"Take this medicine for me, Romeu"

a medicine for your own good, son, a medicine to keep others from taking advantage of you, tell Mommy who were you with, Romeu, don't lie to me, tell me if they gave you wine, if they gave you cigarettes, if they gave you drugs, if the woman from the shoe store shut you up in the back room and took off her dress, and the widows spitting through their loose dentures

"Some people don't even respect innocents"

and after dinner I watch a little bit of TV while my mother clears the table, washes the dishes in a tub, and winds up the felt parrot that shouts for five minutes while shaking back and forth with complicated glee

"Who's in charge? Salazar Salazar Salazar"

over and over until it slows down and stops in the middle of its speech and dance with a moronic expression, I watch a little bit of TV and try to keep still so as not to break any of my mother's clay figurines that clutter the apartment, I watch the vase of flowers tremble on top of the refrigerator whenever the refrigerator, like a person in bed, shifts position and starts snoring, and as soon as the tin clock on top of the doily belts out ten o'clock, scaring the wits out of Alcácer, my mother announces, without interrupting her crochet

"Time for bed, Romeu"

as my dumbstruck father, whom everyone says I took after, looks on from out of the photo on the wall, my father wearing a tie but with his shirt collar hidden by his plump jowls, the clock's hands waving as it shakes with rage on top of the doily, and my mother

"Time for bed, Romeu"

and it was the same thing on Saturdays, Sundays, and holidays, always the lawyer, the courtyard, the widows, the TV, except in September when we went for two weeks to my mother's home town, where to this day her relatives feel sorry for her because of my father, not because he was a big spender, he wasn't, and not because he beat or mistreated her, he didn't, but because he didn't know how to take care of himself, because he gave her as much work as a child would, as I did, her relatives shaking their heads at me for fourteen days straight

"A clod just like Januário"

I likewise dumbstruck, likewise big and fat, likewise with jowls that hid my collar, not knowing what to do among my displeased aunts and uncles, I on the back step counting olive trees, fifteen sixteen seventeen eighteen, to the horror of my mother's family

"Exactly like Januário, Lord help us"

and two weeks later the train back to Alcácer, the parrot with a gleeful wriggle

"Who's in charge? Salazar Salazar Salazar"

the caravels from India and Brazil waiting for me in the sea, two weeks later, I rushing off to the pharmacy to buy aspirins for Miss Filomena

"I've got an absolutely splitting headache, Romeu"

two weeks later Miss Paula at her desk, the light shining on her hair like a saint's halo as she typed a brief with her glasses practically glued to the paper, her hair wasn't black like I thought, it was brown with a few white strands, the weather wasn't sunny, it was cloudy, gray skies and with a breeze in the trees, it was raining in Alcácer and the office was even gloomier, even sadder, the floorboards whining under our footsteps like sick animals, I counting Miss Paula's white hairs as I'd counted the olive trees, fifteen sixteen seventeen eighteen, and Miss Paula

"What are you looking at, Romeu?"

it was raining in Alcácer, my mother cursed her gout and got impatient with the parrot that danced and squealed even without us winding it up

"Who's in charge? Salazar Salazar Salazar"

and at the office a seagull

correction

two seagulls on the balcony were shaking off the rain, three seagulls, because another cawing creature showed up, the lawyer with a scarf and raincoat coughed from the flu in his private office, and Miss Paula, annoyed as when someone looks over your shoulder to read your newspaper, raised her glasses from the brief

"What are you looking at, Romeu?"

two seagulls, because the third one went back to the river wall, I feeling a draft hit my throat every time the door opened,

I imagining herbal teas that burned my tongue and tasted terrible, my mother shaking down the mercury in the thermometer

"Stick this under your armpit, Romeu"

twenty-four white hairs plus a long one next to her ear I wasn't sure about, it looked white or light brown, depending on the light, I got closer to find out exactly, and Miss Paula perfectly still, with an expression that slowly changed and that I didn't understand, an expression as if she'd died or was going to resurrect, an expression that seemed somehow grateful, Miss Paula who was after all smaller than I'd thought, her fingers resting motionless on the keyboard and her mouth opening beneath her glasses, Miss Filomena had gone to pay her gas bill at the bank, and there was no one else around except the lawyer sniffling in his office, there were no clients, no phones ringing, and she swiveled around in her chair and looked straight at me, grabbing my wrist

"Romeu"

the hair was white, twenty-five, twenty-five white hairs on the left side of her head, which, added to twenty-five on the right side, made fifty, with my thumb I pushed on her chin to turn her head and remove all doubt, and Miss Paula obedient, soft like wax except for her hands, within inches of my nose

"Romeu"

her knees against my legs, the hard tip of her shoe crushing my foot, her chest advancing and retreating, and her chain with a little mother-of-pearl heart, her chain

how funny

advancing and retreating with her chest, her breathing making my throat tickle, and after I'd reached eleven white hairs and was still searching among the brown ones, pushing aside tufts, Miss Paula keeping her eyes closed and calling for me as if she didn't know where I was

"Romeu"

a gust of wind blew open the window, causing papers to fly and the door to slam, I shutting the window, picking up the papers, hooking the door on the doorstop, straightening the piles of papers by hitting them vertically against the desktop, the lawyer in his office between sneezes and sniffles

"Did something break?"

I thinking

"Eleven, don't forget, eleven"

Miss Paula a hectic red, Miss Filomena, who lamented her lot in life every time she paid her gas bill, returning from the bank and hanging her coat in the closet where my coat hung and also an overcoat which belonged to we didn't know whom but which we didn't throw out lest the owner show up one day and accuse us of being thieves, an overcoat with a moth-eaten collar and a torn sleeve, Miss Filomena to Miss Paula while leafing through the time book

"You look a bit funny, do you feel all right?"

eleven white strands on the right side above her forehead, so probably thirty or forty total, which meant thirty plus twenty-five equals fifty-five, or forty plus twenty-five equals sixty-five, and zero seagulls on the balcony, zero on the river, zero in the sunlight, the seagulls that, when the equinox comes, take shelter in the church or on the porch of the boardinghouse, the lawyer bundled up in his scarf, unwrapping candies for his bronchial tubes, the lawyer who hated to suffer alone, piping up in a gleeful tone of voice

"Are you coming down with the flu, Paula?"

Miss Paula who if she got sick had no one to make her herbal teas, shake down the mercury in the thermometer, tuck her into bed, or bring a parrot to her room to distract her from the fever, Miss Paula who would soon be old and alone and almost crippled like the priest's mistress, wrinkles were already forming at the corners of her mouth, paler than the rest of her skin, Miss Paula who didn't make any calls or get any calls, whom no one thought of at Christmas, and who never received postcards from the mailman, the rain letting up and the seagulls once more scavenging the sewers that emptied into the river, a blue diamond opening between the clouds, people now without umbrellas on the square, the trees regaining their composure, my mother removing the plastic cloth from her clay figurines, drying the furniture with a rag and a sponge, and at the office Miss Paula, who if I carefully counted all the strands of her hair would no doubt have more than a thousand, who had given up hiring attorneys and harassing her brother who lived I don't know where or with whom, and Miss Filomena said he was a crook because of some farm near Setúbal, a huge city with lots of people on the street and enormous cafés and a park and a stadium and a military base where I went with my mother seven years ago to be inspected for military service, my mother who forbade me to take off my clothes

"Keep still, Romeu"

right as I was about to strip like everyone else, and who argued with a soldier in a smock until he let her into the gym full of naked young men who, embarrassed by her presence, cupped their hands over their privates, my mother walking forward like a man until another soldier in a smock, older and with gold stripes on his shoulder, blocked her way with those rubber tubes that doctors stick in their ears to listen to people's lungs

"What the fuck is going on?"

and the first soldier

"I told her she wasn't allowed, Major, I told her she wasn't allowed"

the young men hiding themselves with their hands, my mother on tiptoe whispering secrets to the soldier with gold stripes, the soldier with gold stripes calming down and looking over at me, twice his size or anyone else's and weighing at least three times what any of them weighed, the gold-striped soldier shutting us inside an examining room without windows and with a machine that people stand against so doctors can see their liver and intestines squirm and struggle, I can feel mine squirm at night, and the gold-striped soldier to me as he stuck a cigarette into a cigarette holder

"Show me what you have there"

a sound of boots running by, a distant bugle, I looking at my mother to see if it was okay, and my mother turning the key in the door just in case

"Show him, Romeu"

the gold-striped soldier brought in two more soldiers who were also older, also used cigarette holders, and also had gold stripes, one of them squatted, touched me some, and then washed his hands with alcohol while the other two remained standing and observed the examination, commenting in a foreign tongue as my mother kept close watch, ready to threaten them, to scream for help, to defend me with her umbrella, her fingernails, and her heels if they tried to hurt me, and the soldier who'd washed his hands with alcohol wrote something on a pad, handing it to his colleagues to sign

"Get dressed"

a van with rattling crates and bottles passed by the gym, I looking at my mother to see if it was okay, and my mother, handing me the clothes she held in her lap

"Get dressed, Romeu"

I remember that I got my shoes mixed up and had a hard time walking, I remember the three graying soldiers smoking cigarettes in the examining room and staring at me as if I were an animal, I remember limping through the gymnasium, my mother leading the way past the naked young men, dozens and dozens of naked men whose bodies didn't resemble mine, whose nakedness wasn't like mine, and once again Setúbal, lots of people in the street, the stadium, the park, the widows waiting for us and feeling sorry for me, the customers in the tavern interrupting their dominoes and feeling sorry for me, my mother winding up the felt parrot to entertain me and the parrot shaking back and forth with obstinate glee

"Who's in charge? Salazar Salazar Salazar"

the parrot slowing down until it stopped in the middle of its speech and dance

"Salazar Sala—"

with a moronic expression, leaning toward the picture of my father, likewise big and fat, likewise with jowls hanging over his collar, the parrot in a last desperate shudder

"A clod just like Januário"

my mother in an apron taking the pot off its hook, taking the bottle of olive oil from the shelf trimmed with a strip of tissue paper, cutting carrots and potatoes for the evening soup, my mother among her ladles and clay figurines

"Go change out of your suit, Romeu"

my father's suit with trousers like no one uses anymore, a jacket like no one uses anymore, a striped vest like the syrup vendor wears, my father's polka-dot tie and lavender shirt, exactly what he wore for the photo that looks just like me, the photo in which they painted his lips and accented his eyebrows with a dark pencil, I just like my father in the little round shaving mirror, the sympathy of the widows huddled together in a single cluster of shawls

"Just like Januário, poor boy"

my mother ironing the suit, reinforcing the creases, checking the buttons, cleaning a mildew stain with the tooth elixir, putting away the tie clip in a canvas pouch that she mixed up with the onions to fool burglars, turning on the TV, and I in my pajamas waiting for the soup while the tavern went dark, the river went dark, torches were being lit around the gallows and on Prince Henry's caravels, and the oxen, pulling on the cannon, plowed the foam with their horns, the clock's hands started waving ten o'clock in a frenzy, and my mother announced, without interrupting her crochet

"Time for bed, Romeu"

a divan stuffed with corn husks and with a plush dog on the pillow, and my mother shutting off the alarm clock which, left to itself, would bleed like a slaughtered pig all night long

"Do you have your doggy, Romeu?"

I, who couldn't fall asleep without my dog, crushing the animal with my weight, the animal that had varnish eyes and no tail and that was getting thinner as its kapok slowly escaped through a hole in its tummy, the room pitch-black and my mother pitch-black against the lighter door, and beyond the door, the stove and the table and the dish tub, and I holding on to the animal's paw so that it wouldn't take advantage of me sleeping to run away

"I have my dog, Mom"

and then the door turned pitch-black, the stove and table and dish tub were swallowed by the darkness, and I heard the sound of water against the river wall, the sound of no wind in the trees, the television talking, then playing music, then talking again, the television far away, my mother far away, the apartment far away, my mother so far away from me that only my dog and the ballast of urine in my bladder prevented me from flying, I didn't get up to take a pee for fear I'd float away from Alcácer like those fluffy seeds that float and for fear of losing my mother, because I don't know how to mend clothes or cook, and since I give her my entire salary I can't buy meat or shoelaces or soap, the widows never stop sighing and wondering

"What's going to become of you when your mother passes away, Romeu?"

and the tavern owner, using chalk to add up his customers' tabs on the blackboard

"What's the problem? There are plenty of clinics for abnormals like him"

the tavern owner who during the feast of Saint Anthony led me away from the rockets, firecrackers, and sparklers, ordered Dona Liberdade's son to pull down my pants, and pointed his flashlight at me so that they could make fun of me, both of them sloshed from the wine, staring at me

"You've got a reason to live that would make any man envious, Romeu"

both of them laughing, slapping their palms on their knees, I surrounded by pine trees, by the tunnel-like echo that the pine needles carry on as if a train were rushing by in the darkness, I standing on one foot, then the other, laughing with them and slapping my knees like them, having fun with them and accepting their brandy, accepting their beer

"Give me a little of what you're short on, Romeu"

yellow and red rockets bursting over the castle, blue balls exploding over the keep, corollas weeping teardrops in the battlements, I lolling on the ground with a bottle in my mouth, with the needles pricking my rear end, and lo and behold my mother, appearing out of nowhere, thrashing Dona Liberdade's son with her umbrella

"Scoundrel"

rockets, exploding balls, weeping corollas, the band playing a tango in the bandstand decorated with paper flowers, a stick from a rocket that stank of gunpowder lying next to me and Dona Liberdade's son

"It wasn't me, Dona Olga, it was Senhor Levi, don't tell my stepfather, Romeu pulled his pants down because he wanted to, look what fun he's having"

I laughing and slapping my palms on my knees, but out of discomfort, not fun, I felt sick to my stomach, my mother lit the burner on the stove to heat up some coffee, she gave me a spoonful of olive oil, then another and still another to make me throw up, but try as I might I couldn't throw up, I could only slap my knees and laugh the way Senhor Levi and Dona Liberdade's son laughed, laughing so hard that I knocked over a porcelain panther that was ready to pounce and a plaster cow-boy sticking a toothpick into a hunched baby bull with a lamb's snout, the band that played tangos banging cymbals in the band-stand, Senhor Vergílio singing out of tune above the trombones, and my mother tying a towel around my neck

"Drink some more coffee, Romeu"

my mother paying a visit to Senhor Levi's wife, who woke up at 3 A.M. every morning to help sell the day's first catch, had muscles like a man, and didn't mess around, Senhor Levi's wife marching into the tavern, kicking domino players and stray dogs in search of scraps out of her way, Senhor Levi's wife going for her husband's gorge

"You fucking, no-good faggot"

I tired of slapping my palms on my knees, tired of laugh-ing, tired of brandy and beer, I falling asleep on top of the plastic tablecloth with the TV still on, I waking up in the morning hugging the kapok animal that my mother had placed in my lap to help me sleep, the felt parrot on its perch yelling

"Who's in charge? Salazar Salazar Salazar"

the wild turkeys flying northeast, a crystal shimmer of sun-light in the trees, I remembering the rockets, the exploding blue balls, and the corollas that wept teardrops in the battlements, I feeling a catastrophic shudder in my gut, the taste of all the olive oil I'd swallowed, I at last throwing up on my father's dumbstruck jowls as my mother jockeyed, in between two heaves, to take the kapok animal away

"Careful with your doggy, Romeu"

the caravels at anchor in the sea, the gallows, the king, men in doublets carrying sacks and barrels, a count unrolling maps to explain India, flags, banners, and emblems, I skating through the kitchen like a penguin, radiantly exclaiming to my mother

"Look at the caravels, Mom"

and Miss Paula, who had given up hiring attorneys and harassing her brother who lived I don't know where or with whom, and Miss Filomena said he was a crook because of some farm or other, Miss Paula's fingers resting motionless on the keyboard and her mouth opening beneath her glasses, her expression slowly changing in a way I didn't understand

"I left a box of proceedings at home, Romeu, will you help me go fetch it?"

Miss Paula with no makeup on her face or eyelids, smaller than I'd thought, mulberry trees, buildings, seagulls, the truck drivers' square, her godmother's apartment with the light fixture hanging loose from the ceiling, a wooden sofa that must have been a torture to sit on, a plate from Castelo de Vide on a buffet with teacups missing their handles, a kind of sad indifference in everything, Miss Paula with brown hair and a few white hairs mixed in, twenty-five white hairs on the left side alone

"Romeu"

her chest advancing and retreating, her chain with a little mother-of-pearl heart likewise advancing and retreating, her knees against my legs, the hard tip of her shoe crushing my foot, Miss Paula within inches of my nose, soft like wax and ready to faint except for her hands, which grabbed my wrists

"Romeu"

Miss Paula with eyes closed, turning her eyelids this way and that as if she didn't know where I was

"Romeu"

I who was right there, in her apartment, leaning against a chest of drawers or a buffet that trembled under my weight, turning her face toward the light, separating tufts to remove all doubt, Miss Paula digging her hip bone into my belly, grabbing me around the back so that I couldn't escape

"Romeu"

but I didn't want to escape or to do her any harm, I was only interested in finding out how many white hairs she really had, I was only interested in looking past her and the trees and the café on the square and the bridge for the Algarve and the strip of sand prolonging Alcácer, past all that to where Prince Henry's caravels, looming black on the black waters, were anchored in the sea.

REPORT

My son was born three months after my father's death, when all that was left of the house and farm in Palmela were a couple of German shepherds ranging over the mountains in search of the disappeared kennels, and in the maternity ward I didn't feel sad or happy, I felt indifferent as I looked out the window with a bit of sky beyond the curtain, and the midwife to me, while listening to my belly with a stethoscope

"How goes it with the pangs, Dona Paula?"

there was no more house or farm, there was a uniformed gatekeeper, villas, golf courses, gardeners to care for the grass, a restaurant where the swamp used to be, a building called "Administration" where the barn had once stood, and a tower called "Bar" in the place of the stable, my father's death merited no article in the newspaper, no mention on the radio, no picture of him on television, and as we took him away in the coffin from the clinic in Alvalade, his room even before the staff workers had changed the linens was being occupied by the next client, an old man who dragged half his body as if he were dragging suitcases, with his pajamas and his slippers in a piece of newspaper under his arm, the sky beyond the curtain as the midwife pulled the blanket up to my chin

"Sleep here tonight, Dona Paula, and we'll see what the doctor says tomorrow morning"

I who didn't feel sad or happy, I felt like on Sundays, sitting on the wooden settee, turning the TV on, turning it off, getting up, leafing through a magazine about actresses and their divorces, thinking about seeing a movie in Lisbon, rummaging in the drawer for the bus schedule whose numbers and letters were too tiny to read, fetching the magnifying glass from the bedroom and discovering that the schedule was from last year, I, my brother, the good-looker and the good-looker's brilliant and hyperactive daughter who wouldn't leave even the deceased in peace, tap-dancing on their tombstones, wiping their framed photos with the hem of her skirt, rearranging their flowers, and climbing on their crosses like a chimpanzee, the good-looker

"Tania"

the grave-diggers lowering my father's casket as a widow close by used a handy whisk broom to sweep chrysanthemums off her husband, and the good-looker's daughter jumped around flapping her arms as if flying, as if she would break through the vaults and wake up the dead

"Peek-a-boo"

the grave-diggers pouring the sack of quicklime over my father's casket as the widow, sneezing from the pollen, began to sweep the chrysanthemum petals from herself, chiding her husband

"Even now you cause me problems"

the good-looker's daughter clapping her hands in between the mahogany shelves

"Peek-a-boo"

the good-looker, proud of her little girl's antics

"Tania"

the yellowed cadavers, shriveled fingers on their chest, blinking their startled eyelashes

"Go away"

my brother with a rope for a belt, shoes unpolished, his tie like the noose of a suicide who hangs herself from the ceiling lamp in her bedroom, a suicide whose wide-open eyes looked at me

wait, hold on, that's wrong, that's not what I wanted to say, don't write that down

my mind wandering from the TV, thinking that if I went to the kitchen and made a cake or if I took up my knitting and finished the scarf or if I did my weekly ironing, time would go by faster and it would be Monday, phone calls, people, petitions, Filomena with her elbows on the typewriter, rubbing her temples

"I'm sorry, Romeu, but could you please get me some aspirin from the pharmacy?"

poor clumsy Romeu, knocking over chairs and going down the stairs to the square, but at least people breathed and talked, at least clocks moved, and the midwife finding me awake, looking at the now black sky in the window while my body was becoming a throbbing sack

"You want a sleeping pill, Dona Paula?"

Romeu, disheveled and out of breath, with the aspirin and the change, telling Filomena to make sure it was correct, you never know, filling a glass with water from the bathroom faucet, bringing the glass on a trembling saucer, taking small, cautious steps as if the floor were a wire twenty feet off the ground, a silence in the office like the silence at a circus when the band stops playing, the spectators holding their breath, I with my heart in my mouth

"There's going to be an accident, he's going to fall and break a leg"

the grave-diggers gathering their shovels and going away, this part of the cemetery still without marble slabs, just fresh earth, future pathways indicated by pieces of brick and iron posts with squares of cardboard, the good-looker's daughter

"Eeny meeny miney mo"

hopping among the graves, a blackbird weighing itself on a twig as if it were a scale pan, Filomena swallowing the aspirin with a frown and lots of water, closing her eyelids with relief and reopening them as if coming to after having fainted

"Thank you, Romeu"

the sky now black in the windowpanes, my blood throbbing under my toenails, in my ankles and knees, membranes breaking one by one, the whistle of the freight elevator, the bell in the next ward over, César startled by the electric alarm clock

"Ten o'clock, shit"

quickly getting up, putting on his shoes, pecking my neck with his lips

"A sleeping pill, Dona Paula?"

the old man who occupied my father's place in Alvalade had two or three strands of long hair positioned with a jeweler's precision between one ear and the other, standing out against his baldness like the lines on ruled paper, two or three precious strands gleaming with hair lotion that were supposed to cover his whole head, the old man who occupied my father's place wearing neat and clean clothes, a smart tie, and a monogrammed ring on his pinkie, and the staff workers yanking off his clothes, removing his wallet, glasses, and dentures

"Wee-wee, sir, it's time to go wee-wee"

the old man with trembling lips and wobbly legs, his precious hairs wilting, hanging down from one ear, the old man asking me to help him, to take him with me, the old man to the staff workers, who were forcing him into a wheelchair, bearing down on his shoulders

"No"

the old man who, as we banged my father's coffin into the hallway cabinets on our way out the main door, could be heard whimpering like a frightened dog in a godforsaken hamlet

"No"

the sky now black in the windowpanes, the freight elevator stopping with a metallic jerk, the light in the dispensary turning on and off, I didn't feel sad or happy, I felt like on Sunday, leafing through magazines about actresses and their divorces, the woman on duty left the sleeping pill on the table, a sleeping pill for me to swallow and forget the night

"You know how Adelaide is, Paula, you know what happens when I'm not home by suppertime, she badgers me all night long"

Romeu worried about me, circling my desk with his huge torso, his bulging stomach, his wrinkled shirttail hanging out over his belt

"Don't you want an aspirin, Dona Paula?"

I at the typewriter, ill at ease, and Romeu just a few inches away, looking at me with his enormous head, his hands close to my hair as if checking for lice, friendly, meek, frightening, Romeu who lived with his mother in a pensioner's hovel, and I remembered when I was little, I remember it perfectly, I was little and my godmother was still alive, and a neighbor man who was also huge and fat and had an enormous head went crazy one day, he started foaming at the mouth, smashed all of his furniture, and jumped over the garden wall, scaring away the chickens, then entered our kitchen waving a heavy wooden bar, I was five or six years old, without a father to defend me, my godmother in the bedroom, I holding on tight to a doll without daring to cry, I with one of my eyes covered by a Bakelite gizmo that the doctor had prescribed to correct my cross-eyes, my schoolmates fascinated

"Can I touch it?"

the neighbor man calming down, taking me in his arms, I with my doll in his arms, sniveling and thinking

"I'm going to die"

the good-looker's daughter, with a satin ribbon in her hair, playing hopscotch among the graves to the horror of the widow with the handy whisk broom who had brought a bottle of Carvalhelhos to change the water in her husband's flower vase, since mineral water perks up flowers, a quarter pound of blackbird bouncing on the twig, my brother next to our father's grave, number eighty-seven in white numerals against a blue background, just like house numbers, eighty-seven eighty-seven eighty-seven, my godmother's is thirty-five and I'll bet there won't be anyone to worry about my grave, the blackbird evaporating from its twig as the widow with the whisk broom began to grumble, the good-looker, who was attractive in mourning clothes, glancing over at the widow with hatred while reluctantly saying

"Tania"

a night in the hospital is like a night keeping watch over a corpse, muffled noises, whispers, cold drafts, discomfort, I reached for the sleeping pill, the firemen were called to come tie up the neighbor man and haul him off to Lisbon in an ambulance whose siren whisked cars and wagons onto the shoulders, they found the madman holding me in his arms, oblivious to the smashed furniture, the wooden bar, and his family, asking me my doll's name, which was Rosa Maria and she was later stolen from me, the madman, with Romeu's same expression, caressing the doll with clumsy passion, and I placing the doll, placing the typewriter, between the two of us, I in a loud voice so that Filomena would hear

"Don't you have some case proceedings to copy, Romeu?"

and Romeu, the neighbor man, Romeu wrapping himself in apologies like the homeless who wrap themselves with newspapers in winter, deathly afraid that he'd offended me, that I was angry at him and would never speak to him again, Romeu who didn't bathe enough, who probably didn't eat well, and whose solicitude touched a soft spot in me, returning to his desk with its broken lamp and rotting papers, the poor slob ensconced there like a hibernating bear

"Of course I do, Miss Paula, I'm sorry"

and the neighbor man, Romeu, the neighbor man to the firemen who'd brought a jacket with sleeves but no holes for the hands, my godmother peering from behind their helmets

(eighty-seven comes after eighty-five and before eighty-nine who's still waiting to die and what happens to a person in a coffin underground?)

the neighbor man, who was the first person in the world besides me to take an interest in my doll and to think she was pretty, grabbing the wooden bar in a sudden frenzy while one of the firemen raised his ax

"I'll only go peacefully if the girl comes along"

after the funeral my brother, who was beginning to get on the good-looker's nerves, invited me for lunch in Odivelas, where there were more miniature scales and more bamboos than before, and in the enclosed balcony there was a wall clock whose minute hand was a knife and whose hour hand was a fork and that instead of dingdongs emitted the sound of a wooden spoon in an empty casserole, the daughter, full of affectations, pressed her lips into a kiss to spit out olive pits, and given my brother's silence and the good-looker's crankiness, she complaining about having to work like a slave to feed three mouths and he sighing at the head of the table without answering her, I began to suspect that he hadn't lied about the inheritance and that what our father

(eighty-seven a mound of sunlit earth with the number eighty-seven next to the cemetery wall since there's hardly a square foot left for the dead so many dead people my God) and that what our father had left us were crows and wind and my hatred for him, my brother sheepishly making excuse to the good-looker as the bright light of Odivelas, the kind of light I wish there was in Alcácer, illuminated his mustache

"Just last week I answered six want ads, honey"

I missing the smell of César in my bed, on the weekend when Adelaide went to Mértola for her nephew's baptism I left the door unlocked, César arrived like a burglar at midnight with the idea of leaving at four in the morning, because Alcácer is small and word gets around, and on that weekend I didn't turn on the TV, it was César who turned it on, yawning next to me, César who leafed through the magazines about actresses and their divorces, César who spent the whole time bored on the sofa because the channels went off the air too early, pushing away my leg if I tried to snuggle up to him, lying down without wanting to do anything with me, and getting dressed at three in the morning as if it were five, I listening to him sleep in the dark, hoping he would forget about the time and have breakfast with me, I understanding but not understanding, letting him take me for a fool

"It's only three o'clock, sweetie"

not wanting to get the bus to go to the movies in Lisbon, not wanting to face Monday, Romeu, Filomena, the clients, and the lawyer, and the good-looker to my brother while impatiently clearing the table

"Do you really think that any company in this country will hire an old man?"

my brother's mustache illuminated by the bright light of Odivelas, the kind of light I wish there was in Alcácer, along with Odivelas's buildings and streets, its shops that sell shoes, knickknacks, and cosmetics, which we can look at even if we don't have any money, my brother who looked older in the bright light of Odivelas, and the good-looker's daughter making fun of him, mimicking a cripple with a dragging foot, twisting the fringes of the rugs while bleating

"Old man old man old man"

marching like a soldier blowing on an imaginary bugle

"You're an old man an old man an old man"

I who could spend every weekend with César if he wanted to, every weekend and weekday and holiday in whatever season, and I'd never get bored, I'd gladly go on outings to Grândola and Sines, I'd love to hold hands with him at the movies, I'd love to have a picture of him on my dresser and a picture of us in a brown velvet frame on my bedroom wall, if he showed a bit of interest in me I'd ask for an advance at work to buy a bigger TV and a parabolic antenna so that he'd have more channels to keep him entertained, the sports channel, the American news channel, the channel with naked women, I wouldn't make scenes or give him the third degree if he told me that on Friday night he had a dinner with the guys and don't wait up for me because I'll be late, I wouldn't sniff for perfume or look for telltale lipstick on his shirt, God forbid, César with all his clothes on and a satisfied look on his face that suggested he was glad to be going, César like a strategist giving lessons

"Imagine if someone sees me and tells Adelaide, just imagine the stink she'd make"

I with tons of leftover food, almonds, chocolates, cheese, because he ate like a bird, or I made him lose his appetite, I calling him several days later at his office

"May I speak to César, please?"

other voices and then César, whose voice I recognized immediately, curtly hanging up the phone

"Wrong number"

I storing everything in Tupperwares in the refrigerator, hoping that there'd be more baptisms in Mértola and that he'd want to come back, the good-looker's daughter howling like a Comanche while dancing mazurkas around the smoked-glass tabletop for me and my brother, and I very nearly whacked her over the noggin with one of the scales

"You two are as old as the hills you two are as old as the hills you two are as old as the hills"

kids on skates and skateboards going up and down the street, in the apartment opposite, a girl was watering geraniums, the good-looker perfectly aware of what her daughter was doing but keeping mum in another room, without moving a muscle, like my father in the coffin that the grave-digger opened so that we could kiss him before the shovelfuls of dirt and the sack of quicklime, my father's hands all shriveled, as if those mixed-in roots that were made to look like his fingers belonged to him when they didn't, since if they'd belonged to him he would have ordered the grave-digger to be arrested, as he would have ordered the good-looker and the good-looker's daughter and all who hurt us to be arrested, as he would have ordered César who hung up the phone like a jerk

"Wrong number"

to be arrested, César bragging about me to his coworkers and I without the courage to face them in the pastry shop, where they pointed at me with their chins and whispered lies to each other, I in my usual place, with a view of the square, lemon tea and a sweet roll, suffering the weight of their stares, their jeering, Romeu with his mother buying a small slice of pound cake from Senhor Vergílio, so small it would be gone after two bites, taking it home as if they were treating themselves to a real dessert, Romeu noticing me and waving good-bye while the customers for whom he was just a butt for jokes covered their giggles with their napkins, Romeu waving good-bye to me and reeling with joy while his mother, proud of her cake, pulled him by the sleeve toward the door, his mother who used her umbrella to defend him from the young men who were forever playing pranks on him, making fun of his innocence and his fat, getting him drunk on beer during the feast of Saint Anthony, and he holding on to the trees for support, tripping on front steps, tumbling in the square, laughing with the others, slapping his palms on his knees with the others, accepting a cigarette and coughing, as rockets and firecrackers shook the walls, and the midwife congratulating me

"You took the pill, Dona Paula, good girl, tomorrow the doctor will come and get you all squared away"

but I still didn't feel sleepy, even as I didn't feel sad or happy

(eighty-seven number eighty-seven I mustn't forget eighty-seven)

you're not going to understand this but I felt like on the day they came to tell me that the ceiling lamp had come loose, and my first reaction wasn't to be angry with my godmother, or to wonder why, or to ask where she got the rope, it wasn't surprise, it wasn't grief, it was

"I'm all alone, what am I going to do now?"

my godmother who never complained, whose pension from Angola had been increased, who had a good appetite, sometimes I heard her whistling as she washed the dishes, she was apparently doing well, César returned there with Senhor Vergílio who, pencil behind his ear, wanted to say something to me but couldn't, César grabbing the scissors for cleaning fish and climbing on a stool, César almost losing his balance and falling to the floor

"Give me a hand, Ferreira"

more and more people at the door, faces I knew but whose names I suddenly couldn't remember, I remembered my father sitting on the wooden settee years ago, when he was a minister who ruled Portugal, every day his picture was in the papers, people feared him, respected him, my father wearily sighing

"What a bore"

and the hoopla would continue until Romeu's mother found him, chewed out his drunk companions, threatened them with the police, and took her boy home, if home is the right word for some shacks around a squalid courtyard, freezing rooms permeated with the stench of the river and full of cheap statuettes purchased at fairs and from the gypsies' stalls in the public market, and you needn't worry about chipping or cracking them because they're already chipped and cracked, Romeu's mother pulling him by the sleeve and he laughing and reeling uncontrollably, giving endless farewell hugs to those who made fun of him, his mother shooing away the friends with her umbrella, his mother as if she were talking to a child

"Time for bed, Romeu"

a woman who wore her wedding band on her middle finger, suggesting that in her younger years she'd had more to eat, and who wore clothes donated by ladies to the prior at Christmas and Easter, a woman who spent her days protecting her son from the kids at school, from the do-nothings at the tavern that would stick a bottle of cheap brandy in his hands and take down his pants to see who knows what, I mean I think I don't know but I'm not sure, all right, all right, I do know, write down in your book that I know and that it's not worth mentioning, the tavern crowd slapping him on the back, choking with laughter

"King-size Romeu"

identical to the mad neighbor man from when I was little whom the firemen put in a jacket with closed sleeves that made it look like he had sausages attached to his body, the neighbor man who could hardly breathe asking for my doll

Rosa Maria

asking me to go with him to Lisbon, the firemen discussing, the neighbor man who wanted to kill me and didn't want to kill me now advancing, me squeezed between the stove and the pots, my godmother

"Stop right there"

Romeu identical to the neighbor man who stared at me from the ambulance so as to remember my face, so as to enter the kitchen and hit me with the wooden bar

bam

as soon as they let him out of the asylum, Romeu circling around me in the lawyer's office like a kite, I pretending not to see him and placing the typewriter between us, the rain in the plane trees on the square, the castle walls hidden by the clouds, Filomena's telephone ringing constantly, the lawyer talking to a client in his office at the back, and Romeu with a grimy smile that was missing teeth

"Do you have a headache, Miss Paula, do you want me to bring you some aspirin from the pharmacy?"

Romeu who at least took an interest in me, who worried about me, who would leave a caramel on my desk before going to his dusky corner

"This is for you"

making sure I unwrapped the sticky paper that obliged me to wash my hands to get it off, making sure I placed the square of sweet rubber into my mouth, where it stuck to my gums and caused a piercing pain in my molar, I cursing Romeu because I couldn't get the piece of rubber out, I had to shut myself into the bathroom until the caramel finally abandoned my mouth and stuck to my fingernail instead, I scrubbing my nail with a brush to no avail, sucking on my nail until the caramel, smaller than before, again hurt my tooth with cruel insistence, and more scrubbing, more sucking, half an hour until I was free of the sugary nightmare, and back at my desk I'd find a second caramel on top of a file folder and Romeu winking at me with joyful complicity, he must have filched money from his mother to buy me those lethal cubes, I pretending to love caramels and tossing them into the wastebasket with the swift hand of a pickpocket, and it wasn't just caramels, it was packets of horrid candies that ravaged my intestines, spearmint gum that had me spitting out bits of wrapping paper all afternoon, cat-shaped chocolates that tasted like mold, and Romeu, while my tongue contended with the animal

"How does the cat taste, Miss Paula?"

Romeu, who when the office was empty, with no clients nor Filomena nor the lawyer, would advance toward me like the neighbor man while I simply froze, thinking about the jacket without holes in the sleeves, the firemen, my doll named Rosa Maria that somebody stole from me, I don't know who

(he's going to kill me he's going to squeeze me in his arms and kill me)

me shrinking with fear and he with his belly propped on my desk, breathing in E-flat like a church organ, touching my hair, separating the tufts, running his finger along my hairline, around my ear, moving his lips in a wordless prayer, and about this same time last year, after the storks and wild turkeys had flown south, I was changing the bottle of butane gas as the radio played waltzes on the shelf with the cumin and oregano when I heard a noise as if someone were jumping over the garden wall, a sound of footsteps trampling the vegetables, I thought

"It can't be burglars, it must be the chickens or a rabbit that got out of its cage"

the waltz ended, there was a pause with static because the radio is old, another waltz began, the kind that begins softly and slowly, then gradually swells, more footsteps trampling the vegetables, the doorknob turning, Romeu looming in the night, seeming even larger in the windowpanes, Romeu smiling while extending his open hand with a chocolate cat still wrapped in the silver foil painted with stripes and a nose and a tail but soft and misshapen from the warmth of his skin, Romeu hesitating in the kitchen, too big for my stove, for my furniture, swinging his arms forward and backward as when the drunks at the tavern and the kids at school pulled down his pants to make fun of him, Romeu touching my hair with his finger

"Miss Paula"

the glimmer of the teacups emerging from the buffet and disappearing, my godmother long gone, and no one, no firemen no Senhor Vergílio and no César, no one to keep him from hitting me with the wooden bar and killing me, I in the living room and Romeu showing me his cat, the shapeless silver foil with chocolate inside, and showing me his other treasures that he pulled from his pockets, namely those sticky caramels and the gum that made me spit out bits of wrapper, I afraid of dying in the bedroom and he placing the cat, the caramels, and the spearmint gum on the chest, moving closer to me as I pleaded

"Don't hit me, don't hurt me"

turning on the lamp with a red glass shade that I bought in Santiago do Cacém, grabbing the nape of my neck, turning my head toward the light

"Miss Paula"

I sitting on the bed with Romeu's hand on my shoulders, his breath in my ear, his leg breaking my leg, Romeu fondling my hair, pushing tufts this way and that, counting

"Thirty-eight, thirty-nine, forty"

I struggling to escape, and the sheets winding around my ankles, the pillow smothering me, I trying to flee to the square but I couldn't, because the midwife was holding on to my hands, on to my thighs, pushing me against the mattress, telling me to sleep

"Easy, Dona Paula, take it easy, the doctor will be here in no time to deal with your baby."

COMMENTARY

I don't know what more Paula wants, Doctor, I don't know what she's complaining about, she's got an apartment handed down to her by her godmother, with deluxe furniture like I wish I had, a good job, her father who was what he was before the

Revolution, but no one ever held that against her except once
or twice, since, with the excitement of democracy and the Communists running around, things didn't always go like they should
have, I'll bet she's got money in the bank, the family of her
brother's wife is filthy rich and ready to help her out in a pinch,
so don't try to tell me that I'm to blame if Paula doesn't go out,
if she spends her Sundays gathering dust in her living room, if
she doesn't go on holiday to the Algarve or abroad, and above
all don't insinuate that it's my fault if Paula is unhappy. For that
matter whatever Paula told you is none of my business, I don't
care to know, so you might as well stuff those papers back into
your briefcase, because I'm not going to read them, I've got better
things to do, either you believe what I say or you don't, and
you're lucky I'm even talking to you, for if Adelaide should leaf
through your book and find my name there along with Paula's
lies about me, then my goose is cooked, Paula whom I haven't
really seen since long before her son was born, because when I
run into her it's just hi, how are you doing, bye, without so much
as a kiss, a handshake, or a smile, Paula whom I'd get together
with once in a blue moon, just for the hell of it and because she
inundated me with phone calls, I'd do my duty with her and
then scram, I met her through one of my cousins when I was a
young man working as a cab driver until I could take the quali-
fying exam for the tax office, and she took a liking to me, she'd
talk to me and give me neckties, and so on my days off I'd drive
her in the taxi to Grândola or Montijo to see the birds that arrive from Africa in May and build nests among the reeds and
rotten husks, I'd park close to the water and turn off the engine,
the flamingos would stand up in the grass that the ebb tide ex-
posed and start shrieking, threatening each other and fighting,

and past the grass and one or another submerged olive tree I could see chimneys and rooftops drowned in the Tagus River, a shipwrecked housing complex for workers whose bones whispered in the sludge, and Paula opening her patent leather purse and cleaning her glasses with her hankie, she always carried a patent leather purse, just like the hairdresser's godmother, Paula who was more homely than pretty, in fact downright homely, and with glasses so thick you could hardly see her eyes and eyebrows, Paula uninterested in the flamingos, snuggling up to me

"César"

and as soon as I began to get passionate I'd hear knuckles hitting the windshield

"Are you free?"

we quickly straightening up, and it would be an old couple who wanted to go to Alcochete, or a group of discalced Franciscans whose monastery van had broken down and who sat there and prayed while waiting for us to take them to Lisbon, Paula buttoning her blouse and adjusting her bra, the submerged olive trees with floating branches the color of iodine, the wild turkeys waddling in the gulfweed like skaters outside the rink, I pulling up my zipper and suppressing a swear word when it caught on my privates, I trying to free my skin from the metallic teeth, Paula pulling down on the zipper to help me and getting me even more caught, the old couple, whose nasty disposition protected them from rheumatism and high blood sugar, getting impatient behind us

"How much longer are your obscenities going to take?"

and so without committing myself

(you get the picture)

without declaring that I loved her, God forbid, I'd drive around with her on my days off, but these were infrequent, and Adelaide, then pregnant, was on my tail to boot, until one afternoon when, turning in the taxi, I found the corporal of the National Guard waiting for me with the air of a detective or FBI agent, leaping out from a plane tree like a toad, not the current National Guard corporal, who also happens to be a chump, but the previous one, with pocked skin he thought would get better with garlic pills, which did nothing for his skin but made him stink to high heaven

"Get moving, there're some people to see you at the guardhouse"

and outside the guardhouse there were three government vehicles nuzzling the flagpole like puppies sharing a tree trunk and five or six plainclothes policemen who inspected the truck drivers' beers, plus another who was climbing up the church tower to make sure the storks weren't plotting something, inside the guardhouse there was a picture of Salazar as a young man, a picture of the Admiral as an old man, a pile of empty demijohns next to the filing cabinet waiting to be redeemed at the tavern for the deposit money that would buy a nice lunch in Seixal, grade-school desks occupied by soldiers with their tongues sticking out of the corners of their mouths as they wrote out parking fines like kindergartners practicing their letters, and plainclothesmen from the secret police who eyed my armpits for hidden platoons of Russian paratroopers, farther on there was a window that looked onto a garden hedged in between stands where street vendors sold casseroles, Band-Aids, and busts of Beethoven, and circus tents where a forgotten lion was being eaten up by moths, a garden where the guards lovingly raised weeds and rats, and finally an office where a man with a hat chewed on a cigarillo stub without paying attention to me, accompanied by the sergeant I sometimes caught at night sleeping off his brandy under the pigeons who took him for a fallen statue, and accompanied by the Major in charge of the secret police, who was leafing through a notebook of photographs, and the hat to the corporal, who stood firm as pudding at attention

"Is this him?"

a trawler walked on the water like an apostle, disturbing the albatrosses, the waves wrinkled and unwrinkled their worried foreheads, the sergeant emitted a troubled burp, a speech from his soul about cirrhosis and solitude, and the Major showed the notebook to the hat, whom I knew but couldn't remember from where

"That's him, Minister"

whom I knew, I finally realized, from him awarding medals to firemen on TV, from him reassuring blind people in the newspaper, from him promising the blacks that they'd be as Portuguese as us provided they kept clapping their thankful hands for dying of hunger, and from him explaining on the radio that the first of the horrors resulting from a Soviet invasion would be an end to bicycle touring and open-air Mass, the plainclothesman who was checking out the storks' patriotism hurled insults at his coworker who'd playfully walked away with the ladder, and the hat to me, without looking at the notebook of photographs

"Why did you lead my daughter astray?"

the playful coworker walking away from the church tower and waving good-bye while the plainclothesman with the storks sent his family to hell, I thinking that there must be some mix-up, some mistake, unable to imagine who his daughter might be, since I'd only finished primary school and was too humble to know engineers, let alone government ministers, I who didn't dare shake hands with the judge's or veterinarian's grandsons, addressing them by their full names while they just called me "hey you" and referred to me as "that guy," "the fellow with the beard," Custódia's nephew, and the Major waving what looked like reports in my face

"Didn't you hear the Minister's question, buddy?"

the breathing of the stones and pebbles in the river where my uncle Zé Francisco claimed there were suicides from long ago who talked to us from the depths, my uncle listening to the water, telling me to keep quiet

"Don't you hear your name?"

I didn't hear my name, I heard the flapping of wet wings, the factory whistle, the school bell, the stones that fell one by one from the river wall, but I didn't hear the dead

"I don't hear any dead people, Uncle"

my uncle Zé Francisco pressing his finger to his lips, because suicides are shy and get scared off by words, they'll only talk to us when there's peace and quiet, we can wait for ages and not hear a peep out of them, hidden like fish among the roots of the seaweed, the plainclothesman in the storks' nest leaning down from the tower and threatening to jump headfirst if his coworker didn't bring back the ladder immediately, and then I want to see the look on your face, you moron, the Major sticking the notebook in front of my nose

"Didn't you hear the Minister's question?"

and the photographs were of Paula and me in Grândola, in Montijo, in the quarry where we did, you know, for the first time, and I remember that, contrary to the suicides, I could hear the pine trees, the exalted humming of their resin, the soft concert of their sighs, Paula and I in the taxi with our elbows and legs out of focus, I with my tattoo, Paula blankly staring at the camera with her glasses as thick as the lenses on tubes for inventing planets, a piece of naked shoulder, of naked stomach, and contrary to the suicides I could hear the pine trees, needles, and more needles, and their branches all startled, the windows down, the meter ticking, her sweater rolled up to her chin, the hooks that wouldn't come undone, my trousers getting caught on the gear stick, Paula strangling me with her shoes

"César"

the pine trees could be heard, just as a workman hammering in the dust could be heard, as the rockroses could be heard, as a snake's hissing could be heard, photographs of Paula and me in the chapel yard at the cemetery of Santiago with a woman selling buttercups peering at us from behind her petals, Paula and me next to a stone wall in the woods of Sintra, surrounded by peacocks and dappled by the trees' tar-colored shade

"César"

and I to the Major

"That's not the daughter of a government minister, that's poor old Paula, a pathetic creature who works at the lawyer's office and lives on the square with her godmother Dona Alice"

I who before I went home would sniff myself all over, look for stains, check my coat for telltale strands of hair, go to the bathroom at Ferreira's pastry shop and scrub myself with the liquid blue soap, smooth down my beard, which Paula nibbled at when she got passionate

"César"

straighten my collar, fix the part in my hair with my comb, wink at Ferreira as I ordered a coffee, and Ferreira, dying of envy as he made my espresso

"Scoundrel"

and I'd march through the front door talking in a loud voice and giving Mário Jorge a good whack for drawing on the new wallpaper with his colored pencils, Mário Jorge howling, the TV howling, the dog howling, and Adelaide, looking up from her *Marie Claire,* which I sometimes read because of the cute girls in the ads

"What's the problem?"

a broomstick when I met her, but with age and her pregnancies she'd put on weight, filled out, and become a knockout, Adelaide who, on top of that, earns more at the bank than I do at the tax office where I verify forms like a mindless idiot, not to mention her benefits and bonuses, Adelaide who if I don't play straight and keep in line will dump me just like that, the Major with his fist in the air and Mário Jorge kicking on the carpet and ruining the pile with his sneakers

"Daddy hit me"

the plainclothesman in the storks' nest at last climbing down the ladder, shaking off leaves and dirt, going after the playful coworker with his gun cocked, and the hat snapping his suspenders, saying

"Stop right there, Major"

the hat looking at the photographs one by one, turning the pages with his fingertip like a connoisseur of rare books, Paula and I walking arm in arm into a cheap hotel, walking arm and arm out of a different hotel, close-ups at odd angles, indefinite shapes, what appeared to be a bare buttock, what appeared to be a smile, the hat with the spent cigarillo in his mouth and a lit lighter in his hand but miles away from the cigarillo and the lighter, engrossed in the photos, focusing on details, going back, slowly closing the notebook while turning to the Major

"Major"

and the Major without enthusiasm, tired, bored

"Yes, Minister"

the hat noticing me for the first time, looking at me without anger or curiosity, with what seemed like a smile but wasn't a smile, just teeth, languidly fanning the cigarillo smoke with his hand, the hat reopening the notebook and looking at the pictures while repeating in a distracted, almost friendly, almost affectionate echo

"Poor old Paula, such a poor, pathetic creature"

and then someone must have entered, because there was a change in the air, the slight whistle of a breeze, because although neither the hat nor the Major moved, the ceiling lamp swayed, I felt no pain, I felt a strange sleepiness, a kind of surrender, an indifference, my tongue tied, something slowly oozing in my mouth, and the hat, the Major, and the photographs no longer existed, nor the guardhouse, nor the sergeant, nor the corporal, nor the faucet that kept bleeding, or rather, not a faucet but something I knew without knowing what it was, or rather, not something I knew without knowing what it was but my throat, my torso, me, wanting to take a shower to wash off the blood and bits of teeth but without the strength to act, without anyone to help me, groping my way toward Paula

"Paula"

Paula, I think it was Paula, or rather, I thought it was Paula but it wasn't Paula, it was a man so far away I couldn't see him

"Poor old Paula, such a poor, pathetic creature"

my bones split open, a certainty of peace and calm, my Uncle Zé Francisco pressing his finger to his lips and telling me to be quiet

"Listen, César"

a drowned man calling me from the stones in the riverbed, a man my age and with my height and my face sinking into the sand, I reached out my hand to him but he slipped away, I reached out my hand to him but couldn't touch him, and the cement floor was cold against my face, the plainclothesmen staring at me and then blackness on blackness and the years going by, so many years, I swear I'm not exaggerating, my bed and my bedroom emerging piece by piece, even as I felt myself emerging in a painful coming together of tendons, phalanges, nerves, muscles, and veins, fragments that converged and fused together, hurting me, the radio planted itself into the nightstand and hurt me, the picture of a Douro riverboat that I bought from my brother-in-law hung itself on the wall and hurt me, the portière strung itself on the curtain rod with a muslin giggle and hurt me, fleshy bulges, scattered colors, creaks, and echoes congealed to form an incomplete Adelaide, a rough outline of Adelaide, her contours slowly coming into focus, with Mário Jorge holding on to a toy train and tugging at her skirt, an Adelaide who was and wasn't Adelaide

"They left you as pulp on our doorstep"

an Adelaide who on closer inspection was indeed Adelaide, if only for the disaffection in her voice, the wedding ring, the gold chain I gave her for her birthday, and the Beagle Boys stamped on her apron, just as it was indeed Victor, an old friend and nurse, who bandaged my knee, put my hand in a splint, appeared and disappeared with a sewing needle, smeared some cream on me that stung, me trying to find out the purpose of the cream, the needle, the cotton, the splints, trying to find out how I'd ended up as pulp on our doorstep, and Victor, wearing rubber gloves and pulling at my left ear with forceps

"Keep still"

and not just the bedroom, not just Adelaide, but also the dresser, the Virgin with her halo, the wardrobe with its sad smells of a decrepit old woman, me whom the plainclothesmen had dumped on the doormat

"Poor old César, such a poor, pathetic creature"

like a dead dog, unwanted clothes, table scraps, poor old César looking at Victor, looking at Adelaide the way drowned people looked at me

"Be quiet"

from the stones of the riverbed, I trying to swim up to the surface

"Be still"

because Mário Jorge was drawing on the wallpaper with a red pencil and they didn't even notice, expensive wallpaper with blue medallions and baskets that I spent an entire Sunday hanging up, I wanted to warn them that the pencil marks wouldn't come out with bleach and that there was no more of that paper in stock, I tried to get up to give the boy a slap, and Victor stuck a roll of prickly sponge into my nose that lacerated my cheeks as if they were being trampled on

"Be still"

with Adelaide looking over his shoulder, Adelaide's hand on his back, Adelaide's thigh against his thigh, Adelaide's thumb on his neck, and I aware of her audacity, her lack of respect, her shamelessness, not to mention Mário Jorge with his rupestrian vocation of covering the wallpaper with one bison after another, I who felt like biting their three heads off

"What's going on?"

and instead of my anger, out came a dribble of purple-red saliva, a dead spurt, Mário Jorge with pencil in hand and seized by Neolithic inspiration, drawing primitive animals on my pajama, Adelaide's lips pressed against Victor's lips, and both of them denying it in a hurt tone of voice

"You're imagining things"

I not knowing whether to believe them but pretending I believed them, thinking

"I'll do the same thing with Fátima, let it go"

but unfortunately Fátima isn't filled out like Adelaide, Fátima is a hairy dwarf, a nice person, sure, a good cook, sure, but one who would scare away a dog, Adelaide's lips pressed against Victor's lips, and Victor wrapping me in bandages and adhesive tape as if he were wrapping a mummy after having stuffed it with his cottons and his cold Egyptian fluids

"Your husband is so out of it from the drubbing he got that he can't even see us"

Mário Jorge in a creative trance on all fours on the bed, drawing mammoths all over the sheets, I sucking up soups through a straw for two weeks, oxtail soup, minestrone, and gazpacho, all with the same yucky taste of their aluminum containers, I navigating around the house with a cane like a gondolier, first the stick and then me, plowing the floor inch by inch with my heavy feet, I with a blanket over my lap, eating mush for retirees in front of the TV, entering Ferreira's pastry shop all out of breath, with no energy, no life, unable to talk, I in a painful wheeze

"A coffee"

the number of customers growing around the tables, with bottles, teacups, and toast, growing at the counter as the plane trees of the square were growing, as the Algarve-bound trucks and the rooftops and the river were growing, as the castle on top of the hill was growing, and fortunately Paula didn't notice me, I prayed to all the martyrs in heaven that she would never notice me again, because if she smiled at me, if she called me, if she greeted me

"Hi, César"

then Adelaide was bound to look once more over Victor's shoulder, with her hand on his back, her thigh against his thigh, her thumb on his neck, and I won't stand for such audacity, such shamelessness, such lack of respect, and much less can I stand to see Mário Jorge drawing bisons all over the expensive wallpaper with blue medallions and baskets that I spent an entire Sunday hanging up.

fourth report
(two unshod shoes in ecstasy)

REPORT

My mother and I, used to the neighborhood around Praça do Chile, never dreamed we might one day live on the Rua Castilho, in this chic building in a chic neighborhood with a pricey French-clothing boutique on the ground floor, a uniformed doorman, a Romanian viscount on the floor below us, and the assistant bishop of Lisbon on the floor above, a five-bedroom apartment furnished like in the movies and with views of King Eduardo VII Park, such that when we opened the window in the morning we saw the statue of the Marquis of Pombal and had trees waving their branches right in our living room, as if they were part of the décor, and my mother thought they were, and when we opened the window at night we had a flurry of neon lights from the airlines and insurance agencies inside our bedroom, along with the transvestites wearing patent-leather boots and hiding their whiskers under a layer of glazing putty, as if they belonged to the ornaments on top of the dresser, but my mother, shooing them away with her hand, thought they didn't, a building on the Rua Castilho with the streets of Lisbon descending toward the Tagus, and the boats on the river reminded me of the plastic ducklings on the mirror that was supposed to be a pond in the manger at the parish hall, a manger with sheep, wise men, martyrs, Mickey Mouse's nephews, statuettes of Father Cruz,* and hills made of brown paper, with a makeshift sign that said MADE IN ITS ENTIRETY BY THE BOY SCOUTS OF PRAÇA DO CHILE A BLESSED CHRISTMAS TO ALL, I'd stare at it for hours, wanting to touch the terra-cotta Baby Jesus who blessed us from the straw with a crumbled knee and with his right foot held on by Scotch tape, and my mother slapping my fingers

"We're not to touch Baby Jesus, Milá"

a building on the Rua Castilho that my mother brought the rest of the family to see, and the family dumbstruck as if before a high altar, not daring to sit down, not daring to accept so much as a chamomile tea, the family stepping softly and whispering as if at a funeral watch, bowled over by the crystal teardrop chandeliers whose sorrows were frozen in glass, by the sterling silver platters with a hallmark on the back, and my exultant mother, in case they hadn't noticed

"Did you notice the hallmark on the silver, Rogério, did you notice the hallmark?"

bowled over by the silk bedspread with naked women and goats that embraced them and played the flute

"Good God Almighty"

my proud mother boasting

"My rich, rich daughter"

leading my aunts and uncles from one marvel to the next, as if she'd charged them admission at the front door, showing them the chinaware Buddha that sported a belly as round as my grandfather's and that smiled blissfully just like him after his sixth cherry brandy, when he began to sing and to hit us, showing them the tiger-skin rug with the tiger's head baring its teeth at one end, explaining to the little ones while winking at the adults that the animal ate people who touched its teeth, and the children squealed in fright, showing them the picture of Francisco arm in arm with the queen of England, my mother who practically crossed herself and genuflected before the photo, full of faith, with the voice of one who knows

"Milá's protector, the Minister, something tells me they'll get married next year"

and the family members instantly putting out their cigarettes, taking their hands out of their pockets, and straightening up as if Francisco were there in person, the family members craning their necks to see the picture frame, craning their necks to see me, imagining me with a crown on my head, even more ceremonious with me than with the tiger or the Buddha

"Good God Almighty"

while my mother, who felt infinitely privileged to be on intimate terms with me and to live with the Minister's girlfriend, whirled around to save me from an invisible speck of dust on my skirt, my mother placing kisses on my cheeks like suction cups

"My rich, rich daughter"

my mother in a confidential, just-between-us tone of voice, telling how Professor Salazar and the Cardinal visited us every other day and addressed her as Dona Dores, how we had a policeman who patrolled the sidewalk to protect us from the Communist threat, and how when Professor Salazar and the Cardinal were here, our block would fill up with dozens of soldiers and officers who saluted her and were so considerate, helping her with her grocery bags

"I'll take those vegetables, Dona Dores"

and the family members, who lived with cats in basement apartments, pressing their hankies against their gaping jaws

"Holy cow"

my mother, who when Francisco appeared in the shop for the first time, with his hat and cigarillo and sheepskin boots, snapping his suspenders in his down-home way, because that's how Francisco was, without the least bit of vanity, as if he shined shoes or sold newspapers for a living, my mother

how people change

started pounding her fist on the counter

"What kind of clod did you hook up with this time, Milá?"

and a customer who was purchasing some ribbon, an elderly customer who knew how my mother was and knew all about illnesses thanks to her niece that was a nurse, a customer forever worried about the possibility of a stroke, a contorted mouth, a crutch

"Watch your blood pressure, Dona Dores"

the Praça do Chile in permanent ferment, the TB victims from the Diagnostic Center so skinny they flew about like the leaves swept up at dawn by the municipal cleaning crew, the hairdresser's assistants making eyes from the balcony at the owner of the mattress shop, who gave them rock-hard orthopedic pillows that quadrupled the number of stiff necks and bad backs among the rheumatics treated at Public Health, the Praça do Chile inundated by retirees in slippers who could barely walk and by blind people who bumped into them, stepping without mercy on their swollen, ostrichlike toenails, my mother standing smack in front of Francisco, sizing up his white hairs, wrinkles, and double chin, sniffing his old man's smell and returning to the counter with the jerky movements of a frantic chicken

"A fantastic choice, no doubt about it, after being in every man's pants in the neighborhood you hook up with a wretch even more decrepit than your wretched father, just what we needed, Milá, an invalid"

Francisco whom I met at the bus stop in front of the cemetery at Alto de São João, where a marble sign says CEMETERY OF EASTERN LISBON, and sloping down from the cemetery are buildings full of people like me and my mother, cockatoos in tin cages hanging out the windows, and then the river, not the river seen from King Eduardo VII Park, with ocean liners and warships, but a humble river that was within our means, with freighters, containers, and loading docks, a river which even I, with my earnings from the notions store, could have bought in installments and brought home to the Praça do Chile, placing it on top of the TV to decorate the living room, I standing at the bus stop with Carlos, whom my mother hated because his only occupation was pool-playing at the Academy Pool Hall, when an older gentleman inside a car driven by a corporal in uniform took his glasses from his pocket to get a better look at me, the car moving closer, just two or three yards away, the older gentleman sticking a cigarillo in his mouth as if it would help him to see me more than his glasses did, and Carlos muttering as he turned his back to the car, unnerved by the man ensconced in the upholstery and afraid the corporal might nab him

"Who could that old codger be?"

the car following our bus down the Rua Morais Soares, stopping and going, stopping and going, while all the cars behind it furiously honked, and it kept following us after we got off the bus, façade after façade, street vendors, tiny shops, the horns in a rage, the older gentleman indifferent to the horns, pointing at me with his cigarillo, his glasses, his red eyelids, and Carlos

"Who could that old codger be?"

afraid he worked for the Justice Department and was following us because of five boxes of Japanese stopwatches that a friend asked him to hold on to for a week so that he could surprise his wife on her birthday and that Carlos, being an obliging sort, held on to, though I couldn't understand why anyone would give his wife four hundred twenty-seven stopwatches at once, and since the police couldn't understand it either, they wanted Carlos to do some explaining before a judge, the police periodically leaving his apartment in Santos with their wagon loaded with TVs and radios that Carlos, to help out a billiard partner, had agreed to cover with a plastic cloth to protect them from dust, not to hide them, while the partner, an honest office clerk whose boss had given him a raise, was in the process of moving to a house in Rebelva, I to Carlos, who kept nervously eyeing the street while we ate snails at the Mimosa bar and grill near the Praça do Chile

"Why does your friend need so many TV sets, love, what does your friend want all those radios for?"

and Carlos, who always picked a table close to the back door, where he claimed it was airier and more agreeable, especially when the back door opened onto a dark alley, Carlos pulling the little beasts out of their shells with a trembling pin and exasperated by my ignorance

"If you buy a big house and live with your mother-in-law and four kids, it's good to have various TVs in each room to avoid arguments about which channel to watch" and I, squeezing Carlos's ankle with my legs as I chewed on a salty-tasting snail, touched by his concern for family harmony and the welfare of children, Carlos

how unfair the world is

whom they called a dangerous convict in the paper last week that reported his escape, amid shooting bullets and falling corpses, from a penal colony in Oporto, where he'd been cruelly confined just because he defended, for clinical and sociological reasons, the liberalization of heroin use, but to get back to what I was saying about the older gentleman and the corporal following us in their car from Alto de São João to the Praça do Chile, Carlos, afraid that the older gentleman worked for the Justice Department and was after him on account of the misunderstanding surrounding the five boxes of Japanese stopwatches that were a birthday present for his friend's wife, suddenly dropped my arm

"I'll write, Milá"

and ducked around the corner of the Praça Olegário Mariano without telling me he was going away, disappearing into the labyrinth of cross streets, into the no man's land of tricycles with vegetables for sale, crates of rotten fruit, and dilapidated buildings beyond the bridge, Carlos who never wrote or phoned me again, nor sent any more messages through his partner with a bum leg from the Academy Pool Hall, "I'll be waiting for you at four o'clock at Anjos Church," "Meet me at Rua da Palma during your lunch break," "Find a way to pass by the Arroios Deeds Office after you get off work," messages written in pencil on crumpled scraps of paper that his partner with the bum leg, as soon as my mother started to talk with a customer, would slip to me while pretending to choose buttons or to buy satinet cloth, and I at Anjos Church, the Rua da Palma, or the Arroios Deeds Office, and Carlos

"*Pssst-pssst*"

from a doorway, his eyes darting left and right and his shoe in the air, ready to run, because the police, due to the unfortunate meanness of the human spirit, didn't like him being so generous to other people, helping out with birthday surprises and house moves for friends who were rising up in the world thanks to their honest labors, Carlos didn't write, didn't phone, and didn't send messages through his partner with the bum leg from the Academy, but the corporal began to bring flowers, earrings, and rings for me and my mother, explaining as he motioned toward the street that they were gifts from the Minister, and in the car parked outside the shop sat the codger, pointing at me with his cigarillo and his red eyes, and the corporal would click his heels, get behind the wheel, and drive the cigarillo and inflamed eyes down Avenida Almirante Reis as my mother, leaning over the counter, examined the basket of gardenias wrapped in cellophane and a pink ribbon as if she were examining a dead rat, my mother suspicious, brandishing the yardstick

"What's the meaning of this, Milá"

opening the velvet cases, picking up the jewelry, and biting on the earrings, biting on the rings, incredulous, outraged, imagining that I was collaborating in Carlos's charitable endeavors, my mother's blood pressure rising and she breaking the yardstick on my back

"This is genuine gold, Milá, what have you gotten yourself mixed up in?"

and it wasn't just gardenias and earrings and rings, it was necklaces, bracelets, and liter bottles of perfume that smelled better than the incense in the cathedral, it was liqueur-filled Belgian chocolates, crystal dromedaries, a mantilla, a hot-water bottle, and fur-lined slippers for my mother, it was Indonesian gods, watercolors of sloops, a brooch with tiny yellow stones the size of a cream puff, a stove with six burners, and a refrigerator so big it wouldn't fit in our kitchen, the corporal clicking his heels

"From the Minister, Miss"

the codger silently focusing his glasses and cigarillo on me from the car's plush upholstery, my mother using the shawl on Sundays, even at the height of the August heat, and it made me sweat just to see her wear the fur-lined slippers that looked perfect for an Eskimo, my mother, as soon as she opened the shop shutters in the morning, standing behind the counter with the jeweled brooch on a strap of her smock and waiting, without answering the customers, for the impeccably uniformed corporal to enter with his packages wrapped in star-studded paper, my mother who when she walked up the hill to Penha de França to pay the landlord his rent was surprised to hear him promise new plumbing, the roof repaired, the apartment repainted, the landlord who had always treated her rudely and threatened eviction when we got behind, raising his voice and puffing out his chest on the landing

"One of these days I'm going to set all your junk on the sidewalk, you welsher"

now courteous, deferential, bending over backward for us, inviting us in, taking the newspapers off the easy chair, the landlord overflowing with friendliness, telling his maid to bring vanilla wafers and a glass of port for my mother

"The Minister has already paid your rent, Dona Dores, how come you never told me that you're a relative of the Minister, Dona Dores, it would have spared us a lot of headaches, Dona Dores, we would have avoided a lot of problems, Dona Dores, just yesterday I wrote the Minister assuring him that next week at the latest I'll change out your toilet tank and faucets and re-place your carpeting with parquet, Dona Dores, I hope the Minister is aware of how patriotic I am, Dona Dores, I've al-ways voted for Professor Salazar, word of honor"

my mother, wearing her mantilla and genuine gold ear-rings, removing her fur-lined slippers to massage her feet, and the landlord running toward the door in a touching show of affection

"I'll go get you my wife's corn-salve, which works won-ders, Dona Dores, I'll go get some warm water for you to soak your feet, I'll go get you some large-size Band-Aids"

my mother demanding rustproof aluminum windows, venetian blinds, a double lock, bathroom tiles with gold swans, and a crackled-glass ceiling light at the entrance, and the land-lord pale white, afraid to say no, taking down notes instead of telling her to go to hell right then and there

"Why certainly, Dona Dores, why certainly, Dona Dores, the workmen will ring your doorbell tomorrow morning at nine sharp"

my mother's ankles basking in the warm water as she held out her glass for a second helping of port and took advantage of the landlord's cue to request a modern doorbell like you see in American movies, one that intones chords from Kashmir and plays a minuet or a waltz, the landlord pouring her the vintage

port, bringing her a clean towel for drying her bunions, and
continually bowing like a servant while walking her to the door

"We'll fix you up with an American doorbell, Dona Dores,
we'll fix you up with a nice minuet, greetings to the Minister,
Dona Dores, call me if any of the tenants gives you trouble"

and one afternoon, after I'd delivered three yards of serge
to a customer at the Paço da Rainha, close to Campo de Santana,
where I liked to sit on a bench beneath the trees and watch the
beggars with long beards that looked false and the swans in the
pond whose necks asked me why, the car with the older gentleman pulled up next to me, his glasses and cigarillo observing me
from the depths of the upholstery, and the corporal with a stalk
of spikenard in his hand

"The Minister would like to speak with you, Miss"

the Minister's sweaty fingers squeezing the cigarillo, squeezing me, squeezing the funereal spikenard that released its sickly
perfume in my lap as the car drove past the morgue, past Martim
Moniz, and past the shop windows with artificial limbs and
naked mannequins that looked like suicides ready to be laid
on marble tables for the autopsy, until we reached the dock at
Commerce Square, teeming with passengers for the ferryboats
to Almada and Montijo, and on the square the ministry building, full of portraits of Professor Salazar and the Admiral, the
older gentleman ignoring all the people who bowed and telling
his secretary, whose hair was much nicer than mine, who was
much better dressed, much prettier

"I'm not here for anyone, Amélia"

a flag on the wall, a map of Portugal, shelves of books, telephones, piles of letters, the chrome lion of the paperweight ready

to pounce on an unsuspecting ashtray, the older gentleman seen from up close, his eyes magnified by the lenses of his glasses, his eyelashes resembling the wiggling feet of insects, his eyes looking all set to run away from his face, down his jacket to his trousers, down his trousers to the floor and then under a piece of furniture, to hide there like frightened cockroaches until I left and they could return to their place on either side of his nose, his sweaty fingers on the spikenard, on my hand, on my shoulder, feeling my neck's tendons, and pleading like a child

"Milá"

the older gentleman not hugging or kissing me, not touching me or fondling my ears like Carlos, who squeezed me so hard I'd get scared and feel like crying

"Carlos"

Carlos ripping my chemise and my slip, oblivious to me, his knees on my knees

"Oh God, oh God"

no flattery, no sweet nothings, just his fever, his urgency, his selfishness

"Oh God, oh God"

whereas the older gentleman would graze me with his sweaty fingers, insisting

"Milá"

his sweaty fingers touching that place behind the neck that arouses a feeling of swooning and tickling and pleasure but that the touch of his fingers didn't arouse, it aroused an odd sensation akin to weeping but weaker, and the next day I had to go to the Praça Paiva Couceiro to make a delivery, and when I came out there was the car with the uniformed corporal blocking traffic, with a row of honking horns behind it, the cigarillo, the eyes, and the red eyelids framed by the back window, again the spike-nard, the fingers sticky as snail's drool, the car driving past arti-ficial limbs and naked mannequins to reach Commerce Square, and his childish pleading

"Milá"

and again, when he touched the nape of my neck, that odd sensation akin to weeping, and the next day the car found me in the neighborhood of Desterro, the next day on the Rua Barão de Sabrosa, and the next day outside the Bolero Bar which is now being remodeled into something else, plus there were the phone calls with me answering

"Hello?"

and on the other end no answer, no voice, nobody, or rather, there was somebody's breathing, a sigh, a pause, the click of the receiver, and I all flustered

"Hello?"

and on Friday, when there were no errands to run, I sat at the cash register wondering where the car with the corporal, the glasses, and the red eyelids might be, I imagining the codger with the spikenard in his fist

"Turn left, Tomás, turn right, Tomás"

as he looked for me on the sidewalks, at outdoor cafés, in pastry shops, in discount stores, I remembering Carlos in spite of everything, in spite of myself, I missing Carlos, our secret meetings on the bridge in the slummy no-man's-land, in dark doorways, at the cinema where I'd show up at the start of the movie and he in the middle, with dark glasses and raised coat collar, I entertained by the gangsters who fell dead by threes and fours, and suddenly a wet tongue wriggling in my ear as the spectators behind us

"Why I never"

squirmed in their seats, I wondering where in Lisbon the car might be meandering, when the older gentleman suddenly entered the shop, with hat and cigarillo and sheepskin boots, snapping his suspenders and holding a stalk of spikenard in his fist, blinking his swollen eyelids as he walked straight up to the cash register that jingled with change

"Milá"

a stunned pause that lasted centuries, the second hand of the wall clock frozen between two notches, my mother's face not grasping, my mother's face dumbstruck with vexation, my mother's face grasping, her features twisting this way and that as if reflected in water

"What kind of clod did you hook up with this time, Milá?"

and the customer who was purchasing some ribbon, an elderly customer who was like a neighbor, who knew how my mother was and knew about illnesses thanks to her niece that was a nurse, a customer forever worried about a stroke, crutches, a limping leg

"Watch your blood pressure, Dona Dores"

my mother who hated Carlos for the same reasons she'd hated Fernando and Américo, because they didn't dance by the rules at the Clube de Estefânia, they didn't work as junior clerks in the civil service, they didn't ask her permission to go out with me, they didn't want to hear about her ulcer, nor did they offer advice or herbal teas to alleviate it, they brought me home after midnight with my hair mussed up, my hair band out of place and a few dress hooks missing, and they didn't even give her a Spanish liqueur for Easter, my mother walking out from behind the counter and standing smack in front of the codger, sizing up his white hairs, wrinkles, and double chin

"A fantastic choice, no doubt about it, after being in every man's pants in the neighborhood you hook up with a wretch even more decrepit than your wretched father, just what we needed, Milá, an invalid"

my mother already envisioning me with a gypsy scarf on my head and a cart of lettuces and smelly eels, hawking vitamins in the Bairro das Colónias, my mother envisioning me living in a tent on the outskirts with a kerosene stove and a mule, blowing flies off my face in my sleep

"A wretch even more decrepit than your wretched father, just what we needed, Milá, an invalid"

the corporal standing at attention at the shop entrance, ready to come to the aid of his master, the older gentleman, whose spikenard tickled his nose as he stuttered embarrassed apologies, and I on the throne of the cash register, in which the coins danced a polka every time the lever was pulled, as if it were the crank of a barrel organ

"The Minister, Mother"

the Minister, Mother, the sweaty fingers of the Minister who never went with me to the cinema, or to the bridge in the slummy no-man's-land, or to the Constantino Garden, the Minister who would place the spikenard in my hand as he looked at the ships, at the Tagus, at the greenish bronze king astride a greenish bronze mule, the Minister, the codger, his voice tarnished by tobacco smoke

"You remind me of someone I knew years ago, Milá"

the customer who recognized him from TV and the newspapers, explaining with hand motions who the clod, the wretch, the invalid was, the second hand resuming its movement, the corporal standing perfectly straight at the door, the cash register, with the fickle and inscrutable self-will of inanimate objects, opening its drawer and spreading around bills and coins when I hadn't touched a single button, I swear, my mother answering the customer's hand motions with her own motions, lifting up her leg and pointing at the slippers, her earrings flashing, rings flashing, the brooch with yellow stones securing her mantilla, grabbing the clod by the sleeve and bowing as if before a miter or whatever it is a bishop wears

"They're the best slippers I've ever had, Senhor Minister"

my mother balancing herself on just one foot to show off her plaid slippers with fur lining, my mother, egged on by the customer, walking around the shop like a fashion model for the wretch to see, turning the doorknob to our apartment, straightening out doilies, discreetly kicking a plate of food under the sofa

"Excuse the mess, Senhor Minister"

and it wasn't just the plate of food, it was pots, tableware, and the soup pan on the sofa, it was old almanacs, cardigan sweaters, and a burned-out lightbulb on the floor, it was a dishrag on the windowsill, a bucket with a mop leaning against the buffet, cobwebs on the umbrella stand, and what appeared to be rat fur on the table, my mother dusting, scrubbing, sweeping, beating rugs, stuffing drawers with spoons, pieces of bread, bones, fruit rinds, and trash, spraying deodorizer, airing the rooms, washing dishes, while the Minister, the older gentleman, the codger, the clod, the wretch, stood on the floor mat of our tiny living room with his funerary spikenard in hand, my mother in the kitchen placing glasses, teacups, and saucers in the drying rack with the clattering sound of dishes hitting each other, falling, and breaking, my mother

"It's a humble abode, excuse the mess, Senhor Minister"

and I, out of embarrassment for my mother and out of pity for the older gentleman, moving closer toward his sweaty fingers without saying a word, taking him by the arm, leading him to my room, and latching the door behind me, night had fallen on the Praça do Chile, and in the darkness I couldn't see him, I couldn't make out his features nor his expression nor his eyes, I thought it was Carlos, I forgot about the old man and I thought it was Carlos, I thought with all my might that it was Carlos, and I felt myself being born.

COMMENTARY

When my daughter told me she was going to marry a state minister, I frankly didn't believe her, and such a wealthy and powerful and important minister to boot, the Admiral and Professor Salazar's right-hand man, who appeared every day on TV and in the papers, so that when my daughter told me she was going to marry a state minister, the first thing I thought was

"Another of Milá's lies, another ruse so she can go and rendezvous God only knows where with Carlos"

a ne'er-do-well who only caused her pain and disappointment, he'd disappear for two, three, four weeks, and she'd wait for him like an idiot, moping all day and running to the phone every time it rang, desperately hoping he'd come back, standing on tiptoe at the shop every other minute to peek outside, I worried about her being so on edge

"What is it, Milá?"

my only daughter, born in Seia a year before my husband found work in Lisbon, you've no idea how hard it was to leave my hometown, not because of the people I left behind, and not because of my relatives who died there, they say it's the dead who hold us to a place

it's not true

they don't hold us, what held me to Seia was the shade of the trellised vines, the path among the raspberries, and the blue pine trees in summer, my only daughter, we put her crib in the kitchen to protect her from the wind, but she still had ice-cold skin and wide-open eyes, just like the corpse of a doll, and I, who am horrified by corpses of dolls

"Get her out of my sight, Augusto"

one Christmas my godmother gave me a cardboard box with something that shook around inside, I cut the string, removed the tissue paper, and found

how disgusting

a dead doll that smiled at me, I tried to run away but my godmother grabbed me by the arm, bewildered

"Don't you like dolls, Dores?"

I'd like dolls if they were alive, but dead dolls horrify me, especially if they keep batting their eyelids, if they keep repeating

"Mommy"

my godmother leaning the doll backward and forward, the doll batting its eyelids, repeating

"Mommy"

my godmother trying to reassure me, forcing me to hold the doll in my lap, a doll with a cloth body, a pasty head, and

blond curly hair like on the angel who announced to the Virgin
that she was pregnant with Jesus, if someone made such an an-
nouncement to me I wouldn't care about God or about being
blessed among women, I'd faint from fear, my godmother proud
of the purchase she made in Viseu, pointing out the package to
her seat companions on the bus

"Be careful"

tucking the doll between my knees

"Don't you like dolls, Dores?"

the doll with a pale white mouth, rolling its eyes, rotting
in my lap, and I kicking, struggling, shouting

"I don't want a dead doll"

I, worried about Milá being so on edge, waiting for Carlos
like an idiot, moping all day, writing letters, running to the
phone full of desperate hope, standing on tiptoe when not even
a blind man or a tricycle with vegetables was passing by

"What is it, Milá?"

and she retreating to her corner, pulling on the lever, and
pretending to be sorting the change in the drawer's compartments, to be putting the coins in rolls, to be stacking the bills in
order under the weighted springs, she making the machine jingle,
pretending to be busy, pretending to be working

"Nothing"

Milá who invented birthday dinners in the homes of friends
who happened

of course

not to have telephones and who had celebrated enough
birthdays to be great-great-grandmothers or Egyptian mummies,
Milá who put on makeup in secret, rolled on deodorant in secret, doused herself with perfume in secret, put on her new coat

in secret, and said good-bye to me from the hallway, not entering the living room to give me a kiss, so that I wouldn't see how she'd primped up, Milá reduced to a fleeting hand

"See you later"

and her perfume leaving such a stench I had to open the window and shake towels to shoo it away, her bedroom a complete mess, stockings here, belts there, the hair spray on its side, a tube of uncapped shoe polish blackening the sheets, her little basket of charms on the floor, and the hair dryer on high, vomiting out hot air, I on the doormat yelling at the unanswering statue in the Praça do Chile

"Milá"

but there was no one on Avenida Almirante Reis, no one on the Rua Morais Soares, no one waiting for the streetcar that goes up to Largo do Leão and the Technical Institute, just her perfume dissipating in the air like a fading trail, just the TV antennas standing out against an absent sky, and I waking up in the dark at one or two or three in the morning, thinking

"Burglars"

hearing the key in the door turn quiet as a mouse, then a rustle of fabric, and naked feet crossing the floorboards, I getting out of bed, hitting the light switch, and finding Milá with her shoes in her hand, fabricating excuses

"I got back a while ago, I got back a while ago"

Milá with lipstick smeared up to her forehead, mascara streaking her cheeks, runs in her stockings, her blouse buttoned in the wrong places, her hankie hanging out of her purse, and teeth marks on her neck, Milá straightening her hair while pointing at some magazine or other

"I got back a while ago but couldn't sleep, I've been reading"

I to myself, You were reading on a park bench, you were reading on some steps, your were reading at the cinema, you were reading with Carlos at a scuzzy hotel on the Avenida Defensores de Chaves, in a crummy room let by the hour and ridden with lice

Milá rolling her eyes, mouth wide open, reminding me of a dead doll, of my godmother forcing me to hold the doll in my lap

"Don't you like dolls, Dores?"

Milá, who if I leaned her backward and forward would have repeated, in an inhuman squeal

"Mommy"

and I, terrified, pushing her into her room as if shutting her inside her cardboard box, covering her with tissue paper, and tying her with twine to get rid of her, to be at peace

"I don't want a dead doll"

Milá with the smell of Carlos's smuggled American cigarettes on her breath, with seafood from a bar and grill on her breath, with rings under her eyes stretching down to her chest, and I can imagine

it isn't hard

where she got them, and Milá, who didn't understand a thing about dead dolls, protecting herself from me

"Leave me alone"

batting her eyelids, her pasty head on the pillow, her cloth body under the covers, I afraid she'd sit up in bed and start repeating in hollow tremors

"Mommy"

and the next day Milá like a zombie, with a damp napkin on her face as she sleepily skated around the living room, losing her slippers, bumping into chairs, asking for aspirin, holding out a tilted, trembling mug in my direction, and chewing on her syllables like caramels

"Coffee"

I wishing I could have sliced off Carlos's balls, and Américo's before Carlos's, and Fernando's before Américo's, ne'er-do-wells who spent their afternoons shooting caroms at the Academy Pool Hall and looking out the window, propped against their cue sticks as against shepherd's crooks, glancing over at the hairdresser's assistants who were all bangs and braids and come-ons, their tanned legs hanging over the balcony and with a silver ring on every finger, whereas Milá was a bit hunched, without bangs or braids or rings, snuggled up against the cash register as if it were a pillow, the sun beating down on the lemons and pineapples of the fruit carts, the fish of the street vendors gleaming like daggers with eyes, the black newsboy selling earthquakes in Tunisia, I who was measuring lace at the counter

"Milá"

and Milá in a whisper, fiddling among the cent keys, pushing away my voice with an arm that wasn't an arm, it was the dress strap of a lifeless tentacle

"In a minute, let me just sit here for a bit"

Milá in a crummy room on the Avenida Defensores de Chaves and I with a mind to show up at the Academy, a hall full of characters with chalk in their fists, grave as astronomers, squinting as if through a sextant to determine the planetary path of a final shot, I with a mind to call Carlos aside and inform him that if he continued to get my daughter upset, I'd go straight to the police station and tell the deputy chief who it was who prowled at night with a cat under his arms on the Rua Cavaleiro de Oliveira, who tossed the cat up to the tenants' clotheslines, who caught the shirts and long johns the cat's claws pulled from the clothespins, and who got rich selling the tenants' trousseaux to the gypsies, and Carlos, with his fingers pressed flat against his necktie in a show of infinite innocence

"Who, me? Who, me?"

the astronomers telescoping their red and white planets, the hairdresser's assistants puffing up like pink and gold pigeons on the balcony, the statue of Magellan pointing down the avenue at the shopping district of Martim Moniz with the stiff tip of his beard as if Martim Moniz were a lost island of his own discovery, an island of discount stores selling wooden knick-knacks, toy horses, toy cars, games with missing pieces, dolls, and I, suspicious of dolls, touching them on the chest to see if they still breathed

"Don't you like dolls, Dores?"

dolls that emit sad giggles if we squeeze their tummies, and if we throw them on the ground they bleed sawdust and stare at us like an unpardonable shame, Carlos's fingers pressed flat against his necktie in a show of infinite innocence

"Who, me? Who, me?"

Milá snuggled up against the cash register as if it were a pillow

"In a minute"

and in walked a government soldier, a corporal with medals and colored braids who saluted me, while outside there were plainclothes policemen standing guard, jeeps here and there with machine guns to divert traffic, the hairdresser's assistants staring in awe, the astronomers running out the back door, and the Minister strolling into my shop like a prince, a man my husband's age but much better preserved, much better looking, much more distinguished, with an obviously different upbringing, a different demeanor, a different air, a man my husband's age but without swear words or a drunkard's nose, and the customer who was at the counter buying some zippers, a customer who lived on the Rua Pascoal de Melo, owned a stationery store, and was more like a friend than a customer, said so softly I couldn't hear

"It's the Minister, Dona Dores"

a man with a hat, a cigarillo, and elastic suspenders, just like a small-town barber, the barber in my town was called Mateus, his wife was Olívia, and around the time my godmother gave me the doll he was the one who would cut my hair, muttering

"Little girl, little girl"

I with a cloth around my neck and scared stiff, because he also pulled teeth and set bones, Mateus and Olívia, Olívia and Mateus, Mateus and Olívia at the cemetery in Seia, you wake up one morning and suddenly everyone starts calling you Aunt Dores, suddenly everyone's younger than you, how unfair, and the people you grew up with are six feet under a marble slab and a jar of flowers, an array of uniforms, jeeps, policemen, the Minister in my shop and I to Milá, my mind on Carlos, not hearing the customer

"It's the Minister, Dona Dores"

you wake up one morning and suddenly everyone treats you with ceremony, from a distance

I imagining the Minister to be one of the billiard astronomers who knocked around planets and who used their paychecks to cushion the end of the month with record players, girlie magazines, and contraband whiskey with no excise stamp and more alcohol from the pharmacy than actual whiskey, I

you can imagine my wrath

imagining that my daughter, disillusioned by Carlos or Fernando or Américo, had changed boyfriends without telling me

"What kind of clod did you hook up with this time, Milá?"

and the customer despairing at my obliviousness, my disrespect, my ignorance, the client afraid I'd be arrested

"It's the Minister, Dona Dores"

and the barber lifting up my head

"If you move, I'll take the pincers from my pocket and yank out your gums, little girl"

we had a well with a bucket and pulley, and above the well a chestnut tree, and if I shouted, my voice echoed in the well for the longest time, like a dropped pebble, if I leaned forward I saw a wavy, miniature me down below, and I'd get confused, wondering, Which one is me, which one is me, Milá now awake, staring at the policeman and the soldier, the customer afraid they might stick me on a plane to Cape Verde, the Minister ever so gentle and with flowers in his hand, nard for a wedding, a bride's white nard, I hadn't seen nard for ages, because my husband never gave me any nard when he was alive, and after he died I never gave him any, what a silly thought, I not listening to the customer, thinking only of the astronomers, imagining my daughter going with them from door to door in search of whiskeys and naked women in black mourning bras, I counting the minister's wrinkles on my fingers and having to continue on my toes

"A fantastic choice, no doubt about it, a wretch even more decrepit than your wretched father"

the customer, terrified, imagining herself also being shipped off to Cape Verde to die of sunstroke inside a barbed wire fence on a deserted beach, the customer about to pass out, in a faint voice

"For God's sake, Dona Dores"

and the Minister trembling with passion, poor man, I saw from the start that he was an honorable, upright sort, the spikenard wavering between Milá and me, the Academy Pool Hall deserted, the planets immobile, the cue sticks on the floor, the customer so nervous she screamed in my ear

"For crying out loud, it's the Minister, Dona Dores"

the smell of the nard filling up the shop, the smell of a church wedding, the smell of a bride, organ music, candles, my tears of joy, Milá on TV greeting the Cardinal, Milá on TV kissing the Pope's stole, Milá on TV between her husband and Professor Salazar, Milá wearing natural silk and a wide-brimmed hat by a French fashion designer as she embraces soldiers who are so unkempt and badly dressed, poor things, departing for Angola with rifles on their shoulders, Milá presenting them with holy cards of the shepherd children of Fátima to protect them from malaria and the mischief of the blacks, Milá visiting me in a chauffeured car escorted by motorcycles blaring their sirens, scattering the TB victims with their exhaust fumes, and Milá just ravishing, a perfect doll, and my godmother

"Don't you like dolls, Dores?"

I serving the octopus stew in my only tureen that was still

intact, ashamed of my home, whose dinginess was only accen-
tuated by the smell of the nard, of a church wedding, of a bride,
the paper friezes around the ceiling all yellowed, the curtains gray
from smoke, the spots I thought were small now looming enormous, the rooms I thought were spacious now minuscule, and
my relatives on the street, trying to make out the Minister who
held my daughter's hand, the Minister with a napkin round his
neck

"Milá"

who became his own father when he took off his hat, his
cheeks sagging, his eyebrows thinning, his skin with brown
splotches, the crown of his head bald, the Minister whom Professor Salazar visited at the Rua Castilho to decide this and that,
wiping his soles on the doormat while giving me a sparrowy wrist
with veins that twitched

"Good afternoon, good afternoon"

giving Milá a knotty wrist resembling a withered vine

"Good afternoon, good afternoon"

Professor Salazar, who had saved Portugal from the Ger-
mans and no doubt knew that my daughter and the Minister
were engaged, who prevented the Communists from killing us
all and no doubt knew that Milá and the Minister were to get
married the following year, and in case he didn't know, since
with an entire country on one's back plus Africa and Macao, a
man

it's only natural

could easily forget, I, while helping him remove his overcoat

"Did you know that the Minister and my daughter are
getting married next year?"

Professor Salazar attentively nodding yes in the shadows of the foyer

"Good afternoon, good afternoon"

where there was a table with a bronze woman emerging from her bridal tunic, like Milá coming away from the altar under a hail of rice

"Did you know that the Minister and my daughter are getting married next year?"

from the balcony of the front living room we could see the heart of Lisbon, stretching from the Marquis of Pombal's statue down to the Tagus River, trees, avenues, boats, the grass in the park, and Professor Salazar, as if he wanted to get away from me

"Good afternoon, good afternoon"

as if he didn't believe in the marriage of the Minister with my daughter, who would one day kiss the Pope's stole on TV, who would

I was sure of it

become friends with the queen of Belgium and have a couple of those bizarre little dogs whose fur is cared for by a veterinarian, just like countesses and actresses have, my daughter on magazine covers surrounded by furry barks and I standing behind her and smiling, the living room balcony gave us all of Lisbon, rooftops, cinemas, hotels, the buildings that looked even whiter at night, the mystery of the lit windows with people's lives in the cracks between the curtains that unsettled me

what do they do, what do they talk about, what bores them

and I to the Minister in the presence of Professor Salazar, walking without ceremony into the living room where they drank tea and went over papers

"Tell Professor Salazar if it's not true that you and my daughter are going to get married next year"

the old codger who was minister talking to the head honcho, the boss, who was even more of a codger, a pair of old fogies who almost made me miss Carlos and the other astronomers, who at least didn't walk slowly and smell sour, a couple of codgers governing the country between sips of herbal tea and toast with unsalted butter, I shaking the Minister's shoulder, offended by his embarrassed silence

"Tell Professor Salazar if it's not true that you and my daughter are going to get married next year"

in the living room where he and Professor Salazar, such old codgers that I wondered why people obeyed and feared them, were drinking tea and going over papers as I considered breaking one of the porcelain cats from the sideboard over their heads, I who should never have let them in the shop, should never have invited them into my home

"Tell him if it's not true that you and my daughter are going to get married next year"

I so gullible, so foolish, ingenuous to the point of taking the Minister for a true gentleman, a distinguished individual, a man of his word, and what I got in the end was a first-class scoundrel, I holding the porcelain cat in the air over the teapot and the toast, the cat that looked horrid but was Chinese and worth a fortune, and the Minister

"We'll talk after Professor Salazar has left, Dona Dores"

an old bumpkin with a cigarillo in his mouth and elastic suspenders, it's a wonder that the doorman, so hard on beggars, on Jehovah's Witnesses, and on the transvestites hiding out from the police, instantly showing them the door with his finger

"Out you go"

allowed him to enter the building on Mondays and Fridays to visit Milá, the burly doorman who, when he saw me for the first time, jumped up from the desk where he was leafing through a newspaper and blocked my way to the elevator

"What do you want, ma'am?"

supposing that I'd come to ring the residents' doorbells and ask for money, or push Bibles, or read their fortunes, the doorman who, when he saw Milá for the first time, objected to her makeup and low-cut dress and red pocketbook and seashell necklace

"You're at the wrong place, honey, the nightclubs are on the Avenida Duque de Ávila, now get moving"

shooing her out with his newspaper as if he were shooing away a turkey, calling over to a policeman and asking him to take her to the station

"Three in the afternoon and already hawking her ovaries, can you explain to me how this country is supposed to make progress?"

the doorman who gritted his teeth when my family visited me on Sundays, eyeing them as if they were a band of jugglers or hobos, afraid they'd spit on the tropical plants or have a picnic on the stairs with thermos bottles, mess tins, radios, and loud discussions on top of a ratty blanket, littering the steps with peach pits, the doorman imagining that we lived in trailers amid domesticated ponies and boa constrictors or that we raised peas and cabbages behind a shipping container near the industrial port, the doorman who didn't dare cross me after the codger had a word with him, but he pretended not to see me, he answered me with grunts, he'd barge into my kitchen with a repairman or the chimney sweep without even knocking, the doorman who, whenever he saw Milá, would start punching his newspaper while crossing and uncrossing his legs, as I was all too well aware

"With a dress like that, you might as well go naked"

and Milá as elegant as could be, blond-haired, dressed in tutti-frutti leather, and with impeccable manners, because I knew how to bring her up, even if I wasn't born in a palace, Milá saying

"See you later, Senhor Vargas"

and the beast, red with rage, drumming his fingernails on the desk

"You'll see what I do once the old man drops you"

but I didn't worry about his threat, since there was no danger of the old man dropping my daughter, because even if he didn't marry her as promised, he would still come on Mondays and Fridays after finishing at the ministry, with his hat and cigarillo, his hillbilly clothes, his elastic suspenders, and nuptial nard, he would still come on Mondays and Fridays, ceremonious and sad, to sit down on the sofa next to Milá, fondling her neck and shoulders with his sweaty fingers as night slowly fell over the city and I watched them from the hallway, I watched them from my room, I watched the codger take my daughter in his arms, my daughter who smiled, blinking as her body leaned backward and forward like a dead doll.

REPORT

I don't know quite how to describe it but it wasn't passion, mind you, that I felt for the Minister, it wasn't like when you fall in love with someone and you miss them, you want to see them and talk to them on the phone, you think about them for hours while staring at the wall, you smile when they smile, you write silly verses and the like, and the Minister knew that I felt no passion, that I wasn't in love, because when we were in my bedroom, for instance, with him fondling me and I detesting every minute, not moving a muscle in the hope that it would end quickly, stiff as a board in the hope that the Minister would hurry up and finish, he would notice my wide-open eyes and perfectly still hands, he'd realize I didn't like it, and he'd let me go, reaching for his cigarillos, not angry at me but disappointed, covering his face with his elbow

"You never liked me"

and I not answering, unable to contradict him, not daring to insist

"But I do like you, really"

I who didn't want a flabby chest weighing on my chest, scrawny legs between my legs, a withered tongue in my mouth, an old man's smell mixed in with my smell

(the smell of drawers, of an herbarium, of an old dictionary)

the afternoon rustling the curtains with a breeze from the Tagus, a trawler drifting across the balcony, flapping its wings like a bird, I feeling sorry for the Minister and telling myself, If I think about Carlos, I can do it, if I think about Carlos, it won't be so disgusting, I thinking about Carlos, about nights at the movies with Carlos, nights in stairwells with Carlos, nights in the garden of Campo de Santana with Carlos, I frightened by the drug addicts and the swans, thinking about Carlos, slowly moving my foot closer until it touched a scaly ankle, then pulling it back as if I'd gotten a shock, and the Minister at my side blinking his eyelashes like moribund centipedes

"You never liked me"

picking up his clothes like the immigrants from Timor picking up debris left by the tide, his shirt like a crumpled newspaper, his trousers like a frazzled basket, his shoes like gaping fish, the Minister walking slowly behind his navel like someone behind a baby carriage, the afternoon rustling the curtains with a breeze from the Tagus, the trawler drifting across the window flapping its wings like fins, the Minister groping for his cigarillos on the carpet like a blind beggar groping on the sidewalk for the spare change he dropped, strangling himself in his shirt collar as if resigned to suicide

"The woman you remind me of never loved me either"

the distant sound of the front door slamming, not with violence but with the listlessness of a coffin lid over the last cadaver, I with my nose flattened against my nose in the mirror, astonished at how what I saw didn't seem like me, astonished at what I was on the outside and repeating, so that I'd get used to the idea, "This is me, this is me, this is me," my mother suddenly appearing next to me in the frame, my mother who at least was the same inside and out, lucky her, wearing the brooch with yellow stones, and I ready to bet that she slept with the brooch, took her bath with the brooch, and made sure every other minute that she hadn't misplaced that horrendous millstone I would have paid a fortune not to use, my mother wearing a gauzy black evening blouse under her apron

"What did you do to the codger, Milá, that he went away looking like a man doomed to die?"

my mother, who was always on pins and needles for fear we'd have to go back to the Praça do Chile to sell buttons and satinet to irksome customers, insisting every day that I ask the Minister to buy the apartment on the Rua Castilho and put the deed in my name

"The codger isn't going to live forever, Milá"

insisting that I get the Minister to open a bank account for me and increase my monthly allowance, my mother whom no one in the building, not even the doorman, ever exchanged greetings with much less invited in for tea, whom the other residents passed on the steps without seeing her, passed on the elevator as if she were a maid or a beggar, pushing the buttons for their floors even if they came after ours, and for three or four or five floors they'd remain silent, serious, jingling their keys as they studied the ceiling, and if the doorman's wife was watering the plants or scrubbing the marble in the lobby when we entered, she'd find a way to sprinkle our legs or make us trip on her brush

"I hope your shoes get ruined"

and if I turned around, I'd see her triumphantly grinning with two hundred canine teeth, her hands defiantly placed on her hips, my mother without the courage to protest, wiping her stockings with a handkerchief, I without the courage to protest, wiping my coat with a handkerchief, I stretched out across the bed, my nose flattened against my nose in the mirror, marveling, This is me, this is me, this is me, wondering, Is this really me? because it made no sense for me to be who I was, with those eyebrows, those cheeks, that chin, it made no sense for me to be that girl, twenty-three years old, hair dyed blond, looking like a gushy cancer victim in my ID photo, it made no sense for my mother to panic

"What did you do to the codger, Milá, that he went away looking like a man doomed to die?"

and behind my mother hung the drapes through which the trawler with its birdlike wings peeked in at me, and next to the drapes stood the dresser, which they'd lowered off the delivery van like a piece of crystal while the doorman huffed

"A period dresser for one of the Minister's hussies, that tops everything"

and on the dresser a silver dish with rings, an ivory maiden leaning toward a swan with an incredibly long neck, and the Minister when he gave it to me, his sweaty palm resting on my thigh

"It's a Greek legend, Milá"

the legend of a maiden in love with a duck, how ludicrous, the duck ravenous and lustful, nuzzling his beak into her back, my mother clapping her hands on the sofa as the Minister, utterly ridiculous, hopped around me flapping his elbows

"Quack-quack"

the Minister waddling around and pointing his protruding lips in my direction, stimulated by my mother's exaggerated glee

"I can't take any more, Milá, I can't take any more"

the Minister convinced he was a born comedian, rubbing his lips into my neck

"Quack-quack"

and soon the neighbors banging broomsticks on the floor, soon the Minister keeling over as if from a stroke, I fed up with so much foolishness, so much silliness, so much bawdiness, begging them with my hands to be silent, my mother laughing her head off to humor the Minister, my mother deathly afraid of going back to the notions store, holding on to happiness, pressing her hand against her chest as if happiness might break loose from her body

"I can't take any more, Milá"

the Minister still hopping around, his waistband coming unstitched

"Quack-quack-quack-quack"

wading around me in the pond of the Persian rug and almost touching my mouth as he shook his head no

"Give your little ducky a kiss, Milá"

I appalled by the pathetic spectacle but deciding, at great sacrifice, as if making a flying leap, to grab the duck's head and give it a quick peck, and I felt like wiping my mouth on my sleeve at once, like brushing my teeth at once, I, and here's the hitch, thinking again of Carlos, of Carlos's promises, of Carlos's lies, my mother making sure the brooch with yellow stones had withstood her howls of laughter

"Give your adorable ducky another kiss, Milá, give him another hug, don't be shy"

the adorable ducky sitting down at the table to write me a check and my mother counting the zeroes while giving me complicitous kicks, looking over my shoulder, grabbing the check, folding it with her thumb, and tucking it in the gauzy black evening blouse that infuriated the doorman

"Give me a break"

my mother, adroitly

"It's better if I hold on to it, Senhor Minister, you know what a birdbrain my daughter is"

and as soon as I'd undressed, put on my bathrobe, and turned on the TV for a little peace and quiet without an old man passionately hopping in front of me, my mother would pull the check from her apron strap and glue it to my eyes

"If you'd been a wee bit nicer to the codger, he would have given you double the amount, Milá, what would it have cost you to give him another kiss or two?"

and so it wasn't that I felt passion for the Minister, it wasn't that I missed him, wanted to see him, or lost my appetite on his account, it wasn't that I thought about him for hours while staring at the wall, smiled when he smiled, or giggled at the things he said, it was that I could live in a fancy apartment like in the movies, have gorgeous necklaces, go to a masseuse, and wear slippers like actresses use in exchange for two or three hours every Monday and Friday imagining Carlos while the Minister, who always respected me, pawed my arms and urgently whispered

"You remind me of someone I knew ages ago, Milá"

someone who might have been his mother or wife or daughter or lover, it doesn't matter, the Minister who showed up one day with a plastic bag containing an old dress like the ones our aunts wore in the photos from when they were young or like those worn by 78 rpm singers, the Minister who talked in circles, faltered, stammered, and I saying the words for him, since it was all the same to me if I dressed up in masquerade and since the sooner the tomfoolery began the sooner it would end

"You want me to put this on, right?"

he presented me a belt, a purse, and a pair of moth-eaten crocodile high heels, and I could never keep my balance in those crooked stilts

"You want me to wear these, right?"

and flashy necklaces, operetta earrings, musty perfumes, a tiny case of petrified rouge, a clown's almost purple lipstick, and a grandmother's gold rings worn thin from rubbing against fingers, the Minister wanted me to dye my hair platinum blond and do it up like a marchioness in a painting, to wear stockings streaked by runs and a whalebone corselette that choked my chest, and to carry a silver-handled parasol riddled with holes, I walking around the living room in the Carnival outfit as the Minister, covering my hands with a pair of lace gloves, joyously proclaimed

"Isabel"

my mother in the doorway

"Holy Mother Mary"

the Minister obliging me to treat her as if she were an old, trusted housekeeper

"Let me introduce you to my wife, Dona Dores"

sure of himself, without seeming pathetic, without any silliness, without any quack-quack, removing the brooch with yellow stones from my mother's apron and pinning it on my low-cut dress

"We're going to spend the night in Palmela, Dona Dores, so you needn't worry about dinner"

as if she worked for us at our apartment on the Rua Castilho, as if she were his housekeeper who took care of the shopping and cleaning, and my mother staring at my getup with endless astonishment

the worn-out shoes, the shabby handbag, the threadbare dress, the bizarre hairdo with pins and bangs, and my makeup like a flamenco dancer's, my mother afraid they'd lock me up in an insane asylum

"Are you going out like that, Milá?"

disappearing from head to toe as the elevator descended

"Holy Mother Mary"

and in the lobby the doorman's wife was shuffling in her slippers among the potted daffodils while I limped across the marble on a broken heel, with earrings that pinched my ears, with a ring that made my finger purple, and reeking of perfume, the tenant from the sixth floor, an engineer who worked for the gas company, looking as ready to faint as the doorman's wife, and the Minister holding my arm as energetically as Carlos, as confidently as Carlos, the Minister pushing me into the backseat more forcefully than Carlos pushed me into our seats at the movies, the Minister in an even more imperative voice than Carlos

"Palmela, Tomás"

his arm around my shoulder, his knee on top of my knee, his hand crawling over my thigh like a crab, and for the first time I didn't mind kissing him, for the first time I leaned against him like a helpless convalescent, sighing through the moth-eaten veil, with a taste of dusty cobwebs on my tongue, I becoming swampy, you know, slimy, as the crab's pincers ripped through fabrics and pushed aside my garter straps, and perhaps I could have felt passion for the Minister, like when you fall in love with someone and you miss them, you want to see them and talk to them on the phone, you think about them for hours while staring at the wall, you smile when they smile, you buy a notebook and write silly love poems and the like, perhaps I was beginning to like him, perhaps I was falling in love, his house in Palmela was huge, a woman with a bun and raised eyebrows waited for us, shaking her head as in the face of a disaster

"Say hello to Isabel, Titina"

Palmela was me limping on a broken high heel through a series of rooms with dozens of smocked maids as the sea on the other side of the mountain rocked like a cradle, and the Minister

"Isabel"

his lover or mother or wife or daughter to whom the Carnival garb belonged, and I, dying to get out of those rotting tatters that made me itch, loosening my collar, and hearing the fabric giving way, I with an aching right ankle and my finger black and blue from the ring, Titina slowly shaking her head with disgust behind us, serving us the lamb in silence, and in a mirror I saw my red cheeks, I who looked ever less like myself in mirrors, I who cease being myself in those glass ponds, the Minister worried about me

"Are you tired, Isabel, are you sleepy?"

I not thinking about Carlos, my mother, the Praça do Chile, or the shop, I looking like a 78 rpm record sleeve or a picture postcard bordered by doves and carnations, finding myself in a bedroom that smelled of mothballs and mortuary lavender just like me, and next to a vase of spikenard there was a picture of a girl my age with the shoes I had on, the purse I carried, and the ring, the earrings, and the dress I was wearing, a girl holding hands with a man who, on close examination, proved to be the Minister, a picture identical to what I saw in the mirror, and I on the bed, with my nose flattened against her nose, This is me, this is me, this is me, so engrossed in the photo that I didn't even notice the Minister tiptoe over to me, cover me with the bedspread, and kiss me tenderly on the forehead

"Titina said it would never happen, but I knew you'd come back, Isabel"

so engrossed that I didn't notice myself falling asleep over the spikenard, with mascara running down my cheeks like the tears of a lonely clown.

COMMENTARY

As if it weren't enough to have to put up with whores, pimps, transvestites, drug addicts who shoot up, and the scandal of married men who drive their wives to the park to watch them fornicate with other men, as if it weren't enough to have to put up with lesbians, pickpockets, and old men in raincoats who call us over and open up their coats to reveal not a scrap of clothing besides their shoes and socks, as if it weren't enough to have to put up with the drunks, beggars, and young men in the park who for a couple of bucks will do anything a pervert asks them to, as if it weren't enough for me to have to continuously chase them all away with a broom, call the police, and live with my wife in a crummy cubicle when everyone else in the building lives in luxury, a cubicle in the back of the building where mating cats howl all night long, and when I can't sleep I place a spoonful of poison in a pot of meatballs, coaxing the animals

"Here kitty kitty kitty"

in the vengeful hope of shoveling a few of their corpses into the garbage can while my wife wipes a tear or two with her sleeve

"Poor things"

my wife who's just begging for a nice hard smack that would knock out a couple of teeth, thereby increasing family harmony and giving her a good reason to cry, because I'm sick of her whining over nothing, and particularly over dead cats, let her weep over the plants in the lobby, so that I at least won't have to water them, as if it weren't enough to have to put up with the air-force brigadier forever complaining that the stairs are dirty, and I can just imagine what his barracks looks like with all those rural recruits who are used to living under the same roof with goats, as if it weren't enough to have to put up with the bishop who mumbles that the elevator smells funny, who would presumably like to travel up to the seventh floor with hands pressed together in a cloud of incense and Saint Peter waiting for him on his doormat with open arms, as if it weren't enough to have to put up with injections at Public Health for my aching back that just laughs at the syringes, as if all that weren't enough, the Minister had to saddle me with a couple of wenches, a mother and daughter, unearthed from one of the city's dank basement apartments in which the sewing machine, when not tacking on buttons, doubles as a card table or dining table, the older wench using pendants and pins to disguise herself as a younger wench but ready to keel over, her ankles so covered by varicose veins that they looked like blue screws perfect for screwing on slippers, and the younger wench disguised as an operetta soprano, rubbing her buttocks together like castanets on the stage of the Rua Castilho to the great consternation of the transvestites, since she lured away their clients, a pair of wenches who were ruining the reputation of the building, I explained to the building manager, who glanced around while motioning me to lower my voice

"Do you want to get tossed into the clinker, Leandro?"

the manager pulling at my arm and explaining that if the Minister so much as suspected that I wasn't keen on the wenches,

I'd be sent straight to the prison fort at Peniche, where I'd sleep on urine-drenched straw when I wasn't being tortured, the manager whispering into my ear that if the Minister suspected that I wasn't keen on the wenches, then he would also be sent to Peniche, for having hired a Communist spy as doorman

"If you don't treat them with due care, we'll both end up in the clinker"

the whores sauntering on the edge of the park, and they happened to be fine-looking lasses, so that if I were twenty and single, and my diabetes permitting, I'd surely indulge, I with a screwdriver pretending to fix the door lock while my diopters were fixed on their cute rear ends, and my wife, who was born with a setter's muzzle and makes my life hell when she's not whining

"What are you looking at, Leandro?"

fine-looking lasses, like the one last winter who crouched among the plants in the lobby to hide from the vice squad, three wagons that were plucking girls from the public gardens like so many lilies, and the lass pointing at her colleagues who twirled around their handbags

"As soon as the police clear out, I'll leave, don't tell them I'm here"

my wife in bed with the flu, swallowing jars of honey and effervescent aspirins, sprawled out on the mattress in a pair of my pajamas, and the lass right under my nose

"Don't tell them I'm here"

I had come out to the lobby to change a lightbulb when, lucky stars, this juicy and smooth-skinned creature grabbed my arm

"Don't tell them I'm here"

I, who would have run a razor over my chin if I'd known I'd be so lucky, leaning into her without believing it was true, feeling her scent of grass and trees, her firm skin, with no flab, the police loading her colleagues into the wagon and I pressing my shoulder against the lass's shoulder without her objecting, without her noticing me, too busy looking out for the vice squad, afraid one of the policemen would come with his stick raised to take her away, and suddenly my wife from her mound of blankets

"My lemon tea, Leandro"

as if she were ruthlessly knifing me to death

"My lemon tea, Leandro"

I, sorely defeated, marching as if in a funeral toward our crummy cubicle, seeing my wife's face twisted like a wet rag, all wrinkles, red splotches, swelling

"My lemon tea, Leandro"

I lighting the gas, which always made a loud pop and will one day blow everything up, I heating up the water, putting some lemon peels and sugar in the mug, hurriedly setting it on the nightstand

"I'll be right back"

and running to the lobby, but the wagon of the vice squad was already on its way to the station and there was no lass observing the night from the rubber plants on the steps, just a smoldering cigarette stub on the ground, its smoke swirling up to me as if in mockery, I staring at the swirl or at where the swirl had been as the building manager finished his warning about the wenches

"I, for one, wouldn't last a month on bread and water"

the older wench whose family visited the Rua Castilho en masse on Sundays, like a busload of hicks on a pilgrimage, to marvel like savages in loincloths at the electric system of the entrance door, at the elevators, at the wall tiles, at the mailboxes with the names of lawyers, assemblymen, and generals, the wench's family with little boys in suits and ties who only needed hats to pass for army recruits, pressing the switch to see the cut-crystal ceiling lamps light up, pulling the fire alarm to see the whole block quake with howls of panic, the firemen hacking away at the façade with their axes, the tenants rushing out onto the landings with porcelain vases and cases of silverware, and it wouldn't have surprised me had the wench's family brought maps and dictionaries, like Americans do, to find their way in the maze of corridors, and the manager, with a broomstick in hand to help me clean up the damage done by the firemen, making sure no one could hear us

"Not a word of complaint to the Minister, Leandro, don't forget about the prison fort of Peniche"

and as I surveyed the smashed flowerpots, pieces of brick, and cracked marble, with puddles of carbonic snow seething here and there, suddenly the younger wench, dressed up as if for a pope's coronation, emerged from the Bentley with the corporal walking behind her, weighed down by shopping bags of fine ladies' apparel, the manager ready to kiss her feet like an adoring page boy, smiling obsequiously

"Good afternoon, Miss"

and behind the corporal there were secret police, causing the alarmed transvestites to try to blend in with the plane trees, while the drug addicts galloped toward the park like a herd of terrified skeletons, and the manager to me, ingratiating himself to the wench

"Help Miss Milá with her bags, Leandro"

I, who if work weren't so scarce would have sent the building to the devil, silently cursing her while lugging her junk on my back like an African boy on a safari, and the older wench, with a brooch as big as an archery target on her chest, leading me to a room with a tiger skin on the floor and giving instructions as if talking to her slave

"Put that in the second drawer, Leandro"

the older wench sliding carved mahogany doors

"Put that on the right-hand shelf, Leandro"

and her Spartacus, namely me, beholding hanger after hanger of dresses, slacks, blouses, bodices, shawls, coats, leather jackets, printed cottons, sequins, and linen shirts, her Spartacus thinking of our ground-floor cubicle with a single closet made of dented metal and no tiger, the older wench putting a copper coin in my hand as if I were a disabled war veteran plying the sidewalk cafés with packs of paper hankies, lottery tickets, or stain remover

"That's for you, Leandro"

I who was beginning to like the Communists, since as soon as they came to power they'd hang all the rich people, since at least they wanted one and all to freeze in the snow and live in overcrowded apartments, sad and orphaned and wearing one of those fur caps, I thanking her for the humiliating coin when I should have pried open her jaws with forceps and dropped it down her gullet

"Thank you, ma'am"

I entering our apartment like an enraged beast and throwing the penny down the toilet with so much force it left a mark, and my wife

"Are you stoning the toilet, Leandro?"

my wife, on whom I should have kept a tighter rein, examining the damage

"Why don't you destroy the wineglasses on top of the buffet while you're at it, Leandro?"

I who, if it weren't for my age and my diabetes, would destroy her with the scaling knife, my wife who on Thursdays has her blind sister over for dinner, identical to her but with mica glasses, so that when I'm finally free of the tenants, the bill collectors, and the mail, when I finally cross my legs and open my sports journal to read up on national affairs, my blind sister-in-law, parked in front of the TV, tugs my sleeve and asks, with her nose tilted back

"They're showing a film, aren't they, Leandro?"

my blind sister-in-law, a culture hound, tapping me with her cane, tapping me with her foot

"Tell me how the film goes, Leandro"

and as if I didn't have enough troubles aggravating my diabetes to the point of my having to switch from pills to capsules, not to mention a cataract that throws the world out of focus and a blocked kidney that means no more cherry liqueur, with the wenches came the secret police, causing the lasses to flee to the far end of the park and leaving me to languish in solitude, and to add to my troubles, I was polishing the mahogany in the lobby with cedar oil and still hadn't taken my bath when the trees stopped rustling and a dead hush fell over the street, over the city

cars, people, voices, Dumpsters, horns

and in walks Professor Salazar with his soft, nunnish footsteps, waving his translucent fingers at the flowers in the lobby to make sure they cheered, and with Professor Salazar the inevitable Admiral, cutting invisible inaugural ribbons with a huge pair of scissors and followed by a retinue of sailors decked out like Vasco da Gama, and with the Admiral the inevitable languishing Cardinal, pale from so many fasts and saintly mortifications, offering his ring to be kissed by the mailboxes and wall lights, and with the Cardinal the inevitable Major in charge of the secret police, gray and cagey and lonely, like a widowed bank employee, all of them meeting in the wenches' apartment to make decisions about miracles in Fátima and concentration camps, the manager calling me aside, pointing at the ceiling, and whispering in panic

"Have they already left, Leandro?"

the red ampoule of the elevator lighting up, the ground-floor arrow flashing, the larva of a figure in the cocoon of the elevator dimly visible through the glass, the manager buttoning his coat, I at my desk buttoning my coat, pissed off at my wife for not having ironed my shirt, the manager tuning his throat to belt out a good evening, sir, but it wasn't Professor Salazar, nor was it the Admiral or the Cardinal or the Major or the Minister, it was that goddamn older wench with a brooch as big as an archery target pinned to her apron, the wench puffing up in my direction like a countess in difficulty

"Do you by any chance have a tea bag of green tea, Leandro?"

all year long in fur-lined slippers and a black blouse with floral patterns and sequins that was the envy of my wife, who adores trash

"Do you by any chance have a tea bag of green tea, Leandro?"

as if she owned the whole world, just because her daughter was the Minister's mistress, just because her daughter was maintained by Professor Salazar's friend, a close-mouthed bumpkin who didn't even reply to my good day, sir, who flicked ashes into the plants every time he walked in and snuffed out his cigarillos in the soil of the flowerpots

you can write down bumpkin, don't worry, you can write down bumpkin, I'm not afraid

and the manager, treating the older wench with every courtesy

"Don't you have a tea bag of green tea for Dona Dores, Leandro?"

the manager, who dropped the courtesies and the "Donas" after the Minister stopped paying the rent and two police vans arrived to remove tables, buffets, sofas, and watercolors from the apartment, after the gas, water, and electricity were cut off, after employees from the shoe stores, clothing stores, jewelry shop, hairdresser's, and butcher shop started showing up with unpaid bills, threats of lawsuits, and writs of attachment, after the wenches no longer dared to leave the apartment, answer the doorbell, talk loudly, shuffle their slippers, clack the dishes, let a drawer squeak, or make any noise whatsoever, and the manager entering our cubicle where my blind sister-in-law was asking me to explain the film

"We've got to evict the wenches, Leandro"

my blind sister-in-law anxiously pulling at my pants leg and turning her nose toward the voice

"Is it a Portuguese film, Leandro?"

the wenches' apartment door tightly locked and the manager pulling keys out of his pocket

"Miss Milá, Dona Dores"

and I began to smell the spikenard, in the same way you can smell the sea before reaching the sea I began to smell the spikenard, the manager trying one key after another, "Goddamn, goddamn"

"Miss Milá, Dona Dores"

if I had looked out the window, I would have seen the statue of the Marquis of Pombal floating in a low tide of streetlamps, the Marquis with his back turned to me like the manager, who kept repeating "Goddamn, goddamn" while separating the keys, inspecting them, uselessly inserting them into the lock, the manager, "Goddamn, goddamn," wiping his neck with his handkerchief

"Miss Milá, Dona Dores"

and I thinking, "Maybe the wenches aren't answering because they passed away, they left the gas on or took pills and are dead," I smelling the spikenard's melancholy fragrance and imagining bodies lying facedown, joints turned inside out, the unexpected intimacy of nakedness, the legs more inanimate than the shoes, I imagining empty medicine bottles and a fermenting red puddle on the floor, I thinking, "I don't want to see them," and the manager with a new bunch of keys, "Goddamn, goddamn," the statue of the marquis falling off its pedestal and floating down the avenue toward the river, the statue of the marquis swaying back and forth

goddamn, goddamn

as it passed by anemic monuments on its way to the sea, sailing over houses that had been leveled and salted by his order,* and the spikenard's fragrance increased, the latch finally clicked open, and we found ourselves in the foyer of the apartment that was now just nails in the wall, cracked plaster, and places for pictures without any pictures, the place for a hat stand without a hat stand, the place for a table without a table, scraps of paper on the floor, the dust of abandonment, the filth of disorder, what had probably been a sweater and was now a rag that the draft caused to flutter on the spindle of a chair, the manager, "Goddamn, goddamn," while crossing through room after deserted room, windows without curtains, the remains of a glazed earthenware pitcher in a niche whose shelves were in pieces, a fringed shawl in a corner, the head of the tiger-skin rug without its crystal eyes, facing sideways like my blind sister-in-law

"They're showing a film, aren't they, Leandro?"

a film about a home with nobody illuminated by the fragrance of flowers and the shadows of July, illuminated by the neon advertisement for an insurance company that alternately flashed the time and temperature, its light sliding down from the ceiling to the floor, perfume bottles, tortoiseshell cases, fingernail polish, combs, brushes, and tubes of cream piled up haphazardly, and then the kitchen with no stove, no hot water heater, casseroles, or tureens, a counter with nothing on it, a pantry with cans and empty cartons, the manager with his hand over his mouth, "Goddamn, goddamn"

"Miss Milá"

examining chests, examining nooks

"Dona Dores"

the spikenard's fragrance spreading, growing, exploding when we entered the bedroom where there was a bed but no mattress, no sheets, no pillows, no pillowcases, just the headboard, springs, and slats, and the rest of the furniture amounted to just the nightstand with a stem poking out of an enamel vase and the photo of a girl with blond hair the way girls wore it when I was young and single, the way they wore it at the theater, at the casino, a girl dressed in an old-fashioned polka-dot skirt, staring at me bashfully, staring at me mockingly, staring at me from out of the frame with a kind of docile pity.

REPORT

How long ago did everything I've been telling you happen? Fifteen, twenty years? More? Twenty-five? Thirty? If you say thirty, okay, maybe it's thirty, I don't know: I could never keep dates straight, and since my mother died my mind's always somewhere else, I live alone and run the notions store by myself, since it's not worth hiring a helper, weeks can go by without a single customer, the shop deserted and me staring at the Praça do Chile from behind the empty cash register, waiting for the shade to creep across the floor and reach the shelves before I get up, place the shutters across the front of the shop, padlock the door, and go home, to an apartment that has become much larger since I live alone, in a neighborhood that's now much smaller: there's a supermarket where the mattress warehouse used to be, there's no more hairdresser, the stained and faded heads cut out of magazines and pasted on the window having disappeared along with the assistants in clogs who used to show off their legs and smile at men from the balcony, the assistants who've all gotten married or died or moved far away, the pool hall gave way to a pastry shop that specializes in baptism parties and wedding receptions, with cakes that resemble Chinese pagodas, four or five stories high and topped by a happy couple made of sugar and surrounded by orange blossoms and marzipan roses, I know almost no one around here except old women, not aging women but old, old women, definitively old women, old women wearing scarves that are black or that were black and are now gray, suspicious old women who are angry at the world, who hang their necks out of tiny windows, baring one or two resentful teeth to the indifference of the street. Old women who don't talk to me and whom I don't talk to, a row of old women hanging out of a row of tiny windows, all of them cruel, all of them on the lookout, all of them equal, each with her parakeet in a cage with a squid bone stuck between the wires, old women whose number I'll soon join if I keep living, old women in whose lungs air passes through dusty caverns before coming back out as words, speeches they spit out and no one listens, bitter complaints and no one pays attention, old women who exchange their minuscule pensions for wormy apples and slices of eel displayed on the street vendors' tricycles, their pensions that they keep in tiny cloth bags, counting out penny by stingy penny, with lapses of memory that prompt fits of rage

"I've been robbed, it was you, you robbed me, I've been robbed"

old women who limp to the 7 A.M. mass in straggly herds, hunched as if they carried their own weight on their backs, old women who ceremoniously bring their parakeets in at night as if they were treasures, parakeets that resemble them with their squeaky murmurs and hooked beaks and halting gait, old women at the pawnshop opening pieces of tattered quilt and foisting unmatching forks, statuettes of Father Cruz, and ivory rosaries on the proprietor

"The Virgin Mary will understand, Dona Anunciação"

old women who dream of having dentures so that they can dream of walking out of the butcher's at Christmastime with a half-pound of steak wrapped in brown paper, old women who sleep fitfully and struggle with aching joints, the sponge of their asthma, failing hearts, frightfully pulling back their feet from the edge of their graves, old women holding on to life with wrinkled tenacity, and except for old women and parakeets I know practically no one around here, it's been fifteen, twenty, twenty-five, thirty years, okay, thirty years, let's say thirty years, I won't argue, I never counted them, thirty years since my mother and I returned to the Praça do Chile from the apartment that the Minister rented for me on the Rua Castilho, and we found the shop invaded by the stench of broken pipes and the gluttony of moths, thousands of moths with white wings like angels, thousands of larvae crawling over the counter, thousands of clusters of eggs in the woodwork, and there were the swaths of serge and velvet and chintz and a fabric with a label that said wool and that we guaranteed was wool

"Look at the label, do you think the English would lie, I'm not talking about the Portuguese but about the English, do you think the English would lie?"

but of course it wasn't wool, it was synthetic, the swaths all reduced to a skeleton of threads, a ribwork of filaments, fringes of veins that disintegrated in our fingers, my mother spraying so much poison against the seraphim, the larvae of the seraphim, and the eggs of the seraphim that the old women in the windows and the old women's parakeets coughed till they choked, and the TB victims from the diagnostic center fell onto the asphalt flailing their scrawny legs every which way, and the next week my mother, after sweeping up all the dead angels and the

dead angels' offspring, settled in behind the counter, and I sat
on the throne of the cash register, my mother still with her fancy
evening blouse and the brooch with yellow stones, and I wearing a hat with Bakelite peaches and pineapples and a tattered
veil, a polka-dot dress, see-through stockings, a black garter belt
sliding down my hips, a purse without the clasp, crocodile shoes
with a broken heel, and a ring so small it made my finger turn
blue, the two of us in the shop and not one customer, not one
lousy customer to buy one lousy pack of buttons, or a pack of
needles, or a few inches of ribbon, what ever happened to the
two or three women who used to buy from us or who didn't
buy anything but who spent all afternoon talking, what happened to Carlos, Américo, and Fernando, who waved at me from
the doorway, who gave me knowing winks, who signaled that
they'd be waiting for me by the freight trucks at the Largo do
Mitelo, or next to the geese and the plaster saint crowned by
candles at Campo de Santana, Carlos, Américo, and Fernando,
who would pound me in a hurry, kiss me in a hurry

"Oh God, oh God"

Carlos, Fernando, and Américo, who were now perhaps
in jail, or on the run in Spain, or hiding out in the Alentejo hills,
chewing on stones for the sin of having temporarily held on to
a few jewels for some friends, a few TVs, a few dozen transistor
radios perhaps stolen by mistake, perhaps stolen by accident, and
intended as surprise presents for relatives in the interior, my
mother at the counter and I on the throne of the cash register,
pushing on the drawer that continually opened its mouth as if
hungry for a few bills, my mother and I looking at each other
and at the empty street until 7 P.M., and at 7 P.M. the Praça do
Chile deserted, the old women sticking one or two teeth out their

tiny windows, Dona Catarina, Dona Mercês, Dona Aninhas, Dona Anunciação, old women moving about in the darkness amid sighs, photos of sergeants with mustaches, bunches of lavender, eyeglass frames held together by Scotch tape, rusty medals, my mother and I looking at each other and at our cramped apartment wedged between other cramped apartments, at the tiny windows of Dona Lurdes and of Dona Sara, at the windows between cages of clumsy, half-crippled parakeets that squeeze their heads into sad kisses, at the laundry tank where the wasps buzz in summer, and when my father couldn't sleep he would sit with his elbows on the plastic tablecloth, hating me in silence, my father whom I can scarcely remember because I scarcely remember my childhood, I remember a file of ants marching in both directions along a crack in the wall, I remember my ailing grandmother asking for a glass of muscatel, convinced that glasses of muscatel would make her get better, I remember walking on tiptoe to increase my height and age, but most of all I remember the file of ants disappearing one by one between two floorboards and reappearing one by one with the same relentless and useless determination, I remember the ants and don't remember my father, neither his gestures, nor his voice, nor what he liked to eat, whether pork slices, cuttlefish, snails with onions, or salt cod, the ants frantically hard at work, the same ants after all these years, my mother and I in this cramped apartment between other cramped apartments, and after my mother's death just me in this cramped apartment between other cramped apartments, without any photos of sergeants with mustaches, without bunches of lavender, without eyeglass frames held together by Scotch tape, without rusty medals, I who'd lived in a six-bedroom apartment on the Rua Castilho, with a tiger rug that grinned at me ferociously and with no parakeet in a cage chewing on a squid bone stuck between the wires, my mother stepping toward the stove and frowning at how I was done up

"You no longer need to dress up like that, Milá"

the polka-dot dress, the crocodile shoes with a broken heel, the hat with a veil, the circles of shiny rouge on my cheeks, I with the face of a chinaware girl from the Minho, of a Catholic martyr, of a fairy-tale princess, and my mother stepping toward the stove to stir the spaghetti while the ants marched with zealous obstinacy along the baseboard

"You no longer need to dress up for that shameless Minister, Milá"

the Minister who the day before he sent us away took me to Estoril to visit Professor Salazar in a castle next to the Tagus, a castle built on huge rocks penetrated by the rushing waves and the waves' foam, and the heavy earrings made my ears sore, I saw the world through the grid of my veil, a nail from a high heel dug into my foot, and the wind blowing through the palm trees that whined on the battlements loosened my hairpins and scattered my perfume, a castle built on huge rocks next to the Tagus

(Dona Catarina, Dona Mercês, Dona Aninhas, Dona Rita, Dona Anunciação)

with one, two, three bronze cannons dripping seaweed onto the stone wall, the Minister snapping his suspenders and grabbing me round the waist with his pincers

"Isabel"

the Tagus was obviously distressed, raging against the huge rocks in between the whining of the palm trees, there was a pond full of bearded goldfish with transparent whiskers on their chins like on the old women hanging out of their tiny windows, the fish hiding in the shade of the grass like the old women in their shadowy hovels crammed with worthless treasures, tarnished marvels scorned by the pawnbroker

(Dona Adozinda)

and behind the pond Professor Salazar and the Cardinal waiting for us, I holding on to a stalk of spikenard, a broken stalk with wilted flowers, the Minister proud of us

"My wife"

the Minister whose age kept changing as he looked at me, he gaining or losing hair, wrinkles, and stomach according to whether or not I smiled at him

"You love me, Isabel, don't you?"

searching for his lighter with a nervousness that made me feel sorry for him, the Minister illuminated and extinguished by the time and temperature of the insurance company, by the streetlamps, by the park's trees and the boats' lanterns refracted on the ceiling, the Minister suspended on the pillow, questioning like a child

"You love me, Isabel, don't you?"

the Minister to Professor Salazar, proud of us, yelling over the waves' crashing and the palm trees' whining

"My wife"

(Dona Lavínia, Dona Ortelinda, Dona Ester, and my mother's cousin who lived in the neighborhood of Campolide and who even wore proper shoes, she was called Guiomar da Conceição Pedrosa and always had a tin of cookies that she shared with no one, Guiomar da Conceição Pedrosa munching with her calloused gums on cookies that were mostly crumbs, suspiciously clutching her tin lest someone steal it, Guiomar da

Conceição Pedrosa dressing up for her doctor visits in a paisley shawl that was once a curtain and using her husband's denture that was too big for her, Guiomar da Conceição Pedrosa getting on the streetcar at Arco do Carvalhão with the tin of cookies under her arm and a dozen false teeth from her late husband that she kept pushing back into her mouth with her hand and tongue, Dona Guiomar, Dona Lídia, Dona Celeste, Dona Maria do Sepulcro)

and Professor Salazar in a sparrow's cheep, touching me with the fluttery silk of his fingers

"My pleasure"

Professor Salazar, who ruled over the whole country, over the military and the Church, asking me questions and delighted by my answers, concerned about me, offering me toasts, fruit drinks, cakes, dishes of strawberries, Professor Salazar, with his skinny legs pressed together and a napkin on his knees, wanting to know all about the Praça do Chile, about my mother, about the notions store, Professor Salazar treating me with respect, addressing me as miss, the waves rushing in and out of the castle's tunnels, the lighthouse shedding green tears for I don't know whom, the palm trees whining outside, Professor Salazar, who seemed incapable of having people arrested, tortured, and shipped off to Africa to die from poisonous snake bites, Professor Salazar so helpful, so gentle, so considerate, taking my hand in his own delicate hand, the delicate and insecure hand of a little girl, Professor Salazar hanging on my words, begging me to go on whenever I stopped talking

"Is that right?"

Professor Salazar, who couldn't have hurt a flea, holding a miniature custard tart between his fingers, lamenting that the

Americans and the English didn't understand and that the Pope was ingenuous, that he didn't realize what the Communist bishops were plotting in Rome, that he defended blacks in Africa who were knifing white people to death, the waves hurling albatrosses against the windows like so many pebbles, the beam from the lighthouse casting a green tint on the Cardinal who deplored the students' ingratitude and then vanishing into the horizon, taking with it the Cardinal, the palm trees, the castle, the Minister, the English, the Americans, the toasts, the fruit drinks, the cakes, the dishes of strawberries, the general who ran against the government* in the elections, and the supporters of the general who ran against the government in the elections, I wishing it would take everything with it and leave me alone, as I am now in the notions store at the Praça do Chile, completely alone, I who one day soon

(Dona Milá, Dona Milá)

will stick one or two teeth out the window and hide in covered pots my worthless bibelots, a glass paperweight with the Tower of Belém

(Dona Belém)

a dried-out starfish, a picture of me when young with an oil stain, curtain rings, postcards from a cousin in Vila do Conde

(Dear Cousin, I hope that this)

white metal earrings missing the clasps, I sticking a squid bone through the wires of the cage and the parakeet squeezing its little head into a kiss, I rushing about with gout-rusted joints, with ankles as stiff as a hippo's, and the Minister introduced me to the Admiral, to the Major in charge of the secret police whose eyes weren't to be found on his face but on his glasses, glued there like two tiny cardboard circles

"My wife"

the Major, toast in hand, breaking into a smile as if he believed it, a smile in which only his lips smiled, his eyes remaining spent

"My pleasure"

the Major who, as soon as the Minister drew away, helped Professor Salazar decide the fate of the general

("Kill him, arrest him, kill him, it's better to kill him, kill him")

who ran in the election against the government, and I sat still on the sofa, teacup in hand, surrounded by albatrosses, snipes, palm trees, and waves, I with a polka-dot dress, a hat with a veil, spikenard in my lap, and a nail from a high heel that dug into my foot, tearing at my muscles, tendons, and bones, I without the courage to remove my gloves, to loosen the strings of my corset, to lift my veil, I with torn see-through stockings

("My wife")

struggling to get spoonfuls of whipped cream through the openings of my veil, the waves pounding at the floor and making the furniture rattle, destroying floorboards, making books fall from the shelves, and the Major approaching me with his spent-eyed smile and an air of respect, speaking softly out of the corner of his mouth

"If you don't play along, you're going straight to the prison at Caxias, my dear hussy"

the Major still smiling, stepping on me, pressing his thumbnail into the back of my neck, dumping the whole sugar bowl into my tea

"If you don't play along, you're going straight to the prison at Caxias, my dear hussy"

a horizon of seagulls and foam topped by tugboats, a tanker sailing up the Tagus, dragging itself forward as if with crutches, swollen, and lopsided like the parakeets of the Praça do Chile limping in their cages, and Professor Salazar talking to me again, laughing with me, excusing himself for a moment as he ordered the general to be arrested

"Arrest him, kill him, arrest him, it's better to arrest him, arrest him"

the Major attentively removing a hair from the Minister's lapel, the Major gallantly extending his arm to help me stand up, the Major bowing to the Minister and smiling his spent eyes at me, kissing the ring that strangled my finger and feeling around with his shoe for my toe, so that he could step on it yet again

"You have a charming wife, Senhor Minister, you can't imagine how I envy you"

the Major who would pretend to be looking at the mannequins in the shop windows when I walked out of the building on the Rua Castilho, who would pretend to be looking at the homosexuals when I walked into the building on the Rua Castilho, whom I would see at night if I looked out the window, an orange figure lit up and swallowed by a blinking neon sign, the Major who didn't talk on TV, who didn't greet foreign dignitaries, who didn't inaugurate hospitals or schools, whose picture didn't appear in the papers, who existed without existing, who lived without living, taking his leave of me and the Minister with a carnivorous appetite

"Miss Milá"

his spent eyes, crowned by snipes, warning me

"Straight to Caxias"

I with the nail digging into my foot, limping on the shoe heel that got stuck in the gravel, measuring the ten yards that separated us from the car as if they were ten miles, thinking, I can't do it, not one more step, I can't walk, the palm trees whining, the castle listing under the onslaught of the waves, Professor Salazar and the Cardinal like drowning men bidding farewell from the battlements, I wanted to go back, to save them, to bring them with us, but my feet were unwilling, I still made out a cassock before it sank out of existence, I still saw a man before the beam from the lighthouse swept him out of sight, the earrings were torturing my ears, the see-through stockings were unraveling on my legs, the corselette crushed my ribs, the spikenard drooped in my hand, the ring was making my finger gangrenous, and the Minister, placing his hand in mine

"To the farm, Tomás"

the Minister into my ear

"You love me, Isabel, don't you?"

while at the Praça do Chile there's nothing but tiny windows, parakeets, and old women

Dona Lúcia, Dona Andrelina, Dona Flávia, Dona Benilde, Dona Alzira

whetting their teeth on their sniveling resentment, when Dona Natividade passed away her door was left open, the coffin was placed in the middle of the living room, with a candle in each of the four corners and a bouquet of cheap flowers propped against the wall but no one to keep watch, the candlelight revealing pictures of saints on the wall, an enamel bidet, a bicycle tire, and a tiny stove, Dona Natividade's parakeet staggering around its cage, puffing up its feathers, chewing on its squid bone, stretching its body to squeeze out a kiss

"Peep"

and Dona Natividade all alone in a child-size coffin baring her one tooth to the ceiling, her door remaining open for an entire week, until gypsies or else beggars from the no-man's-land made off with the stove and the bouquet of flowers, leaving a whirl of blowflies in their stead, the parakeet forever chewing its squid bone and warbling in its cage, one step here one step there, outside the tiny window

"Peep"

and the same thing will happen to me one day, when I also chew my soup with toothless gums, I who used to be different, I to whom Professor Salazar would pay his respects, nodding his head

"My pleasure"

to whom Professor Salazar offered toasts, cakes, custard tarts, and herbal teas, I who knew the Admiral, I peeling a sprouting potato over a casserole, distrusting the street vendor's scale when I exchange my minuscule pension for a few wormy apples and slices of eel, I mumbling prayers to a plastic, glow-in-the-dark Virgin on the shelf with an empty package of macaroni, an empty package of beans, an empty package of rice, prayers mixed in with nonsense phrases, my mother's reprimands, scraps of children's ditties, "Who wants to see the beautiful boat that's setting out to sea," forgetting the year, the month, the hour, and my own name, losing my temper at my parents who died ages ago, whistling for the dog that I never had, that I'm sure I never had, that maybe I did have, that I definitely never had, that I must have had, I arguing with dead people as if they were right here, dead people who opposed me, who wouldn't let me leave, who accused me, I getting lost on my way to church and spending the whole afternoon wandering around Martim Moniz, kneeling on street corners, crossing myself before banks, sticking my fingers in the holy water of public fountains, gesticulating at the truck drivers and card players of the Largo do Mitelo when they make fun of me

"Hey there, good-looking"

showing them my cane that will weigh more than me, losing my balance, steadying myself on a step from where stray cats will flee, spitting out a street urchin's obscenities heard by no one and learned I don't know where

"Faggots, motherfuckers, sons of bitches"

flustered by the neon signs of the bars and discothèques, by all the dark glasses, by the colorful T-shirts and chain bracelets of the Cape Verdean construction workers, I reaching the Praça do Chile in the wee hours, led back there by scent or by a change in the air, like turtledoves returning to their dovecote, settling into the nest of my gutted mattress with drooping eyelids and a piece of bread in my dirty claws that I'll soak in some leftover broth, my parakeet tearing at the squid bone with swaying motions, as if drunk on cheap wine

"Peep"

and the Minister straightening the spikenard, sniffing it, leaning back in the seat, straightening my hat and the clasp of my necklace as he probingly whispered

"You love me, Isabel, don't you?"

don't call me Isabel because that's not my name it's your mother's or your lover's or your daughter's or your wife's name I don't care whose but don't call me Isabel, my name isn't Isabel it's Milá, Dona Milá, I live on a cross street of tiny windows with other old women who have just one or two teeth and moldy, lacy vertebrae, Dona Catarina, Dona Mercês, Dona Aninhas, Dona Rita, Dona Anunciação, and the elms of Palmela, the mountains of Arrábida, the unemployed on the square, the woman with the bun

(Titina, I think it was, Titina)

shaking her disgusted head on the front steps, the arbor, the greenhouse, the chapel, the table all set, and the phone suddenly ringing, the Minister's features suddenly changing, his wrinkles getting deeper, deep with hatred, the Minister looking at me

"Since when do you want to leave me, Isabel, don't lie"

and the woman with the bun

(Titina, I think it was, Titina)

wringing her hands in her apron, all embarrassed, shooing the maids into the kitchen like a pack of turkeys, the phone ringing with monotonous insistence and the Minister throwing down his napkin and advancing toward me in a furious whirl

"It's your boyfriend waiting for you at the square, Isabel, it's your boyfriend who's come to get you, don't lie"

the Minister, who was talking not to me but to his mother or lover or daughter or wife, whoever, as he packed a mildewy suitcase and a dusty trunk with dresses as old as my polka-dot dress, with purses and gloves and shoes as old as the purse and gloves and shoes I was wearing, with ridiculous hats adorned with Bakelite flowers and fruits and as old as the ridiculous hat that kept sliding down my forehead, the Minister to a man whom I'd never seen, who wore a rope instead of a belt and who stared in bewilderment from the doorway

"Your mother wants to go away and leave us, João, your mother doesn't care about us"

the man staring at me in confusion, whining like an orphan on the verge of tears

"Titina"

and the plaster angels turned their heads to watch me as I went down the steps dragging the mildewy suitcase, dragging the dusty trunk, the angels with their heads still turned as I hurried down the drive through the cypress trees, limping on my broken high heel and pursued by the dogs' barking.

COMMENTARY

I honestly have no idea what you're talking about. I'm an officer in the army, a lieutenant colonel in the reserve, and if I didn't rise any higher it wasn't for lack of merit but because I enlisted as a buck private with just a third-grade education, having moved up in the ranks to private first class, then corporal, then sergeant, second lieutenant when I was forty, first lieutenant at age forty-six, and captain at fifty, if I didn't rise any higher it's because my way was blocked by the rich brats of the military academy, who never knew hard times and never went hungry, they had it easy from birth and looked down their noses at me as if they were viscounts, treating me with rude arrogance, humiliating me, not talking to me in the officers' mess, not asking me to play cards or dice when they needed a partner, keeping me from being promoted through stealth, schemes, conspiracies, hush-hush talks with their godfathers who controlled the military, with their brigadier fathers-in-law, with their uncles who were generals

(my wife's grandfather was a turner in Viseu and my uncle a drunk in Serpa, he spent most of the year sleeping off his beer in the local jail, and I doubt that either of them, however handy they were with an adjustable wrench and a long-neck bottle, had any great influence on the decisions of the Minister of Defense)

so that I, having no high-placed godfather, uncle, or father-in-law, finished up as a lieutenant colonel in the reserve, and how you discovered me in this house in Madre de Deus is beyond me, since our address and phone number aren't listed in the Lisbon directory under my name but under that of my wife's father, who died a few months before I met her, this house which, for being a low-income duplex, is really pretty nice, with a bed of begonias in front, a bed of begonias out back, and a row of lettuces that I planted next to the fence, in the late afternoon I bring out a chair, the *Artillery Review,* and a beach umbrella, I put on my sunglasses and dab some sunscreen on my nose and forehead, and until suppertime I look at the lettuces, learn about mortar shells, and reminisce about Serpa, not that my memories of Serpa are so great, but between thinking back to Serpa and thinking about the life I lead today, Serpa wins hands down, in Serpa at least no one scornfully compared me, twenty times a day, to a dead section head from the phone company who weighed two hundred forty pounds, and my wife carries him around her neck in a gold, heart-shaped locket, God knows how she can breathe with all that lard pressing down on her chest, a section head from the phone company who communicates with his daughter every Thursday via long-distance calls over the switchboard of a three-legged table operated by a clairvoyant in Chelas, who justifies charging a fortune to connect to paradise with the argument that if it costs a lot to call the United States, then you can't expect calls to heaven to be cheap, "Compare the number of miles, Dona Emília, multiply the number of units, add up the total and you'll see," so that her father's pension is frittered away on calls to the beyond, leaving it up to me, with my pension, to maintain her and the house, which entitles me to hear her complain without letup about the day she met me and I filled the house with my gun collection, such that you never know when one will explode through the roof, not to mention the noise, the smell of gunpowder, and the inconvenience to our next-door neighbors, who got upset when a shell fell in their yard and pulverized the chickens, leaving behind just these feathers, look, and a clucking from an unidentifiable source, and besides pulverizing the chickens it riddled the laundry on the clothesline

"Come here and look at this, Dona Emília"

beyond recognition, because I happen to spend a lot of time wiping my guns, because everything in this world gets dusty, as you know, I mean if even the most concealed feelings gather all kinds of dust, then imagine the dust on objects not stored in cases, so I spend lots of time wiping the dust from my guns and *boom,* a loud noise, a column of smoke, and the Church of Beato becomes a bonfire, a car lot becomes a scrap heap, and the barbecued chicken place in Marvila turns into smoldering embers, which at least saves the owners money on charcoal, my wife praising her lately departed who, in spite of his enormousness, was peaceful and loved silence, who never bothered anyone, entertaining himself with stamps and butterflies, which fortunately make no noise, and he so abhorred charred chicken, blazes, and explosions that he didn't even bathe, being afraid to turn on the gas for the hot water heater, and so in the late afternoon, when I'm tired of putting up with her, I bring out a chair, the *Artillery Review,* and a beach umbrella, I put on my sunglasses and dab some sunscreen on my nose and forehead, and if a shell zooms out the window I shrug my shoulders, if a mortar should do away with the train station and the Jewish cemetery, making a purée of train cars and tombstones, I raise my arm with glee, and until suppertime I look at the lettuces, read up on mortar shells, and reminisce about Serpa, the amaryllises, the wood pigeons, the thistles, and goiters, dozens of goiters getting fresh air on the bandstand, but as to the matter that brings you here, I'm afraid I don't know what you're talking about, I don't understand all this jabber about Salazars and the New State, or about ministers, ministers' girlfriends, and Ruas Castilhos, but if that's what interests you, then okay, I was indeed a sergeant at the time of the revolution, and before becoming a sergeant I was naturally a corporal, a corporal who worked as a chauffeur, but I don't see how the opinions of a thirty-year-old corporal who had just been promoted from private first class could be of interest for your book, yes my name is Tomás, yes I was stationed many years ago at Commerce Square, but instead of us talking, wouldn't it be better if I bring you a chair and a beach umbrella so that we can enjoy the late afternoon, we don't need to talk, we can listen to the peacocks in the woods, and when it gets so dark we can no longer see each other, you can stick your papers and tape recordings in your briefcase and go away without asking any questions, since it's useless to dig up the past, you can forget everything and pretend you never saw me in your life, you can leave Salazar who's already kicked the bucket in peace, leave the Minister who's rotting away at some hospital in peace, when it gets so dark we can no longer see each other, just forget about me, as I'll forget about you, and presto, case closed, I'll keep looking after my vegetables in peace and keep on getting old in peace, have you noticed the sheen on vegetables as night begins to fall, the shimmer of the lemon tree, how everything becomes clear and sharp just before nightfall, the outline of the rooftops, the outline of the windows, the startled rippling of the curtains, a mossy growth or microscopic crack in the wall that we'd never noticed and that now looms enormous, have you noticed how sounds and voices change color, how they become intimate, close and unsettling, how we seem to live in a bell jar of silhouettes and echoes, I'd sometimes drive the Minister to the farm in September and feel myself floating among the cedars, hanging from an invisible wire like the sparrow hawks and kites over Serpa in summer, exactly in the same place each morning, day after day, the sparrow hawks and kites that are probably still there, like me in Palmela stationed between the kennels and the rose-bushes, with the German shepherds panting against the iron grating, looking at me with their sad, resigned eyes, and Dona Titina calling me from the steps with a feather duster in one hand while she straightens her bun with the other

"How about a bowl of soup, Tomás?"

I at the kitchen table between the gardener and the tractor driver while the Minister strutted around the house with a girl dressed like a scarecrow that he dug out of a seedy notions store at the Praça do Chile, a girl half his age who wasn't pretty, or even cute, or even very clean, a girl you wouldn't even notice if you passed her in the street, a bit dumpy, a bit awkward, a bit lethargic, I can't imagine what the man saw in her, if at least she were intelligent or charming, but she wasn't, she was a bashful dishrag, a frightful blob, a fearful shiver down the spine, the Minister strutting around the house with the scarecrow who hobbled about in worn-out, moldy shoes, doting on her, pampering her, waiting on her, hardly daring to touch her lest she shatter, the Minister who at Commerce Square, next to the Tagus River and without the dishrag, would regain his fury, authority, and disdain

"You're going with the police to Spain to nab the general,* Tomás"

three cars with foreign license plates and the head of the police squad at my side, a huge Indian who told me stories about the prisons in Tarrafal and Peniche, about the guy who went crazy and claimed he was King Afonso Henriques, about the guy who hanged himself, about the guy who drank his own urine from out of his cupped hands, the Indian who slapped me on the back during the whole journey, and we came to the sparrow hawks and the kites hovering motionless since my childhood over fields of cork and yellowish olive trees, we came to the well at the bottom of which we found my uncle one day, we looked down and there he was, smiling up at us, when I shave in the morning he sometimes grins at me from out of the mirror with his blue teeth, a row of blue teeth planted in blue gums that sneer at me, sparrow hawks and kites, yellow olive trees, rats, silence, the identical squalor of the Serpa I once knew and whose mere memory makes me want to vomit, and the guy who drank his urine, the guy in the inferno of Tarrafal who crawled around in circles growling, groping for his own feces to assuage his hunger, until the olive trees finally gave way to scattered hills, dry wheat singed by the frost, a wooden bridge over a river that amounted to a few reeds with a useless boat tied to a stalk, and after the river

(look at the sheen on the lettuces now, at the shimmer on the lemon tree, the window, the crocheted curtains, the fence, notice how everything becomes clear and sharp and tends toward the night)

after the river there was a windmill amid boulders, two or three stone pines full of bees, tiny golden dots as if the trees had sneezed, sun-bleached sentry boxes on the border, the Indian exhibiting passports, the guy who ate his feces crying with his head between his hands, a matching windmill on the other side, along with more golden bees and two or three stone pines, so that it seemed like we were repeating the trip we'd just made, through olive trees, wheat singed by the frost, birds with splayed wings pinned to the sky, and the Minister, who's now rotting away at some hospital, calling me to his office, where the Major was showing him documents, photos, and letters

"You're going with the police in my stead to Spain to nab the general"

the potbellied general, with a toupee and a false mustache, holed up in a cheap hotel with his secretary, we saw them arrive there on foot like leisurely tourists, we saw them walk through the front door, we saw them go up to their room, drinking urine, eating feces, answering questions on their feet as a flashlight glared in their eyes and contorted figures screamed in the darkness, we saw the blinds lower, the balcony go dark, the Indian who told stories about Tarrafal and Peniche no longer talking about the arrival of prisoners on ships from Lisbon nor about diarrhea, malaria, and the stench of dead people, the Indian no longer exulting in the memory of corpses nor slapping me on the back, the Indian seething with inexplicable hatred for the potbellied general with a toupee who was somewhere behind the darkened blinds

"Fucking swine"

the Indian hissing into my ear

"I'll kill him"

and I could hear his fingernails growing, his beard growing, the Indian searching in his jacket for his gun and wanting to enter the hotel to make the general cry with his head in his hands, us holding him back, imploring

"Wait"

and early the next morning we waited at the spot on the map where the Major said we should wait, near a factory smokestack, with partridges flitting from bush to bush, a herd of goats trotting up a rocky incline, I dead tired and the Indian furiously jumping around on the seat

"I'll kill him"

hoopoes in an oak tree, a rat snake, the buildings and antennas of the city in the distance, my uncle smiling at me with his blue teeth from the well, the ancient echo of a rooster or a dog in the backyard, the men using a rope to hoist him up and laying him in front of the house with his pocket watch, whose lid opened by pressing it with the thumb, stopped at six o'clock, my grandmother pulling on my uncle's tie

"Afonso"

my uncle indifferent to her, to us, to the priest, my uncle laughing in silence and my grandmother pulling on his tie

"Afonso"

hothouses of tomato plants two hundred yards away from us or three hundred at the most, their plastic coverings gleaming silver in the sun, boulders, tall grass, a crossroads, there must have been a lake somewhere to judge by the uncertain breeze, no sound of a car engine, no smell of exhaust pipes, the Indian or my grandmother pulling on my clothes, the Indian with blue teeth pulling on my collar

"I'll kill you"

the inspector filling the ashtray with the wrappers of his stomach pills as he checked the map, following the line of the roads with his index finger, stopping at a penciled *X,* adding up miles in the margin, using the belfry of a church to take his bearings, stuffing the map in his pocket while the Indian picked up a grasshopper, held his lighter beneath it, and watched as its hairpin legs fell off one by one, and finally the partridges took fright and disappeared into the brush, there was a metallic flashing that came and went, the sound of an engine a hundred feet away, fifty feet, twenty feet, and the inspector jumping out of the car, the Indian out of the car, I out of the car, watching as when I watched my uncle being hoisted out of the well, with the same bewilderment and the same horror, and the man with the newspaper frowning as he ordered

"Kill him"

the potbellied general, with a false mustache and a toupee, dressed in a brown or gray lawyer's suit, and next to the general a woman with a purse slung across her shoulder, the general and the woman walking toward us, once more the ancient echo of the rooster and the dog, the plastic coverings gleaming silver in the sun, my bladder letting loose, my legs all wet, my shoes and socks soaked as if I were walking in a swamp, a partridge flitting here and there, and the general holding his hand out

"Companions"

the rat snake lurked between two rocks, the birds that seemed like hoopoes because of how they flew were definitely hoopoes, rising together out of the oak tree in a tempest of shrieks and flapping wings, my grandmother poking at my uncle's chest with her sandal

"Afonso"

the grass trembling, the belfry of the church not sounding any alarm, the woman with the purse slung across her shoulder staring at the inspector, staring at the Indian and finally grasping, her mouth opening wide in speechless protest, the potbellied general slipping on the grass, getting up, wiping his trousers, straightening his hair and mustache

"Companions"

and the Indian

"Fucking swine"

cocking his pistol and nailing the brown or gray lawyer's suit, a bevy of eyes, a bevy of dark bodies, and feathery commas flying away at full speed, my uncle's watch stopped at six o'clock, his blue teeth smiling impassively throughout the funeral watch, and I'll bet they're still smiling six feet under, the woman with a purse slung across her shoulder

"What's the meaning of this, what's the meaning of this?"

and no shots were heard, or at least I can swear that I heard no shots, it all happened in an aquarium silence, with the slow motion of eels, with delayed gestures, delayed movements, delayed falls, the general bent over and draining out of himself, with a strange foam leaking out of his nose, the general with one shoe off and facedown on a slope, lacking his toupee, his false mustache, and a third of his cranium when the inspector, or rather the Indian, I think it was the Indian, took him in his arms, the worried voice of the Minister blowing sweet kisses to the scarecrow

"You love me, Isabel, don't you?"

the hoopoes depluming the oak tree, thousands of hoopoes in the white, white sky depluming the oak tree, the belfry of the church moving back and forth, back and forth, like a pendulum, the woman sitting on the ground and warding us off with her open palms

"What's the meaning of this, what's the meaning of this?"

a pistol in her mouth and she jerking backward like a disjointed doll, my coat covered by red gobs, a red gob sliding off my chin and falling like a slug, and instead of stepping on it I leaned against the car and began to cry, and the Minister at Commerce Square, with the Admiral's picture on one side and Professor Salazar's picture on the other, speaking in a calm voice while continuing to write

"And what did you do with their corpses, Tomás?"

the hothouses of tomato plants retreating into the distance, the oak tree vanishing behind a hill, the hoopoes falling silent, the buildings of the city invisible, a forest of cork trees within reach of a shout, the hothouses of tomato plants retreating into the distance but the reflection from their plastic coverings blinding me to where I hardly noticed the Indian open up the trunk and hand each of us a shovel

"Dig"

the plastic coverings blinding me to where I hardly noticed the Indian open up the trunk and remove a sack of quicklime from among the shovels, I hardly noticed the lime dissolve the red gobs, devouring a sleeve, a belt, what looked to me like a ring, a piece of neck, the woman's purse, and although I hardly noticed, due to the blinding reflection from the plastic coverings, we covered the grave with dirt and branches to keep the dogs from picking up the scent, the Indian gathered up the shovels and the sack of quicklime, and during the whole trip back I was dazed by the oncoming headlights, by the lights along the road, by the lights in the small towns, by the lanterns of roadside restaurants, and by the arm reaching out toward us

"Companions"

and at Commerce Square the Minister, with the Admiral's picture on one side and Professor Salazar's picture on the other, speaking in a calm voice while continuing to write

"Quicklime, Tomás?"

I wanting to tell him about the oak tree, the hothouses of tomato plants, the plastic coverings that blinded me, and the belfry moving back and forth, I wanted to tell him about the red gob on my coat, on my shirt, sliding off my chin, falling like a slug, and instead of stepping on it I leaned against the car and cried, I wanted to tell him about the toupee, the false mustache, and the Indian opening up the trunk and handing me a shovel, I wanted to tell him about the arm reaching out toward us in the aquarium-like silence

"Companions"

but the Minister stood up, motioned me to keep quiet, snapped his suspenders while walking out from behind his desk, and stepped over to the armchair, which was occupied by the scarecrow with the polka-dot dress and those shoes and those gloves and that perfume from an old chest that reminded me of the pharmacist's wife in Serpa when I was a kid, the Minister hesitating, nervous, shy, placing his hand in hers, I standing at attention as the Minister blew kisses to a creature who rubbed her sore ankle without paying him any heed, ignoring him, despising him

"You love me, Isabel, don't you?"

the Minister squatting in front of the armchair, indifferent to the general and the woman with the purse slung across her shoulder, indifferent to the shots, the inspector and the Indian, indifferent to the quicklime poured over the bones and bodies that jerked backwards like disjointed dolls, the Minister stroking a pair of stockings full of runs

"You love me, Isabel, don't you?"

the scarecrow who wasn't pretty, mind you, who didn't have a nice figure and wasn't good-looking, she looked like a housemaid from the interior and worked behind the counter of a notions store at the Praça do Chile, her name wasn't Isabel but Milá or Mina or Micá or some other fool thing, and she had a bride's spikenard that was wilting in her lap, the scarecrow who didn't answer him but just kept looking out the window at the boats from Seixal, and the Minister in her ear

"You love me, Isabel, don't you?"

and it's not worth your while to bore me with tape recordings, photographs, and dossiers, to tell me about this or that, or to pester me with questions, because I don't know what you're talking about, I'm an officer in the reserve of the army who lives in this low-income duplex of Madre de Deus, with a bed of begonias in front and a bed of begonias out back, I'm an old man who only asks to be left in peace, to be left definitively in peace with his chair, his *Artillery Review,* his beach umbrella, his sunglasses, and some sunscreen for his nose and forehead, looking at the lettuces until suppertime and reminiscing about Serpa, all I can do for you is bring out another chair, another beach umbrella, another pair of sunglasses, more sunscreen, and invite you to put that microphone in your briefcase and join me in watching the onset of night, have you noticed how everything becomes clear and sharp just before nightfall, the outline of the rooftops, the outline of the windows, the startled rippling of the curtains, a mossy growth or microscopic crack in the wall, have you noticed how sounds and voices change color, how they become intimate, close and unsettling, and how we, I mean you and I, seem to float, hanging from an invisible wire like the sparrow hawks and the kites, we float and we forget everything, the important thing is that we forget everything, we forget everything forever and ever, you forgetting your book and Salazar and the Minister, and I, who didn't tell you anything, who you know very well didn't tell you anything, who for all the money in the world wouldn't have told you anything, I forgetting not Serpa, not my wife, and not the late husband she makes celestial phone calls to but Spain, all I care about forgetting is Spain, all I care about forgetting is a false mustache and a toupee, all I care about forgetting is a sleeve reaching out to us

"Companions"

and being dissolved a minute later in a sack of quicklime.

fifth report
(quasi-mortal birds of the soul)

REPORT

When my son was little I used to walk with him around the farm on Sundays. The rudder of the windmill would turn right and left in search of the wind, and it bothered me to see my features perpetuated in his, even as I'm bothered by this body I'm told is mine but that doesn't belong to me, because I'm not like this, sitting next to the window overlooking a tiny square with a slide and a swing

"Wee-wee, Senhor Francisco, time for wee-wee, you don't want to wet your nice clean pajamas, do you, Senhor Francisco?"

hands that lift me up, lay me down, wash me, feed me, stick a bedpan between my legs, I flowing out of myself into the pan with the tinkling sound of marbles, and they pinch me on the chin with satisfaction before vanishing down the hall, taking me with them in the bedpan

"Hooray, Senhor Francisco, who's the good little boy who made a nice wee-wee?"

I next to the window overlooking a square with a slide and a swing like the prisoners at Moçâmedes who were next to the sea but didn't see it, five slatless bedsteads for ten prisoners here, five slatless bedsteads for twenty prisoners there, and it disgusted me to walk among them with the warden, among their scabies and coughing, I in the zinc-roofed administrative office ordering them to kneel on a board placed over their fingers while I interrogated them, the prisoners like tattered baskets, like worn-out leather trunks, like cages made of broken ribs, like I am now, they saw the sand and sea through the walls, they didn't see me or the warden, they didn't see the blowflies and worms in their open sores, they saw the sea without noticing it, as if the sea were a slide and a swing

"Here's your soup, Senhor Francisco, a nice vegetable soup passed through a strainer, a piece of fried fish with no bones because I spent half an hour removing them, you rascal, and a yummy boiled pear, eat this for Daddy, come on, this spoonful for Mommy, chew faster, this one for me, you old cad, because I also deserve one, and this spoonful for your goofy son, so he won't think you're too skinny on the day he comes to visit, we don't want to frighten your son with a face that looks like a skull, we don't want to frighten your son with a mummy's face, we want to be obedient, Senhor Francisco, now swallow, you bugger, open up your mouth and swallow, are you going to swallow or not, you scamp?"

the peace of the sand and sea of Angola through the walls of the prison at Moçâmedes in spite of the scabies, lice, and coughing, in spite of the rats, I kneeling on a board placed over my fingers, I in the zinc-roofed administrative office with the spoon bruising my gums, the fork bruising my gums, the knife forcing my jaws open, with a condemned man as old and scrawny as me in the next chair, blue grass, the swing, the slide, the geese waving their spaghetti necks at me

"We'll see if you swallow, you bugger, we'll see if you swallow, you scamp"

Titina shooing away the geese with her broom, the steward looking thoughtfully at the sky, even when cloudy, and saying what time it was, my son arriving with a bag of vanilla wafers but not daring to kiss me, unsure whether or not I could understand him, faking a smile I'd repay with a good slap if I could move my arm

"It's been a long time since I've seen you looking so chipper, Dad"

beyond the wall the languid waves, the jeep that had brought me there rusting in the sun, ragged palm trees shaking their cretonne tatters, and the warden, afraid I might sack him, poking the prisoners in the stomach with his stick

"It's just put-on, Senhor Minister, they want us to think they have dysentery when they're all in perfect health, there's not one patient in the prison infirmary"

as if I cared whether or not the prisoners died or whether the infirmary, a tent with a jar of dirty cotton and a single dismantled bed in a corner whose broken springs served as a wasps' nest, was or wasn't full of Communists with dysentery, I, who when one of the German shepherds in Palmela stopped eating and whimpered all curled up in a flower bed or lay prostrate in an irrigation channel, would tap the animal with my shoe or poke it with a stick, yell to Titina to bring me my shotgun and a couple of cartridges from my desk drawer, yell to the tractor driver to dig a hole next to the well, Titina would shudder once or twice, and I, glad to have saved money on medicines from the veterinarian, would go back to the house, lean the shotgun against the nightstand, and then go out to the arbor and sit, gazing at the farm once more in perfect order, gazing at the slide and swing on the square while my son squatted down and hugged the dead dogs, wanting to run away with them so as to save them from me, my son begging the tractor driver not to drag them by the tail to the hole next to the well, my son afraid that I, gazing at the square with a slide and swing, might pull a pistol from my pajama and shoot him in the guts, my son for whose sake they dressed and washed and shaved and fed me and went away all satisfied

"Who was the good boy who did his wee-wee, Senhor Francisco, who was it?"

with what flowed out of me into the bedpan with the tinkling sound of marbles

"My father lost some of his brain with the stroke, didn't he, my father doesn't understand anything we tell him, does he?"

I who, as soon as my wife decided she was leaving me, long before she shut herself in the bedroom and started taking clothes from the dressers and opening suitcases and trunks, should have done to her what I did to the German shepherds, instead of humiliating myself, instead of letting her spend hours whispering on the phone, not answering me, not talking to me, pulling away when I tried to touch her

"I'm having my period, I've got a headache, I'm tired, leave me alone"

I who should have yelled to Titina to bring me my shotgun and a couple of cartridges from my desk drawer, who should have yelled to the tractor driver to dig a hole next to the well, and Titina could have shuddered all she liked, the turtledoves could have flown away for as long as they liked, at least then they would have stopped mussing up the shrubs, or else I should have had the Major ship her straight down to Moçâmedes, she in the hold kneeling on a board placed over her fingers throughout the voyage, I should have done to my wife what I should have done to the Major when he refused to help me

"Official instructions from the Prime Minister, I'm sorry"

the Major, who wasn't at all sorry to get rid of me over the phone, "There are certain people we can't afford to antagonize under the present circumstances, certain supporters we can't afford to lose right now, the Prime Minister appeals to your understanding, to your patriotism, to your better judgment," and I full of patriotism and better judgment yelling to Titina to bring me my shotgun and a sack of cartridges so that I could kill them all, I ordering the steward to drag them to the well by what was left of their heads and to bury them with the dogs, there where the lard from their carcasses makes the grass grow, I who should have sought out her lover boy at the bank and prevented him from laughing at my expense with national assemblymen, regional governors, and city councilmen instead of seeking her out after he'd dumped her, my wife in a one-room apartment without an elevator, without a cook, without any maids, a room in need of painting, a photograph on a desk that she hurriedly hid, my wife looking thinner, her hair disheveled, her fingernails neglected, wearing a cheap men's bathrobe with margarine stains on the sleeves and shoulders, without any makeup, no lipstick, staring at me the way the German shepherds, sick and shedding their fur, stared at me from the irrigation channels, begging me to kill them with my shotgun and bury them next to the well before the veterinarian stepped in

with his useless medicines, a poor animal with no money holding the bathrobe against her chest

"Don't kiss me"

a poor animal who'd grown old all alone, sitting on a little
wicker sofa with her legs crossed and arms crossed as if to defend herself from the shotgun, to defend herself from me, with
a can of food and an empty bottle of perfume on the windowsill, a poor animal staring at me from toe to head, like the moribund German shepherds with their mouths hanging open in the
flower beds

"Don't kiss me"

as if, gentlemen, I'd thought of kissing her, as if I wanted
to kiss her, as if I'd care to kiss a scrawny, haggard dog on her
last legs, without the strength to bark or crawl or lift her snout,
as if I'd care to kiss the ants and flies that strolled over her back
without her even trying to shake them off, as if I'd care to kiss
the bloody drool of her snout, a can of food and an empty bottle
of perfume on the windowsill, dirty dishes in the sink, she barefoot, and a child hurling Carnival streamers on the balcony
opposite, as if I'd care, imagine, to kiss a mangy, worn-out dog,
if I'd had my shotgun, if I'd brought some cartridges, if I could've
yelled to Titina to bring them, and my wife on the little wicker
sofa

"It's no use crying, don't cry, it's no use crying"

as if I were crying, as if I were a man of tears, as if my life
hadn't improved without her, without having anything to worry
about, without having to return home by dinnertime, to offer
explanations and invent excuses, me cry, just think, me cry,
imagine, me cry before a can of food and an empty bottle of
perfume in a squalid apartment where a sad seamstress might

live, the tractor driver would push the German shepherds
with his shoe until they rolled into their graves like bundles of
clothes, then he'd pick up the shovel, and I'd watch him from
the purple clusters of the arbor, a dog with field spiders lodged
in gashes on her chest, gashes on her belly, sitting on the little
wicker sofa with her legs crossed, hair graying, an old dog waiting for me to aim my gun at her with a steady wrist, a bathroom with a plastic shower curtain, a glass shelf without facial
cream or an eyebrow pencil, a mangled tube of toothpaste, a
toothbrush stuck in a glass like a blue-jay feather in a Tyrolean
hat, a wad of hair plugging up the sink, a suitcase next to the
umbrella stand, why aren't you with me, why don't you come
home with me, Titina will change the sheets, change the towels, lay out the good china, and put the boy to bed so that we
can relax, she'll buy papayas in Setúbal, she'll make you French
toast, baked codfish with carrots, poached eggs with parsley, soft-
crust meat pies, you need to put on weight, go to the beauty
parlor, take care of yourself, and have me take care of you, you
need to go downtown to buy new clothes, but since I'm talking
to a deaf animal lying prostrate in an irrigation channel, a sick
dog ready to vanish under the fig tree, since I'm talking with
crossed legs and crossed arms that spurn me, refuse me, defend
themselves from me

"Don't kiss me"

"Who made a nice wee-wee, Senhor Francisco, who was it?"

"Don't kiss me, Francisco, don't kiss me"

"Here's your soup, Senhor Francisco, a nice vegetable soup
passed through a strainer, a piece of fish with no bones because I
spent half an hour removing them, you rascal, and a yummy boiled
pear, eat this for Daddy, come on, this spoonful for Mommy,

chew faster, this one for me, you old cad, because I also deserve one, we want to be obedient, Senhor Francisco, don't we,
now swallow, for Christ's sake, swallow, you bugger, open up
your mouth and swallow, are you going to swallow or not, you
scamp?"

"It's useless to cry, Francisco, don't cry, I'm okay, I swear
I'm okay, don't worry about me, I'm not going back to you,
don't insist, don't say anything, it's useless to cry"

not even a maid, a cook, or a cleaning woman to tidy up
this mess, to help you, to mend and iron your clothes, to take
care of you, no one to take your trash out to the street, since
this building has no doorman, no one to sweep the stairs and
water the plants at the entrance, to fix the elevators when they
go on the blink, the pipes when water floods the floor, the leaky
toilet tank, the worn-out washers on the faucets, and the broken toilet seat, no one to pay your bills, for I can't imagine you
standing in line at the electric company for hours smoking cigarettes, sighing, and agreeing with the other customers' protests,
shaking your disgusted head in solidarity when the others in line
shake their disgusted heads, no one to call the doctor when you
need a doctor, the nurse when you need a shot, no one who
phones to ask how you're doing, no one who takes an interest,
who cares, let me write you a check, send you some food, send
someone from the ministry to paint your apartment, to change
out this hideous carpet, to fix the drapes, to bring you some
decent Austrian chairs, to service your refrigerator and hot
water heater, to talk with your landlord so that he'll repair the
roof, solder the gutter, get rid of this dampness, but since I'm
talking with a can of food and an empty bottle of perfume on
the windowsill, since I'm talking with a little wicker sofa with

crossed legs and crossed arms that spurn me, refuse me, and look at me with pity

"I feel so sorry for you, Francisco"

Titina holding back tears with her hands over her eyes, the tractor driver pulling me by my paws, by my tail, by what was left of my head, pulling me with one hand while shooing away flies with the other, and my son

"He doesn't understand anything we tell him, does he?"

grabbing the shovel to help the tractor driver bury me, my body hanging over the grave, teetering, and finally falling in like a bundle of clothes, the staff workers impatiently lifting me off the floor, sitting me up again by the window overlooking the square with the swing and the slide, tying me to the chair the way a suckling pig is tied, my wrists, stomach, and feet, wiping the drool from my face with my pajama sleeve

"The geezer won't sit still until he breaks a leg"

disinfecting some bruise or other on my forehead with a compress that turned pink, cutting a piece of adhesive tape with scissors

(a piece of adhesive tape that stuck to their fingers, that stuck to everything, like a song you try to get out of your head but can't, I spent an entire year helplessly singing an atrocious jingle from a coffee commercial at cabinet meetings, in the Assembly, at the National Union,* at foreign service receptions, and during the Pope's visit, people talking about politics, the war in Africa, the overseas provinces, student unrest, the unfortunate but inevitable need for censure, people asking me what I thought, and I stepping up to the microphone, clearing my throat, raising my hand to my chest, and belting out "Say good morning with Mokambo coffee" to a stunned audience)

the staff workers pulling back on my straggly hair
"Hold still"
and applying the adhesive tape to my forehead with a vindictive slap, tightening the straps on my wrists, stomach, and feet
"You can turn purple but you're not going to budge from here"
a room even smaller than my wife's room, with a lower ceiling, more dirt, and the smell of excrement, cold food, and syrup reminiscent of kerosene, with a chair where they make me sit and a chair where they made my roommate sit until yesterday, when he dropped dead, my roommate who moaned the whole day without letup
"Teresa"
the staff workers in their compartments unable to sleep
"Teresa be damned"
and as soon as he fell silent they started talking in a buzz, they scurried up and down the hall, huddling here and there, then rolled him up in his blanket and carried him away, as stiff as a tin soldier, a room with two beds, with a dresser filched from a beggar's shack and full of expired pills and capsules, clogged syringes, broken catheters and irrigation tubes, and with a light on all night that magnifies the night outside, making the buildings enormous, the swing huge, the slide gigantic, the sky like gray paper over the blue grass, and dozens of old men ensconced under their sheets, flowing out of themselves into bedpans with a tinkling sound like marbles and moaning one after another
"Teresa"
like roosters in their separate backyards vying with each other, if you're willing to leave your can of food and empty bottle of perfume, the wicker sofa, the plastic shower curtain, and the

photograph you hurriedly hid, it doesn't mean you have to stop liking him, meeting him, calling him up, and seeing him, I miss having your home-decorating magazines in the living room, your clothes in the closet, the rings you take off before going to bed, your necklaces hanging on the mirror, I carry your wedding ring in my pocket, here, put it on for just a moment or two, you don't have to keep it on if you don't want to, I won't force you, I won't insist, put it on for a moment just so I can see how it looks

"Don't kiss me"

"Open your mouth, you bugger, thanks to you I'll miss the five o'clock bus, Jesus, I'm always behind in everything, open your mouth, sir, open your frigging mouth and swallow"

"Don't cry, Francisco, please don't cry, it's useless to cry"

the elm trees on the square of Palmela, the melancholy Major spreading wide his dismayed hands

"I'm afraid there's nothing we can do, official instructions from the Prime Minister, we can't antagonize supporters, the internal situation is complex, the regime has commitments"

the Major seeing me to the door as if I were a widower, with exaggerated sympathy, exaggerated friendliness, grabbing my coat to help me along as if indignation provoked arthritis, as if mourning made canes necessary, as if solitude had made me an invalid, the Major opening the storm door with a show of pity barely disguising his urge to laugh

"I swear we won't let him go, we won't forget, as soon as things have cooled down a bit we'll find a discreet way to take care of your problem"

the inspectors nodding their noses in agreement, likewise holding back their laughter by tightening their facial muscles, making cuckold's horns with their fingers behind my back, and

I without the courage to turn around and face them, I leaving as quickly as possible to cut short the mockery of the Major's condolences, I surrounded by jeering laughter as I marched down the Rua do Alecrim toward the Tagus, the pigeons scampering out of my path, I in my bedroom in Palmela yelling at Titina to bring me my shotgun and a couple of cartridges from the drawer as I gazed at the sick dog in the mirror, a dog with a hat, a cigarillo, suspenders, and eyes that begged me to kill him, a dog lying prostrate in an irrigation channel with ants and blowflies all over him

"It's no use crying, don't cry, please don't cry, it's useless to cry"

a dog with his mouth hanging open in a flower bed, staring at me but unable to bark, unable to lick my fingers with humble gratitude, unable to protest or to run away, a dog shedding its fur and covered with cuts and sores, I yelling at the tractor driver to open up a grave next to the well, I aiming straight at the mirror, Titina shuddering once or twice, the orange trees shuddering once or twice, the man with the hat, the cigarillo, and the suspenders, I mean the dog, I mean the man, I mean the dog, shattering onto the rug in a cascade of glass bits, and I leaned the shotgun against the nightstand, then went out and sat in the arbor, gazing at the farm once more in perfect order, forever in order under the squawking protests of the crows.

COMMENTARY

I have no one to play chess with since the Minister disappeared from Palmela. It was through my cousin that I met him, when he was already an old man who would inadvertently flick his cigarillo ashes onto his tie, then blow them off and into our faces, for which he profusely begged pardon

"Sorry about that, sorry"

my cousin, primped up in lace, sequins, patent-leather pumps and hair spray, quickly wiping his shirt with loving care

"Honeybun"

entangling him in spidery solicitudes, wedging pillows behind his back to imprison him, squeezing him into an arm-chair so that he couldn't escape, hovering over him with the voracity of a bat showing its teeth and casting its hooked shadow on the wall, her bracelets jingling a death knell

"Honeybun"

piling potatoes and gravy onto his plate with a criminal concern to fatten him up, and the old man, like an innocent steer at the slaughterhouse, marching to his death under the eyelashes of the plaster-of-Paris cat and the raving appetite of the apostles in the low-relief Last Supper, all starving at a long table, ready to fight over the crumbs like shameless hyenas, I feeling sorry for the Minister, whose knees were being crushed by his fiancée's impassioned buttocks, whose cheeks were pinched by her praying-mantis pincers

"Honeybun"

the poor old man turning purple for lack of air as the Span-ish dancer's earrings, all sparks and flashes, threatened to blind him, and my wife throwing herself in the middle to separate them

"The poor man's going to keel over"

the Minister who lived on a farm in the part of the Arrábida range that's now a resort for the English with a riding school, a golf course, and tennis courts, the farm where he spent his afternoons drinking sweet wine with a shotgun under his arm amid maids and dogs, the old man who had been a state minister during Professor Salazar's time and bitterly resented not having being named his successor, who held it against the Admiral for not having pleaded

"Govern this piece of crap for me, Minister"

for not having pleaded

"Whip this rabble into line for me, Minister"

the idle and innocuous old man conspiring in the greenhouse with other, equally idle and innocuous old men, passing out titles of honor, municipal posts, administrative posts, and cabinet posts to a band of decrepit geezers, aiming his enraged shotgun at stone angels suspected of treason, the idle and innocuous Minister at the top of the steps sending away other idle and innocuous ministers with the scepter of his index finger

"Get out"

disillusioned by his army of good-for-nothings who rowed with their canes, step by step, down the path covered with orchid leaves and turtledove droppings, the old man at my cousin's house complaining about the world's ingratitude to the chinaware dwarfs with chipped hats and chipped pickaxes that dotted her garden, the old man swearing that he'd go to Commerce Square to demand that the Admiral hand over what he'd stolen from him, namely an entire nation plus parts of Africa and India and some peninsula or other with a bunch of Chinese, and my cousin, outraged that her boyfriend wasn't governing this pile of crap and whipping this rabble into line, smothered him with consoling endearments

"Honeybun"

my cousin who I'm quite convinced killed her pharmacist husband with her onslaughts of affection, for no sooner did the poor, unsuspecting soul arrive home from his medicine bottles, wrapped in a healing mist of sodium perborate that improved the digestion and cleared up the bronchial tubes of whoever happened to be near, no sooner did the poor soul turn his key in the door than his wife, covered with treacherously glittering jewels, would jump out from behind the refrigerator and overwhelm him with an avalanche of hugs and kisses

"Honeybun"

burying the pharmacist under shovelfuls of necklaces, pendants, pins, bracelets, shoulder pads, and rings until he lay gasping on the rug

"Help"

the pharmacist, whose miner's destiny caused him to be fatally buried one day under his wife's alluvium, later that night under a pyramid of chrysanthemums at the church in Palmela, and the next morning under a slab of marble with his name and a cross, the pharmacist forever condemned to a subterranean existence that my cousin, armed with more chrysanthemums, ensured through monthly visits, my cousin ever ready to shower him with renewed hugs and kisses

"Honeybun"

to prevent him from returning to the surface, and after five years, when it was unlikely that the pharmacist would come back to lodge any complaint, my cousin moved him from under the tombstone, whose weight had increased with added Virgins and flower vases, to a bolted drawer amid other bolted drawers, like safe-deposit boxes at the bank, thus freeing her from the specter of a pernicious resurrection or an annoying head sticking its nose out of the grass and smiling at her from the roots of the poplars, and she exchanged her crêpe mourning clothes for an effusion of low-cut dresses, tight skirts, red satins, and talismans, she bought the cat for the center of the table and the dwarfs for the garden, she banished her photos of the pharmacist to the back of a closet, replacing them with pictures of the Minister in tails and a top hat and with medals on his chest, pictures from the time of Salazar, when the Minister's name had clout in municipal governments, sanitoriums, recreational clubs, the police, the Minister whom my cousin dug up God knows where, or perhaps it was the Minister who dug up my cousin, likewise God only knows where, the old man who back then was heftier, had droopy eyelids, and muttered with disdain, sitting with her on his farm's terrace next to the beech trees and the astonished crows, my cousin's laces shaking like an excited turkey

"Honeybun"

and the old man to me, frowning at the chessboard and moving a pawn forward at random

"Is it your move or mine?"

the old man, without waiting for an answer, snatching my queen from the board before I'd had a chance to move and announcing with an apologetic smile

"You lost"

when there were still knights, castles, and bishops he hadn't captured, when I had surrounded his king and was winning, I just needed to move some pawn or other and victory was mine, the old man magnanimously

(and my cousin's costume jewelry glittering as she beamed with pride

"Honeybun")

setting up the pieces again, making two moves at once, and I without the courage to object

"I'll give you a chance to get even, Martins"

the Minister pissed off at the Admiral who hadn't shown him any consideration, who hadn't pleaded

"Govern this piece of crap for me, Minister"

who hadn't called him to the palace, hadn't grabbed him by the lapel and pulled him aside from everyone else, sliding a few conspiratorial steps across the waxed floor into a corner while lowering his voice, cautiously looking right and left while cupping his hand over his dentures

"Whip this rabble into line for me, Minister"

a pack of wimps without the strength to win a war in Africa against a handful of blacks who couldn't even speak proper Portuguese, a pack of wimps without the courage to give the Communists a few good whacks and lock them up in jail, the prison of Caxias practically empty, the prison of Peniche practically empty, of Tarrafal practically empty, of São Nicolau practically empty, an absolute disgrace, with almost no one starving and almost no one dying, if you can imagine anything so amateurish, the Admiral pleading with alarm

"Govern this piece of crap for me"

alarmed by the laxness of the censors, by the National Guard's failure to clobber the unions, by the informers' silence, by the secret police lolling about playing cards instead of earning their pay and torturing a few people, making them stand for hours with their arms in the air, depriving them of sleep, and applying a few electric shocks, by the newspapers saying whatever they pleased without fear, by the opposition holding up immoral England and Sweden as models, offering suggestions and ideas that were warping the minds of the common people, and by the unskilled workers who handed out leaflets claiming that they didn't get paid and went hungry, as if, for Christ's sake, going hungry and living in crowded rented rooms amid a pandemonium of children and junk, without windows or running water, wasn't exactly what the workers wanted, the Admiral worried that the country was edging toward moral collapse

"Whip this rabble into line for me, Minister"

the Admiral who not only didn't call him to the palace, he didn't even deign to answer the Minister's phone calls, letters, and memorandums, not even through a counselor, administrator, aide-de-camp, or goddamn cleaning woman, the Admiral who didn't beg him in desperation, while cupping his hand over his dentures

"Govern this piece of crap for me, Minister"

and my cousin sympathizing with the Minister, flapping rubies and lamés while flitting around him in a pizzicato of kisses

"Honeybun"

the old man with the shotgun under his arm, pulling me by the coat, I holding the white king with my thumb and index finger to defend it from the five or six pieces he'd move at once as soon as my cousin backed off to catch her breath before attacking him once more with her tons of chokers and lace, the old man taking me to the busses at Palmela's square, pointing to a seat next to his in a bus crammed with peasant baskets and aprons

"Sit here, Martins"

showing me his shotgun and the inscriptions on the butt

"You'll see, Martins"

and before I knew it we were at the arcaded buildings of Commerce Square in Lisbon, next to the ramp that descended into the water with its sickly, incurable stench of low tide, the old man groping for cartridges in his pocket before the stony indifference of the dozing ministries

"I'll finish off all these traitors in nothing flat"

we stepped off the bus in a hubbub of cardboard boxes, burlap sacks, suitcases, caged chickens, and caged rabbits to find ourselves amid government vehicles, policemen, beggars with saxophones, bookkeepers, and archivists carrying file folders this way and that, bulletin boards with announcements, orders, lists of prisoners, prohibitions, and recommendations, the Minister snapping his suspenders in the direction of a corridor with a red carpet

"I'll finish off all these traitors in nothing flat"

a final flurry of pigeons between the freighters and the train station, and then a tunnel with stairs, the click-clack of type-writers, the ringing of phones, the squeaking of file drawers, a uniformed guard brusquely stopping the old man with his out-stretched hand as if he were stopping a beggar

"Where do you think you're going?"

the old man taken aback, letting go of his suspenders as his cigarillo fell from his mouth, I stooping down to pick it up, but it rolled away, I crawling out to the street in pursuit of the cigarillo, bumping into shoes, socks, ankles, military gai-ters, and startled legs that jumped, the uniformed guard jab-bing the Minister in the gut with his knee

"Get lost"

and the Minister descending, like the cigarillo, step by step toward the street, the hat on his head at the same height as the people's shoes, socks, ankles, military gaiters, and startled legs that jumped, above us a final flurry of pigeons flying between

the freighters and the train station, and the Minister facedown
on the sidewalk, using his shotgun as a cane to hoist himself up,
brushing the dirt off his pants, accepting from me his cigarillo,
mangled but still lit, pointing the smoldering tip like a proud
smokestack toward the pigeons overhead, thrusting it between
his teeth like a nail, couching the shotgun in his armpit, straightening the brim of his hat, straightening his tie, walking toward
the bus crammed with peasant baskets and aprons, sitting on
the seat next to mine, and puffing smoke against the window
that looked out onto carts and bicycles, goats and streams, restaurants in ruins and grade crossings with blinking red lights
where girls pointed red flags at wheelless and doorless train cars
rusting away in the grass, the Minister to me, in his voice from
the days of Professor Salazar, when his name had clout in the
sanitoriums, the national ID office, the repatriation office, and
the jails, the Minister snatching my queen from the board before I'd had a chance to move and announcing with an apologetic smile

"You lost"

under the shadow of the cypress leaves, under the shadow
of the magpies' wings.

REPORT

My God how clear it all is now. I'm not at the farm and yet
I see the farm, I'm not at the house and yet I see the house, I'm
not with you and yet I see you, your back to me, sitting in front
of the bedroom mirror and tilting your head to remove your earrings, brushing your hair with your right hand on this side of the

mirror and with your left hand on the inside of the mirror, I see you smiling at me in the glass, and behind your smile

(my God how clear it all is now)

lurk other smiles I thought were lost, other houses, other hands, other voices, behind your smile there's a dead pigeon in the courtyard, a drizzly Sunday, I in the backyard and my mother calling me to the table

"Francisco"

the dining room lights so tiny in the pitcher and the glasses, a napkin tied around my neck

"Don't make a mess, don't spill the soup"

my father rolling little balls of bread that turned gray, my father getting up to wind the wall clocks with the key in his vest, the prisoner stepping over to the fourth-floor window without any of us having touched her and saying

"Good afternoon"

saying to me

"Good afternoon"

in a calm voice devoid of fear, devoid of resentment, the prisoner leaning out over the sill and crashing to the street, my God how clear it all is now: your hair, your smile, your smell, the shadow inside your eyes that was the only wrinkle you had, the prisoner whom two agents dragged by her arms and legs into the cubicle in the entrance hall, and the doctor, feeling her soft skull and broken vertebrae, his coat stained with her blood

"Call the ambulance to take her to the hospital"

the cubicle for the officer on duty, with a desk, a chair, and a folding table in the corner, the inspector, with phone in hand, asking for my go-ahead with his chin, the doctor turning the prisoner's neck, looking into her pupils with a tiny flashlight

"Call the ambulance immediately"

and I

(my God how clear it all is now, you facing me on this side of the mirror but with your back to me inside the mirror, slowly holding out the hairbrush to me as if the hairbrush were you, a hairbrush with a sculpted bronze handle that prolonged your smile)

and I accepting the hairbrush, touching your fingers with mine, and likewise answering the inspector with my chin

"We're not calling anyone"

fingers over fingers over fingers, your watch on the nightstand, my watch and tie pin on the nightstand, a piece of bosom showing between your shirt buttons, your smell suddenly moving away to draw the curtain

"I don't like the neighbors seeing us"

your smell drawing the curtain and turning around to me with tiny dance steps as I took off my vest, took off my shoes, your smell forever dancing as it pushed the big pillows and the bedspread to the floor, as it pulled down the sheets, the inspector putting down the phone and the doctor, with the prisoner's blood on his trousers, marveling as he switched off the flashlight

"You're not going to call anyone?"

your smell stretching out on the mattress and pretending to sleep, your closed eyelids trembling, your stomach, your buttocks, your separated knees, my mother calling me to the table

"Francisco"

my father rolling little balls of bread that turned gray, the doctor looking at me as he put away his flashlight, the doctor looking at the inspector, then at me again while he checked to see if the prisoner was still breathing

"You're not going to call anyone?"

a guard in civilian dress, with a bucket and mop, chasing away the people on the street

"Don't you have anything better to do than mill around?"

until it was empty, then washing the sidewalk so clean that not even the pigeons could find a telltale sign of the prisoner, a shred of clothing, a shoelace, or a hairpin, just a stain of water that was evaporating between the stones, an insignificant stain that would soon cease to exist, I putting my arm around the doctor's waist

"Why burden the hospitals with useless complications if the woman died as soon as she hit the sidewalk?"

your smell stretching out on the mattress, your stomach, your buttocks, your separated knees, while in the mirror a second you stretched out the opposite way toward a second me and moved her stomach, buttocks, and separated knees, the first me, naked, looked at the second, likewise naked me, who looked at my smiling body as I looked at his, in a bedroom that was mine but with everything in reverse, and the time was different, twenty past midnight outside the mirror and twenty to one inside the mirror, the doctor turning on the flashlight and taking the prisoner's pulse, afraid of me, squirming as he sighed in a sweat

"The woman didn't die, Minister"

and

(my God how clear it all is now)

and the first me lying down looking at the second me lying down while the two you's stared at them back-to-back, the inspector pushing the doctor aside and grasping the prisoner's neck as if probing, or fondling, or stroking, or squeezing it, squeezing its cartilage with a frown, as if he were straining to uncork a bottle, the agents turning their heads and looking into space, the guard putting the bucket and mop into the closet, I enthralled by a crack in the ceiling that looked just like the blue line of the Guadiana River on maps, the doctor transparent with horror, pulling out his handkerchief with jerky movements, the doctor so transparent you could see his veins contracting beneath the skin, his tendons, his muscles, the prisoner's hand closing and opening, the prisoner's features in peace, the inspector's frown giving way to a beatific innocence, and I, lowering my gaze from the crack in the ceiling to the doctor

"Did the woman or didn't the woman die as soon as she hit the sidewalk, doctor?"

both me's struggling in vain, pedaling between the sheets without success, notwithstanding your efforts, your help, your kisses, your hands, and your thighs opening up to us, both me's taking a breather, lighting a cigarillo, trying again, and it was like pounding against a latched door, like searching for an opening where no opening existed

(my God how clear it all is now)

both of you with a quizzical look, questioning us, and the two me's consulting each other, with triangles of sky showing through the drapes, two skies without clouds or buildings, two hollow tunnels, and the two watches asserting categorically and contrarily I don't know what time

"Did something happen, Francisco?"

"Are you tired, Francisco?"

"Aren't you in the mood, Francisco?"

the prisoner on the bed of the official on duty, with a dark clot in her ear, a dark clot in the corner of her mouth, hair curls spread over the pillow, curls that looked like oakum, like a mannequin's or a doll's curls, with purple streaks below her jaw, a cheap ring that I couldn't stop looking at, one of her legs shorter than the other, like on a cripple, a cheap ring imitating a wedding band but not even made of real silver, already worn out and ready to break, darkened by time and by contact with human skin, the prisoner with an ordinary gray sweater and an ordinary gray skirt, her earlobes pierced by a needle when she was little, she crying as her mother or grandmother held on to her in some small town in the interior

"Hold still"

("Did something happen, Francisco?")

whining no, protesting no, yelling no, I'll give you anything you want but don't hurt me, don't make me cry, don't pierce my ears, let me go, an ordinary gray sweater and skirt, not of a peasant woman but of an office worker, nurse, or schoolteacher, her nails trimmed and polished, eyebrows well cared for, teeth in good shape, legs shaved, no corns, the inspector gripping the doctor under his armpit and the doctor agreeing with me in a strained whisper

"She died as soon as she hit the sidewalk, Minister, she obviously died as soon as she hit the sidewalk"

the doctor having forgotten about the flashlight in his coat pocket that was still on, causing a bright green dot to show through the fabric, the inspector turning it off with a playful slap, then straightening the doctor's collar like a doting wife, pinching the doctor's chin with his thumb and index finger

"If I were a pretty young girl, I swear I'd fall in love with our good doctor, Minister"

and the doctor too fainthearted to pull away his chin, to free himself from the inspector, the doctor who had been working at secret-police headquarters for four or five years, giving digitalis injections to stimulate those who flagged during interrogations, measuring their blood pressure, hiding behind the white sleeve of his coat, wearing dark glasses before those deprived of sleep or those forced to stand for hours with their arms in the air, controlling the voltage of the shocks, encouraging denunciations with a dentist's drill, facilitating confessions with enemas and laxatives, setting bones, dressing wounds, and curing bruises for appearances in court, where the casuistic lawyers would mention the bandages, and the judges, saying the bandages were irrelevant to the case, would threaten them with contempt and advise us, in private, to give them a good scare at the first opportunity, the doctor putting up with the inspector, chuckling with the inspector, thanking the inspector for his flattery as pea-size beads of sweat ran down his face, and I, instead of wrapping up the matter and taking my leave

(my God how clear it all is now)

extending my hand toward the prisoner's cheap ring, a ring imitating a wedding band but not even made of real silver, already worn out and ready to break, darkened by time and by contact with human skin, a cheap ring which, if you looked at it with glasses, would prove to be etched with designs, a snake, a lizard, phony Egyptian signs, a cheap ring bought for peanuts at a North African bazaar with her boyfriend, after one or two years of saving up for the plane, for the hotel, for those copper pitchers whose copper rubs off the tin after a month, for those rugs that fray down to their skeleton in a month and are tossed out, a week in Tunisia or Algeria or in Morocco eating meatballs with her hands, eating greasy cookies and being outrageously happy, wearing a straw hat over her black curls, a leather necklace, a long dress in bad taste, and I

("Did something happen, Francisco?")

envious of her, or no, not envious, but wishing I could stroll hand in hand with her, you can write those very words, I'm not ashamed, I was so ashamed for so long that I can no longer get ashamed, go ahead and write wishing I could stroll hand in hand with her down filthy narrow streets full of filthy swindlers hawking filthy junk, and we excitedly putting together our spending money, giving up lunch and the excursion to Tangier, using mathematical jugglery to count up our pennies and bring the junk back to Portugal, to decorate my two-bedroom apartment in Pedrouços with woolen tapestries and wicker baskets that, except for being shoddier, are exactly like the ones sold at any outdoor market or subway station, I putting the ring on her finger but then, come winter, gradually ceasing to call her and to take her to the movies, I canceling our Saturday dinners at a bar and grill in Alcântara with idiotic excuses

"I think I caught the flu, and I'm afraid I might give it to you"

"I have to go see my parents in Santarém, what a pain"

"I've got a bookkeeping job on the side that's tons more work than I expected"

avoiding her, running away from her, not answering her letters, or her messages through friends, or her invitations to birthday dinners in Cruz Quebrada where her cousin would no doubt be playing guitar amid the seagulls and sewers emptying into the Tagus, I telling my coworkers

"I'm not here"

I

(my God how clear it all is now)

I returning home in the rain and finding her black curls and cheap ring waiting for me inside my building, all dripping wet, so dripping wet that her tears couldn't be seen, they would never be seen, she wringing her hands and biting her lower lip as her wet curls dripped, the cheap ring reaching into a canvas handbag for a wet pack of cigarettes and a box of matches that wouldn't light, she shaking her head and turning on her heels, the cheap ring going away without a word, going out into the rain without running, without hurrying, without even curving her head as she walked toward the bus stop, and when I opened the apartment door I was met by the rug and the peeling copper pitchers, by a picture of her on the shelf, from Tunisia or Algeria or Morocco, I contemplating it all in a melancholy archeology, I to the inspector

"Have the doctor sign the death certificate"

the obedient doctor, afraid we might suicide him, writing myocardial infarction or brain cancer or pulmonary embolism, wooed by the agents' sarcasm, by the guard's prodding elbow

"If you were a girl, I'd hound you day and night"

and it goes without saying that there was no autopsy, that the coffin was given to the family already sealed, that we oversaw the watch and burial and dispatched agents to make sure it wasn't opened, and I took the ring to the ministry and hid it in the box of cigarillos on my desk, a cheap ring that I'll bet someone, taking it for a child's plaything or a pigeon ring or a prize from inside a Christmas cake, had thrown out just like I throw out my papers, pens, notes, books, and the first and second me

(my God how clear it all is now)

moving their mouths at the same time, articulating syllables at the same time, begging pardon at the same time to the you in this bed and the you in that one, two identical you's in two identical beds, looking at me with identical surprise

"I don't know what happened, I don't know what's wrong with me, don't be mad, I'm sorry"

both me's lying stomach-up in defeat, head against the pillow, the second you vanishing from the mirror and deserting me, the first you in the bathroom, I hearing the sound of objects banging, drawers opening and closing, water running with so much force that I couldn't hear the sound of the body hitting the sidewalk and the doctor's pen writing out the death certificate, the two me's looking at each other all alone, and they continued to look at each other when you reappeared dressed in a raincoat in the mirror and disappeared from it, telling me as you turned the doorknob

"I'm coming home late"

and

(my God how clear it all is now)

and I think it was then, hold on, I'm sorry, correct that, I'm sure it was then that I began to lose you, that we began to lose each other, to spend the evening not on the sofa but in armchairs, so as not to run the risk of touching each other, of your leg grazing my leg, of my arm grazing your arm, you with your section of the newspaper and I with my section, each of us hoping to have the section with the bridge column and the crossword puzzle, you taking a sleeping pill with your glass of water, and I taking a sleeping pill with my glass of water, each of us yawning theatrically and pretending to be sleepier than we were, and I think it was then, change that, I'm sure it was then that you met the other man, accepted his compliments, his flowers, his overtures, his cards, the meetings he proposed, that you started returning to the farm much later than I, with lame excuses such as horrendous traffic when there was no traffic, the car breaking down after it had just been serviced, the severe depression of an old high-school friend I'd never heard of who refused to go to the psychiatrist without you, and yet you couldn't remember the name of the psychiatrist, whose address changed every five seconds

"Why strange? It's perfectly normal, you know how bad I am at remembering streets"

I'm sure it was then that the phone calls started, the soft whispers into the receiver, the giggles, the sighs, the phrases in code that even the maids deciphered instantly, phrases like

"Me too"

like

"Of course"

like

"I swear it"

like

"You know the answer"

your sugary voice whispering sweet nothings and I trying to read the paper while overhearing you, trying to do the crossword puzzle while overhearing you, and the softer you spoke the louder I heard you, the less you said the more I understood, piecing together your plans, feelings, promises, and neither the you in flesh and blood nor the you in the mirror bothered to draw the curtain anymore or to look at me while stretching out on the mattress, you stopped having a stomach, buttocks, and legs, you became a disheveled profile, a silhouette that floated by with weary indifference, and when I finished my day's work at the ministry, instead of muttering to my driver to take me to the farm, where I wouldn't find you in the living room or the greenhouse, just some of your clothes strewn on the floor and Titina's distress and embarrassment, I had him go up the Avenida António Maria Cordoso to secret-police headquarters, where the Major looked at me with stupefaction from inside his office

"What brings you here, Minister?"

the Major who opened my letters, recorded my phone calls and conversations, followed my friends, had informers who kept tabs on me in Palmela (perhaps the gardener, the shifty veterinarian, or the chauffeur I didn't fire so that he wouldn't know I knew), had photos of me in restaurants, of me outside the apartment building of a girlfriend in Campo de Ourique, of me outside the building of a girlfriend in Praça do Chile, the Major miffed by my suspicions, the poor Major all pouty

"Please don't offend me, Minister"

leading me down corridors and pointing with sad resignation at all the file cabinets lining the walls

"If you don't believe me, Minister, then look around all you like, I'll ask the head of the department to help you around in this maze"

the Major

(my God how clear it all is now)

with the whole country on file in his metal cabinets, not just the Communists, foreigners, and enemies of the state but us, we ourselves, even Professor Salazar, even the Admiral, even the Cardinal, us, we ourselves, our gallstones, our hay fever, our cavities, the offended Major with sad resignation

"If you don't believe me, Minister, then look around all
you like, I'll ask the head of the department to help you around
in this maze"

instead of muttering to my driver to take me to the farm,
I had him go up the Avenida to secret-police headquarters, the
Major following me with piqued curiosity, making signs left and
right, the gray Major with a gray forehead, gray mouth, gray
glasses

"What's the matter, Minister? What's the matter, Minister? What's the matter, Minister?"

up the Avenida to secret-police headquarters, where I
searched floor after floor, I entered the interrogation rooms,
the jail cells, the administrative offices, the restaurant, the snack
bar, and the secret passage to Rua Ivens, I flung open closet
doors, ransacked drawers, scoured hat stands, looked under and
behind machine guns, and found nothing, the Major following
me with piqued curiosity, the inspectors following me with
piqued curiosity, the police chiefs taken aback, the doctor
stopping short in the middle of drilling a prisoner's tooth, you
stretching out in a seaside hotel in Sesimbra, you smiling in a
seaside hotel in Sesimbra, you stark naked in a seaside hotel in
Sesimbra, in a room that was two rooms, with everything in the
second room turned the opposite way, and yet it wasn't the flesh-
and-blood you or the you in the mirror that I was searching for,
it was a cheap ring imitating a wedding band purchased in
Tunisia, Algeria, or Morocco, a cheap ring already worn out and
ready to break, darkened by time and by contact with human
skin, a cheap ring which, if you looked at it with glasses, would
prove to be etched with designs, a snake, a lizard, phony Egyp-

tian signs, stop, wait, that's wrong, correct that, let's start over, let's be perfectly honest, at this point

"Wee-wee, Senhor Francisco, it's time for wee-wee, who made a nice wee-wee, who was it?"

it's all right for me to be perfectly honest, it costs me nothing to be perfectly honest, write that it wasn't the ring I was searching for, it was an ordinary gray sweater and gray skirt, it was black curls dripping with rain, she wringing her hands and biting her lower lip on the steps of my building, it was a canvas handbag and a wet pack of cigarettes, it was a box of matches that wouldn't light, that left red streaks on the box and broke, it was the prisoner shaking her head, turning on her heels, and going away without a word, the doctor gulping as if he were swallowing himself, his flashlight glowing through his coat pocket as he agreed with me in a strained whisper

"She died as soon as she hit the sidewalk, Minister, she obviously died as soon as she hit the sidewalk"

the prisoner going out into the rain without running, without hurrying, without even curving her head as she walked toward the bus stop, and when I opened the apartment door I was met by the rug and the peeling copper pitchers, by a picture of her wearing dark glasses on a shelf, I contemplating it all in a melancholy archeology, hesitating, thinking

"I can still catch her"

feeling my head spin, feeling troubled, antsy, confused, should I go after her or not, yes or no, walking over to the door and backing off, walking over to it again, grabbing the key in the lock and letting it go, sitting down in a chair while a Lisbon-Cascais train whizzed by between trees and buildings along the

Tagus, a rosary of yellow boxes whose trembling spread to the floorboards and my bones, I returning to the interrogation room where two agents sat at a desk and a man waved back and forth on his feet, stinking of sleeplessness and vomit, I stopping in my tracks, thinking

"If she missed the bus, then she's probably still at the bus stop waiting"

I frozen in my tracks, thinking

"I'll go down to the street and make up some excuse, I'll ask her to come up and she'll come, even if it's a dumb excuse, she'll accept me and come up"

she wearing my bathrobe and wrapping her wet hair in a towel to dry, barefoot, with those bunions and widely separated toes that I unfortunately abhor, why in God's name do I care so much about feet, about piddly details, a scarcely noticeable varicose vein, a white island of unpigmented skin on the shoulder, a scar from an appendix operation, why in God's name do I invent utterly ridiculous, childish pretexts to reject people, the way their lips move when they talk, the way they handle their knife and fork, the way they blow their nose, pretexts that I immediately transform into enormous defects that prevent me from touching others, from enjoying their company, from making love, I furious at myself for being all alone, feeling sorry for myself and feeling good about feeling sorry for myself, as if feeling sorry for myself could console me, pretexts so powerful that even somebody's skin, tone of voice, and mannerisms can repel me, everything about them getting on my nerves, irritating me, disgusting me, how was I able to feel attracted, fascinated, potentially in love, enchanted, by a cheap ring bought from beggars in the subway and not even made of real silver, how could

I be touched by an ordinary gray sweater and gray skirt, how charmed by the black curls of a run-of-the-mill girl like you can find on every street corner in town, you need only enter a coffee shop, a government office, a neighborhood beauty parlor, you need only scan the lines for the 6 P.M. streetcar, how in God's name was I captivated by a threadbare rug, by pitchers coated with peeling copper that not even the most down-and-out gypsies would take for free, I going every day to police headquarters like an idiot instead of muttering to the driver to take me to the farm, where perhaps she would have been waiting for me in the living room knitting, reading a magazine, or playing solitaire, where perhaps she would have been waiting for me in the bedroom, which is to say that the you in flesh and blood and the you in the mirror would have been waiting for me, your closed eyelids trembling as you pretended to sleep, stretching out in the sheets, I, without grasping my motive, searching in the jail cells, in the administrative offices, in the corridors, in the closets, the Major following me with piqued curiosity, making signs left and right, with his gray forehead, gray mouth, and gray glasses, with my whole life on file to use against me, as if I had ever done anything else in life but use my own life against me, the Major reassuring the police chiefs with his palm

"What's the matter, Minister? What's the matter, Minister? What's the matter, Minister?"

I in the interrogation room, where a man was standing before two seated agents, as he had been standing for hours or days or weeks, swaying back and forth, with a black eye and a smashed nose, a Communist, a traitor, a son of a bitch who liked to spend his holidays in North Africa, in Tunisia, Algeria, or Morocco, a son of a bitch who was probably the boyfriend of that daughter of a bitch with a cheap ring on her finger, and I started insulting him, punching him, pushing him toward the window, bending him over the sill to make him crash to the sidewalk, until the agents grabbed him from out of my hands.

COMMENTARY

On Saturday afternoons, after everyone had gone away

(my aunts and uncles, my godmother, my cousins, my father's army buddies, his friends from the military academy who were still alive, plus the humbler people for whom it was a privilege to be there, holding glasses of wine that they didn't dare drink any more than they dared sit down and take part in the conversations, old orderlies from the barracks who addressed my father as "sir" and "lieutenant colonel," while my father addressed them by their first names)

on Saturday afternoons, after everyone had gone away, leaving the chairs and sofas out of place, newspapers on the floor and the ashtrays full of ashes, plus a strange sensation that some objects were missing, a sensation of emptiness, of sadness

after everyone had gone away, my father and I remained alone on the verandah that looked out onto the mountains of Sintra, and beyond the mountains of Sintra the sea at Azenhas and the sea at Adraga, two angry seas with birds jumping on their sandy cheeks like tears of rage, seas we couldn't see but could feel in the pine trees' trembling

my father who kept drinking, with a glass of whiskey in one hand and a bottle in the other, looking at the garden wall without noticing the wall, at the trees without noticing the trees, at me without noticing me, my father with red eyelids talking to himself as he slumped in the canvas stool with liquor dripping from the corners of his mouth, from his chin and from his shirt buttons, in the complete abandonment of someone talking in a dream

"There's nothing in the world as slow as sheep and clouds"

the sheep that passed behind our house along the road to Ericeira or Mafra and the clouds that passed in flocks over the mountain ridge, getting caught in the fir trees, I'd help my father as he staggered to his bed still clutching the bottle and his glass, pressing the neck of the bottle against his chest

"There's nothing in the world as slow as sheep and clouds"

turning sluggishly toward the wallpaper's faded flowers, his shoulders shaking like those of a weeping child as the glass from the bottle struck his teeth, and I, worried

"Dad"

bending down toward him on the bedspread, and only then did I realize that he was laughing, hugging his glass and bottle and laughing, laughing like on the morning when he came home to Sintra in his uniform without saying a word or giving me a kiss, placed his hat and switch on the armchair, and walked straight over to the liquor on the buffet, with the cartilage in his neck moving up and down as if a mouse trapped under his skin were desperately trying to escape, and I, alarmed

"What happened, Dad?"

my father on the verandah looking at the garden wall without noticing the wall, at the trees without noticing the trees, at me without noticing me, my father with red eyelids surveying the empty sky and the angry sea of Adraga

"There's nothing in the world as slow as sheep and clouds"

and from that day on he never again wore his uniform and never returned to the barracks, a week later two fellows I'd never seen before walked through our gate without ringing the bell, found my father, whom they addressed as "you there," and warned him

"Don't try anything"

shutting themselves up with him in the living room, uttering various threats, and taking his sword, a stack of papers, and the cases with his medals, the fellow who seemed to be in charge lowering the car window to point his finger at us

"Don't try anything"

they knocked over a flowerpot with the bumper, ran over the brick border of the flower bed, and vanished in a windstorm of wood chips as a finger pointed at us from out of the smoke like a pendulum of doom

"Don't try anything"

they had ransacked the drawers, overturned objects, ripped up photos, and read through letters, my father on the canvas stool on the verandah, with a glass in one hand and a bottle in the other, laughing uncontrollably, laughing so hard his shoulders shook, my father tickled to death

"The scoundrels have kicked me out of the army, Isabel, I'm a civilian"

my mother's letters in shreds on the rug, the pink ribbon in shreds, my grandparents' letters in shreds, the letters from my father's brother who was a pilot in the navy until his plane fell into the Tagus estuary in shreds, the brother whom my father never talked about, so that it seemed like he'd never had a brother, and yet he wore his brother's ring next to his wedding band, and I'd sometimes catch him fondling it with his pinkie, my father tickled to death

"The scoundrels have kicked me out of the army, Isabel, I'm a civilian"

I at least glad to see my father glad, laughing because my father laughed, the mouth of the bottle hitting his glass without making it over the brim, I, worried

"Dad"

my father trying to piece together letters but giving up, ripping them up even more as he kept laughing so hard his shoulders shook, gleefully lifting his head toward me in the midst of his laughter

"Scoundrels, scoundrels"

my father spending years on the verandah looking at the garden wall without noticing the wall, looking at the trees without noticing the trees, looking at me without noticing me, my father who when night fell became invisible except for a glassy shimmer clinking in the darkness

"There's nothing in the world as slow as sheep and clouds"

and the two fellows in civilian clothes, one of whom was in charge of the other who was in charge of nothing, periodically returned, entering unannounced through the gate, knocking over flowerpots with the bumper and running over the brick borders of the flower beds, pulling me by my elbow to the kitchen

"Wait outside, Miss, wait outside"

railing at him I don't know why, warning him about I don't know what, sticking him in the car and bringing him back to Sintra a day or two later with a gash on his forehead, his wrist bandaged up, and his beard unshaven, and the inevitable finger would point out the window in a whirlwind of wood chips

"Don't try anything"

my father with his trousers torn at the seams, placing a wet towel on his differently shaped nose, taking comfort in the bottles on the buffet, cleaning the gash with a cotton ball and the alcohol he used as aftershave, the wind blowing through the amaryllises out back where I played as a child, and beyond the amaryllises the footpath to the fountain whose water danced beneath the ferns, a policeman on the path waving at me if I appeared at the window, throwing me kisses, whistling at my legs, I complaining to my father

"Dad"

and the policeman smiling at me in front of him, complimenting me on my looks in a sugary voice, asking if he could get a special rate for an hour with me, and my father not answering, my father with the whiskey bottle in one hand and his glass in the other, dressed in a uniform without stripes, like a seller of lottery tickets, the wind blowing through the amaryllises, something like the sun in the treetops, I furious with the policeman

"Dad"

my father laughing so hard his shoulders shook, struggling against the wiles of gravity to stay on his feet, the policeman tossing him out with his cigarette stub and returning to the footpath

"Poor slob"

and one afternoon when the car with two fellows in civilian dress entered unannounced through the gate, knocking over flowerpots and running over the brick borders of the flower beds, the fellow who was in charge of the other who was in charge of nothing wasn't accompanied by the other in charge of nothing but by a fellow in charge of him, a fellow who was younger than he was and had a hat, polka-dot suspenders, and a cigarillo between his teeth, the fellow in charge of the other who was in charge of nothing was in the driver's seat and got out first, trotted around to open the door for the fellow in charge of him, and led the way to the front porch, heedlessly trampling the daffodils as he went, as if my father and I were plumbers or construction workers or the like

"This way, Director General"

the Director General not hearing him, snapping his suspenders in front of me and coughing from the tobacco smoke, forgetting about the older fellow, forgetting about my father, forgetting about shutting himself up with him in the living room to rail and warn, I fascinated by his suspenders' polka dots that expanded and shrank, depending on whether the elastic was stretching or contracting, the policeman from the footpath hiding in a tree, wishing he'd never waved at me or whistled at my legs

a blackbird flitting among the pine trees, the water pump groaning with arthritic pain, the suspenders continually exploding in the cloudy world of cigarillo smoke, the older fellow to the Director General while grasping my arm and trying to hide me from view, as when we try to keep visitors from seeing embarrassing objects such as a towel with a hole or a raveled fringe

"This is his daughter"

the Director General to the older fellow, who pulled at me as if I were a heifer

"Just a minute, Camilo"

the Director General with us on the verandah that overlooked the hills, showing my father every consideration, setting our flowerpots upright, repairing the brick borders, apologizing for the trampled daffodils and any trouble caused by the police agents, the older fellow in the car writhing with indignation and scribbling desperate memos to his superiors while the Director General politely, respectfully looked at the picture of my mother on the chest of drawers

"Your wife, Lieutenant Colonel?"

as if my father were still in the army, as if he weren't wearing the uniform of a seller of lottery tickets, my father blotting out my mother's picture with a wave of the hand, blotting out the past with a wave of the hand, shaking his shoulders as he laughed, the Director General returning to visit me with spikenard, chocolates, perfumes

"Call me Francisco, Isabel"

taking me to Palmela, showing me a horizon of mud marked out by a horizon of frogs

"Our farm, Isabel"

so that a year later I was being woken up by stone angels somersaulting into lemon trees, I was being woken up in the middle of the night by a cigarillo singeing my cheek

"You love me, Isabel, don't you?"

so that a year later I was bumping into magpies, crows, and a housekeeper in mourning clothes who ordered around the maids, the cook, the tractor driver, and my son, while I listened to the beech trees and the insects in August gnawing away at the house's foundations, sick of German shepherds and solitude and windmills, dying my hair and painting my nails to make myself into a different woman with a different life, longing not to wake up in the middle of the night with a worried cigarillo singeing my cheek

"You love me, Isabel, don't you?"

I who'd never thought about what it means to love, to love my father, my husband, my son, as if loving were important, as if it were necessary, as if the simple fact of loving made life any easier or less sad, I with a mind to ask the cigarillo that closed in on me in the bedroom amid anguished shadows

"What do you call love, Francisco?"

so that I could answer him back, so that I could also wake him up in the middle of the night full of anguish, my father, in all the days he counted sheep and clouds on our verandah in Sintra, clinking his bottle against a glass while sliding off his stool, never once asked

"You love me, Isabel, don't you?"

even as my son, while dissecting his toys on the rug in the living room, never asked

"You love me, Isabel, don't you?"

I hesitating to say

"I love you"

as I hesitated to say

"I hate you"

because "I love" and "I hate" are two sides of the same nothing, the nothing of the insects gnawing at the house's foundations until the walls fall down or become perpendicular shadows over a horizontal shadow with our two shadows moving around inside, my mother died without ever having sworn that she loved us and without us having sworn that we loved her, on our return to Sintra after the funeral we found no change in the bibelots, nor in how the furniture was arranged, nor in the tone of light, her absence consisted in there being no change, in it raining as it had rained the day before and would rain all week, the rain after her death identical to the rain when she lived, the amaryllises murmuring the same indifference as ever, the same bemused indifference without loving and without hating, or beyond loving and hating, since loving and hating are something outer, something previous to people, not between them or after them, something like a wrapper, the crumpled bits of a shriveled plastic coating, and so on the day when Pedro, speaking the way my father and son never spoke because there was no need to speak, wanted to know

"You love me, Isabel, don't you?"

I decided to say

"I love you"

I decided to let his hand hold my hand, to pretend not to notice when he stuck a love note in my handbag, even though I thought he was ridiculous, phony, theatrical, not only in his acts but in his expression, his gaze, his tone of voice, his enthusiasm, I decided to talk to him on the phone and to read his letters, which was like hearing him on the phone except that his voice was replaced by ink and his lies were more pathetic, I agreed to meet him in the square under the elm trees, his elbow against mine, his hand on my leg, his breathing on my neck

"Isabel"

and I felt nothing, I wanted to feel something but felt only as if I were in a theater politely putting up with a dreary play, from the square we went to a hotel in Sesimbra, he crumpling my dress with his hand as he drove and giving me meaningful looks that made me laugh, the hotel in Sesimbra on a beach with five or six boats and boatmen mending their nets, the scene of a cheap painting like the ones sold in chinaware shops and they're

so awful no one buys them, Pedro filling in the registration card
and winking at the employee who smiled at him deferentially

"Let us know if you need anything, sir"

while I absently looked at the waves, thinking

"So this is what they think love is, so this is what they mean
by love"

and for Pedro, in fact, love was little more than this, than
shop windows with cloth dolls, fishwives, fishermen from Nazaré,
Minho peasants, leather-bound books, maps, postcards, some
foreigners in shorts at a café, a pianist with a ponytail, an elevator up to the seventh floor, and a room with a balcony facing
the beach that to me

I don't know why

looked frightfully ugly, the beach with the boatmen and
the five boats, the same beach I'd seen down below, I discovered in that hotel room that for Pedro love meant a bed with a
print over the headboard, a print that was no doubt by the same
artist who invented the beach, I in the bed and Pedro in bed
with me, talking about things I paid no attention to, about love,
I suppose, when for him love meant only that, a mattress and
me staring at the flaking plaster of the ceiling the whole time,
until he finally pulled away from me, checked the time, and
became frantic

"It's horrendously late"

his love was after all just like Francisco's except quicker,
more selfish, and even less affectionate, love for Pedro meant us
grabbing our clothes and getting dressed in a hurry, he impatiently combing his hair in the mirror as if he didn't know me
or knew me too well

"Let's go, let's go, it's horrendously late"

his love was after all just the kiss of one cheek grazing against another on Palmela's square

"Get out here and catch a taxi home, it's horrendously late, I'll call you, get out of the car, I promise I'll call"

I who hadn't asked him for anything and who didn't want anything except to be alone, without any men harassing me with their absurd interrogations

"You love me, Isabel, don't you?"

alone on the verandah in Sintra watching the sun setting on the amaryllises, the sun setting on the forest, completely alone, without the unbearable weight of men who thought they loved me, without them waking me up in the middle of the night with questions that got me all flustered

"Isabel"

alone, without the farm's angels and without prints in a hotel room, forever alone on the verandah, without any sheep and without any clouds, it was so I could be alone, far away from them, from their anxiety and their haste, from their anxiousness beforehand and their hurry afterward

"Get out here and catch a taxi home, it's horrendously late, get out of the car for your own good"

it was so I could be alone that I accepted the apartment in Lisbon, a kitchenette with an enclosed balcony where they finally stopped pestering me, stopped boring me, stopped visiting me, pawing at me, and asking me questions, where they left me in peace, where they fortunately left me in peace except for a visit or two from Pedro and a visit or two from Francisco in which tears of their supposed love were mixed with tears of their supposed hate, in peace next to the window, waiting for the buildings across the street to give way to the sheep and clouds of Sintra, waiting for the buildings across the street to give way to the sea.

REPORT

Before going away, I'd like to ask you to explain to my idiotic son that it's not difficult. Tonight, as soon as the staff worker on duty falls asleep, I'll pull the bandages and IV tube from my arm, get out of bed, put on my clothes that were stowed in the closet, my shirt, pants, jacket, boots, hat, and suspenders, adjusting the clasps since I may have lost a little weight, I'll walk down the hall and out the door on tiptoe, flag down the first taxi I see on the square, and have him take me to the farm, where Isabel and Titina will be waiting for me in a tizzy, calling up the ministry, the hospitals, and the police in search of me, I know how Isabel and Titina are, they'll be pacing the terrace, peering through the geraniums to see if I might be arriving, imagining at the slightest sound that it's a car driving up through the cypress trees, Isabel and Titina running toward me with the rainbow of a smile behind their tears, finding me in great shape, ruddy, and without rings under my eyes, without a haggard face, Titina warming up dinner in the kitchen and Isabel sitting next to me on the sofa and asking what happened, and I, so as not to upset them, saying nothing about the rest home in Alvalade, about the old men, the bedpans

"Wee-wee, Senhor Francisco, it's time for wee-wee, who made a nice wee-wee, who was it?"

the napkins that were tied around my neck as if I were a

sick man, an invalid, the soups and boiled fruits that were forced down my throat, I naturally not telling them about what I've been through here, as I trust you won't tell anyone, as I forbid you to tell anyone, I'll blame my absence on an unexpected trip, on some conniving generals and thankless civilians who conspired against Professor Salazar in Elvas or in Braga and on all the work it took to set everything aright, promises, threats, detaching troops here and there, arrests, my dinner getting cold on the table, I forbidding Titina to rewarm it, I eating the tasteless meatballs topped with cold gravy while the German shepherds cough in the kennels, I in the living room with Isabel, lighting up a cigarillo and listening to the wind in the beech trees, I feeling happy, you understand, happy, and so when my idiotic son comes by on Saturday with a useless box of cookies to look at me from a distance, to scrutinize me, to seek reassurance from the staff workers

"My father doesn't understand anything we tell him, does he?"

please explain to him that I've gone away, that I've returned to Palmela and wouldn't come back here for all the money in the world, tomorrow morning at nine sharp I'll be at Commerce Square going through papers, I no longer feel pain in my chest or pressure on my heart, the difficulty I had breathing is gone, explain to my idiotic son that it's as if I were thirty years old again, with all my hair and good health, without a wrinkle or any sign of a potbelly, as if I were thirty years old, you understand, before Isabel left, I always felt certain that this business of her falling in love with someone else was just a lark, a whim, a bunch of nonsense, I always felt certain that she needed me, loved me, and would grow old with me, the two of us in the arbor with no need for words, for silly endearments, for romantic mush, Isabel returning to the farm with her suitcase, nonchalantly returning to the farm with her suitcase, as if nothing had happened, because in fact nothing did happen, I reading the paper on the terrace, and instead of Titina it's Isabel who brings me tea, sits down in her chair next to the rosebushes and that's that, at most a word or two about the heat, about the lack of wind, about the gardener not pruning the dead branches and letting the greenhouse go to pot, and my life as it should be, as I'd like it to be, it's a matter of quietly waiting until the staff worker on night duty falls asleep, it's a matter of letting them wash me, change my pajamas, shave my beard, give me pills, run a wet comb through the straggly hair around my ears, it's a matter of finding out if the Major's and Professor Caetano's policemen are spying on me from the glowing blue grass of the square, the same police chiefs, inspectors, and agents who used to frantically straighten the knots of their ties, button their jackets, and stand at attention to salute me and whom I'll bet have instructions to shoot me on sight to prevent me from going downtown and taking my rightful place in the palace, from putting a halt to all the abuses, from kicking the army into shape, from whipping this rabble into line, from governing this piece of crap, with a few cuffs here and there, the newspapers mum and the people mum, because that's what they want, that's exactly what people want, to keep mum, tow the line and on we go, because there must be someone in this country who's with me, someone who remembers and respects me, if you would only take this bandage off my wrist, if instead of just listening to me you'd help me remove this IV tube from my arm, because the way they've rigged me up, with only my left arm free, it's hard for me to do much, you could make up some excuse to stay longer, you could say that you're my godson and came from the interior to see me, or that you immigrated to Canada and are going back there in two hours, you could stay and help me get up, because I've probably gotten a bit weak, because in spite of my resilience, all this time in bed eating soup and canned peaches has probably made me a bit stiff, a bit rusty, you don't have to carry me, all I need is a little help with the first few steps from here to the closet, until my muscles loosen up and my body gets used to moving again, a little help putting on my clothes and walking down the hall amid the old men's groans without turning the light on, because once I get out to the square I'll manage, don't worry, I can spot the police from miles away, I know their tricks, I know their disguises, and there may not even be any police waiting for me, because when the cat's away the mice will play and since I left the ministry it's total chaos, complete apathy, no one works, no one lifts a finger, no one cares, fortunately I'm still alive to keep this mess of a country from falling into the hands of foreigners, I can still save this strip of dirty seacoast and cathedrals, it's not true that Isabel isn't in Palmela, Isabel has returned, it's not true that my daughter-in-law's family ended up with the farm, over my dead body, it's not true that I fired everybody, I'm no fool, I may have every other defect in the world but I'm no fool, you think I'd give up the farm or let it be sold off, a farm where a man can single-handedly defend himself, where a man with a shotgun and a beltful of cartridges can single-handedly fend off tanks and cannons, can fend off an entire battalion if necessary, the crows giving the signal

"Caw caw"

at the sight of the first outsider, just one foot inside the gate and the crows

"Caw caw"

just one foot inside the gate, just two feet inside the gate

"Caw caw"

and who would ever find us in the swamp, tell me who would ever find us in the wild grass, I'll lend you a pistol, we'll take Isabel and Titina with us, now peek out the window to see if there's anyone on the square, to see if a car is parked between the slide and the swing, I've spent endless afternoons tied to this chair looking at the slide and the swing, and whenever I shouted at the staff workers

"No"

they stuck a pillow behind my back and patted my hair with a look of pity

"The poor dear doesn't even complain"

pretending not to hear me, pretending that I couldn't talk, my idiotic son, a brainless good-for-nothing who squandered himself on the first clever broad to come his way, my idiotic son to the nurse who was putting away his nurse's instruments with the efficient and serious air of the ignorant, recommending syrups and injections, my idiotic son to the nurse as if I couldn't utter a syllable, how absurd

"A debilitated pleura, a debilitated pleura, how did my father's pleura get debilitated if he never leaves his room?"

the moon shining on the blue grass and crowned with bats like the street lamps, exactly like the street lamps, a tin moon with smudges that Titina would immediately wipe off if she could reach that high, a moon that they forgot to unscrew so that it would stop glaring in my eyes and I could sleep in peace, and in spite of me ordering them to be silent the nurse kept up the inane conversation with my idiotic son, who will be sorry when I leave here later tonight and lay my hands on him, the ignorant nurse to my idiotic son

"We'll be lucky if we can control his fever, sir"

and perhaps now you can understand why I'm so anxious to get out of here, before they torture me with syrups and injections by order of Professor Caetano, by order of the police, before a phone call from the Major instructs them to suffocate me with my pillow, perhaps now you can understand why I'm so anxious to escape, if you insist that Isabel hasn't returned to Palmela, then forget Palmela, if you insist that I've been cheated out of the farm, then don't worry about the farm, any place in Lisbon will do, a street corner, the subway, a stairwell, or a park bench, drop me off where you like and adios, who's going to notice an innocuous old man who can hardly move, a half-blind scarecrow squatting on a step, just straw and bones, without any meat or fat to fill up his suit, any place in Lisbon will do, a street corner, subway, stairwell, or park bench, as long as my son doesn't know and the nurse doesn't know and the staff workers don't know, as long as Professor Caetano and the Major don't know, after Isabel ditched me for someone else

"Don't cry, Francisco, it's useless to cry, don't make a scene, please don't make a scene, don't cry"

I had no one to go home to at the farm, so I started to work late at Commerce Square, I and the inspector deciding whom we'd banish to Cape Verde to die quickly and who would die slowly in Peniche, these nine people to the islands, those six to the fortress, and that fellow there can wait in Caxias, where next month he'll have a stroke and we can send him home to his family in a coffin, and when I'd take my leave of the inspector

"Good night, Carvalho"

and walk down the street, there were no beggars or cripples or saxophones playing wrong notes under the arches, just the deafening echo of my footsteps against the stone, and my elongated shadow, the shadow of a sleepwalker, the shadow of a clown with a tiny hat topped by the sunflower of my cigarillo, a clown at my side whose shoes struck the ground at the same time as mine but sounded like a poor man's sandals or like slippers, as if half of me were what I thought I was and other people thought I was, and the other half of me were what I really was, the driver doffing his hat and holding open the door for me, who dismissed him with a wave of the hand that was more like a refusal than a wave, and I'd walk among the statues of kings and Neptune-graced ponds of a deceased city, shrouded in columns and trees, its quivering streets prolonging the striations of seashells, I'd enter an apartment perched over the shadows of King Eduardo VII Park, an apartment I'd rented and decorated and paid all expenses for, pretending that it was my home, as I pretended that the woman who opened the door and dressed like Isabel, wore her hair like Isabel and used Isabel's perfume was in fact Isabel, not the Isabel from the time of our separation but the Isabel from the time when we met, a woman I rented and decorated and paid all expenses for just like the apartment, with the meticulous detail of a stage setting, with the precision of a watchmaker, a bedroom just like our bedroom, a living room just like our living room, the same pictures, the same flowers, the same mirror in which she accepted and rejected me, with green curtains that gave the illusion of the farm's beech trees, the illusion of birds, I caressing Isabel through that woman whom I called Isabel and who dressed and wore her hair and smelled like Isabel

"Do you like me?"

the girl stiff, intimidated, bothered by the earrings, the rings, the shoes that pinched her toes, the wilted spikenard in her lap, the girl answering in a faint, reluctant whisper

"Yes, I like you, Senhor Minister"

while her mother made hand signs and twitched like a huge bird, flitting around me with nervous enthusiasm

"Say that you adore the Minister, Milá"

the mother who, if I'm not careful, will show up here pulling the recalcitrant wrist of her daughter, still wearing the hat with a moth-eaten veil that I found in a trunk and asked her to put on, still hobbling in the crocodile high heels with a heel coming loose that I found under the bed and asked her to use, the daughter struggling with her mother

"Let go of me"

and the mother, irrepressible, marching down the hall and stirring up the old men and the staff workers, dragging her daughter to the armchair from where I gaze at the blue grass with the swing and the slide, the mother brandishing the spikenard like a switch, slapping her daughter with it and forcing her to bend forward until her nose touches mine

"Say that you adore the Minister, Milá"

and her daughter wringing the satin gloves with time-yellowed buttons running up to the elbows, her daughter wrapped in an odor of moldy velvet and ancient perfume, her ears sore from the large earrings, her hair flung upward like a cock's comb, and with a bit of mascara running down her eyelid like a black tear

"Yes, I like you, Senhor Minister"

and so you have to get me out of here before the two of them show up, imagine the scandal, the daughter decked out like the queen of clubs and the mother presenting the queen of clubs like a ringmaster, how mortifying, you have to get me out of here despite my debilitated pleura, despite my cough, despite my fever and this dreadfully cold afternoon, I don't know how you can stand to be in short sleeves, without an overcoat, a scarf, a muffler, I don't understand why the heaters are turned off, why the staff workers aren't wearing stockings, why the people on the square are dressed for summer, I don't understand why the same name keeps coming to mind, keeps coming to my lips, the same name, the same memory that's slowly fading

Isabel

write that down

Isabel

to see if I can understand, write it in your notebook in large capital letters and show it to me letter by letter

Isabel

to see if I can understand what it means, why it matters, to see if I can recover a smile, an expression, a gesture, but no, just crows and magpies, just burning oranges glowing with blood in the orchard, a barefoot girl whom I don't even know coming out of the stable with bowed head and a pail of milk in each hand, a man with a shotgun at the top of the steps, dogs barking as he sends away the maids, the gardener, the tractor driver, and the housekeeper, trunks and suitcases helter-skelter down the cypress-lined drive

wait

Titina, the housekeeper, that's right, Titina, stay with me, Titina

trunks and suitcases helter-skelter down the cypress-lined drive, the man burning up papers and photographs, sitting at the piano and waiting in the shambles of the living room, hair disheveled and beard unshaven, a man identical to the one you're going to drop off tonight at a subway station or else leave in a stairwell, by the trucks at the Largo do Mitelo, or on a park bench, a different man from me, whose wrist they've tied up with a bandage, whom they've so weakened with boiled food that I can't even dress myself, at the beginning of the war in Africa, in 1961, when blacks murdered whites in Luanda and mounted their heads on poles, forced teenagers to eat their fathers' testicles, decapitated children, yanked fetuses from wombs and hung them from branches like balloons for the feast of Saint Anthony, and strung intestines between the columns of houses like streamers at outdoor fairs, in 1961, when whites murdered blacks and mounted their heads on poles, forced teenagers to eat their father's testicles, decapitated children, yanked fetuses from bellies and hung them from branches like balloons for the feast of Saint Anthony, and strung intestines between the columns of houses like streamers at outdoor fairs, Professor Salazar sent me to Angola with the Major, and even the bay where the scrawny and long-legged seabirds with no name eyed the trawlers with cruel delight, even the bay, take note, was infected by the smell of slime and decaying flesh, by a humble, sickly sweet stench of rotting dogs, a mist of bent knees and bowed heads, a wet stickiness like vomit under a vomit-colored sky, a rain of vomit, I wanted to return straight to the ship and sail back to Lisbon, to get away from bullets all night long, spilled guts, devastated neighborhoods, the Major pushing me with his knee

"Don't be a coward, Minister"

despising me the way the staff workers despise me when changing my wet sheets, my wet pajamas, furiously showing me the mildewed straw in the mattress, blaming me for making them miss their bus home

"Blasted old fool"

the Major shoving me into that blurry silence crossed by shots, the bay's long-legged birds, gray guts in ditches, human fingers lopped off by pruning shears

"Don't be a coward, Minister"

the Major and I on patrol in a jeep as dusk fell and it rained over the stench of the dead, our jerking headlights exposing walls, corners of buildings, embankments, adobe constructions, shadows on the run, and a village of corpses, corpses of dogs, calves, and mules, corpses of casseroles, buckets, drawers, and stoves, horrible, mutilated corpses of stoves, our gunshots and their gunshots that were also ours, I in the seat next to the Major, hiding behind his shoulder and holding back my tears in sheeplike whimpers as wet goo filled up my pants, and the Major straightening me up in the seat, grabbing my shirt with his angry hand

"Pull yourself together and be a man, Minister, don't force me to hit you"

at an intersection of two narrow streets we heard music playing on a windup phonograph in a shack ravaged by war and rain surrounded by other shacks ravaged by war and rain, the Major got out of the jeep with pistol in hand, I got out of the jeep and followed the Major, my feet sinking down in filthy sludge as I tried to determine where the shots were coming from, one of our men approached the music and used the butt of his gun to open the hingeless board that served as a door against the shivering wind, we stormed into the dirty room where dishes and utensils were strewn on the floor and a few clothes hung from a cord, into the dirty room that was the entire shack, and in the middle of the room stood the old phonograph, which was playing an old record, a phonograph consisting of a wooden box and a dented horn resembling an angel's trumpet and blowing forth the "Internationale" in fits and starts as the needle hopped around, the Major fired his pistol at the music and the wooden box, transforming it into confusionofspringsandncylindersandstrangemechanisms, and as he pointed at the walls made of mud, rags, and cardboard, as he pointed at the wild grass, broken brick tiles and used tires that constituted the roof

the roof, the roof

the roof, as he pointed at the other shacks, the wind, the rain, and the corpses of things, the horrible, mutilated corpses of stoves, as he pointed at me along with the chairs and casseroles and buckets and drawers, as he pointed mainly at me, the Major, forgetting about the phonograph and pointing only at me, gave orders to the police agents

"Burn all this crap to the ground"

the agents, whose faces loomed or shrank depending on how their flashlights pointed, brought cans from the jeep, uncapped the cans, doused me with kerosene, tossed a lit match, and I started to burn, I swear I started to burn, I literally started to burn, so that it's too late for me to leave this place, too late for you to untie the bandage on my wrist and help me get up and walk to the closet, too late for me to take my clothes off the hanger, get dressed, and have you help me down the hall without waking up the woman on duty, I almost hanging on you as I stumble along, too late for you to take me to the farm, where no one's waiting for me, where Isabel isn't painting her nails or playing solitaire or reading a magazine in the living room and Titina isn't all set to run to the kitchen and warm up dinner for me, some soup that smells of gas and tasteless meatballs topped with cold gravy, the farm without the greenhouse, the barn, and the orchard, inhabited by the rage of the eucalyptus trees, by the skeleton of the windmill and by the crows' screeching, too late for you to pull me out of your car and leave me on a street corner, at a subway station, in a stairwell, on a park bench or by the freight trucks at the Largo do Mitelo, too late for me to go home, because the agents brought cans from the jeep, uncapped the cans, doused me with kerosene, tossed a lit match, and I started to burn, I literally started to burn, the walls made of mud, rags, and cardboard burning, the roof made of grass, broken brick tiles, and used tires burning, the palm trees, the rain, the wind, and the corpses of things burning, the horrible, mutilated corpses of stoves burning, and casseroles, and buckets, and drawers, so please tell my idiotic son when he comes on Saturday, please tell my idiotic son who doesn't know how to manage his affairs or take care of himself, a good-for-nothing, a washout, a kid who's afraid of the dark, afraid of gypsies, afraid of wolves, afraid of burglars, tell my idiotic son

how can I say this, how can I make it clear, please tell my idiotic son that I may not have been but that, tell him that I may have made mistakes but that, tell my idiotic son, do you hear, tell my idiotic son

please don't forget to tell my idiotic son that in spite of everything I

notes

128 *Professor Caetano:* Marcelo Caetano (1906–80) held various posts in Salazar's cabinet and was rector of the University of Lisbon from 1959 to 1962. He became Portugal's prime minister in 1968, after Salazar was incapacitated by a stroke.

131 *the Cardinal:* Manuel Gonçalves Cerejeira (1888–1977), a university classmate and lifelong friend of Salazar's, was the cardinal patriarch of Lisbon from 1929 to 1971. He negotiated the 1940 Concordat that made Religion and Catholic Morality compulsory subjects in Portuguese schools and promoted the cult of Our Lady of Fátima, who allegedly appeared to three Portuguese shepherd children in 1917.

143 *Nab that jerk for me, Major:* Major Fernando Eduardo da Silva, chief of Portugal's secret police during much of Salazar's regime.

168 *furious that the Admiral:* Admiral Américo Tomás (1894–1987) was president of Portugal from 1958 until the 1974 revolution. He had little real power, since the prime min-

ister ruled as a virtual dictator, but it was up to him to name Salazar's successor, Marcelo Caetano, in 1968.

175 *I'll have Barbieri:* Agostinho Barbieri was for many years the assistant director of Portugal's secret police.

205 *the prison at Tarrafal:* This concentration camp, located on the island of Santiago in Cape Verde and in service from 1936 to 1974, was the grimmest and most notorious detention center for political prisoners created by the Salazar regime.

292 *statuettes of Father Cruz:* Francisco Rodrigues da Cruz (1859–1948), a Portuguese priest known for his work among prisoners, the sick and the poor, became a highly popular figure of devotion.

340 *leveled and salted by his order:* The Marquis of Pombal (1699–1782), an autocratic prime minister famous for rebuilding Lisbon after the catastrophic 1755 earthquake, was ruthless toward his adversaries.

350 *the general who ran against the government:* General Humberto Delgado, opposition candidate in the 1958 Portuguese presidential elections, was assassinated in Spain, near the Portuguese border, in 1965.

362 *to nab the general:* General Humberto Delgado (1916–1965), mentioned in the previous note.

381 *the National Union:* A civic association and the de facto to-
talitarian political party of Salazar's so-called Estado Novo
(New State).